The
WINDS *of* GRACE

Best Wishes!

Marilyn Kus

The
WINDS *of* GRACE

Book One

MARILYN KING

CROWN LEAF PUBLISHING

Published by Crown Leaf Publishing, functions only as book publisher. As such, the ultimate design, content, editorial accuracy, and views expressed or implied in this work are those of the author.

Unless otherwise noted, all scriptures quotations are taken from the King James Version of the Bible.

This is a work of fiction. Names, characters, incidents, and dialogues are products of the author's imagination and are not to be construed as real. Any resemblance to actual events or persons, living or dead, is entirely coincidental.

ISBN: 13: 978-0996725835 Trade paperback

ISBN: 10: 0996725830

Library of Congress Catalog Card Number:

Cover design by Ken Raney
Cover artwork copyright ©2017 by Ken Raney

Printed in the United States of America
2017–Third Edition

THIS BOOK IS dedicated to my mother, Verdean LeRoy, who was a constant inspiration my whole life through. She wanted to see my book in print. Are you looking through the portals of heaven, Mother? It's done. Thank you for believing in me.

ACKNOWLEDGMENTS

Many thanks to the wonderful writers and editors of the High Desert California Writer's Club who helped me bring this story to life. My sincere thanks to my critique group who helped keep my historical facts, points of view, storyline, and tenses straight. My peers have become great friends. I am deeply grateful to Roberta Smith, Mary Thompson, Jim Elstad, Bob Isbill, Denny Stantz, Carol Warren, Hazel Stearns, Curt James, Evelyn Blocker, Holly LaPat, Willard and Suzanne Holbrook, Winnie Rueff, Anne Fowler, Liz Pye, and Harold Meza.

A special thanks to my sister, Theresa LeRoy, who worked with me every step of the way. I appreciate all the hours you spent when we hashed out the story over the phone, through the mail—and in person when we could.

Many thanks to my editor, Ann M'teer, and to Mary DeMuth's Writing Spa. Your insights were both educational and invaluable. Thanks go out to Mike Foley, who not only edited the story the first time around, but also gives monthly online advice.

Also my love and gratitude go out to my husband, Bob, who has been my backbone, advisor, and ear throughout the building of this book. He didn't know how much I'd depend on him for research. I so much appreciate his thorough dedication.

To my four children, Janine, Rick, Andy, and Sam, for the years of patience as I worked and pecked away at the keyboard. They have been a constant encouragement as they waited to see my book on a bookshelf. Thank you, my children, and my precious grandchildren, who make my heart smile.

I thank God, who gave me strength and lifted me up when I was down. Without Him I couldn't have done it.

Grace and Blessings,
Marilyn

ONE

Charleston, South Carolina
December 8, 1829

GRACE COOPER CLUTCHED her skirt as she and Josie flew like the wind up the South Battery, not slowing their steps until they reached the row of townhouses.

The surgeon's buggy sat in front of the town house, with Aunt Katy's carriage parked behind it. The driver sat straight, watching the girls. He motioned with the horse's whip for them to go on into the house.

Fear gripped Grace's heart as she climbed the staircase with Josie close on her heels. Concern for her mother was paramount. When Grace had left earlier that morning, her mother claimed she felt better and said Grace could step out for a spell and not worry about her. Now Grace's heart pounded in her ears as she reached the door to her mother's bedchamber. Aunt Katy stood outside, speaking in low tones to two doctors in a tight, confidential circle. One was her mother's doctor, the other, Ethan Boyd, a surgeon who'd spent the last six months calling on Grace.

Grace approached the small group, trying to hide her dismay at seeing Ethan standing outside her mother's door. His growing interest in her had accelerated to the point that he turned up at the most inopportune moments. It was time to let him know she had no interest in him as a suitor. But more urgent matters faced her at the moment.

The threesome turned to look at her. Aunt Katy motioned Grace to come stand by her side.

"Olivia asked to see you," Aunt Katy said in her smooth, southern drawl.

"What happened? She was fine this morning." Grace felt as if her world were spinning out of control.

"Do go in. She needs you," her aunt said with a small push forward.

Grace slipped into the room almost on tiptoe and walked to the foot of the bed. Her mother lay sleeping, her head resting on a pillow. Her grandmother smoothed the crisp linen sheet in a plaintive manner. Her mouth grim, she moved to sit by Grandfather, who watched solemnly. At the foot of the bed their orange-and-white cat, Smitty, lay curled in a circle, his tail lifting and falling in rhythm.

"Grace, is that you?" Olivia whispered.

"Yes, Mama." Grace looked down at her mother's frail form.

"I seem to be at the bottom of my strength." Even in her weakness, her strong southern drawl was evident.

Olivia glanced at her parents. "Could you leave us? I want to talk to my daughter alone."

They looked startled at the request. Grandmother's hand went to her lips, and she stared at her weak daughter as she touched the foot of the bed. "Fred, I can't leave her . . ."

"Come along, Adeline." The door closed softly behind them.

"Take my hand." Olivia reached for Grace.

Grace held the frail hand. "Mama, please don't leave me."

"I will always be with you. Remember this when you feel alone."

Grace's eyes smarted and a tear slipped down her cheek.

Her mother closed her eyes. After a long moment she started a bout of harsh coughing. She twisted under the covers as the hacking consumed her.

Grace flinched. "Maybe it would help if your pillow were raised." She placed a hand behind her mother's shoulders as she stuffed another

2

pillow under her back. "Is that better, Mama?" She slid onto the bed, scooting her slim frame next to her mother.

Olivia put a slender hand over her chest in an attempt to stop the painful wracking. It was several moments before she spoke again.

"Grace?" Her mother's voice was barely audible.

"Yes, Mama?" Grace leaned down to hear her.

"Please forgive me."

Grace raised her face to search her mother's eyes. They remained closed, her brows furrowed.

"Mama?" Grace took her mother's hand and held it to her cheek.

"Forgive me," her mother whispered.

Olivia's hand relaxed.

"Mama?" Grace gently shook her mother's shoulders. "Mama? No! Don't leave me!"

For the first time in months her mother appeared at peace. A sick chill pierced the center of Grace's being. She couldn't lose her mother.

"Somebody! Come quick!"

Hours later, Aunt Katy took Grace aside. "I know you have your servants here at the house, but would you like to come stay with us? It will be difficult staying here with your mother gone."

"As odd as it may sound, I can't leave the townhouse just yet. I appreciate the offer, Aunt Katy." Grace bit her bottom lip. "Could you send Peter to stay with me until I know what I'm going to do?"

"That's a fine idea. Your cousin Peter shouldn't mind helping out temporarily. I'll talk to him."

Grace hoped Peter would come. She wasn't ready to leave the lingering scent of her mother's presence. She needed to touch the things that were so dear to Olivia. Somehow, she had to keep the memory of her mother alive within her.

Olivia Cooper was laid to rest in the parish churchyard. Grace watched as her mother's casket was lowered.

Mama!

The pain and grief cut like a knife. Her eyes misted and tears fell. Never in her life had she spent a night apart from Mama until yesterday, and now she faced a life of separation. *God, I can't!*

She heard a stifled sob and turned. Grandmother had a handkerchief pressed to her mouth, trying to contain the agony of burying her child. Grandfather stood at her side, a hand on her shoulder, his face pale and furrowed with pain.

The sound of dirt falling on wood drew Grace back to the wrenching sight of Mama being buried.

How can I leave her here, cold and without light? Grace saw Mama sitting on their veranda, her face lifted to the sun, smiling at its light and warmth.

Grace turned to Aunt Katy in panic. "She'll be so cold!" Tears flooded her vision.

Katy slipped a lace handkerchief underneath the black veil of Grace's hat and gently dabbed at the tears escaping her eyes. They held hands.

"Now let us pray," the minister intoned, bowing his head.

Grace heard the minister's call to prayer, but the words didn't register. *"Please forgive me,"* the last words of her mother echoed, drowning out all else.

A murmured chorus of amens signaled the conclusion of the graveside service.

The afternoon went by in a blur while people filed by to give their condolences. Many of the town folk offered kind words of wisdom for the days to come. But the ones who stood out in Grace's memory that gray, foggy day, were the ones who said her mother owed them a debt.

"Sorry about your mother, dear. You *will* come see me in a few days to cover your mother's outstanding balance at the millinery shop," Mrs. Prichett said.

Wouldn't good manners require these people to wait at least a day or two to remind Grace that her mother had left debts behind?

Grace stared into the face of the plump woman. She wore a hat with feathers flared out like a peacock's tail. She knew her mother had a penchant for hats, but she didn't know her mother owed a balance at the hat shop. She wished the feathery-hatted woman would move along.

"I will do my best." Grace bit her bottom lip.

"See that you do, first thing next week." Mrs. Prichett winked and gave a sharp click of her tongue.

Several people filed by before another guest brought up a debt her mother owed.

"Sorry for your loss, Miss. Your mother was a grand lady."

"Thank you, Mr. Hopkins." Grace gave him a quivering smile.

"Uh . . . your mother . . . has been behind on the payments for the townhouse—" He stopped.

Grace frowned. *Another debt?*

"I've not had a chance to see how much money is in the bank. I will try to make good any debt she owes."

"Good, good." He mopped his brow with a white handkerchief. It was obvious this was an awkward moment for him. He quickly moved on.

At the end of the day, Grace climbed the stairs of the townhouse, anxious to peel off the dreaded black dress she would wear for the next few weeks. Her heart and head felt numb, and she moved her body without thinking. She stepped into her bedchamber and lit the kerosene lamp at the side of her bed.

Smitty, the family cat, lay at the foot of the bed when Grace entered the room. At her appearance the cat stood, blinked indifferently and turned its head to look elsewhere. With a flick of its tail, Smitty jumped down from the bed and ambled out of the room.

Too weary to care that Smitty had received little attention lately, Grace pulled the thick covers down to the foot of the bed. She slipped into a white flannel nightgown. She lifted the warm blankets and crawled under them. Her mind went back to the many people who mentioned her mother owed them a debt. She hoped with all her heart her mother had sufficient funds in the bank. If not, how would she repay all these people?

She would sleep on it. Maybe the answer would come in the morning. A moment later, she heard the front door close softly. Peter's footsteps echoed to the downstairs spare bedroom. The sound was comforting. She was grateful he had agreed to stay for the time being. The last thing she heard before she fell asleep was the click of his bedroom door. The house was secure. But was her soul? She wouldn't know peace until she found a way to pay her mother's debts.

TWO

BY MID-MORNING, GRACE sat at the desk in the drawing room, sorting through mail. Smitty curled near her feet and flicked his tail contentedly.

Grace gazed at the stack of unpaid debts in disbelief. How had her mother fallen so far behind? Many of the notes were for frivolous things. However, the house payment was also past due. How long had she fallen behind in payments?

Mother had worked at Grandfather's mercantile until she became ill with tuberculosis. Grace worked for her grandfather as well. She had a knack with the books, so a portion of the bookkeeping landed in her lap. Between her mother and herself, she thought their income met their needs. How wrong she'd been! Would she be able to keep her servants?

A knock at the front door interrupted her train of thought. The chair scraped as she scooted back. Smitty jumped and ran to stand where a sunbeam streaked the floor. Grace opened the door. A courier held out a note. "A letter, Miss."

"Thank you." She closed the door and glanced at the inscription on the envelope. "Aunt Katy." She opened the small envelope and read the short note. "Please join us for lunch at noon." Grace rubbed the back of her stiff neck and placed the note on the hall table.

She glanced at the desk piled with bills and shrugged. She could do nothing about them now. She would accept the invitation.

Grace slowed her steps just in front of the bank. Curious as to the amount of funds in her mother's account, she'd only take a moment to find out how much was available to pay the unpaid debts. The jitters that had consumed her since the day of her mother's burial would certainly diminish once she talked to a bank teller.

Mr. Pettis shook his head and said, "Your mother didn't keep a positive balance for long. She spent all she had from paycheck to paycheck. This isn't what you hoped to hear, young lady. But the fact is, your mother's been living on a thin thread for some time."

Grace frowned. "You mean to tell me there isn't anything left in her account?"

"Not a dime."

In her dazed state, only one thought resounded in her mind: *I must get out of here.* Grace leaned forward, "You might as well close her account then."

"I'll do that. You, on the other hand, have kept a few dollars in your account. You'll keep it open?"

"Yes." Grace pasted a smile on her face before standing and reaching a hand across the wooden desk. "Good day, Mr. Pettis."

An hour later Grace sat across the table from Josie and her aunt, and spilled her dilemma of the debts her mother owed.

"I don't know what to do, Aunt Katy. The wages I earn don't compare to the debt she's left behind." Grace held her face in her hands and peeked out between splayed fingers.

"I wasn't aware my sister accrued such a mountain of debt." Aunt Katy shook her head, then poured more lemonade into her dainty, iced glass.

"I've been to the bank. Mr. Pettis says there's nothing left in her account." Grace drank the cold lemonade and licked her bottom lip.

"It's only been a few days since your mother's passed. You mustn't worry. Something will work out." Katy glanced at Josie. "Why don't you spend the night with Grace tonight? Get her mind off all this serious business."

Grace focused on a droplet of water working its way down the side of the iced glass in her hand. Her world had changed. With the passing of her mother, she had become aware of their dire financial state. And her mother wasn't here to fix it. For the first time, she faced what her mother had faced all along. There were not enough funds to pay the bills. What was she to do?

"Grace?"

Grace popped her head up, tears smarting her eyes.

"Would you like to have Josie spend the night with you?" Aunt Katy asked in a soothing tone.

"I'd love to have her company." She pulled the napkin off her lap, dabbed at the corner of her eyes and stood. "I'm going home if you don't mind." She scooted around the ladder-back chairs and pulled on her long overcoat. She glanced at Josie. "I'll see you tonight."

"At six o'clock. I'll bring Grandma's leftover chicken pot pie." Josie quickly stepped to Grace's side and swung a gentle arm over her shoulder.

"Good then," Aunt Katy said. "The good Lord said we're not to be in a spirit of fear or worry. Lend it to Him, dear."

"I know you're right." Grace sighed. She gave her aunt a peck on the cheek and glanced back, "See you tonight, Josie."

Grace slipped out the door and walked the seven blocks back to the South Battery. Each step she took matched the slapping water that hit the wall holding back the Atlantic Ocean. The walkway, a narrow strip of cobblestone that stood above the street and was hemmed in by the long stretch of wall, let one look out over the waters that ran along the side of the South Battery. Right now, the weight of her problems seemed as vast as the sea. When she neared the end of the street she saw Ethan Boyd sitting on her doorstep waiting for her. He stood when he caught sight of her, his tall frame slim and lanky.

Grace groaned to herself as she hurried up to him. "How long have you been sitting here?"

"Pretty near an hour." He looked down at her with an easy smile. "I didn't mind."

"You must have come shortly after I left. Aunt Katy invited me to lunch."

"Well, I've come to invite you to supper." He slipped his hand under her elbow and led her to the front porch.

"I can't." Grace pulled her elbow out of his hold. "Josie is spending the night with me." She smiled apologetically. "Aunt Katy thinks I need some cheering up."

"I can cheer you up." A cheeky grin followed his words.

"I'm afraid you can't this time, and I wish to be alone to work things out."

"Pray tell, what can be so serious as to send me walking?" He put his arm over her shoulder.

Grace leaned out from under his arm and turned to face him. "Mother's left me with a fine mess." She flinched. "I didn't mean to say that."

"What is it?"

"I don't want to talk about it. It's personal. I'll find a way to work it out."

He hesitated before he asked, "Is it financial problems you're dealing with?"

Grace stared at the crack in the sidewalk, her cheeks burning.

"Marry me." His light brown hair, usually combed into a perfect part, fell over his forehead. He brushed it back with long, slim fingers. "I can pay your mother's debts with you as my wife. I've been meaning to ask you for some time now. I wanted to wait for the right time, the right setting." He looked down with sincerity in his light brown eyes.

10

"Obviously, that time is now."

"I won't marry you under these circumstances. My mother's debts are not your concern." Grace stepped back.

"I had already planned to ask you to marry me."

Grace shook her head. "Your offer is quite tempting, given I don't know how I'm going to get out of this predicament. I do, however, have enough propriety and decency to know it isn't right to marry you to save my financial reputation. I'm honored you asked me." She reached into her black-stringed purse and pulled out the townhouse key.

"Give it some thought." He shoved his hands into his tweed pockets. "Who cares what everyone else thinks about us getting married under these circumstances?"

She turned back to face him. "I do."

Ethan's shoulders straightened and his cheeks blushed deep red. The color rose to his forehead, where the unruly hair fell once more. She'd known for a while the day would come when he'd pose the question of matrimony. Truth to tell, she didn't want to marry him. As one of the town's physicians, Ethan would be a good provider to some woman someday. She'd argued this point to herself a hundred times. But the spark she anticipated when she fell in love just wasn't there.

Ethan folded his arms across his chest and glared at her for a moment. "I won't give up." The muscles in his jaw worked. "I've known for some time I want you in my life. I mean to see my dream come to fruition. I hope you'll give it some thought."

Grace didn't miss the heated glance. "I will think about it, Ethan. But I'm sure I already know the answer." With that, she entered the house. Once inside, she leaned her back against the closed door. *Why does life have to be so complicated?*

THREE

GRACE DELIBERATELY KEPT her eyes from straying to the desk in the drawing room. Instead, she climbed the stairs and stood at the entrance to her mother's bedchamber. She missed her mother terribly. Her gaze settled on the wardrobe. "Mama." She crossed the floor, opened the wardrobe, and looked over the long gowns. A perfumed fragrance wafted out from the pretty dresses, all arranged by color and duty. Some were day dresses, others Sunday best.

Grace embraced the familiar blue-flowered day dress, crumpling the fabric to her face and drowning in its scent. Tears spilled over onto the blossoms and made dark stains on the petals. More than ever, she missed her mother's soft and gentle touch. Her shoulders shook while she clung to the dress. Its essence was all she had left that truly made her feel her mother's presence in the room.

Moments later, her tears exhausted, Grace held the dress to her and circled the room. She draped the gown over her left arm while she opened drawers to the night stands on either side of the bed. Trinkets and unimportant items lay in them.

Setting the dress on the soft, quilted bed, Grace turned to the chest of drawers. The top drawer was full of ladies' underclothes. She ran her hand through the silky pieces. Her fingers bumped something hard. Grace took hold of the object and pulled out a dark frame the size of the palm of her hand. It folded in half like a small, metal booklet. Curious, she opened the frame and stared at a man who posed in a dark suit near a ship.

"Who might this be?" The inscription on the opposite side of the picture read Phillip Thomas Cooper 1806.

"My father!" She moved to the rocking chair, staring at the picture as if she'd just seen a ghost. *Why didn't Mother ever show this to me?* Her mother had told her that her father was lost at sea, and though her mother never told Grace how he had died, as a child she had conjured up a dozen ways it could have happened. Her childhood version of her father did not look like the man in the picture frame. He appeared too austere, unlike the rough-and-tumble version she had made him out to be.

She was twelve years old when her mother told her the story about her father, a shipping merchant who sailed from one small island to another. Olivia stood on the dock one day, seeing a friend off, when he sailed into Charleston, South Carolina. Their eyes caught and he asked her name. They fell in love and married. Her father had spent months remodeling his plantation house in Jamaica for his new bride.

Grace leaned her head against the rocker, remembering her mother's southern drawl as she spoke about the plantation house. Grace wished to see her father's plantation with its tall palmettos, tropical bushes, and Spanish Oak trees. She wished she could experience the steamy smell that came up from the earth "like a hot, damp blanket," as her mother had described it. She longed to hear the slaves singing at night as her mother had heard them in the distance in their cabins, a soul-searching kind of singing.

It must have been thrilling.

But over time her mother had grown silent, her eyes hard. She began to hate the plantation, the weather, and the small town. She missed the gentle rain. She missed the carriages going by with ladies and gentlemen dressed in their fine clothes. She missed the flower sellers and the fruit stalls. She felt trapped and wanted to go home to Charleston. Before long, Olivia had fled Jamaica and sailed back to her roots. That same year, Grace was born on American soil.

Grace fingered the metal frame in her hand. She had a fear of traveling on a ship. Since her father had died at sea, she grew up promising herself she'd never step foot on a vessel. She wouldn't put herself in that kind of jeopardy. The sea was perilous. It had claimed her father. In a state of hopelessness, she pushed out of the rocking chair and set the picture of her father on top of the tall chest of drawers. She continued to rummage through drawers and clothes closets, trying to discover some small sense of herself through her mother's things. After an hour of tearfully shuffling through Olivia's personal effects and crying tears for her loss, she opened the brown trunk at the foot of her mother's bed.

She and her mother had gone through the trunk many times over the years. Even before she opened the heavy lid, she knew what she would find. She had memorized each piece of treasure in the order they were placed in the chest.

She lifted a quilt sewn by her great-grandmother, then baby clothes Grace had worn nearly nineteen years ago, and a brown, turtle-shell hand mirror that also belonged to her great-grandmother. The list went on: a crocheted baby blanket, a hymn book, and a metal letter opener engraved with a hummingbird. By mid-afternoon, Grace had piled the foot of her mother's bed with relics from the past. When she neared the bottom of the chest, she lifted a white shawl, revealing a bundle of unopened letters tied with twine and a pale blue diary, worn around the edges.

"I don't remember these." Grace lifted the letters and diary out of the trunk. She quickly opened the hardbound cover and read: This diary belongs to Olivia Cooper.

A piece of gold chain slipped out and hung from the pages of the blue diary. She carefully opened the worn book to the middle, where a gold locket lay wedged between the pages. It had been there so long the center of the page had become indented in the shape of the heart.

Her hand shook as she gingerly picked up the jeweled piece and turned it around to find the latch. She pushed a small, round knob the size of a pinhead, and the heart popped open. A picture of her mother and father attired in wedding clothes lay nestled in the gold piece. The young woman staring back at her looked like herself. She'd been told she resembled her mother. This locket proved their strong resemblance. Her father, dark-haired and handsome, stood behind her mother and to one side. His arm reached around her mother's waist and Olivia's hand rested on his. Their eyes shone. They appeared happily in love. She closed the gold piece and hugged it to her heart. With both parents gone, all she had left of them was this gold locket.

Grace sat down on the floor and leaned back on the brown trunk. The bundle of letters tied with twine rested on her lap. With shaking fingers, she pulled at the knot that held the letters secure. The twine pulled apart easily. Grace lifted the first envelope and looked to see who the sender was. "Phillip T. Cooper," she whispered. The date of the letter was July 1810. "Twenty years ago."

Grace peered at the sealed envelope. How odd, the seal had not been broken. She eagerly slit open the first envelope and pulled out a crisp sheet of paper. As she unfolded it, a narrow piece of paper fell to her lap. Wide-eyed, Grace picked it up. A cashier's check for five British pounds! She read the first letter. Eyes moist, she read of her father's love for Olivia. He begged her to come back to Jamaica. The letter explained that she should deposit the check in the bank account he'd opened for her. Had her mother ever used this bank account?

Grace opened one letter after another and finally found a note that contained information about the account her father opened for Olivia. It too contained a cashier's check for five British pounds. Had they struggled all these years for nothing?

Heart pounding, Grace spent the next hour poring over the letters. Her father wrote about the plantation he owned in Jamaica and his adventures of buying and selling goods on island coasts in the Caribbean Sea.

With each letter Grace opened, a slip of paper fell onto her skirt. By the time she'd finished reading all the wonderful letters, a pile of cashier's checks lay on her lap. Her cheeks were wet with tears. Renewed hope burned in her soul.

Many of the letters were written after she was born. Olivia had said he died *before* she was born. Why did Mama lie? Why didn't she read his letters?

The letters slowed down as the years progressed. Grace reached for the last letter, dated November 1829, and frowned. That was only a month ago. As she slit open the letter no cashier's check fell to her lap. The letter was only one page. Her father wrote as if he were a distant friend. Not one word in any of the letters had he spoken of his daughter. Had her mother failed to tell him he had a child?

Please forgive me, was the small plea before her mother died. Holding the letter dated November 1829, Grace now knew the truth. Olivia had withheld news of her birth from her father.

"She lied to me!" Grace glared at the mail that contradicted all the stories she'd ever heard. All this time she'd wanted to believe her father still lived, albeit in an enchanted land. And all this time he *was* very much alive! She'd been cheated of the father she'd dreamed and wished for. What was she to do with this newfound knowledge?

So engrossed was she in her father's letters, that the diary lay on the floor, untouched. Grace picked up the worn book. The first few pages were filled with romantic ideas and Olivia's hope and fantasies for a bright future, Olivia had hoped for with Phillip Cooper.

A few pages over: My bags are packed. I wait with anticipation to sail to Jamaica. Another page: My father-in-law, Grandville Cooper, is none to thrilled to have me in his family. I fear Phillip will pay the cost of marrying me. His father threatened to cut Phillip out of his life and out his will. Phillip's heart is set on making a future for us. He says, no amount of money in the world can separate us. Dear Diary, I do hope he doesn't regret the course he has taken.

Then in the middle of the diary the truth came to light: "I can't bear to be on this island another day . . . I must leave! But can I go with this babe in my womb? I mustn't let Phillip know . . . he'll make me stay . . ." Grace swallowed, her mother's words.

She thumbed through the small book and read the last page of her entries. Tears flooded her eyes as she read: *Grace must never know her father is alive. I raised her with the lie that her father was lost at sea. If she learns the truth . . . will she ever forgive me?*

My father is alive. This enlightenment both invigorated and infuriated her. Too stunned to grapple with her own thoughts, she didn't know what to do. Should she search for him? Would he accept her as his child? Was it twenty years too late? Grace shook her head and glanced at the pile of mail before her. Should she pretend she'd never discovered them? No. She couldn't and she wouldn't. She would not follow her mother's footsteps and pretend her father did not exist.

Olivia didn't have Grace's father's irrepressible spirit. She'd stopped writing in her diary and tucked Phillip's letters unopened into the bottom of the brown trunk, afraid of what? That I would find them?

"Oh, Mother!" She eyed the stack of cashier's checks. "You were so adamant in putting father in your past that you denied me the right to know him, and we lived a hard life. We didn't have to struggle to get by."

She pushed the outdated checks off her lap onto the floor. One note floated back to her side. Grace stared at the paper. Maybe the date on the checks didn't matter.

Grace rolled to her knees and gathered up the strewn paper. She tapped the stack on the floor to align them. Then, one by one, she counted the checks and stuffed them into an empty envelope. For a moment she felt giddy. She wanted to believe there was enough to pay off her mother's debts. She would hide the checks. The thought of this much money sitting in her house frightened her.

She placed the envelope under the silky underclothes in her mother's top drawer. Unknowingly, her father might have paved the way for Grace to see the light of day. There may even be enough left over to buy passage to sail to Jamaica. *Where did that thought come from?* Grace frowned. *I can't sail.*

"Oh, this is all silliness. Sail to Jamaica?" Grace gathered the rest of the envelopes lying on the floor. She picked up the pale blue diary and put it and the envelopes in the middle of Olivia's feather mattress.

A knock at the front door sent Grace's heart leaping into her throat. "Coming!"

She glanced at the clutter on the end of her mother's bed. It could be dealt with later. Grace sailed down the stairs and opened the door. "Josie, do come in."

FOUR

GRACE BOWED HER head against the cold morning chill as she walked the three blocks to her grandfather's mercantile store. She kept a tight grip on her black purse filled with cashiers checks made out to her mother. She didn't have the faintest idea how to go about changing the currency of British pounds into American money.

The cowbells clanged on the door as Grace walked into the spacious store. Her grandfather stood behind the cashier's counter tallying up a customers purchase. Grace held up a finger and pointed, signaling she'd be in the back office. He nodded and turned back to the customer.

Grace sat behind the wooden desk and tapped her foot impatiently. Moments later, she rose and paced the floor. She stood with her back to the door as her grandfather walked in.

"Now what brings you in with your tail feathers in a ruffle?"

"I need advice." Grace opened her purse and pulled out the envelope filled with British pound notes. "Take a look at these."

She watched her grandfather peer over his spectacles at her, then at the contents in the envelope. "What's this?"

"British pound notes."

"I see that. But where did you get the money?"

"Did you see the signature?"

"Yes, that's why I ask." He took a seat in front of his desk.

"They were in Mother's brown trunk. I found them last night."

"Why on earth didn't your mother cash these?"

"She never opened the letters. I went through her things and came across all this mail." She leaned forward, elbows on the desk. "My father isn't dead. He's alive."

"You don't know that for sure. I wouldn't be getting my hopes up if I were you."

"I read every letter he wrote. Mama said he died before I was born. These letters came after my birth. Furthermore, the last letter was only a month ago." She swallowed hard. "Not once did he mention my name. He doesn't even know I exist." Her eyes smarted. "And besides, I read Mama's diary. She didn't tell him about me."

"That's because she didn't want to go back to Jamaica. I suppose she hid all those letters so she wouldn't have to face the truth." He shook his head.

"There are so many questions I want to ask her." Grace's voice quavered as she dabbed at the corners of her eyes. Then she cleared her throat. "If you look further, there's a letter explaining an account Father set up for Mother. I'm inclined to believe it's an account she never knew about."

He glanced over the letter, and then looked up. "Come back at noon. We'll have lunch and visit the bank. Katy told me your mother left you in a pinch." He held the envelope out to her.

"Thank you, Grandfather." She stood on tiptoe and kissed his cheek.

The door clanged again as she stepped out into the crisp morning air. Christmas was only two weeks away, and the shops were full of tempting gifts for their customers. Wreaths hung on the front doors of homes. Wagons rumbled by with pine trees in the back. Walking the three blocks to the South Battery, she sensed a glimmer of hope for the first time since her mother had passed.

After a hearty lunch, Grace and her grandfather went to the bank. Mr. Pettis' brows rose as he sat down before them, a slip of paper in his hands. "It appears this account was opened a good many years ago." He set the paper down and picked up one of the British pound notes. "With proper authorization these can be cashed in. I suggest you see your attorney, Miss Cooper. You'll need a signed letter from him, authorizing you as the legal heir to your mother's account. Until then, there's nothing we can do."

Grace extended her hand to Mr. Pettis. "Thank you. I'll see Mr. Burkley and have the papers drawn up."

Grace and her grandfather stepped out into the cool air.

"Think you can handle this on your own?" Grandfather asked.

"Certainly. You go ahead. I know you're needed at the store. I've other matters to attend to after I see the attorney."

"If you have any questions after you've talked to him, come see me." He tipped his hat and walked toward the mercantile.

Grace turned and walked in the opposite direction to Mr. Burkley's office.

"You are your mother's only beneficiary," Mr. Burkley announced. "I'll write up the proper documentation allowing you access to her funds."

"Thank you, Mr. Burkley. "I've a number of creditors who've peppered me for payments. It will be good to pay them and be done with it."

"Stop by tomorrow. I'll have your papers ready."

"Good day, Mr. Burkley." Grace left his office with purposeful strides.

By the end of the week, Grace was able to sit down and pay the majority of her mother's debts. Setting the pen next to the ink well, she pondered, "There may be enough left to take care of one more thing."

She looked down at Smitty, who was intent on licking his paw and running it over his whiskers.

The discovery that her father was alive filled Grace with renewed hope. She had spent every waking moment thinking about him. After much thought and prayer, Grace gathered the courage to walk to the docks landing and purchase a ticket to Riverbend, Jamaica. She wouldn't think about the perilous sea for now. She'd find the strength to step onto that ship when the day arrived.

With most of her mother's debts paid and a ticket in her hand assuring she'd sail to Jamaica, she had one more hurdle to face. Grace walked to the bank and sat before Mr. Pettis once again.

"What can I do for you, Miss Cooper?"

"I'd like to see the balance on the townhouse."

"Certainly." His brows rose as he walked away.

Grace fidgeted with her stringed purse as she watched Mr. Pettis open a file drawer and pull out important-looking papers. He strode back and sat down.

"You do know that your mother left an outstanding debt on this mortgage?"

"I was told as much. How far behind in payments was she?"

"Five months to the day." He leaned back, gazing at her. "I'm sorry, Miss Cooper. We must start foreclosure procedures if the payments are not brought up to date."

"I . . . I don't have the funds." Heat flared up her neck and over her scalp. "How long before I have to be out of the house?"

"Ten days."

"Ten days?" She swallowed hard.

"Yes. A generous allowance, you must admit, given the delinquency of this account." His mouth was grim.

Grace stood, her knees weak with the harsh news. They nearly buckled beneath her. "I've no time to waste."

"That's true. Good day, Miss Cooper."

Grace stood outside the bank, her pulse racing. *Ten days! How does one box up her life in ten days?*

"You can just forget about sailing to Jamaica, young lady. You've no chaperone. The answer's, no."

"Aunt Katy—"

"It isn't proper for a young woman to sail alone. It just isn't done." Aunt Katy stood with both hands on her hips. She looked like a bull ready to charge its target.

Grace gulped. "I'm not afraid to sail alone. And proper or not, I'm going."

"You would risk your reputation? Surely you don't think I would condone such a thing." Aunt Katy paced, wearing a path on the hardwood floor of her kitchen, her face ablaze.

"What if he's not at the plantation when you get there?" Josie said from her chair opposite Grace. She picked up her iced glass of lemonade and took a sip.

Grace was thirsty, but she couldn't touch her glass. She sat, hands clenched in her lap. "He's there. I wouldn't consider going if I didn't believe I'd find him at the plantation."

"You put all that foolish nonsense aside. I understand your not wanting to live in that townhouse alone. I'm sure Peter's not much company when he gets home."

Grace couldn't sit any longer. She joined Aunt Katy and paced the floor. "I think he's courting someone. He comes in late, but I don't mind."

Aunt Katy winked at Josie, then turned back to Grace. "Josie and I have given it a good deal of thought. The townhouse is too big, and it holds the memory of your mother passing in it. We have plenty of room here. Move in with us."

"Oh, Aunt Katy . . ." Grace raised her petite shoulders. "I want to meet my father. Can't you see that?"

"Of course you do, darlin', and we will send him a letter, post haste. You can explain how you found out about him. He'll likely take the next ship out to see you."

Grace sat down. She put her forehead in the palm of her hands and shook her head. "No, no, no. You don't understand. *I want* to see my father's home. *I want* to spend days, hours, weeks with him. *I want* to get to know him. Don't you see?"

Somehow she had to make Aunt Katy understand how desperate she was to be with her father. She and her father had years to make up for the time they'd lost.

Her aunt stopped pacing. Her shoulders slumped. "Unfortunately I do." Aunt Katy shrugged and gave in. She frowned at Josie. "We both do. We'd hoped to convince you to stay with us. If that is not to be, then there are other things to consider. Have you spoken to your grandfather about this?"

"I wanted to talk to you first."

"Good. You'd better let me handle it."

"Would you?" Grace leaned over and hugged her aunt.

"He won't be happy when he finds out he's losing his bookkeeper indefinitely."

"Josie's learned a bit of it. I can train her before I go." Grace glanced at her cousin.

Josie nodded ascent to the plan and half smiled.

"I still don't like the idea of your leaving." Aunt Katy pointed a finger at Grace. "And I'm not condoning your decision to sail alone."

"But if you were in my shoes—?"

"I'm thanking the good Lord you're sticking around long enough so that Josie can learn the books," her aunt said, as if to ignore Grace's point of view. "You'll have to purchase your ticket for about a month from now. I can't leave before then and you'll not travel alone. I promised your mother I'd look after you and I'm holding to that promise."

Grace froze to her seat. How would her Aunt Katy react when she told her the rest of her plans? Grace bit her bottom lip and looked up. Before she could speak her aunt went on.

"Your Uncle Harold left the Apothecary Shop to me when he died six months ago. Up till recently, I hadn't given it much thought about legally putting it in my name. Mr. Burkley informed me it's going to take at least a month to finalize the paperwork. That being because of the pharmaceutical and health laws." So don't get any harebrained idea about going until I'm free to come with you."

"Well, that's the problem." Heat rose to the top of Grace's scalp. "I've purchased a passage to sail the first of January. That is only two weeks away."

"Have mercy, child." Aunt Katy fanned herself. "You'll have to cancel that ticket. I meant what I said. You are not traveling alone."

"I'm going." Grace lifted her chin.

"Your mother would turn in her grave if she knew what you're up to, Grace Cooper."

"Well she doesn't know, and besides . . . she lied to me." Grace squared her shoulders and eyed her aunt boldly. She sat rigid in her chair.

"Now you hold your tongue, young lady. That she did and Lord knows it's true, but she did it to protect herself from losing you."

"All my life I wished I had known my father. I would never have dreamed in a million years my own mother would keep us apart." Tears stung Grace's eyes. She brushed them away.

"Isn't this a fine kettle of fish," Aunt Katy said. "You've only two weeks to get everything in order. You've got to pack enough clothes for the trip, and what of the townhouse? Who's watching it while you're gone?"

Grace wiped her eyes with the back of her hand and studied a tiny speck of crumb on the tablecloth, wincing.

"Grace?"

She peered at her aunt then back to the crumb on the table.

"All right, Grace. What have you done?"

25

"I gave up the townhouse."

"You didn't!"

"Mother was too far behind in payments. I needed enough money to make the trip. I let it go back to the bank." She glanced first at her aunt and then to her cousin.

"Oh my!" Josie's mouth dropped open.

"Grace Cooper . . ." Aunt Katy laid both palms face down on the white tablecloth and leaned in to study her niece's face. "You've no intention of coming back to Charleston, do you?"

Grace waited a beat. "No, I don't. I mean to find my father and make a home with him." *There, I've said it.* Grace folded her hands in her lap.

"You do beat all, child."

"Yes, I know. But I've made up my mind."

"How long before the bank takes possession of the townhouse?"

"Ten days."

"What in heaven's name!" Aunt Katy said.

"I give them the key four days before I board the *Savannah Rose*."

"The *Savannah Rose*?" Her aunt pursed her lips. "That name sounds familiar," she said in a smooth, thoughtful tone. She drummed her fingers on the table, as if trying to remember where she'd heard the ship's name.

"Well, no matter." Aunt Katy waved a hand as if swatting her thoughts away. "Josie, we've got work to do. Your cousin is going to need all the help she can get. We've got to get her trunks packed and do something with all the furniture in the house. In the meantime . . ." She peered at Grace. "You've got to teach Josie a thing or two about the books at your grandfather's store."

Grace relaxed. "I will. I promise." The worst part of the confrontation was over. She would sail to Jamaica!

FIVE

GRACE LEFT AUNT Katy's house with a million thoughts on her mind. There were dozens of loose ends that needed to be tied if she were to be ready to leave in two weeks. She picked up her step as she headed for the South Battery. She would give the cook the night off. She'd surprise Peter and cook his favorite supper tonight. She wanted to show her gratitude that he'd unselfishly stayed with her at the townhouse.

Grace stepped off the sidewalk and started across the cobbled road, her mind on the side dish she would serve with his meal. All at once two horses pulling a buggy loomed up in front of her. She heard the coachman shout, "Look out!" as the horses whinnied and reared up. Grace froze. Before she could move, the horses sidestepped, but not before the hoof of one horse slammed into her chest sending her flying against the cobblestone street. Pain split her head like an explosion. The world went black.

Grace lay with her eyes closed. Voices rose and fell beside her bed. Footsteps. Someone walked past her bed. Where was she? She wanted to open her eyes. But she couldn't. Pain pierced the back of her head.

"Ooh," she moaned.

"Grace?"

A familiar voice. She wanted to reach out. Climb out of this dreadful darkness. She couldn't move, couldn't speak. Couldn't . . .

It seemed she had slept a million years. Outside of her dark world, the room rustled with soft sounds, and then the familiar voice again . . . was that Aunt Katy? Her eyes snapped open. Josie sat on one side of her bed, Aunt Katy on the other. Glancing beyond them she noted other beds lined up in the oblong room. Nurses came and went.

"What am I doing here?" Grace asked in a weak voice. She tried to raise her head and flinched as pain shot between her side and chest. Her head throbbed as well.

Aunt Katy hovered over her. "Don't try to move, darlin'. You're in bad shape."

"What happened to me?" Grace tried to focus, sedated and groggy. The room swam.

"You had a terrible accident, Grace. You need to lie still and rest." Aunt Katy laid a gentle hand on Grace's shoulder to comfort her.

"An accident?" Darkness threatened to pull her back into nothingness. She couldn't fight it. She fell, fell, fell into the abyss that swallowed her up.

Sounds in the room awakened her consciousness. Footsteps. That's what she heard, and metal. Something scraping metal. Grace peeked one eye open and turned her head in the direction of the sound. Pain shot through her head as she glanced at a doctor checking on a patient in the bed next to hers.

Aunt Katy and Josie were gone. She surveyed the long windows on the far side of the room. Twilight had set in. She tried to raise her head and flinched. "Oh!" she moaned.

The doctor turned at the sound of Grace's voice and strode to her bedside. "Miss, you mustn't move too much." He examined the bandage on her head and asked, "Are you hungry?"

Grace's stomach growled in response. She nodded her head ever so slightly.

"I'll send someone in with a meal for you." He walked to the foot of her bed.

"Wait!" Grace stopped him.

"Yes, Miss?" The middle-aged doctor turned back to her bedside.

"What happened to me? How long have I been here?"

"I'll fetch Dr. Newton. He's your doctor. He can answer your questions." He smiled and left the room.

Grace glanced around the quiet room. Seven other patients shared the oblong room, with four beds on each side. Long, white curtains were pulled around some beds. But the bed beside her was visible. A young woman lay sleeping. She lay on her side with her back to Grace. *What am I doing here? What happened to me?*

Moments later, she heard Dr. Newton's footsteps on the polished hardwood floor. He walked up to her bedside. "Good evening, Miss Cooper. How do you feel?" As he asked, he poked her ribs gently, then reached under her jaw with both hands and pressed lightly.

Grace winced when he touched her ribs. "I ache all over Doctor Newton." The ward doctor stood beside the physician and the two of them eyed Grace.

"You took a hard fall, Miss Cooper, and a hard kick in the ribs from one of the horses you stepped out in front of. When you fell, it knocked you unconscious." He took a stethoscope from around his neck and listened as he moved it over her heart and lungs. "You have two broken ribs. You're lucky to be alive." He patted her arm and smiled.

Her heart sank. "How long will I be in the hospital?"

"Another two weeks at the least, Miss Cooper. Then you must stay home and take it easy for few months. It's best you try not to move too much so your ribs can mend. Then again, we want to make sure you've not damaged your skull. "You have quite a knot on the back of your head."

Grace reached up and touched a tender spot where the doctor indicated. A dull ache penetrated the area. She wanted to shout or kick or do something to let out her frustration. This couldn't be happening. She had purchased a ticket to sail to Jamaica. She was to be on the ship in two weeks. She had to be on that ship!

"I won't be able to sail to Jamaica in two weeks?" She knew the answer but had to ask.

"No, Miss. You won't be going anywhere for the next few months. Get your rest. I'll check in on you again later." He turned to the ward doctor. "Give her something light to eat." Then they were gone.

A tear trickled down the side of her temple. She swallowed the lump in her throat. She wouldn't be sailing to Jamaica for a good long while. She'd be laid up in this dreadful bed staring at four walls. She gave in to the sobs that wrenched her heart. And what of the townhouse? The bank would take possession of it on the first of the month. Nothing was going right. *What did I do to deserve this, God?* She closed her eyes, hot tears sliding down her face. Moments later, she slept.

A few days later, Grace sat up in her bed. She had spent the first hour with her sketchpad. She drew what was around her, a cleaning woman in uniform and cap, the sun's rays through the curtained window, and a glass half-filled with water. She didn't move anymore than she had to. Yet she found if she sat propped just right, she could draw on her sketchpad or read her Bible.

Peter had just left and now she tried to concentrate on the scriptures before her. Try as she might, she couldn't keep her mind on the words. What with all the quiet sounds of the doctors coming and going and the housekeeper sweeping under beds, picking up small wastebaskets, and dusting around tables, she couldn't focus. Grace finally set her Bible down. She needed uplifting, and she knew she would find it in the Word. She would rest and try later.

Just then, Ethan walked in the room. "How's the patient doing?" He leaned down and kissed her forehead.

"The doctor was just here. He said I'm recovering well. The bump on my head has gone down and I'm able to sit up." She wished he hadn't come. Her shoulders stiffened.

"I'm making my rounds as well. I've been in to see you several times, but you've been asleep. I'm glad to see you're awake and sitting up." Ethan pulled up a chair and sat down.

Grace waited for the inevitable. She knew he wanted an answer to his request that she marry him. She focused on the foot of her bed and fingered the top cover of her bedding.

Ethan cleared his throat. "Have you given any thought to our getting married?"

Grace didn't miss the anxious look in his eyes.

"To be honest, Ethan, I have been so busy with Mother's affairs I haven't had time to think about it." She hated herself for sidestepping the truth. She had no desire to marry him. Friendship is all she ever wanted of Ethan. "There's no rush for an answer is there?"

"I want to know where we stand." He turned red from his neck to his ears. "But no, there is no rush for an answer." He searched her face longingly. "You do care for me don't you, Grace?"

"Of course I care for you, Ethan. We've been good friends for the past six months. You've been a perfect gentleman, quite caring." She couldn't look him in the eye. She felt parched in the throat and took a sip of water.

"Friendship is not what I'm asking for Grace." His tone was sharp. "Do your feelings go beyond that?" He had removed his stethoscope and thumped it on the palm of his hand.

"I need time, Ethan. My emotions are all mixed up. It wouldn't be fair to you to ask more than I can give right now." This time she looked him full in the eye.

Ethan stood and nodded his head. "You're right, Grace. You're still trying to heal from your mother's passing, and now this." He held up his hand in a halting signal. "Forgive me for imposing on you at a stressful time."

Grace gazed down at her hands again.

"I'll come back and check on you later." Ethan backed up a few steps.

Grace bobbed her head up and gaped at him.

"I want to see improvement to your health." With two fingers to the side of his forehead, he saluted her and walked out of the room.

Grace leaned back on the pillow and let out a long, weary sigh. She picked up the Bible again. *Lord I need direction, now more than ever.*

Grace was tired of lying around. She'd spent months recuperating from her fall. Now she was back from taking her daily walk that Dr. Newton had suggested to regain her strength. She plopped down on the sofa and picked up a book. She felt good as new. No sooner had she leaned back for a good read than the front door opened and Josie stepped in.

"Are you home for the afternoon?" Grace asked hopefully.

"Yes, Mama sent me home. Business is slow today." Josephine eyed Grace, "And what of you? You look fit to be tied."

"I can't sit here another moment. I'm tired of being confined to this house."

Josephine stepped up to the lounge where Grace lay. "Are you up for a little sword sport?"

Grace leaned forward. "I'd love to go a round with you."

"I'll give you a moment to change. I need to change myself. Meet me in the courtyard."

Grace entered the flagstone courtyard. Her boots clicked across the floor as she went to the wall mount that held a variety of swords. She reached for the rapier she used when she and Josie practiced their fencing lessons.

Josie, dressed in white canvas breeches and a long-sleeved, canvas top, hurried in and scanned Grace with a quick appraisal. "It's good to see you back to your normal self."

Grace gave Josie a peck on the cheek. "You're a dear, Josie. I don't think I could have stood one more minute of sitting around." She pulled her face shield over her long, auburn ringlets and adjusted it to a comfortable fit. After she pulled on her white gloves, she took up the shining rapier and smiled.

Grace liked the feel of the rapier's long, thin, flexible blade. It was most elegant in action and most deadly because of its long reach. She swiped at the air, flicking her wrist the way she had been taught. The blade hissed.

Josie pulled on her face shield. Tawny-brown eyes glinted through the screen.

The two young ladies hugged, then stepped back. Grace held her blade to her face shield in a salute. The girls crossed their foils in the air to form an "X." Each blade wore a thick tar-and-canvas tip to protect them from accidental injury.

Each stepped to the right and circled the floor. In a flash Grace jumped back, then thrust her blade forward for the first move. It came down on Josie's blade, sending a sharp ting through the air.

Josie, ever ready, tilted her rapier. Grace's blade slid off. The girls moved forward and back, their foils flashing in the afternoon sunlight that spilled into the room from the west portico alcove.

Grace loved the sport of fencing. She'd spent countless hours sharpening her skills. When she wasn't working at her grandfather's store, she was watching other combatants in swordplay. She understood the moves for defense. Now she met each thrust and advance with a parry, and moved quickly while Josie's blade swung in long, sweeping arcs.

Grace picked up speed, and in a flash, her rapier knocked Josie's from her hand. The sound of iron clanged on the flagstone as Josie's blade slid across the floor. With mischievous eyes, Grace stepped forward, her rapier pointed toward Josie's right ear. "Swashbuckler, lend me your ear."

For a moment the two stood frozen in place. Then Josie giggled, "Stop, you evil pirate, you." She pulled off her face shield as she laughed. Grace did the same, a playful smile on her lips.

"I think we'd better let you rest for now. Mother will have my skin if she sees us," Josie said, as she pulled her glove off.

A servant came out to the courtyard with a tray of iced lemonade. They each took a glass and clinked them together. "To your health," Josie said.

"And to my long-awaited journey to Jamaica!" Grace smiled.

Grace held the letter tight against her chest as she walked the few blocks to the post office. Her heart hammered to the rhythm of her steps. When she arrived at her destination, she glanced at the letter addressed to: Mr. Phillip Cooper. The contents told him she was coming. Would the letter get there before she did?

The warm, June air filled the sunny bedchamber at Aunt Katy's house. Trunks sat open in every available floor space. Hat boxes lay at the head of the four-poster bed, sitting precariously on a stack of pillows. Neatly folded clothes lay in short stacks in the middle of the soft, quilted bed, on armchairs, and on the table—cleared of its vase— by the window. Gowns draped over the foot of the bed and lay heaped in high piles before each trunk.

Grandmother tapped her foot impatiently. Aunt Katy rolled her eyes toward the ceiling. They were there to help Grace pack her belongings for the two-week journey to Jamaica. The June weather had peaked in its summer heat, and they all dripped with sweat in the crowded room.

"Where's Josie?" Grace asked.

"She went after your grandfather."

"Whatever for?"

"Because, dear girl, you've got to come to your senses. You've far too many trunks planned for this ridiculous trip," Grandmother said.

"Land sakes, you couldn't possibly think I'd leave these perfectly good clothes behind." Grace stood her ground.

At the end of the hall, Grace could be heard giving orders, making decisions, and asking advice. Her grandfather shook his head and gazed back at Josie.

"Our Grace is a bit headstrong at times," Josie said. "As you will see, she has seven trunks crammed into the bedchamber."

He scanned the panicked faces of his wife, Adeline and his daughter, Katy, and the flushed face of his granddaughter Josie, then turned his gaze into the room.

Grace smiled first.

He smiled back. "You'll be needing all of God's help for sure."

Grace put her hands on her hips, about to explain, when her grandfather held up an open palm.

"I will not get in the middle of this." He cleared his throat. "Even you can see it will take nothing short of a miracle to pack all of these clothes for your trip. Please see that it is all done with a minimum of fuss." He grinned reassuringly. "You do have three days to accomplish the task." He placed his hat on his head and disappeared out the door.

Grace sat in her bedchamber. The sunset gave the room a rosy hue as she placed the heart-shaped locket of her parents in her stringed purse, as ready as she'd ever be. Lighthearted, she leaned against the comfortable armchair. After months of recuperating, she was truly going to Jamaica. She grinned at her accomplishments. Six months ago she wouldn't have thought it possible to plan this trip without the help of her mother. The thought of finding her father gave her the courage to forge forward and accomplish the necessary steps to get this done. She had crammed the fear of stepping onto the *Savannah Rose* into the back of her mind a dozen times since she'd bought the tickets. But there was only one way to get to Jamaica: sailing.

The same ship was in port again. It had been months since it had last sailed to Jamaica. Yesterday, out of curiosity, and the need to get over her fear of sailing, Grace had walked down to the pier. The stevedores were unloading old cargo, while sailors pushed carts with new goods up the ramp onto the ship. Though she'd never sailed before, nor did she have a wish to, she loved watching the activity at the docks. A few heads had turned her way, with bright smiles and lifted eyebrows. She didn't stay long. It was enough to see that the ship was in port.

Tomorrow she would chart a new journey. She would leave behind the hurt and pain that had plagued her the past few months. She needed a new direction in her life. Would she find it in that land so far away?

Grace reached for the letter she wrote Ethan. The contents told him she must find her father. The last line read: *"I'm not coming back. I can't marry you."* She signed and sealed the letter. She'd known all along she would refuse his offer of marriage. Her father gave her a legitimate excuse to decline. Surely Ethan would understand. She'd send the note by courier in the morning, before she boarded the *Savannah Rose.*

SIX

Bridgetown, Barbados
June 1830

AWAY FROM HOME, on the beautiful island of Barbados, Phillip Cooper traveled through Bridgetown on his way to Kindra Hall. He would have paid Agnes Cavendish a visit were she on the island, but he'd learned she was not due here for another three weeks. He had counted on the two of them sharing a luncheon or two and swapping notes on the tobacco industry while he was in Bridgetown. Agnes Cavendish had a level head on her shoulders. She knew the trade. She was one of the few plantation owners he trusted when it came to the validity of sales and the growing need for tobacco crops. This was a new venture for him. Tobacco. It had been a while since he'd visited his second plantation, Kindra Hall. He'd spent the last five years hoping that the tobacco trade would be profitable. It had been. It was necessary to diversify his holdings, and it offered a nice change from the sugarcane fields at his home in Jamaica.

Phillip glanced out of the carriage window just as his tobacco plantation came into view. Large-leafed foliage lined the lane, and a row of oak trees, thick with Spanish moss, hung low on each side. The dark green foliage contrasted with yellow and fiery-red begonias lit up the scenery. The Great House loomed up as the buggy circled the drive and came to a stop.

In the distance, Stanley Bernard waved to Phillip as he picked up his pace and walked toward the drive. The blond-haired, blue-eyed foreman and manager of the estate grinned widely as Phillip stepped out of the carriage.

"Afternoon, Mr. Cooper," Stanley said.

"I see you've been out to the fields," Phillip slapped the young man on the back. "How are the crops?"

"I must say the tobacco growth has surprised me. This will make the fifth year in a row that the crops have produced at a maximum."

"Good, good." Phillip's eyes traveled over the vast fields. "I'll be going back to Jamaica in the next day or two."

"I'm sorry to hear that. My wife and I have enjoyed your stay."

"I've enjoyed it too, Stanley. I've not been away from Cooper's Landing more than two weeks at a time until now. A month on the island has given me much-needed rest."

"Glad to hear that." Stanley smiled.

"I'd heard rumors there's a wave of discontent among the slaves on Barbados. I wanted to see for myself." He cocked his head toward the house. "Let's go inside."

The two men sauntered into the Great House and took a seat. The maid set two cold glasses of lemonade on the table and left silently.

Phillip pulled out his pipe and lit it. After a billow of white smoke filled the air, he said, "I've learned what I've heard is true among many of the plantation owners here on the island. Are you seeing any signs of mutiny from our slaves?"

"We've had a rift or two in the last three months. A couple of our own escaped the plantation and joined the mutiny. The overseer put them in solitary confinement. It appears that has quieted any new melee for the time being."

Phillip leaned back in his leather chair. "Are they in confinement now?" He held his pipe at arms length.

"They were released a few days before you arrived." Stanley frowned. "Barely alive."

"I dislike this sort of thing." Phillip shook his head. "But we can't have them running off."

"I agree."

"We've seen signs of discontent at Cooper's Landing as well. I don't know how they're escaping the plantation, but I've lost five slaves in the past three months." Phillip shifted in the leather chair and frowned. "Neighboring plantations have complained that they're missing slaves as well. One owner found his field hand down by the wharf. He brought him home and hung him. Made him a public display for the rest of the field hands to see. Something to think about."

"I sure don't want to resort to that."

"You and me both," Phillip said.

A searing pain woke Phillip in the late hours of the night. He clutched his chest. Sweat beads formed on his brow. He panted and tried to slow his breathing, but the pain wracked his body. It felt as if a boulder sat squarely on his chest, crushing him.

Breathe slowly, he told himself. *Is this the end?* Should he call the valet? Should he call on God? *No!* He clamped his teeth so tightly his jaws ached. *There is no God.* Why had that thought occurred to him?

Little by little, the pain began to ebb. He took a deep breath. He opened his eyes and glimpsed over the dark room, then closed them again. He'd be all right. He'd beat this demon monster inside his chest. When the pain had eased, he rolled over to sleep.

The next morning, Phillip stepped inside the attorney's office. It was time to settle a few things before he left the island. He had an hour before the ship would sail. He'd be on that ship. He was ready to go home to Cooper's Landing.

"Morning, Mastah Camp," Dinah said.

"Good morning, Dinah. Coffee ready?"

"Sure is." Dinah moved to the shelf, pulled down a coffee mug, and then stepped to the stove where a pot of coffee boiled. She filled a mug and pushed the swinging kitchen door with her elbow. "Your breakfast be just about ready." Dinah sat his cup on the dining room table. Back in the kitchen she picked up a wooden spoon to stir the eggs in the cast iron skillet.

Cameron Bartholomew pushed through the swinging door and walked to the far end of the table and sat down. As the foreman of Cooper's Landing, he came to breakfast before dawn. Unlike foremen on other plantations, he moved easily into the kitchen and talked with the cook. The servants had been here long before he arrived as a young boy. They'd nearly raised him. While Phillip was out to sea, Cameron was alone with the gentle house slaves who looked after him. Ever since he was a child, Phillip called him "Camp," and Cameron called his mentor "Pip." It wasn't long before others on the Landing referred to Phillip with Cameron's pet name.

Cameron usually spent the first hour of the morning checking his ledger for the results of the prior day's activities. Nearly 194 slaves worked on the Landing, which made for a vast number of jobs to keep track of. He logged the work done in the cane fields, sugar mill, boiling houses, and provisional fields. The plantation workers maintained a good deal of land where horses, cattle, and sheep grazed. Cameron kept figures for births, deaths, and numbers of cattle butchered for the end-of-the-year accounting.

As Cameron opened the logbook, the clang of skillets and the smell of sausage filled the room. It wasn't long before Dinah pushed through the door with a broad smile on her dark, round face. She carried a plate of scrambled eggs and sausage in one hand and a pot of steaming coffee in the other.

"Now you be putting that book aside and git you some food in your belly." She set the hot plate of food before him.

"Smells good." He moved the log book aside."

"More coffee?"

"Only a fool would pass up your coffee." Cameron smiled. "Fill it up."

A moment later, Dinah made a second trip out to the dining room with a plate of biscuits and gravy and a bowl of sliced, tropical fruit.

"Can I git you anything else?"

"No, I'm fine." He watched her disappear into the kitchen again.

Cameron bit into a biscuit baked to a toasty, golden brown, and tried to focus on the logbook. By the time he finished his work, he had eaten a plate of scrambled eggs and several biscuits and had drunk two cups of coffee. He wiped his mouth with the napkin and dropped it in the center of his dish. He closed the logbook and stood to his feet.

Dinah shoved through the door with her wide hip, the coffee pot in hand.

"You all done?"

"Breakfast was good as usual. Best be moving out to the fields." He held out the logbook. "Mind putting this in the office for me?"

"Be glad to." She took the gray book, slipped it under her chubby elbow and hugged it to her side.

Cameron scooped his wide straw hat off the hall tree and placed it on his dark, unruly hair.

"Mastah Coopah should be home soon."

"I believe you're right. I don't recall his ever being gone this long." He reached for the doorknob.

"Mastah Coopah trust your ability to run things around here."

"Could be."

"He wouldn't be staying gone so long if he didn't."

"I hope you're right." Cameron opened the door, letting in the cool morning breeze.

"I'm baking your favorite pie this afternoon. Got a load of them fresh apples from Morgan's ship."

Cameron spun around and grinned. "You don't say! I'll be looking forward to some of that pie for supper." With that he slipped out the door.

Cameron stood on the porch and peered over the drive beyond the circular driveway. He missed Pip sorely. A month wasn't such a long time, but it felt like ages when Phillip was gone.

He'd come to think of Phillip like a father. The bond that grew between the two could be no stronger had they shared the same blood. Cameron didn't know where he'd be if while a child Pip hadn't taken him under his wing.

As he stood there in the early morning hour, his mind played back to his childhood, before Pip, before living at the Landing. He recalled the night his mother died. The morning hour had grown deathly quiet. His father said the infant was a boy. He didn't see the baby. It was wrapped in a blanket and lay in the crib. But he saw his mother. She lay in the bed as if asleep. She looked like an angel, with softness about her face. He wanted to touch her one more time. He had kissed her cheek and froze. She was cold. A sick feeling had come over him. She'd always been warm, inside and out.

Things got bad after that. Many nights his father came home drunk and beat his older sister. He wouldn't work, and food became scarce. Before long his father told the boys to find food for the house. After a year of this ravaged lifestyle, Cameron ran away.

It was easy to find food from the soiled women who hung around the docks. More than anything, he wanted to get on a ship and sail as far away from his misery as he could.

One night, he crept aboard a ship, hid himself, and fell asleep. In the recesses of his mind, he remembered being yanked from the abyss of darkness. He awoke, kicking and screaming, his heart pounding. "Let me go!" What would they do? Throw him overboard?

Fear engulfed him. If he could only get loose, he could make a run for it.

As the crewman dragged him down the dark aisle and up three flights of stairs, Cameron used every board and post to brace his feet to try to pull back and out of the iron grip of the crewman. His heart plummeted when the sailor opened the last door that led up to the quarterdeck.

Fear gripped him when they found Captain Phillip Cooper standing at starboard, gazing out over the high seas through a black, hand-held telescope.

Captain Cooper lowered the scope and spun around. The crewman held Cameron by the back of his neck while he kicked and squirmed to free himself.

"Let me go, you old croak!" Cameron yelled.

"Not a chance, lad. You been caught stowing away in the cannon room. Best be telling the captain what you been doing there!"

His heart pounded in his ears as Captain Cooper eyed him. This wasn't the first time Cameron had found himself in a precarious situation, and he stared back. Moments passed before he saw a slight twinkle in the captain's eyes. The captain's lips thinned as he strode across the quarterdeck toward him.

"I'd give command to my crewman to let you go," he said, "if I thought you'd give me an honest answer as to why you chose the *Savannah Rose* to make your escape."

Cameron said nothing. His eyes stayed on the captain.

"Let the boy go, Jesse."

This was his chance, Cameron thought. He'd have to make a run for it if he was to save himself from being thrown overboard. He glanced to the left and then to the right.

"Don't disappoint me, son," Cooper said.

Cameron glanced up into the eyes of the man who would set his course. Either the captain would have him whipped, or worse, thrown overboard. If he was lucky, the captain would find pity on him and let him go at the next harbor. His shoulders slumped.

"What's your name, son?"

"Cameron."

"Got a last name?"

"Bartholomew."

"Cameron Bartholomew," Captain Cooper said.

"Yes, sir." He hung his head and gawked at the floorboards as if to study the holes on the worn, wooden deck.

"How old are you, son?"

Cameron straightened his shoulders to gain a few inches in height. "Nine years old, Cap'n."

"How long you been away from home?"

"'Bout eight months, sir."

Cooper cast his gaze to the sailor who stood to the side and studied them. "Take him to the kitchen and tell Cook to give him some grub."

Involuntarily, Cameron's head flew up. He eyed the captain with awe.

"Then get the boy a bath and clean clothes."

" Aye, sir." Jesse reached for the lad's collar.

"Let the boy follow you. He won't run."

For the first time in months Cameron wasn't afraid. He squared his shoulders and walked behind Jesse. When they reached the stairs, he looked back to where the captain stood. Phillip Cooper stood at starboard and peered through the telescope once again.

When the *Savannah Rose* pulled into port at Riverbend, Jamaica, the captain came and got him, and they descended the gangplank together. Phillip Cooper hailed a driver to fetch his carriage to drive them to Cooper's Landing.

"Are we almost there?" Cameron scooted next to the window to peer out at the strange, tropical trees and bushes. Colorful parrots flew past and landed in the tall branches above to watch the carriage pass by. Cameron hardly blinked, lest he miss the wonder of it all.

Since then, life had been good. His nanny, Laulie, not only took the time to clean up the young boy's outerwear, she'd seen to his inner soul as well. She couldn't read a lick, but that didn't stop her from storing up stories from the Good Book she'd learned as a child. Her heart held a wealth of treasures she shared with him. As a child, Cameron loved hearing the stories. By the time he was a young man he had most of them memorized.

Before his seventeenth birthday, he made a commitment to Christ. He couldn't wait to share it with Pip. When Pip came home, Cameron told his foster father the good news. He still remembered the disappointment as Pip stared at him with no emotion. He didn't share the joy.

Laulie helped him through that tough time. She encouraged Camp to pray for Pip. He'd been doing that for the last twenty-four years. Nothing had changed. Had God given up on him?

SEVEN

June 1830

GRACE EMBODIED GENTEEL southern charm in her green traveling dress and hat. The color brought out the green of her eyes, and the contrast easily set off the sheen of her auburn hair.

But the layers of clothes were a bit much on this sultry morning. She would have been happy to discard the hat, shawl, and jacket right there on the spot. She looked heavenward and fanned herself while waiting for all her trunks to find their place in the hold of the ship.

Dust rose from wagons and carriages arriving at the side of the dock. The smell of the sailor's sweat hung in the air, their unpleasant odor clinging to them in the humidity. Not far from the vessel sat a row of fishermen's boats. Their nets, full from the catch of the morning, added a distinct stench to the cool, salt breezes that wafted now and then off the water. Grace wrinkled her brows and inhaled. She hoped she'd get used to all the scents floating through the air. She'd be on the ship a good two-to-three weeks, for better or for worse.

Grace never dreamed she'd leave South Carolina to journey to the Caribbean islands in search of a father she had never met. Now it was the perfect escape from the bleak future ahead. If only she could calm her thumping heart at the thought of stepping onto the massive ship that bobbed in the water.

With mixed feelings, Grace focused on the sweat-soaked crewmen hurrying around the dockyard picking up trunks, luggage, boxes, and freight and scurrying up and down the gangplank. Aunt Katy and Josie stood beside her, waiting for her bags to be loaded.

"Grace, honey, I wish you would reconsider your plans for this ill-advised voyage."

"I will do no such thing, Aunt Katy." Grace kept her eye on her baggage while several sailors rolled them up the ramp on flat, crude carts. One crewman reached for the bulky trunk next to her.

"This is to go to my cabin," she informed him.

The barrel-chested man swung around and chuckled. "This chest is too big for your cabin, Miss. You're gonna have to choose a smaller one for your room."

"I can't do that. I've already packed this container to be with me on the trip." Grace turned to her aunt for support.

Aunt Katy stepped forward. "Just take this trunk to Miss Cooper's cabin. She won't mind the inconvenience."

The sailor's craggy brows creased in disagreement. He grunted at the weight of the chest.

"You don't understand, Missy, this will take up most the space in your cabin. You won't have a speck 'o room to walk around," he said.

"I don't mind." Grace turned her back.

"Now you mind who you talk to on the ship." Aunt Katy's voice rose above all the clamor and noise at the dock.

"I will. Surely I'm not going to be the only woman on this voyage." She eyed the other passengers, but they seemed to be mostly men.

A carriage pulled up and stopped. A footman came around to the side and placed portable steps outside the carriage door. When he opened the door, a young woman with flame-red hair poked her head out and squinted at the noisy dockyard. She glanced at Grace and nodded before she picked up a section of her rust-colored cotton frock, stepped down, and turned to face the carriage. She moved back a step as another petite, young woman exited the door of the coach. She appeared wilted from the heat. Her brown, kid-laced boots hit the first step and she stopped. Her honey-colored ringlets bounced as she squinted toward the crowd, then quickly looked out at the large vessel waiting at the port ahead. Her bright, blue eyes sparkled and she giggled as she clutched a handful of her pale-blue skirt and moved down the next two steps to solid ground.

Grace watched with curiosity and relief. She relaxed and nudged Josie's side when a third woman poked her head out of the coach. The footman pulled luggage and trunks from above and behind the carriage while the gray-haired woman descended the three small steps. She hovered over the younger women giving instructions, her hands waving this way and that, while they waited for their trunks to be lowered to the ground.

"Well, there you are," Aunt Katy said. "You'll have someone to keep you company on the ship."

"Yes, I see." Grace watched the crewmen lift the women's trunks off the dirt road and load them onto the crude carts. Now that she was at the dock, she wished her Aunt Katy or Josie could come along. But it was not to be. She would make the most of this trip. And surely with a minimum of two weeks on the high seas, she would get to know the young ladies who had just shown up.

The three women moved toward the ship. It wouldn't be long before the whistle would blow, signaling their departure from shore.

"I hope I didn't make a mistake bringing that trunk." Grace bit her lip.

"What's that you say?" Aunt Katy asked.

The clopping of hooves and the rattling of a carriage approaching behind them on the cobbled street saved Grace from having to answer her aunt.

Again a footman scurried to the coach door. He reached toward the passenger with great fanfare. A dour-looking woman dressed in a gray satin gown peered out at the crowded boardwalk through a pair of wire-rimmed spectacles. She scowled and stepped carefully down the three small steps. She carried a cane and stood waiting for the footman. He pulled one large and two small trunks from the back of the carriage.

Crewmen from the dock hurried up to the waiting carriage and took the trunks up the gangplank on their strong shoulders. The old woman glanced about and pinned her gaze on Grace and her party. She turned sharply and walked determinedly toward the ship and headed up the gangplank at a slow pace. The three women in Grace's party stared at her motionless, as if bolted to the wooden deck.

"I wonder where the captain is?" Aunt Katy shaded her eyes as she glanced toward the vessel. "Josie, you and Grace follow me. I'm going in search of the captain." Aunt Katy scurried off in the direction of the *Savannah Rose.*

"Why in heaven's name is Aunt Katy looking for the captain?" Grace asked as they each picked up a carpetbag and worked to keep up with her aunt.

Josie shrugged. "You know how she is. Likely she's giving the captain orders to see to your welfare. You'd better walk faster. I've already lost her."

Grace caught sight of Aunt Katy's parasol, held high while she worked her way up the gangplank. When Aunt Katy reached the top, she found a sailor and tapped him on the shoulder.

He turned to her, his bushy eyebrows raised. "How can I be helpin' ya Ma'am?"

"I'm looking for the captain of this ship."

"He can't be bothered." He shook his head.

"Wait a minute, Sailor."

"He's busy gettin' the ship ready to shove off." He looked out over the gangplank. "I can't accommodate you, lady."

"It's imperative that I see him." Katy poked her fingers at his chest. "Your captain will wish you'd found him for me if you don't fetch him now."

Grace and Josie looked at each other with eyebrows raised.

"I'll see what I can do." He disappeared through the mass of traffic.

Before long, a tall, muscular man in a white captain's suit stepped up to Aunt Katy with a scowl on his face. He appeared to be in his early thirties. The captain lifted his wide-brimmed hat and bowed slightly. Grace didn't miss the mass of wavy, blonde-gold hair that gleamed in the morning sunlight. When he stood upright again, hazel eyes peered down at the three of them.

"I'm Captain Drew Harding. How can I assist you ladies?"

"I thought you ought to know," Aunt Katy said, as she handed him a thick envelope, "that one of your passengers is Phillip Cooper's daughter."

A quirky grin spread across his face while he shook his head slightly. "I've known Phillip a good seven years. He doesn't have a daughter in America. I'd know."

Grace stiffened and lifted her chin. She stepped back, but remained in earshot.

"I understand this has taken you by surprise, Captain. We, too, were surprised to learn that Phillip Cooper is alive." Aunt Katy didn't go into detail, and the captain gazed down at her curiously.

"Ma'am?"

"We understood Phillip Cooper died at sea some years back, nearly twenty years to be exact."

"I don't know where you got your information. He's alive and well." The captain gazed down at her, his eyes squinting in the morning sun.

"I'm sure he is," she continued. "Problem is, my niece had been told her father died at sea. Her mother recently passed. It is my niece's intent to meet him in Jamaica. I thought you ought to know, since it's going to be your responsibility to get her safely across the ocean and into his hands all in one piece."

Grace shifted and heat rose to her cheeks. She glanced at Josie then back to the handsome captain. What must he think of her aunt giving him orders?

Captain Harding glanced at the envelope in his hands. "What's this?"

"Documents proving Grace Cooper is indeed Phillip Cooper's

50

daughter. They are notarized by an attorney." She gazed up at the captain. "It wouldn't do for her to sail across the sea to meet her father without proof of her identity."

"May I look at these documents?" He glanced at the red wax seal that held the letter concealed inside.

"That would be wise. Keep the letter and document in a safe place and see to it that it makes it into Phillip Cooper's hands when you get to your destination." She visibly relaxed.

"Are you ready to meet Miss Cooper?" Aunt Katy asked.

"I do wish to meet her." He glanced at Grace. "But it will have to wait." He shoved the thick envelope into his coat pocket and backed away. "The ship will be leaving port soon. I will meet her later this morning, rest assured." Without waiting for Aunt Katy's response, he lifted his hat and turned toward the front of the ship.

Aunt Katy turned to Grace. "We'd best say our goodbyes. I believe you're ready to sail."

Grace gave Josie a tight hug. "Come as soon as you can. I'm going to miss you dreadfully." Tears suddenly blurred her vision. Her throat thick, she laughed with a tremor.

"I'll miss you, too." Josie bit her bottom lip.

Grace turned to her aunt.

"I do wish you would have waited for us." Aunt Katy wiped tears from her eyes. "Now, you remember everything I told you. Don't talk to strangers. And—"

"I've got all the instructions I need." Grace smiled. "I'll be fine." She kissed her aunt on the cheek. A sailor came and retrieved the two carpetbags sitting on the deck by her feet. "Your name, Miss?"

"Grace Cooper."

"I'll put your bags in your cabin," he said.

"Thank you." Grace turned back to see her aunt and cousin descend the gangplank to stand with the others on the wharf. They hooked arms and watched as Grace moved along the rail of the ship. A few passengers waved goodbye to people below. Grace found an empty place and gazed down at her family. Her heart swelled while she waved to them. The tears she'd been able to hold back till now slipped down her cheek as they waved back.

A long whistle blew from the boatswain's pipe and the gangplank was raised from the dock's landing and up onto the ship's side. The vessel pulled away from shore. She waved again and again. She could see her family waving to her. They grew smaller as the ship crept away from the mooring. "Goodbye," she whispered.

A dull ache formed in her heart. She would miss them. She waved one last time, knowing they could not see her. As the vessel picked up speed, the people on the dock appeared like dark spots on the shore. Grace glanced at her ticket and found her cabin number.

With one last glance out over the ship's rail she sighed, "I'm coming, Father. Ready or not, here I come."

EIGHT

GRACE SHOVED THE passage ticket into the same hand holding the umbrella handle. With her other hand, she lifted her skirt just enough to keep its hem elevated. She peered out over the ship's deck. A few passengers gathered in a small group, checking their boarding tickets.

A moment later, a sailor moved to the center of the deck and announced, "Your boarding tickets have your cabin numbers on them. If you will follow me, I will escort you to your rooms." Some of the passengers followed while he moved to a door below the quarterdeck. Others milled on the deck, waiting for the passengers to clear the way to their cabins.

Grace glanced about the dwindling crowd. She noticed a young sailor looking her way as he tightened a thick rope on the iron extension below the ship's rails. He left his task and sauntered over to her wearing a broad smile.

"Do you need assistance, Miss?" he asked with a Scottish lilt, his blue eyes shining.

Gold hair reached his shoulders, bronzed by the sun. Light blue dungarees disappeared into heavy, black boots. His smile carried a lightness about him that gave one the impression he hadn't a care in the world. She judged him to be in his early twenties and liked him instantly. She smiled back.

"I'm waiting to find my cabin." Grace let her skirt drop and lifted her hand toward his. "I'm Grace Cooper."

"Name's Corky, Miss. Corky McGreggor. Do you know which cabin is yours?"

Grace reached for the small ticket and held it out to him.

Peering at the small slip of paper, Corky grinned. "Follow me." He moved to the door below the quarterdeck. She found it led down a short flight of steps to a row of rooms. Five cabins lined each side of the narrow passageway.

"The last two rooms are for single passengers. They are small." He pursed his lips. "I'm afraid you'll find it standing room only. It's best if you can spend some of your time on the main deck. One would likely go mad with cabin fever if you don't venture out and get fresh air."

He stopped at cabin number ten and grinned. "This is your cabin, Miss." He paused, his eyes shining, "I best be gettin' back to work. Captain's sure to be looking for me." Corky flashed her a smile and walked briskly away.

Grace pushed through the door and stopped. Corky was right, she had just enough room to step inside. The large trunk stood squarely on the only floor space her room afforded.

Her heart sank. She glanced around the dim room and swallowed. Grace left the cabin door open as she squeezed between the trunk and narrow bed. She found a box of matches and struck a match on the coarse side of the box. A small flame flickered to life. Lifting the glass bowl from its brass dish, she lit the candle.

She sank onto the thin mattress and frowned. Had she listened to the crude sailor, she would not be in this predicament. She had insisted on the largest of seven trunks. Now she had no floor space. The six small trunks stowed below would remain there until she arrived at her destination.

Her shoulders sagged. The excitement of the last few days dimmed, like a candle snuffed out. She didn't know how she was going to bear being cooped up in such a small cabin for two whole weeks.

Grace moved the two carpetbags off the thin mattress and placed them on the trunk. She pulled off her hat and shawl and then slipped out of the green jacket. She threw the three pieces haphazardly onto the chest. At the moment she didn't care where they landed.

"Well, for cryin' out loud. What have I done?" She bit her bottom lip. Grace pulled her mother's diary out of one carpetbag and curled up on the thin cot to read, aware of the swaying motion of the ship. As the ship moved out into the vast ocean, she tried to convince herself that sea travel was safe and reminded herself that all her fears of sailing had been founded on a lie.

Settling in to learn more of her mother's past, Grace combed her mother's diary. It grieved her to learn Olivia was with child when she fled Jamaica. If Phillip had known she bore his child, he would have made her stay. When she returned home, Olivia asked her family to keep her secret.

It was hurtful to learn her grandparents knew her father was not dead. A flame of resentment kindled in her spirit. How could she forgive them? All of them. Most of all, her mother. They had lived a lie. She'd been deceived.

Olivia admitted Phillip had written countless letters she had never opened. She wrote that she hated the pain she had inflicted on him. But the letters continued to come.

A surge of emotions coursed through Grace—both anger at her mother's deceit and sorrow for her loss. She trembled as she slipped the diary in her carpetbag, hiding it from sight.

She sank onto the slim cot, her heart plummeting. Losing her mother. Saying goodbye to her beloved family. And now this ghastly cabin. She needed a good cry, and cry she did. Then she drifted into a fitful sleep.

Drew Harding slipped into his cabin for a much-needed moment of solitude. Cook sent a roast beef sandwich and sliced fruit to his cabin.

The plate sat on the small table along with Grace Cooper's documents. He leaned back, his feet propped on the edge of the table, and a cup of coffee in his hand while the ship rose and fell on the ocean's swells.

Drew eyed the envelope. He'd known Phillip Cooper a long time. In the seven years he'd worked for Cooper, he couldn't recall ever hearing about a child in America. He doubted the credibility of a daughter showing up out of the blue.

On the other hand, Phillip had said his wife fled the plantation and sailed to Charleston, South Carolina. Perhaps Olivia Cooper was with child when she sailed.

He broke the wax seal and pulled out the crisp paper. His eyes followed the words to the end of the document.

"I would never have believed it."

He swung his feet down. He'd eat, and then find a couple of crewmen to assist him in moving Grace Cooper to a better cabin.

The ocean breeze ruffled Drew's hair as he neared the door below the quarterdeck. Cabin number two was empty. Cabins were assigned by the number of occupants per room or their willingness to pay an exorbitant fee for larger accommodations. Room number two was sizable and furnished exquisitely.

The cabin across the hall had been assigned to Mrs. Cavendish. She had the means to afford the comfortable cabin. She requested this room each time she sailed.

The captain placed his hat on his head and went in search of Erik, his first mate, and Jesse, a crewman who was more trouble than he was worth, but strong as an ox. Before long, the three men stood in front of cabin number ten.

Grace roused herself from sleep. The ship rose and fell, and her stomach lurched. Her hand flew to her throat. *Am I going to be sick?* She waited for the rush of queasiness to pass. When her stomach settled, she eyed the cast iron hooks on the wall. "I'd better unpack." She reached for her jacket to hang it up. At the same moment, someone rapped on her cabin door.

Grace stopped. She opened the door a crack. The handsome captain stood outside.

"Good morning, Miss Cooper." The captain removed his wide-brimmed hat.

"Is there something wrong?" She glanced past the dashing captain to the two sailors who stood behind him.

"Yes and no. I hope you haven't unpacked your trunk." He glanced over her shoulder into the small cabin. "My men are here to move you to another room."

Grace glanced back at the cabin. Would she be moved into a smaller room? Anything less would be insufficient for even the lowliest of passengers. She gaped at the captain, her insides roiling again. This time it was not the motion of the ship that set butterflies squirming in her stomach. It was the uncertainty of where her new accommodations would be.

"Excuse me." Captain Harding reached to push the cabin door open.

Grace stepped back and grabbed her skirts. The crewmen squeezed into the small floor space. The first crewman tossed her hat and shawl onto the narrow bunk. They each grabbed one end of the large trunk, then picked up a carpetbag and stepped out of the cabin before she could protest.

"Take the trunk to room number two." Captain Harding said.

Grace slipped her arms into her jacket, snatched up her hat, shawl, and parasol, and then glanced out into the corridor with a hint of dread.

The captain's eyes sparkled with amusement as he offered his hand to help her over the threshold. Grace accepted.

"This way, Miss Cooper."

Bewildered, she glanced up at the captain and quickly retrieved her hand, clutching her umbrella as something to keep her hands busy.

"Where are we going?"

"We're not going far. I hope we've not inconvenienced you." He raised an eyebrow her way.

The ship rose and dipped making it difficult for her to keep her balance. Flustered, she kept her eyes straight ahead. It was all she could do to keep her footing without bumping into the attractive captain. *Why hadn't she waited to travel with her aunt?* She had no idea she'd feel so unraveled just a short time after taking off from shore.

The captain took hold of her elbow to steady her and led her to cabin number two.

"Was I given my cabin by mistake, may I ask?" Grace found her voice.

The captain's hazel eyes slanted down to her. "Yes and no."

Grace's head popped up at his reply. "I don't understand. I paid for my passage six months ago." She bit her bottom lip.

"Yes, I know." He smiled as they neared the new cabin. "That was before we knew who you were." His eyes gleamed. He opened the door. "After you, Miss Cooper." He bent his head to duck under the low opening and entered a room quadruple the size of the one she'd left.

Grace smiled while she took in the walnut furnishings. The bed was twice the size of the tiny cot in room ten. A tall chest of drawers, a table, two chairs, and a washstand, stood easily on the floor with room to spare.

Grace glanced up at the captain. "Did I pay for such a grand room?" She asked, uncertain.

"Yes and no." Again, that quirky grin.

"Please explain," she said, beginning to feel agitated. His answer was no answer at all.

"Another time, Miss Cooper." He backed out of the cabin into the corridor, replacing his Captain's hat onto his unruly, blond hair. "I hope you find this room suitable." He gave a slight bow and turned to leave.

Grace rushed out. His tall frame strode toward the front of the passageway. "Captain?" He stopped and glanced over his shoulder.

Grace pointed toward her new cabin with her white umbrella, her chin jutting out. Before she could pose her question, the captain placed a finger to his lips, with a gleam in his eyes. "I have a ship to sail." With that he climbed the steps that led to the main deck.

The vessel surged up swiftly and fell again. Grace lunged toward the cabin door and took refuge inside. She lit the kerosene lamp hanging on the far wall and then moved to her trunk.

Grace spent the next half hour arranging her clothes, while a niggling thought played over in her mind. The captain said he moved her to this cabin because of who she was. *No.* He said, *"That was before we knew who you were."* What was that supposed to mean?

NINE

FOOTSTEPS SOUNDED OUTSIDE Grace's room as she arranged her clothes in drawers. She placed the picture of her father on top of the chest, a reminder of why she was on this journey. That finished, she planned to join the passengers who came and went all morning up and down the steps outside her cabin door.

"Well," Grace said, as she ran a hand down the front of her newly-changed dress, "I'd best find my way around the ship." She picked up her parasol, slipped out of her cabin and up the steps to the main deck. Salt air blew gently as she glanced out over the water. People milled about, some heading toward the front of the ship and disappearing down another flight of steps. Grace followed them to the dining room. The dining hall, an expansive room, held several long tables with passengers seated with plates of food before them.

Graced edged into the room and glanced about. The older woman who'd appeared at the dock's landing sat alone at the far side of the room. Grace moved toward the table. "Mind if I sit here?"

The gray-haired women glanced up at Grace through wire-rimmed spectacles. "Don't mind at all." She lifted her cup and took a sip of tea.

Grace moved to the chair opposite the woman and sat down. Sailors moved about the long room taking orders and clearing tables.

A sailor appeared at Grace's side. "Are you ready to order Ma'am?"

"Yes, please. What are my choices?"

"Pot roast and boiled potatoes, or lamb chops and rice. Can I get you something to drink while you decide?"

Grace eyed the cup in the old woman's hands. "I'll have a cup of tea."

"Right away, Miss."

Grace looked up, feeling eyes on her. The woman observed Grace. "I saw you boarding the ship this morning. Are you by yourself on this voyage?" the old woman asked.

"Yes, I am. I know it's uncommon, and even scandalous for a young woman to travel alone." She cleared her throat. "I'm on a mission to find my father."

"How long has he been gone?" Rough brows raised above the rim of her glasses.

"All of my life. It's a bit confusing and it's a long story." Grace turned away, her cheeks warm.

"Don't let my prattling annoy you. It isn't any of my business. We can change the subject. Is this your first time sailing on a ship?"

Grace swallowed and grinned. "Yes. I've never been away from Charleston. I must say I'm looking forward to the change of pace."

"You'll get plenty of that on the ship."

The seaman came with Grace's tea and waited for her order. "I'll have the lamb chops and rice."

"Right away." He disappeared toward the galley.

"Good choice," the woman said. "The cook has an impeccable reputation as one of the best chefs on the sea."

Grace leaned forward. "I take it this isn't the first time you've sailed."

"Land sakes no." She chuckled and reached out a frail hand toward Grace. "My name is Agnes Cavendish. I've sailed often. I'm headed to the island of Barbados."

Grace took the small-veined hand and gently shook it. "I'm Grace Cooper. What takes you to Barbados?"

"That, too, is a long story." She smiled. "I have a tobacco

plantation there. I don't care to live on the island, nor do I care to spend more time than need be with my nephew who tends it for me. But I do travel often to the island. It never hurts to keep an eye on the operation. It keeps the workers in line when I show up." She winked.

"I'm impressed," Grace said. "My father is a plantation owner as well."

"In Barbados?"

"No, Jamaica. That's where I'm going."

"What does your father grow on his plantation?"

"His letters said sugarcane." The server set a plate before Agnes. Then he came around and set another plate before Grace.

"I'm familiar with some of the crop owners on the island of Jamaica. What's the name of your father's estate?"

"'Cooper's Landing.' Have you heard of it?" Grace glanced up.

"My, yes I have. Most folks with high rank, whether they be American or British, who live up and down the coastal lines of the Caribbean Sea know Phillip Cooper. He's your father?"

Grace held a small piece of lamb chop on her fork and gaped at Mrs. Cavendish. "Yes. Do you know him?"

"I've known your father a good many years. Not only because of his prosperous plantation and good reputation, but because he sails to Barbados with his merchant ships and brings supplies to my plantation. I don't know if you know, but your father has bought and sold merchandise all along the Caribbean coast more years than I can count."

Grace laid her fork down and leaned forward. "Truth is, Mrs. Cavendish, I know nothing about my father. When we have the time, I will tell you all about it."

Captain Harding stood with his first mate, Erik watching the two women, young and old, carry on in easy conversation. The captain turned to Erik. "She's in good hands with Agnes Cavendish." He nodded his approval. "I won't interrupt them now. I can wait to speak with Miss Cooper. But keep an eye on her. See that she makes it back to her room safely."

"Aye, Captain." Erik grinned as the captain moved away. "It will be my pleasure."

Grace awoke to the swaying of the ship. She peered out the small window above her bed at the night sky. Stars shone in the distance. *Goodness. I've slept the afternoon away.* She scooted out of the comfortable bed and stopped. The vessel rose and fell. She stepped carefully to the small table and grabbed the back of one chair to steady herself. Fully awake, she freshened up and then slipped out of the room. A dim light lit the narrow passageway. When she reached the doorknob, the door leading out to the main deck flew open. Two young ladies and an older woman stood on the main deck looking down at Grace.

Grace came topside and stood to let them pass. The older woman reached out a hand and touched Grace's arm. "We were just talking about you," she said.

Grace stepped back a tad.

"Don't mind my boldness," the woman said. "Our carriage pulled up when you were about to board this morning. My girls hoped to meet you when we got settled. Girls, come forward."

Grace clutched her shawl to her while the wind blew a steady breeze against her back. The redhead was the first to step forward. "My name's Jacqueline Moore," she said with a strong British accent. "Most folks call me Jackie." She held out a slim, white hand.

Grace took the limp hand graciously. "Good to meet you."

Jacqueline stepped back and hugged herself in the cool breeze. Her nose went up a notch as she raked the length of Grace's fine traveling dress, green eyes hostile.

Goodness! thought Grace.

The blonde woman came forward, "And I'm Violet Moore." She dipped her head, lifting smiling eyes to Grace. "And you?"

"Grace Cooper." She liked the blonde immediately. Were they sisters? If so, they seemed as different as night and day. The redhead appeared to have a bone to pick with Grace, and for what, she could not guess, while the blonde had a sunny, friendly disposition.

"Now I'd be out of line if I didn't introduce myself as well. I'm their mother, Ruby Moore. We're headed home to Jamaica on this fine ship. Where are you headed, dear?"

"I, too, am on my way to Jamaica." The three women waited. Grace continued, "To meet my father."

"Cooper?" Jacqueline leaned forward. "Might you be going to Cooper's Landing?"

"As a matter of fact, I am. You've heard of it?"

"I've been to the plantation a number of times. Her lips pursed together. "I suppose that means we'll meet again."

Grace's pulled her shawl a little tighter. "I'll look forward to it." *But would she? And what connection did Jacqueline Moore have with Cooper's Landing?*

"Now, girls." Ruby Moore signaled for them to go down the steps. "We won't keep you. The supper was superb. The dining room was open when we left. Come along girls, keep moving."

Grace watched the party of three disappear down the steps. Alone on the main deck, she peered out over the sparkling water that mirrored the stars above. She walked toward the narrow passageway that led to the dining hall.

A swell lifted the ship. Grace lost her footing and bumped into the wall. She waited a beat. Further along, light poured out of the dining room. Again, the water undulated the vessel. The sway pulled her to the right. Her hand flew to her throat. An odd sensation set upon her. Was she going to be sick?

"Let me give you a hand, Missy," came a gruff bark behind her. Grace turned. The sailor was one of the men who'd helped move her trunk to her new accommodations. He moved to her side on sure feet.

"The . . . thank you," she said, unsure of the sailor and unsure of her footing. She jerked when he grasped her arm and pushed her forward. She stumbled in his rough hold.

"Maybe I'd better hold you a wee bit tighter." He slipped his arm around her waist and pulled her tight against his side. He reeked of whiskey. Grace fought the urge to be sick.

"I . . . I'm all right. I don't need assistance." She squirmed out of his hold.

"Come on, honey. Let me escort you to the dinning room . . . or maybe below deck . . . hum?" His words slurred. He grasped her shoulder in a strong hold.

Shocked by his implication, Grace went into action. She dug her elbow into his ribs, and stomped the toe of his boots. "Let go of me!" She pushed him away from her.

He stumbled momentarily, but reached back to pull her into his rough hold again. "You little wench! You need to learn a lesson!" He raised a hand to slap her.

"Hey!" A sailor ran up and whirled the intoxicated swab, before he landed a fist in the sailor's jaw. The crewman sprawled on the deck.

The seaman stood before her. "Are you all right, Miss Cooper?"

"I . . . I'm fine . . . he—"

The inebriated seaman picked himself off the deck and lunged the sailor. "Look out!" Grace shrieked.

He whirled in time to receive the full brunt of the intended blow, staggered, fell against the ship's rail and then bounced forward with a raised fist. The two men tumbled and rolled as they pummeled each other, each intending to gain the better hand.

Grace watched. It wasn't long before heads popped out of the dining hall. Men scrambled toward the two sailors who fought against the rail. The intoxicated crewman pushed the sailor back with a strong hold on his neck. The sailor kneed the besotted crewman, who slumped in pain. The onlookers tried to separate the two men.

"What goes on there!" boomed Captain Harding. He strode up, eyes blazing. "What's the meaning of this?" He eyed the two men, the crowd, and then Grace, who shook violently.

The sailor who'd come to her rescue pulled himself out of the hold of a passenger and squared his shoulders. "I came upon Jesse assaulting our guest." He darted a glare at the crewman.

Captain Harding grabbed Jesse's shirt in a tight grip. "What have you got to say for yourself?"

"Isn't true, Cap'n. I be helpin' the lady to the dinning room when Erik jumped me." His lips curled. "I be thinkin' he wanted the lassie for himself." He hiccupped and jeered at the onlookers. "She be a looker this one." He jabbed his finger toward Grace.

Grace wanted to shrivel up and die. The wind picked up. She shuddered. But it wasn't the wind that racked her body with violent shivers. It was the ill-fated crewman who leered at her with crass implications.

"Take him to the hold until he sobers up. I want him in my cabin first thing in the morning." Captain Harding barked, "All right, everybody, break it up!"

He turned to Grace, eyes blazing. "You! Come with me!"

The captain escorted Grace past the dinning room toward the front of the vessel. They stepped down a short flight of steps to a cabin door. When Captain Harding opened the door, light flooded out across the deck.

"After you."

Grace entered the cabin shaking.

He shut the door with deliberate calm and turned toward her.

"What were you doing out on the main deck alone?" His hazel eyes smoldered.

Grace bristled. "I was hungry. I didn't know it wasn't safe to go out for a meal."

"It's never safe for a female to wander around the ship alone after dark."

Grace lifted her chin. "Am I not to have an evening meal?"

"Of course you are. But you won't be escorting yourself. From now on, you'll wait for one of my trusted men, or I will personally escort you to the dining hall. Is that clear?"

She met his gaze. Her jaw tensed.

"Is that clear, Miss Cooper?"

"It is perfectly clear, Captain."

"Good. Tonight I will escort you to supper."

Grace could see he was torn. He had a ship to run. He didn't have time to be a babysitter.

"Shall we go?"

"Lead the way, Captain."

The vessel continued to sway over the large swells in the Atlantic Ocean. The captain held her elbow as they walked toward the dining room. He steered her to a round table near the galley and held out a chair for her.

Grace took her seat and cleared her throat. She was clearly out of sorts and wanted nothing more than to go back to her cabin. She would not, however, give him the satisfaction of seeing her act like a spoiled child who could not handle being put in her place.

A seaman hurried to their table and placed two cups of coffee before them. Before long, the captain leaned back in his chair.

"We are going to be out to sea a good many weeks. Normally, we would sail directly to Jamaica making it our first stop. Unfortunately I've made a commitment to the governor of Barbados. I'm bringing a shipment of rice to their island before we continue on to your destination."

Grace frowned. "That's clear out of our way. I'd hoped to be in Jamaica in two weeks."

"That would be ideal. Charleston exports the highest grade of rice, known to many of the islanders as 'Carolina Gold.' It's the staple the people use most at their dinner tables. Barbados has nearly run out of the rice. The governor is willing to pay a premium per pound if I'm willing to sail there first and deliver the shipment of rice to them."

"How long will it take us to sail if we go there first?"

"A month if the trade winds are behind us all the way. Longer if not. We have two stops in the Bahamas, one in Long Island and one in the British Virgin Islands. We'll need to stop for fresh water and supplies."

Grace bit her bottom lip. "And how long from Barbados to Jamaica?"

"Another two to three weeks." The captain leaned forward. "I hope you brought plenty of things to keep yourself occupied."

"I brought books and a sketchpad. I will manage. But I must say I'm terribly disappointed. Six weeks is a long time to be out in the ocean. I fear I shall feel like a fish by the time we get to Jamaica."

The captain smiled. "You aren't the only one."

Grace seized the moment alone with the captain. "Are you going to explain why you moved me from the single cabin to such an elaborate room?" She leaned her elbows on the table curious.

"Your father wouldn't approve of your traveling in a small cabin." His eyes glinted at her. "You were aware, were you not, that this is your father's ship?"

Grace was not prepared for such information. She gawked in bewilderment.

"I've caught you by surprise, have I not?"

"This is my father's ship?" She glanced about her.

"It is. I'm surprised your aunt didn't tell you." Captain Harding took a sip of coffee and leaned back in his chair. "I read the letter documenting that you are indeed Phillip Cooper's daughter." He grinned at her. "Which is why it is my express purpose to get you to Jamaica all in one piece." He forked a bite of pork roast.

Grace sat with her mouth open and mentally checked herself to close it. "My aunt seemed taken with the name of the vessel. She didn't explain why. It makes perfect sense now."

She thought back to her father's letters. He mentioned his travels as a merchant ship owner. But she didn't remember having read the name of his ship.

"I realize I was stern a moment ago. I do, however, have your father to answer to when we sail into port." He laid down his fork.

Grace only half listened. She was on her father's ship. Never in a million years had she imagined she'd purchased a ticket on her father's vessel. She couldn't fault the captain for his stern behavior. As he said, he answered to her father.

"I would like to tour my father's ship." Her eyes lit up.

"I was afraid of that. But tour the ship you will. Tomorrow. The swells are unusually high tonight. After you eat I'd like to get you settled back in your cabin."

Grace frowned.

"Is something wrong?"

"How long will it take to get my sea legs?"

"We've had cases where passengers are what we call 'green' the whole voyage."

"I am my father's daughter."

"And you may find your sea legs in the morning."

Grace set her napkin on the table. "I thought I'd have to wait until I got to Jamaica to experience aspects of my father's life. And here I am sitting on his ship."

"Which reminds me. I have something for you." He reached inside his coat pocket and pulled out a long envelope.

"What's this?"

"The papers your aunt gave me. You may need them when you reach your father's plantation."

Within the hour, the captain escorted Grace to her cabin. "Promise you'll not take to the main deck in the evenings unescorted."

"I promise."

"Breakfast is at eight o'clock. If the weather is fair, I see no harm in your coming out on the main deck."

"When will I be given a tour of my father's ship?"

"Before noon."

"Good night, Captain Harding."

The captain tipped his hat in her direction. "Lock your door."

"I will." She closed the door and locked it. Leaning against the cabin door, she gazed toward the ceiling, thinking. Should she write Aunt Katy and tell her about the calamity she'd caused this evening? Her eyes sparkled and her lips curved up. *Goodness no! Wild horses couldn't pull it out of her!*

TEN

THE SUN PEEKED through the small, round window above Grace's bed. A perfect day for touring the ship. She buttoned the top of her dress and hurried to the deck.

Captain Harding peered over to find her heading his way.

"Good morning, Captain. I'm ready to tour my father's ship. I would like to see every inch of this grand vessel."

"I've assigned two shipmates to give you a tour. I'm counseling with the navigator this morning. I won't be able to join you."

Grace glanced at the crewmen waiting for her. It was first mate, Erik and the Scottish lad, Corky. "Apology accepted." She smiled with anticipation.

"Right this way, Miss Cooper."

The trio moved toward the front of the vessel where the helmsman steered the ship. Then they walked the quarterdeck and milled with the passengers. The wind caught her hair and tugged it. She shook her auburn ringlets and brushed the shining locks out of her face. When Grace turned toward the men, she found two pair of eyes ogling her. Both of the men swallowed, their Adam's apples bobbing up and down. Heat crept up her neck and over her scalp. The men nearly stumbled over themselves as they resumed the tour.

They went as far down as the hold, took in the wheelhouse, the galley, and a small dining room used by the captain and his officers. An hour later they stood on the quarterdeck.

"Have I seen everything?"

"Just about."

Erik turned to Corky, who held a telescope. He nodded and handed Grace the long, black scope.

Grace peeked through its lens as the *Savannah Rose* sliced through the gray-green waters. A far off vessel seemed to jump forward to where she stood. She jerked her head back and laughed. "Oh, my."

The two men grinned. "Corky sometimes climbs the mast to check for other vessels or to see if we have neared land."

A gust of wind whipped over the deck. Grace pulled her sweater close and walked away from them. She stood near the rigging, pleased with the tour. Corky walked up. "That's about it."

"Which reminds me," Erik said. "We're to bring you back to the captain's cabin when we're done. Come with me."

The men led Grace to a spot just outside Captain Harding's cabin. Corky stayed with her while Erik disappeared toward the front of the ship. Grace waited at the rail. The water sparkled from the afternoon sun.

"Ah, Miss Cooper," Captain Harding said, drawing her away from the water. "You must be famished after the tour."

He held the door open for Grace. "Tell Cook we are ready for lunch."

"Aye, Captain." Corky disappeared into the dining room.

Drew led Grace to the table and seated her in front of a fine place setting. "How was it? Did you scour the ship?" He grinned, his eyes shining.

"I believe there was no corner left unexplored. I'm quite satisfied I've seen it all." She fingered the silver spoon. "I never realized how large a ship this is. Much of it is under water."

The cabin door opened. Cook came in, followed by a seaman with their meal. Cook lifted the lid from a silver bowl. Steam rose as he ladled hot clam chowder into the bowls set before them. Roasted sandwiches, fresh salad, and cut up fruit filled their plates.

"This looks fit for a king." She leaned over to smell the hot steaming soup. "How are you able to keep the clams chilled?"

"We have an ice box in the hold. My men bring aboard blocks of ice. We eat well the first week. The ice doesn't last long. But we do our best to serve the finest to our guests." He snapped his white, cloth napkin open and laid it on his knee.

"Shall we?" He bowed his head and said a short prayer. "Now I want to set some ground rules for the rest of your trip on the *Savannah Rose*."

Grace looked up and wiped her mouth with her napkin.

"I want you to hear what I have to say so there'll be no questions in the coming days ahead. The most important rule is that I am in command of this ship. Not only you, but the rest of the crewman must respect my authority."

Grace pursed her lips and nodded.

"Number two. You will remain inside your cabin with the door locked at night. The only exception is mealtime. I will send first mate, Erik Bishop, to escort you to the dining room.

"Number three. I don't want you talking to strangers. You may, however, talk to the women. I realize you need companionship while you travel."

"Might you explain why these rules are necessary?" Grace set her fork down.

"This ship is loaded to capacity. I know my men to a degree. I do not, however, know the male passengers. Some of the men on this voyage are in single rooms such as you were given at the beginning of your voyage. These men roam the vessel at will and, short of causing havoc with my crew, will be allowed free range for the continuance of this trip. You have already experienced one of my crewmen who was out of line last evening. I cannot guarantee a male passenger will not accost you. For your safety, I have put these rules in place. I need your word that you'll abide by them."

"I understand, Captain Harding, and yes, you have my word."

Grace listened to the water slapping the side of the hull.

"With that out of the way, let's enjoy our meal." He picked up his spoon and scooped the steaming clam chowder. After he'd emptied his bowl, he leaned back, "So you're sailing to Jamaica to visit your father."

"Yes, but it's not just a visit. I have hopes of living at Cooper's Landing with my father."

"And he knows you're coming?"

"I mailed him a letter a month before I left. If he hasn't received it before I arrive, then no he doesn't know." She cleared her throat and picked at the crust of her roast beef sandwich.

Amusement danced in the captain's hazel eyes. "Your father is a noble man. He won't throw you out, in case you've wondered.

"I hope you're right. I've little funds and would be left with no means to return home if he did. I've wanted to know my father all my life."

"Do you have any idea what's in store for you when you reach Cooper's Landing?"

"Not at all. Mother told me stories about the Great House and the weather, the slaves who work the fields. That is all I know." She looked up, "Have you been to my father's plantation?"

"Many times. He usually puts me up for a few days when I pull into port. I have a room at a boarding house near the dock, but I enjoy staying at the Landing. I often visit your father's neighbors, the Borjeaux."

Grace cocked her head with curiosity.

"They have a daughter your age. Her name is Camille. You'll like her." A light flush crept over the captain's face.

Did he fancy the Borjeaux's daughter? "I look forward to meeting her. You might introduce me when we arrive."

"I plan on it." He grinned, deepening the crow's feet at the corner of his eyes. Then sobered. "Things may not be as you suppose when you arrive at the Great House."

"Meaning?"

"Your father has spent a good many years alone. You may want to brace yourself for the unexpected." He cleared his throat and shook his head slightly. "Be patient with him."

"Are you trying to tell me I'm in for a challenge ahead, Captain?" Grace moved uneasily in her chair.

"You may open up a set of circumstances better left alone. I hope they go easy on you."

"I didn't expect my arrival to be placid, but thank you for the warning." She placed her napkin on her plate, ready to retire to her room. She wanted to sketch some scenes she had seen on the ship.

The captain walked her back to her cabin. He gave her a two-finger salute and walked away. Grace thought he appeared utterly exhausted.

The next morning Grace waited for Erik to come after her for breakfast. While she waited, Grace thumbed through her mother's diary. A passage caught her eye: *I never much cared whether Phillip was rich or poor. We could have lived in Charleston, in a modest house, and I would have been happy. It was Phillip I wanted, not his money. Phillip's need to grow his wealth took him away from me. I felt so alone in that big house on the island. I couldn't bear it. In the end, I came home where I felt needed.* Grace closed the book, a sadness in her heart.

She eyed the envelope on the table that shed proof she was Phillip Cooper's daughter. She had only heard Aunt Katy and the captain talk about the contents of the letter. Yet, she hadn't reviewed the letter herself. Would her father believe the evidence? She would read it at breakfast. When three sharp raps sounded on the door, she knew Erik had arrived. She picked up the document and followed him out.

"I have an unusual request." She grinned up at him.

"Unusual?" he eyed her warily. "Try me."

"I noticed a number of rapiers hanging on a wall in the hold. Might I borrow one to practice fencing?"

Erik stopped. "You want me to loan you a sword?"

"A foil. Yes. I am quite good at it. My cousin and I have spent the past year in fencing lessons practicing the sport for competition. You might want to join me in a round."

Erik's face turned crimson, and he cleared his throat. "I will have to bring that up to the captain."

"Please do. I'd like to sharpen my skills, should I need them in the near future."

"The near future?"

"I am going to Jamaica. Who knows what I will come across in that untamed land."

Grace followed Erik out to the main deck. She carried the document in her right hand. As they rounded the corner of the quarterdeck a sharp breeze whipped the envelope out of her hand. It sailed up and circled out over the water before it plunged into the sea. "My papers!" Grace wailed.

"I'm afraid they'll do you no good, Miss Cooper. The sea has swallowed them up." Erik looked on in alarm.

"Now how will I prove to my father that I am his daughter?" She leaned over the rail. Her eyes followed the last blurry piece of the envelope as it dipped out of sight.

"How careless of me! I shouldn't have brought these vital documents out of my room!" Grace looked helplessly at Erik. "I fear the captain is going to think I've not a responsible bone in my body!"

ELEVEN

CAMERON STOOD ON the porch of the Great House and watched the early morning sun come up over the horizon as tall palms gently swayed in the cool morning breeze. The effect made both the carriage drive that led to the plantation house and the circular drive in front of the house welcoming sights. The flowers interspersed between the plants gave off a fragrance that enhanced the early morning air.

Gemma and Penny rounded the corner of the Great House and glanced up at Cameron. "Mornin' Mastah Camp," the two said in unison as they neared him.

"Morning, ladies." He touched the brim of his hat and nodded toward them. The two servants giggled and slipped past him into the house.

Cameron took the porch steps two at time and circled around to the back of the house toward the stable. With long strides he worked his way past a number of outbuildings and neared the side of the corral.

Nate's voice came from inside the rough structure. "Hold still there!"

Cameron heard the black stallion, Scimitar, nicker in response.

Brush in hand, Nate popped his head up when the stable door squeaked open. "Morning, Mastah Camp. Just about finished here with this wild animal of yours."

Scimitar stomped impatiently and swatted flies with his tail. Nate bent to run the curry brush down the horse's hind legs. Cameron reached out to brush the black mane of his tall horse. *Beautiful*.

Dust-coated lanterns spaced at intervals to light the stable's interior hung on sturdy, wooden posts. A vague smell of hay and animal odors permeated the stable, muted by the early morning freshness. In another hour the heat of the day would set in, and the pungent smells in the barn would increase. *The day is well on its way.* Cameron watched Nate with a wry grin. *Best get this beast out on the range and make sure all is well. Pip could well show up today.*

Nate finished brushing Scimitar and slapped him on the rump. Cameron stood at the opening, lead rope in hand. He guided his horse out to the wide aisle where he saddled the gelding. After cinching the last hoop, Cameron led the horse out of the stable and swung easily into the saddle. With a nudge from Cameron, the stallion moved toward the gate.

Already the plantation showed signs of waking up. Slaves made their way to their assigned posts. The Great House garden loomed up and Scimitar walked toward the back of the house. Men and women alike walked toward rows of vegetation with garden tools in their hands.

Further back behind the cluster of buildings lay the provisional field, which fed not only the family in the Great House, but also all of the people on Cooper's Landing.

As Cameron nudged Scimitar past the garden behind the Great House he looked back at the structure, admiring the architectural design. Six white columns stood from ground to roof on the front and back sides of the house, five columns stood on each side. The veranda wrapped around all four sides with a set of French doors leading out from each of the bedchambers. It didn't matter how many times he saw the house, he always marveled at the twenty-three-room structure. It was one of the grandest houses on the island.

Something moved beyond the tall palm trees, on the balcony. The fringe of palm leaves swayed in the morning breeze. Still, his eyes narrowed to focus on the veranda. Then he saw her. A black woman with sleek hair staring down at him from behind the rail. Her gown of bright yellow, splashed with multicolored designs, stood out against the color of her skin and the dark shadows behind her. Gold, hooped earrings glinted in the morning sun. Even from a distance he could imagine the crystal blue of her eyes against her ebony skin. She stood regal and straight, observing the morning activities below her.

For a moment their eyes locked. Her lips thinned. With a wry look, she lifted her chin and turned away from the rail. He watched as she slipped through the doors of the last bedchamber on the east wing.

Cameron's brows furrowed. That bedchamber had been vacant a good many years. It was off limits, having once belonged to Olivia Cooper, Pip's wife. When Olivia fled the plantation, Pip banned the chamber from future use. The only exception was the weekly dusting and the exchange of fresh flowers in the bedchamber's sitting room.

Cameron didn't trust the Cheetah. There was something dark and foreboding about her. She'd acted strange of late, going out after dark and coming back in the wee hours of the morning. Where did she go? He glanced at the vacant balcony one last time. "Git up there, Scimitar." He nudged the horse with the heels of his boots.

Smoke billowed out of the chimney of the outer kitchen and floated lazily into the air. Cameron could hear voices rising and falling from within its brick walls.

He circled his stallion back the way he came and rode down the narrow lane toward the stable.

The profound silence of pre-dawn was now broken. Birds' chirps crescendoed into ceaseless warbling. A rooster crowed somewhere behind the barn. From the stable complex came the murmur of stockmen's voices and the soft clang of gear. The horses demanded feeding and attention. It was as though a great orchestra had struck up, the maestro bringing in each section one after the other.

He felt the pull of the land calling to him. It was home. He had struggled so long and so hard to become a part of it. It was strange to discover that now it felt a part of him.

He loped his stallion out to the cane fields. After easing off his horse, he sauntered over to Mingo, the overseer. He surveyed the first gang of slaves, who were topping the front rows of the sugarcane. Behind them came the men and women with cutlasses, chopping the stalks at ground level.

Mingo held a logbook in his ebony hands and monitored the bundles of cane stalks loaded into waiting carts. He kept track of the number of bundles hauled in each load. A worker stepped into the cart piled high with sugar cane grass. The wagon rolled out onto the worn path, pulled by a donkey. It slowly made its way toward the sugar mill.

"Morning, Mingo."

"Mornin', Mastah Camp."

The two men stood for a moment in silence. Cameron watched the steady progress while the group of slaves methodically moved down the long rows of tall sugarcane grass, chopping the stalks down, while others picked up the fallen grass and tied it into tight bundles.

The gangs of nine to twelve men and women hacked away at the tall stalks row after row. Cameron had grown accustomed to the people who labored in the fields. He knew them by name. The slaves did a good day's work and went back to their shacks at the end of the day to resume their family life.

Recently some of the workers showed discontent, grumbling and complaining as they took up their posts. Knives and cutlasses were used to cut the sugar cane. After a long day's work, the tools were gathered and locked away. With more slaves than white owners, things could get bad. It was expedient that the overseer kept the workers under his thumb. If they turned, there was no telling what could happen. It wouldn't be good.

Neighboring plantation owners had complained that a few of their slaves were missing. Cameron noted a couple of their own were also gone. Where? It was rumored a potential revolt was boiling in the brew. The news had spread throughout the territories of Jamaica and enclaves along the Caribbean coast. It became increasingly harder to keep the slaves happy and working the land. For this reason, Pip kept the slave families together. A man would not be so eager to leave his wife and children behind.

Cameron counted the slaves chopping down stalks. "You're short a hand. Where's Cuffee?"

Mingo hurried to the line of hackers and questioned them in their native tongue. He glanced to Cameron and shrugged. "No one know where Cuffee be. But I be checkin' with the next crew. Maybe he sick or maybe he be lazy in bed. I find out, Mastah."

"You do that." Cameron turned Scimitar toward another section of cane fields. The horse picked up its pace. Up ahead, the mill house came into view. Denzel, the overseer, would be inside. Did he know another slave was missing?

TWELVE

KINDRA CREPT DOWN the front steps and tiptoed stealthily to the side of the Great House. Looking back, she hoped no one would notice her absence. Eager to spend a moment alone with the overseer, she hurried past the outer kitchen, past the lane that led to the outbuildings, and slipped into the mill house. The large building was dark. It took a moment to adjust to the dimness. When she did, it was to find Denzel, tall and muscular, coming her way, a broad smile on his face.

She nearly ran into his arms. As they stood just inside the large, double doors, light streamed in from the opening, casting shadows behind them as they held each other close. They only had a moment, aware that every second counted. Kindra gazed up at him, rapturously.

He held her away from him to devour her with his eyes. "Did anyone see you come?"

"I don't think so. Mother is in her room getting ready to go into town. I made sure she didn't see me leave.

His broad, calloused hands encircled her upper arms, as he pulled her close to him again. "I count the hours for the moment you come to me. But I tremble at the thought of your getting caught."

"Don't talk, my darling. Just hold me." Kindra pressed her cheek against his bare chest.

"You look beautiful." His smile gleamed white against his dark skin.

Kindra stepped back and looked up into his face. "I'd be happy in a muslin blouse and black skirt, if it could have afforded me the right to be out here among the rest of you. Mother insists I dress in these silly frills." Kindra swung around, making her skirts flare out. Then she put her arms around his waist again. "And for what? No one seems to notice.

"I noticed you." Denzel kissed her petite nose.

Kindra longed to spend time with the man who pulled her to him. She touched his face, and ran her finger along the crease beside his mouth.

"We've only a moment. Eyes are watching us."

"I know. I can't stay long." She cast a glance out over the vast building. "The slaves may be spying on us for Mother."

"Can they be trusted not to tell her?"

"You've gained respect as overseer here at Cooper's Landing. But Mother doesn't see you as anything but a slave. I trust some of the workers to keep quiet. The others? They listen to her."

Cameron slipped inside the mill and saw them. He slid into the shadows and held his breath. He'd known of an interest brewing between Kindra and his overseer. He also knew that Tia, the headmistress of the Great House, worked to keep them apart.

Now he watched Denzel pull Kindra against his massive chest and kiss her. She giggled when he let her go, and she lifted a cup to his mouth. Denzel drank his fill. Cameron's heart beat loud in his ears. He tried to stay inconspicuous, sure they didn't know he was there.

Denzel put the empty cup on the table and pulled Kindra into his arms again. She tipped her head and kissed his chin, his face in her small hands. When she lifted her chin, she glanced out toward the mill room. Cameron watched her eyes stray to where he stood in the shadows near the back entrance.

She stepped back abruptly and grabbed her skirt. "I must go!"

"Wait! Don't leave!" Denzel reached out to stop her.

She fled the building.

Denzel's large frame filled the entrance to the mill house as he watched her race toward the big house. He swung around with fire in his eyes.

Cameron stepped out of the shadows. "Sorry, Denzel. I didn't know she was here."

Denzel glanced back at the door, then at Cameron with a wistful look on his face. "She don't trust a soul around here. She fears someone will tell her mother."

"I won't."

"I know. But she ain't gonna take the risk." He shook his head, kicked a clump of sugar stalk across the room, and then swivelled back to the grinding machine. "Sometimes I wish I could take Miss Kindra and run. I'd flee someplace where we can be ourselves, someplace where there would be no eyes watching us."

Denzel's arms glistened with sweat. His muscles flexed as he tightened his fists. Then he cleared his throat. "Enough about us. Let's get to business."

Cameron nodded. "Before we go over the Landing business, do you have information about Tia?" Cameron stood to the side of the grinding machine, his arms folded across his chest. Given the circumstances, he wasn't sure this was the best time to bring up the subject. But he had to know.

"She went into town again last night. Took one of the hands with her. They didn't return until two o'clock in the morning. I followed her to a warehouse on the wharf."

"She didn't see you?"

"No, sir. Having dark skin come in handy sometimes, boss. I stripped off my shirt and waited in the shadows. Almost fell asleep, but she finally come out."

"And?"

"You're not going to believe it."

"Try me."

"Ever heard of Captain Blissmore?"

"He owns the *Bloody Mary*. It's one of the renegade pirate vessels known for raiding ships up and down the Caribbean coast. I know him, all right. So does Pip."

"That burly scallywag come out with his arm slung over Miss Tia's shoulder like she be booty."

Cameron narrowed his eyes. "So did you figure out what they're up to?"

"No. They didn't say a word once they come out of the warehouse."

"What happened next?"

"She kissed that dirty scoundrel and climbed back into the wagon." Denzel scowled. "Cuffee waited in the wagon the whole time. It was all I could do to stay in the shadows and try to get the gist of what she'd come for. The She-cat and Cuffee rode toward the main road back to Cooper's Landing. I slipped further into the shadows, thought Blissmore might give me some information we could use."

"And?" Cameron frowned.

"He walked back into the warehouse laughing like a hyena. I figured there weren't no reason to hang around. I waited 'til I knew I'd be out of earshot. I got on my horse and followed Miss Tia and Cuffee back slow's I could. I figured they'd be heading back to the Landing, so I took my time." He shook his head. "By the time I got back she was nowhere to be seen." Denzel shrugged his massive shoulders.

"Did you see Cuffee when you returned?"

"No. Must have slipped out of the wagon before I arrived on the road."

"Think she knows she's been followed?"

Denzel shook his head again. "I kept a good distance between us."

"What about Kindra? Does she know about her mother?"

"She hasn't said. And I'm not talking to her about it."

"Let's keep it that way." Cameron slapped his big arms. "We can't afford to lose track of what she's up to. Just keep an eye out."

"Will do, boss."

An hour later Cameron stepped out of the boiling house, his shirt sticking to his back and sweat beading on his brow. He walked to the hitching post, untied his stallion, and lifted himself into the saddle with ease.

The sound of carriage wheels and horses prancing down the tall palmetto drive filled the air. He whipped his head around in time to see the carriage with the Cooper coat of arms emblazoned on each side coming into the circular drive. The driver pulled on the reins and the two horses halted in front of the Great House.

Cameron urged his horse to a trot and slid to a stop next to the carriage. Pip poked his head out of the coach, his green eyes bright as he climbed down. Cameron slid off the saddle and covered the ground to the old man. They slapped each other on the back before they embraced.

"You finally decided to come home," Cameron said.

"Yes. I'll be at the Landing for a while," Pip replied.

"How was your trip?"

"I'll tell you all about it after you put your horse away. Come see me in the library. I have lots to tell you, my boy."

The screen door slammed and Zeek hurried down the steps of the front porch. "Welcome home, Mastah Coopah."

The carriage driver set carpetbags on the ground. Zeek grabbed a bag in each hand and held the screen door open for Pip.

Before Pip took one step over the threshold, Tia stepped out, the sun glinting on the large hoop earrings against her dark skin.

Pip's eyes sparkled. He nodded her way. The ebony woman's lips curved up.

Cameron frowned. He hadn't worked it all out yet, but was sure she was undermining Pip by stealing slaves and selling them. Until he had proof, he wouldn't say a word. The last thing he wanted was to make an enemy of his father.

Twenty minutes later, Cameron joined Pip in the library. They talked about the merchant business and discussed what Pip had learned in regards to the slave revolt along the Caribbean coast. Plantation homes had been ransacked and burnt, their owners hanged for all to see. Many of the colonies had lost good workers and had to hire indentured men to work their land. And worse yet, rumors indicated that slaves in Jamaica had gotten wind of the revolt and showed signs of wanting to rise up against their owners. Cameron thought of Cuffee. He still hadn't shown up. It would be a grievous day if Cooper's Landing had to resort to bloodshed.

THIRTEEN

AFTER FOUR WEEKS at sea, it had become a challenge to find ways to spend the days without going utterly mad. Grace found comfort in knowing Mrs. Cavendish's cabin was across the hall from hers. She grew accustomed to the sound of her cane thumping the deck when she neared her room. They spent hours playing games, usually cribbage or cards, a great means of passing the hours at sea.

Against his better judgment, the captain gave in to Grace's request to borrow a foil. On a few occasions, Erik accommodated her in a round of fencing in the dining room as the captain and Corky watched. It gave her an outlet she desperately needed from days of sitting in her room or on the deck. She loved the feel of the light metal in her hand. She even liked it when she saw approval in the captain's eyes. She was good with the foil and it gave her satisfaction to have the opportunity to show that even a woman could wield such a threatening weapon.

But today, Grace snatched up her sketchpad and headed for the quarterdeck. She shaded her eyes against the sun's rays and climbed the short steps to the upper level. The breeze tugged at her hair, and the cleansing winds blew against her face.

She peered up at the cloudless sky and noted the gulls flying in circles. Their broad wings flapped as they shrieked at the vessel. In another day the ship would be landing on the island of Barbados. The birds were the lone sign that land was nearby. It would be the third stop, where Mrs. Cavendish would be deposited for a two-month stay.

Then they would sail west to the island that held out promise to her. She was eager to unite with her father for the first time on his plantation.

Footsteps sounded behind her. "We will be docking on the island of Barbados in the morning."

Grace turned to face the captain. "I'm looking forward to it. Mrs. Cavendish has told me many stories about the island." She stood and gazed out over the water. "Are you sure we will be there by morning. Where is the land?"

"It's there. It never ceases to amaze me how quickly the shore shows up after days out at sea."

"Mrs. Cavendish advised me to bring some spending money to shore. For the peddlers selling their wares."

"It's a sight to see, for sure. Be careful though. The peddlers have an eye for those who are not accustomed to their ways. They'll steal you blind if you let them." He gazed out over the gray water. "The winds are picking up, you'd best settle in your cabin for the rest of the afternoon."

Grace glanced at the sketchpad and shrugged. "Thank you, I will."

The ship tacked south, then east in the warm, turquoise waters. Grace could hear the sounds of the island even before anyone could see it. A haze of clouds lifted off the morning waters. Waves crashed against the rocks in the distance. In a few hours the vessel cleared the rough, windward, wave-tossed coast of Barbados and headed through the steady, sheltered waters to Bridgetown.

Grace stood on the deck, her eyes intent on the shoreline, its colors bright, vibrant, and alive. Scores of peddlers and merchants waited on the dock to greet them. Long tables with palm-covered roofs stood in rows, holding every imaginable kind of relic a tourist might seek.

Within moments the ship docked and the crewmen jumped ashore to tie the long ropes of the vessel to the heavy, iron stakes at the dock's landing.

Grace searched for Mrs. Cavendish as the crewmen's voices rose with their morale. Raising her white umbrella, she lifted her white muslin skirts and ventured down the gangway for a closer look.

When she glanced back at the ship, she found Captain Harding watching her and talking to one of his sailors at the same time. She waved up at him. He touched his wide-brimmed hat in return.

The colors appeared bolder when she neared the first booth. Natives rattled on in a language she did not understand. She thought it best to keep her eyes on the table. Captain Harding warned her about eye contact. "If they get your attention," he said, "you'll have a difficult time getting away from them. Don't look them in the eye unless you want to make a purchase."

Keeping his advice in mind, she lowered her eyes and continued on. She learned quickly that sellers would not follow after her. She picked up a shawl. The colors were bold red, blue, and green. She laid it down. The woven blankets were just as bold in color. She ran her fingers over the fabric. The smells of mounds of fresh fruit in baskets made her hungry. Wooden figurines of carved exotic birds painted in brilliant colors hung in birdcages. Her favorite were the dark-blue-and-red parrots.

Grace carried a few coins in her purse. She found a wide-brimmed hat decorated in small, wooden beads in the red-and-blue, bold colors. On the opposite end of the table a ribbon in vibrant colors was tied around the top of a similar hat. Grace fingered both hats and hung onto the one with the wooden beads. The native girl behind the table said, "Schilling."

As the native girl reached out to accept the coin, a cane flew in between Grace's hand and the young girl's.

Grace snatched her hand back. Mrs. Cavendish wagged her finger at the young native girl, speaking rapidly in her native tongue. Grace waited while the two dickered back and forth. When they ended their debate, Mrs. Cavendish said, "Give the girl half a schilling.

Grace dug in her coin purse for the half schilling and placed it in the waiting hand of the native girl. The girl bobbed her head and smiled, revealing white, shining teeth.

"You need to bargain with these people. Their first price is always double what they will take. No need to give them more than their wares are worth," she clucked, following Grace down the rows of booths. Grace inspected the colorful hat and thought it worth much more than the half schilling she paid.

Standing in hot sun, Mrs. Cavendish said, "I'm hiring a carriage to my estate. Would you like to join me for some fruit punch to cool you off?"

"That sounds wonderful." Grace fanned herself. "I must inform the captain before I accept."

"I will hire the carriage and wait for you," Mrs. Cavendish said. She disappeared through the jumble of tourists. Grace moved through the thick crowd, trying to find someone she recognized.

She spied Corky. "Where might I find the captain?"

"He's gone off to take care of business in town. Can I be helpin' you?"

"Oh, dear." She frowned. "Mrs. Cavendish has offered to drive me out to her estate for refreshments. I shan't be more than an hour. When will we be leaving the port?"

"We'll be off in the morning. I doubt the captain will mind as long as you're back on the ship before late afternoon."

Grace bit her bottom lip. "If he asks for me, tell him I've accepted Mrs. Cavendish's invitation to her estate."

"I'll do that, Miss Cooper."

She turned and wound her way back through the heavy flow of people. A carriage sat by the side of the road, away from the vendors. When she reached the buggy, not only Mrs. Cavendish sat in the coach, but Mrs. Moore and her two daughters, as well. The carriage driver gave Grace a hand as she stepped up onto the vehicle and seated herself next to Mrs. Cavendish, across from Jacqueline. Before long the carriage bounced along the roads of Bridgetown and out to the plantation that belonged to the elderly woman.

Jacqueline stared out the window or at the ceiling of the coach and sighed every few minutes. She fidgeted and fumed and gave her mother sidelong grimaces. Tiny droplets of sweat beaded the redhead's upper lip and forehead. With flints in her eyes, she eyed the white, muslin gown Grace wore. Jacqueline had dressed in layers of blue taffeta that soon had her wilting.

Violet quirked a conspiratorial smile Grace's way, as if she knew a secret. The look also said she'd be willing share it if given the chance. Grace didn't know what to make of it. Jacqueline acted like she'd been eating persimmons. For all the world, Grace didn't know what she'd done to warrant such disapproval. If ears could puff smoke, Jacqueline's would spew like a steam locomotive screaming to a stop at a train depot.

Ruby Moore seemed oblivious to the three girls in the coach. She prattled on and pointed to all the color and activity around them. The horses carried the coach swiftly to the tobacco plantation, serenely nestled in a cove away from the cool waters. The fields fanned out from the Great House like an autumn maple leaf.

Mrs. Cavendish gave the women a tour of her lavish home. Afterward, they sat on the patio with iced fruit punch and sugar cookies while they admired the lawns and tall palmetto trees. Beyond the yard, one could see the vast, framed barns that housed the dried tobacco leaves and smell their tainted odor.

As the afternoon passed, Grace looked up at the sun lowering to the horizon. *What time is it?* she wondered. The women enjoyed the cool breeze that blew in from the shore. They could hear the slaves singing in the fields and the horses nickering while they munched the hay nearby. It wasn't long before the sun lowered to the ground far off in the distance. She glanced at the others. A niggling in her conscious told Grace it was time to head back to the ship.

"Ladies, I believe we have nearly worn out our welcome. Poor Mrs. Cavendish hasn't even had time to unpack."

"Fiddlesticks! I'm enjoying you all immensely!" Mrs. Cavendish said.

"I fear the captain shall be impatient with us if we don't head back to the ship."

The Moore girls groaned. Jacqueline spoke up. "This is such a nice respite from sitting on that boring old ship. Let's stay a little longer. Then we can go."

A servant came out to the back yard and whispered in Mrs. Cavendish's ear. She glanced about her and waved Grace to her side.

"I suppose it is all my fault, but the fine captain has arrived to escort you back to the ship."

Grace looked up in time to see the captain, clothed in his white captain's attire, stride onto the patio. At first glance she could see the flash of fire in his hazel eyes. He seemed to relax his rigid stance when his eyes beheld hers.

"Evening ladies. I hope I'm not interrupting anything of importance."

"Of course not," Ruby Moore answered. "Come join us for a glass of fruit punch. Mrs. Cavendish has been the perfect hostess this afternoon."

His hand went up. "No thank you." He cleared his throat. "I came out to warn you the ship leaves first thing in the morning." He eyed Grace. "The evenings here can be rowdy for unchaperoned women. I'd feel better if you took your leave as soon as possible."

"I had just suggested the same thing, Captain." Grace stood.

"Since we are in agreement, may I escort you lovely ladies to the ship right now?" His voice had a distinctive edge.

The women said goodbye to Mrs. Cavendish. When it was Grace's turn, Agnes embraced her shoulders with strong, wiry fingers. "You are always welcome on my plantation, young lady. Maybe we will meet again, if you should sail with your father."

"I would like that, Mrs. Cavendish. Thank you for opening your home to us." Grace gave her a peck on the cheek and joined the others on the front porch.

The coachman helped her into the carriage while Captain Harding climbed up front with the driver. It wasn't long before the carriage bumped along the cobbled path of the carriageway and out toward Bridgetown.

The lights of the city had been lit in tall lamps along the busy street. Bawdy saloons had filled to capacity, and the sound of pianos floated out to them. The women had talked themselves out during the heat of the day. Now they all gazed out the window of the carriage in silence. The sound of the horses' hooves clopping on the cobbled streets soon had the effect of a lullaby. Grace's eyelids drooped until at long last, the lights of the dockyard beamed out along the wooden boardwalk in front of the *Savannah Rose*.

"Stay together when you move up the gangway," Captain Harding said. There was an edge to his voice. Just as she passed him he grumbled something under his breath.

Grace could have sworn she heard him mumble the word, "babysitter." She picked up her skirts, her chin jutting out as she worked her way up the gangplank behind the trio. Once her foot hit the main deck she did not wait for the scolding that was sure to come.

"Good night, everyone."

"Just a minute!"

"Good night, Captain." She didn't stop. She was not a child and she didn't need him treating her like one. She continued down the steps below the quarterdeck and entered her room where she dropped her purchases on the bed with her white umbrella.

A rap came at her door.

Grace heaved a sigh. "Drat it!"

She flung the door open and the captain walked in. He shut the cabin door with a jolt, his eyes blazing.

"Yes, Captain?"

He strode back to the door and opened it. "You better be glad we're shoving off in the morning. It's high time I get you deposited on the shores of Jamaica!"

Grace's cheeks flamed. "Good night to you, too, Captain."

He slammed the door. "Lock it!"

She crossed the short distance and turned the key.

Grace sat up in bed and hugged her knees, trying to remember all the sights and sounds of the harbor in Bridgetown. She'd spent the last hour trying to find sleep. It seemed to evade her. For the first time since she boarded the ship, she felt alone. She missed her grandparents, her aunt, and Josie. It would even be nice to have Smitty curled up at the foot of her bed. Instead, she listened to the sounds of the water lapping against the hull of the ship. A tear slipped down her cheek.

Father, I need you right now. You said You would never leave me nor forsake me. Help me to feel Your presence in the middle of the ocean. And Lord, help me to hold my tongue. It gets me in trouble every time. Amen

Two weeks dragged by. The sun hardly peeked through the cloudy skies. Then one sunny morning the clouds dispersed and Grace woke up to an odd sound. The rhythm of the swaying of the ship had stopped, and she realized then that it was the ship's lack of motion that had awakened her. She listened again to the sounds outside her window. Horses? Wagons? She rose to her knees and peeked out her window. A busy harbor met her eyes. Her journey had come to an end.

She flew out of bed and pulled her carpetbags out from under the bed. She set them both on the coverlet and set about packing all her personal effects. Then she pulled out the green traveling dress she'd planned to wear when she first met her father. Butterflies took up residence in her stomach. She was sure she wouldn't be able to eat a bite at breakfast.

She pulled out the locket reserved for this day. She worked to hook the clasp and patted the necklace in place. Today she would meet her father and begin her new life. Would he accept her, or send her packing?

FOURTEEN

GRACE GAZED OUT over the dock to the busy activity below. She took a deep breath and tried to calm the frantic beating of her heart. It wouldn't be long now.

Captain Harding came to the rail beside her. He called her name twice before she dragged her eyes from the passing landscape to look at him. When she did, she saw concern in his eyes. Could he read how young and vulnerable she felt?

"You're going to be fine," he told her softly. We'll be descending soon, and when we do, I'll help you acquire a carriage to get you to your father's house."

"You've been more than kind to me. I'll be sure to tell my father I was in good hands on the voyage."

The captain pinned his gaze on her for a fraction of a moment and smiled. "I know I was hard on you, Grace, but I couldn't afford to let anything happen to you that I would later regret."

Grace shook her head, "I understand. I have to admit I gave you plenty to worry about, and for that, I apologize."

"Think no more of it." He turned to leave. "I have business to attend to. I will return when it is time for you to leave the ship. Wait for me."

"I will." Grace leaned on the rail and focused on the scene before her. People, wagons, and carts all moved in pandemonium on the dock's landing. Dock loaders and stevedores waited for the *Savannah*

Rose to pull next to the pier. Crewmen began preparations to unload the passenger's luggage and the ship's merchandise. Passengers milled near the gangway as they waited to depart the ship.

Grace had promised the captain she would wait for his assistance. Soon the gangplank lowered to the ground and passengers began to descend to the dock's landing. *So much color!* Grace thought. She could barely contain her excitement as she viewed the activity below. She bit her bottom lip as she waited for the captain. Should she go on without him?

"That be the *Savannah Rose,* all right," Penny said from her seat on the wagon. Passengers descended the gangplank. "We best tell Dinah we be having company for the next few days. Lord knows the captain sure be liking her food."

Kindra held the reins to the wagon, half listening. She peered up at the beautiful woman who stood at the rail. She seemed familiar. Had they met? The woman looked straight at her.

A dockhand strode up to the wagon. "Move along! We need room for the carriages. Passengers won't be wanting to wait for the likes of you!"

Kindra lifted the reins and shook them. She glanced back at the vessel as the wagon moved out into the streets. She wanted to stay and watch the people descend the ship. The woman who spied her from the ship's rails and held her eyes . . . who was she?

Grace watched the wagon move away from the crowded dock. The woman holding the reins looked uncommonly familiar to her. She was dressed well for a slave. Her day dress was made of a flowered print with ruffles around the neck and sleeves. Who was she? A dockhand shouted to them to move on. There wouldn't be any reason to know anyone here. She'd never set foot on Jamaican soil. Still, she couldn't shake the odd feeling that she'd seen the girl before.

Where was the woman's driver? In Charleston, a woman did not travel without a male companion. Nor did slaves run errands. She had a feeling much would be different here in Jamaica. She had left Charleston behind. She would embrace the changes in this new land.

Corky waved at Grace as he pushed her trunk down the gangplank on a cart. He set the trunk on the wharf near a street pole. Another sailor picked up her carpetbags. Grace gazed over the deck looking for the captain. He was nowhere to be found. She peeked over the rail again. She would stand by her trunk. If the captain came looking for her, he could easily find her there. Grace worked her way down the ramp.

Moments later, Captain Harding strode up to the side of the road. "You were supposed to wait." He seemed exasperated.

She bit her bottom lip. "I thought I'd save you the trouble." She glanced down both sides of the lane. "The carriages have all been taken. How do I go about getting transportation?" She watched a gentleman hire a cart across the street. "I suppose a cart will do."

"A cart?" Drew's eyebrows shot up. He surveyed her flounced skirt, then looked out at the street where the small carts waited.

"I've only a small amount of funds left. If I should decide to sail back to Charleston, I will need every schilling I have left." Her cheeks grew warm.

"I have something for you." Drew reached in the pocket of his white trousers and pulled out a black, velvet pouch. "A refund for your passage."

Her eyes widened. "I don't understand."

"If your father knew I took money from his daughter to sail on his ship, he would be greatly disappointed in me."

Grace accepted the British coins and quickly deposited them in her stringed purse.

"Well then." She took a deep breath. "I think it's time I be on my way. Thank you for the refund. It's a relief to know I'm not completely at the mercy of my father." She frowned. "He may not welcome my coming unannounced."

"I'll help you attain a cart, Miss Cooper." He put two fingers in his mouth and a shrill whistle pierced the air.

A young coffee-colored man jumped down from his cart and hurried through the mill of traffic. He slid to a stop, pulled off his yellow straw hat, and bowed slightly.

"You need a ride, Captain Harding?" His white teeth gleamed in his big smile.

"Not today, Jimmy." He tilted his head toward Grace. "This young lady needs a ride to Cooper's Landing."

"Oh, yes." He beamed. "I give her ride to the Landing."

"Miss Cooper this is Jimmy Downs. He works for the dock foreman. He will take good care of you and your luggage."

"Pleased to meet you, Missy." He tipped his yellow straw hat. "I git my cart. You wait."

Grace watched the short, young man weave through the masses. She glanced up at the captain. "You've been so much help. I don't know how to thank you."

"Give it no more thought. I'm glad I could be of assistance." The captain removed his hat and brushed tanned fingers through his blonde wavy curls. Then he glanced back at the ship.

Her eyes followed his gaze. Crewmen pushed crude carts filled with cargo down the ramp before climbing the gangplank once again. Many carried bulky crates on their muscular shoulders.

"I've got to get back to the ship. You'll be all right?"

"Yes."

Jimmy pulled up beside her hefty trunk.

"I'll be bringing out the rest of your trunks tomorrow, " the captain said with a nod. Then he turned and disappeared through the milling crowd behind her.

Jimmy Downs tackled the job of loading Grace's steamer trunk on the small cart. Shaded by her white, lace umbrella, Grace flinched more than once as her trunk threatened to tumble to the ground. Having chosen the largest of seven trunks to travel with her, she again regretted the choice.

Sweat beaded Jimmy's brow as he braced the heavy trunk on his knees and crouched, his arms hugging the brown chest.

"No worry, Missy. I get it on for you," he reassured her.

A number of times Grace lurched forward to lend a hand, knowing she'd be of no real assistance. She glanced around her at the busy street. *Would no one assist this young man?* With a grunt and determined force, Jimmy shoved the trunk squarely on the back ledge behind the cart's seat.

"See, Missy, I told you I would git it on." A broad smile split Jimmy's face.

Grace smiled back with relief. "You certainly worked hard enough." She gathered her skirts to step up into the small cart. Jimmy's grin remained while he assisted her up. He lifted the two carpetbags. She placed them on the floor on each side of her wide skirt.

"How far is it to Cooper's Landing?" Grace clutched her seat with her left hand to keep from bouncing out. She held her umbrella above her head with her right hand to keep the hot sun from her face.

"It's a ways, Missy." Jimmy's dark head half turned as he spoke. "'Bout eight miles I 'spect." He kept his eye on the rutted road.

"Good heavens," Grace said. "I shall be all undone by the time we reach the Landing."

"What that you say, Missy?" Jimmy half turned again.

"Nothing." Grace rolled her eyes upward. "I'm talking to myself." She held on for dear life.

The cart rumbled and jostled as it worked its way through the dense, tropical road. Often the road narrowed with deep ditches on either side. Her eyes widened in fear as the wheels neared the edge of the road. Jimmy seemed not to care or notice. *He's probably traveled this road numerous times,* thought Grace.

She tried to lean back against the wooden board at her back, but the bouncing cart prohibited any semblance of comfort. Her knuckles white, she clamped the wooden seat with her hand. She tried not to look at the road, but concentrated on the fact that she was near the end of her journey.

All at once the horse reared, his brown eyes big and round. The cart tipped, and teetered at the edge of the road, then rolled into the ditch. Grace flailed her arms as she tumbled, hearing sounds of her trunk bouncing close behind her.

Grace landed with a thud on a large boulder at the bottom of the ditch. "Ow!" she cried. A sharp pain ripped through her left arm as she sat back against the bulky rock. She knew by now she was a disheveled mess. Her straw hat lay some ten feet away, crumpled and cracked. She blew a strand of hair away from her mouth.

Then Jimmy let out a low moan. "Oh, Missy, this is not good."

Her eyes swept the scenery before her. Crinolines and under garments lay strewn all over the ground, her trunk topsy-turvy in front of her. *Drat it!* After all the work it took for Jimmy to load the heavy trunk onto the cart.

Jimmy crouched on his hands and knees, slowly rising, seeming unharmed. The horse stood in a stand of tropical trees stomping his hind hooves, its withers shaking. The lead rope to the cart dragged behind him. The cart lay on its side at the bottom of the ditch, though it appeared unharmed.

"You all right, Missy?" Jimmy's voice came from behind her.

"I think so. What happened?"

"A boa constrictor passed in front of the horse. The horse spooked."

Before she could reply, she heard the thundering of horse's hooves.

"Whoa! Hold up there, Scimitar!" a strong male voice commanded.

The horse stopped, and the stranger jumped down.

In a fleeting movement the man was at Grace's side.

"Are you hurt, Ma'am?" he asked.

"My left arm throbs." Her voice shook. "I believe the rest of me is unharmed."

The broad-shouldered, black-haired man inspected Grace's arm. His calloused hand pressed near her elbow. "Ouch!"

"Sorry." His brow creased in concern. "Just checking to see if you might have broken a bone."

"She took a bad fall, Camp," Jimmy said, his black eyes wide. "The horse and cart seemed to take the plunge all right, but the Missy?" He shrugged.

The stranger tilted her cheek with his thumb. He smelled of the land. And was that a scent of ginger she detected? Her eyes glanced up at the chiseled face that moved close to hers.

Grace moaned as she moved her bottom off a small stone. The pressure on her left hand sent a sharp pain up her arm again. "Oh! Oh no!" She settled back on the stone, resigned to its discomfort.

She peered over the stranger's shoulders aware of his closeness, trying not to look at him.

"There's some swelling beginning to form near your elbow. You may have sprained your arm." He glanced at Jimmy, the cart, and the horse. An amused grin tilted his lips upward.

Grace caught Jimmy's eyes as he slightly shook his head toward the stranger. Then he glanced up over her head.

Grace's eyes followed those of the two men. On a tree limb to the right of where she sat hung her umbrella, as if put there intentionally. Next to it dangled a slim pair of silky white pantaloons. She froze, dismayed by the sight of her undergarments dangling from the tree. Heat burned up her neck and over her scalp.

"H . . . help me up." Grace reached out her right hand to the two men who fought to keep their composure.

"Not so fast," the stranger said, his voice deep. She didn't miss the glint of humor in his smoky-gray eyes. Humiliated, she wished to be anywhere but here.

"I believe I'm unharmed, save for my elbow." She glanced into the face of the stranger who towered above her. "Please." She held out her hand for assistance.

He ignored the outstretched hand. In one fluid motion, he picked her up. He felt strong as she lay against him, his male scent overpowering. For one giddy moment she enjoyed the feel of his muscular arms holding her, but not for long. Propriety told her he shouldn't be taking such liberties with her.

"Put me down." She glanced at the amusement in his eyes. She wanted to strangle him. She stiffened in his hold. "I said, put me down. You're quite bold to be taking such liberties."

"Just trying to be a gentleman, Ma'am."

Cameron gently set the woman on her feet. "Let's get this mess picked up and you back on your journey." She'd felt light as a leaf in his arms. He hadn't wanted to put her down. *This is a fine kettle of fish*, he thought.

"Help me roll the cart upright, Jimmy."

For the next few minutes they worked to right the cart. Then they hitched the horse back to the wooden structure. Next they placed the empty trunk on the narrow ledge behind the seat. When Cameron glanced back at the clearing where the woman once sat, he saw her picking up undergarments, petticoats and gowns. She hugged them to herself until she reached the trunk where she plunked the garments inside, her cheeks red.

Cameron glanced to the tree limb that once held the white umbrella and silky pantaloons. It now stood empty. He chuckled to himself and set out to pick up the dresses that lay crumpled on the ground in a heap. But the trunk was filled to the brim, and he held an armload of crinolines. *How in tarnation are these dresses going to fit into that trunk?* he wondered.

"Allow me." The young woman moved in. After much pushing and rearranging of the garments in the trunk, she relieved Cameron of the crinolines and frocks then eyed him with one eyebrow cocked.

Cameron gauged her as she worked. Petite with long, auburn curls, her eyes glistened like emeralds fringed with long, black lashes. Her cheeks glowed a bright rose, partially from the business of pushing and shoving to fold in all the lace and crinolines to make them stay put. High cheekbones and dimples. A fair complexion. A pert nose with a smudge of dirt on it. She was beautiful. She smelled good, too. Rosewater?

So absorbed in watching her, he hadn't noticed her staring up at him, hands on hips. "If you'd be so kind as to latch the chest shut, sir, we can be on our way."

Cameron reached a calloused finger to the tip of her nose. With a quick swipe the smudge was gone. He noted the slight rise of her rigid shoulders as she stood before him. Her cheeks bright pink, their eyes met and held. He nodded. "That's better." She lowered her eyes, moved to the side of the cart and waited to be helped up.

Cameron took hold of her good elbow and helped her into the cart. Jimmy climbed into his seat and shook the reins. "Gid up," he called to the mare.

Grace glanced back to see the stranger untie his horse from a tree limb and climb easily onto the saddle. He passed them at a trot. A moment later, he disappeared around the bend of the road.

For a fleeting moment, she felt disappointment that he'd left. He seemed such a gentleman. She let out a sigh. No time for such matters now. She had a father to meet.

The cart rocked and bumped along the rutted road once again. She clamped the seat with her right hand. The jostling sent a pain up her arm. She hoped they would reach their destination soon. Jimmy slowed the cart a half hour later, then let it roll to a stop.

Bobbing his head toward the scenery before them, he said. "This be Coopah's Landing."

Grace sat awestruck at the beautiful scene before her.

The lane leading to the plantation was a quarter of a mile long. On each side of the drive in straight lines stood tall palm trees. Their enormous leaves waved gently in the quiet breeze.

Far off in the distance the carriage lane veered to form a circular drive for easy access to the large three-story house rising up from the knoll. The massive house stood white with black shutters that opened on each side of the many windows. The long drive led past the sprawling lawns. Tall palms and Spanish Oak trees stood scattered in front and all around the house.

Grace tried to take in the enormity of the plantation. Numerous buildings stood within walking distance from the house, neatly painted white with shake roofs. The slave shacks were not painted. They appeared stark and crude.

As far as the eye could see, barns, stables, and outbuildings speckled the landscape. Further on, rows of sugarcane and provisional fields skirted the buildings, and beyond that the ocean shimmered in the sun. Sitting on the rise of the road gave her a good glimpse of the plantation.

"All of this belongs to my father?"

"Yes, Missy." His dark eyes gleamed.

"Alla this be the works of Mastah Coopah. He been working them fields for nigh on thirty years."

"Yes," Grace whispered.

They sat silent for a few minutes. *Lord, help me in this new venture. I've wanted this for so long.* Then Grace raised her parasol and ended the silence. "You may continue to the Great House, Jimmy. I'm ready."

FIFTEEN

GEMMA ENTERED THE large dining room and snapped open the starched tablecloth. She shook the white cloth and raised it over the table and let it settle softly on the polished surface. As she worked her way around the table, pulling here and pushing there, she glanced out of the leaded-glass window framed by dainty, lace curtains parted to each side and held by a Basque ribbon. She could see from the front porch to the driveway lined with tall palmettos. Dust rose as a horse pulling a small cart trotted steadily toward the house. Gemma quickly straightened the last wrinkled edge and went to the window to peer out more closely.

A handsome woman holding a white umbrella high over her head sat in the cart.

"Well, who could that be?" Gemma said, as she stood with her nose close to the windowpane. The cart came around the circular drive and stopped.

"That can't be her. Dinah! Come quick!" Gemma jerked away from the window and looked back toward the kitchen door, her eyes big and round. "Dinah! Come quick!"

The driver leaned back and spoke to the young woman.

"Dinah!" Gemma whirled around and fled into the kitchen, sending the swinging door swaying back and forth as she did.

"What's all the commotion?" Dinah turned from kneading bread. "Why, you be looking like you seen a ghost!" She spilled flour on the kitchen floor as she raised both hands in the air.

"I be thinking I did seen a ghost. Come quick!" Gemma motioned Dinah to follow and then hurried back to the dining room window.

Dinah moved up beside Gemma at the window. Jimmy Downs moved to the side of the cart to help a young lady to the ground.

"Lawdy, have mercy! I be thinking we both be seein' a ghost!" Dinah rubbed her floured hands on her apron as she sailed out of the dining room to stand in the roomy entryway.

"Zeek! Come quick!"

Before Zeek arrived, the downstairs housekeeper came flying out of the drawing room with a feather duster in her hand. "What's all the noise 'bout, Dinah?"

Dinah grabbed hold of the housekeeper's arm and dragged her to the dining room window. The three women peered out in time to see Jimmy lift the two carpetbags out of the cart and set them on the ground. The housekeeper's eyes grew round as she gawked out the window. "Land sakes a-livin'!"

Grace stood at the side of the cart with butterflies in her stomach. She was glad Jimmy kept talking. It helped to calm her nerves. She peered up at the Great House. When she did, curtains moved by the window on the right side of the porch.

"Thank you, Jimmy. Maybe you should wait to take my trunk off the cart until they know I've arrived."

"Don't mind waiting, Missy."

Grace closed her parasol with difficulty, as her left arm throbbed, and moved toward the porch. She lifted the hem of her dress and advanced up the steps to the front porch. "Lord," she whispered, "I've waited for this all of my life. Give me peace and strength as I enter my father's home."

She lifted her hand and rapped three times. The door swung open and a black servant stood before her. Eyes round, he gaped at her. "How-do, Miss."

"Is . . . is . . . Mr. Cooper home?" She stumbled on her words.

"He be home, all right. Please come in." The butler stood aside as Grace entered the house. He closed the door behind her.

"Who may I say be calling?" He stared down at her.

"I'd rather not say. I've traveled all the way from America. May I see him?"

"Stand right here." The butler's shiny, black shoes clicked on the marble floor as he walked away.

Grace glanced around the foyer while she waited. The interior felt cool. An expansive staircase leading to the second floor swept across the right side of the room. An alcove sat back to the left of the room with a round table and a vase of flowers. A grandfather clock stood beside the dining room entrance on her right.

To the left of the front entrance was a large drawing room with double, glass-paned doors. Grace peeked down the hallway to her left, past the stairs. Faint sounds came from beyond the dining room.

A mahogany table sat in the center of the dining room with twelve chairs around it. A portrait of her mother hung in a gold-domed, oval frame above the sideboard. Grace gaped at it, stunned. It looked like a painting of herself.

When had the painting been done? Until now, she hadn't realized the likeness between herself and her mother. Seeing this early version of her mother, she now knew there was no question they shared a strong resemblance. All these years her father left the portrait hanging on the wall. He must have loved her very much.

What was taking the butler so long? She glanced down the wide, dark hallway. He'd disappeared behind one of the doors. Feeling someone watching from above, Grace glanced beyond the polished handrails to the upper landing.

A black woman gripped the smooth banister and peered down at her.

Her manner seemed regal, her build slight, yet her stance seemed hard as steel. Her hair was combed back into a chignon, her ebony face smooth. Strikingly beautiful, the sheer blue eyes enhanced her already aesthetic features. Large, hooped earrings hung from her earlobes and she wore an ivory gown, embroidered with gold jungle animals. Grace noted the woman didn't wear a servant's uniform. Who was she? Discomforted by the woman's brazen stance, Grace casually moved to the left, out of the woman's vision.

She stole another glance upward. She had the odd sense this woman was miffed with her.

A door closed down the dark hallway. The butler returned alone, wearing a slight frown.

"I apologize, Miss, for taking so long. Mastah Coopah had a trying morning and wishes to rest before seeing anyone." He cleared his throat and glanced up the stairs. The dark woman had disappeared as silently as she'd appeared. "The Mastah would like you to rest, as well, seeing as you have traveled a long way. He won't be ready to see you for another hour." He gave Grace a kind smile and bowed.

"But did you tell him I've come an interminable way to see him?" Grace had waited for this moment all too long. Was she to wait yet a while longer? Disappointment assailed her.

"Yes, Ma'am, I did. He be saying he has an awful headache and not good for company at the moment. He be resting before he be seeing you." He glanced at another house servant who'd appeared.

"Gemma can show you to a room upstairs where you can rest before Mastah give you some attendance." An older maid stood in the arched entrance to the dining room and lowered her eyes when Grace turned toward her.

"I don't wish to be any trouble," Grace said.

"You sure be no trouble at all." He nodded toward the maid, whose salt-and-pepper hair poked out from under her white, ruffled cap.

"Gemma, show Miss—" He glanced back at the young lady who stood by the front door, his brows raised.

Grace grabbed her skirt ready to ascend the wide staircase. "My name is Grace Cooper." She smiled at the two servants, whose eyes had gone wide.

"You are related to Mastah Coopah?" The butler cocked his head sideways.

"Yes" was all she could muster for the moment. Her left arm throbbed and rest sounded wonderful to her bone-weary body.

Zeek glanced out at the cart laden with the hefty trunk. "You'll be staying with Mastah Coopah a few days?"

"Yes." Grace believed she was coming apart at the seams. The tumble from the cart and the pain in her elbow had caught up with her. She knew at once she needed to lie down.

"You be asking too many questions, Zeek," Gemma said. "Can't you see the lady is plum worn out? Leave your questions for later." Gemma's arm went around Grace's waist to steady her as they climbed the stairs. "And tell Amos to bring her trunk up to the porch. You can leave it there until we know what room Mastah Coopah be having her stay in."

With the maid's arm moving Grace forward, they climbed the stairs.

Grace heard the butler call out the front door to the waiting cart driver. "Hold on a moment. We'll git some help with that trunk."

As they came to the top landing, Grace glanced down the halls on either side of the stairway. The two women turned right, looking down the east wing. "Let's use this first room to the left, Miss Coopah. It's small, but comfortable. I'm sure, Mastah Coopah will have you moved to a larger room after he be rested."

Gemma yanked draperies aside to let in some light and then pulled down the coverlet to the bed.

"Now you be making yourself comfortable, Miss Coopah. I'll fetch some fresh water for your wash basin."

Grace didn't care what the room looked like. The noon hour had passed, and she had not eaten a meal since leaving the ship. Her stomach growled as she sat down on a nearby chair and unlaced her hot, kid boots. She pulled out tired, cramped feet and let her toes caress the soft rug that lay on the hardwood floor. Too weary to slip out of her traveling clothes, Grace climbed into the bed and fell asleep.

Phillip sat with his hands over his chest, sweat beading his forehead. He tried to measure his breathing as he inhaled, taking it slowly. He remembered the feeling from before, from when the pain had wracked his chest weeks ago.

The world swirled around him a he sipped the glass of water Dinah had brought. The pain eased. He laid his head back on the dark leather chair and closed his eyes. He needed to rest. If he allowed himself to settle back and sleep, he would wake up and be fine. He listened as the clock ticked to the rhythm of his heart. The house grew quiet.

SIXTEEN

AN HOUR LATER Grace awoke, slipped her feet into her boots, laced the buttons, and ran her hands down her wrinkled skirts. Her arm still throbbed and she ran her hand over her left elbow, trying to assuage the pain. She tiptoed to the mirror and glanced at her reflection. Tendrils of curls escaped the combs that swept her hair away from her face. She moved out into the hall and stood at the top of the landing.

The house was quiet. She slipped down the stairs. When she neared the bottom, she heard voices beyond the dining room. She waited and listened.

Gemma entered the foyer with an arm full of soiled bedding. "Why Miss Coopah, you're up." Then she peered down the hallway at the dark woman moving toward them. Grace recognized the woman who'd watched her earlier from upstairs.

"Tia, she be wanting to speak with Mastah Coopah."

Other servants appeared from the kitchen. Their presence gave Grace some comfort as the ebony woman stood before her in a cold stance, her shoulders squared.

"Who may I say is calling?"

"She be—"

"I'm talking to the young lady, Gemma."

"You may tell him his daughter, Grace Cooper, is calling."

Tia's gaze raked over Grace before she turned and walked down the hall as graceful as a panther. When she came to the office, she paused, lifted her chin and knocked twice.

A male voice called, "Come in, Tia."

Phillip watched Tia enter the small room. Evidently something was wrong. Her countenance was like that of a cat about to pounce. Her eyes flashed blue fire.

"You have a guest waiting to speak with you in the foyer."

Phillip put his pen down and gazed at the woman before him. Even in her darkest mood, Tia was astonishingly beautiful—her skin glistening like black satin, her face striking, with a straight nose, a hint of broadness to her nostrils, and wide, thick, shapely lips. Her eyes were not dark like those of the rest of the African slaves at Cooper's Landing. They were a piercing blue that captivated and held anyone who saw her for the first time, as they had captivated him so long ago.

Instead of the formal housemaid uniforms, he'd let her wear gowns. Though she usually preferred bold colors, she looked elegant now in her ivory gown embroidered with jungle animals. His eyes followed the length of her before he looked at her sullen face.

"Zeek said as much earlier. Who might the gentleman be, Tia?" He leaned back in his leather chair and folded his hands in his lap. His left eye winced a bit.

"It isn't a gentleman, Master Cooper." She called him by his surname, her lips grim. "The young lady standing in the foyer says her name is Grace Cooper. She claims she is your daughter."

Phillip pushed his chair away from his desk. "You must have heard wrong."

Tia's eyes narrowed. "I did not misunderstand the caller." She stepped aside while Phillip passed through the door.

As he neared the foyer his gaze fell on the young woman. All at once the room spun. He reached the banister for support. Tia had said her name was Grace, but she looked every bit like his Olivia.

Grace locked eyes with the gray-haired man. He faltered and grabbed the banister for the space of a moment, allowing her to take in his tall frame, stocky build, and clear, green eyes.

Then he drew near. He scanned her from her head to her kid boots and back. He seemed at a loss for words, a look of astonishment on his face.

Grace sucked in her breath.

"Remarkable," he said in a low tone. His eyes pinned her to where she stood. "You are the spitting image of your mother, child." He started to reach out and touch her but took a step back, his mouth grim.

"Tia says you claim to be my daughter." He paused. "It is quite obvious you are Olivia's. But I have no reason to believe you are mine. When she left, she was not with child." He frowned. "She would have told me if she had been."

Grace missed none of the hesitant gestures, and his remark stung to the very core of her heart. She stepped back as well and her hand flew to the locket at her throat. Phillip's eyes darkened, and he clenched his jaw. Coldness came over his expression.

She held her breath for what seemed an eternity, staring at the man before her, an older version of the man in the picture she'd found in her mother's drawer. She brought that picture. It lay secured in the tapestry bag at her feet.

"You didn't receive my letter?"

"What letter?"

"I wrote that I was coming, a month before I sailed."

"I received no letter." His eyes remained cold.

"I . . . I shouldn't have come," she stammered, feeling like the air had become too thick to breathe. Her cheeks grew hot and she faltered backward.

The butler jumped forward and laid a strong hand on her back. "Easy, Missy."

Phillip Cooper stepped forward and grabbed Grace's left arm, grimness on his lips.

She flinched in pain.

"What did you say your name was?"

Grace shuddered inwardly from his firm grip on her injured arm. It throbbed. She felt faint. It took all her reserve to steady herself and not pull back. "My name is Grace . . . Grace Cooper," she drawled.

For a fleeting moment Phillip's eyes brightened and a look of sheer delight spread across his face. "You also have you mother's voice." For an instant he appeared hopeful as he pulled her toward him. All at once he glanced about the foyer and back to Grace, his gray eyebrows creased. "Where is your mother, child?"

The pain in her arm was more than she could bear. She pulled her arm out of his grip and took a step back, her face pale.

"She passed away six months ago." Her eyelids dropped. Sweat slicked her brow.

"Passed away?" She faintly heard her father's whisper, as the room grew dark.

Zeek lurched forward and caught her before she fell to the floor. "She done fainted!" she heard the butler say, before the world went black.

Someone shook Grace's shoulder. She blinked open her eyes.

"Miss Coopah, you wake up now."

Grace squinted. "Where am I?" She tried to sit up on the rose-patterned sofa, but a servant woman laid a firm hand on her to hold her down. "Not so fast, Missy. You 'bout gave us all a scare."

"My arm," Grace moaned.

"What about your arm?" The servant inspected the arm Grace held.

"Why your elbow be swollen!" She stood up and placed her hands on her hips. "What happened to you?"

Her father moved the dark woman aside. And bent to look at Grace's arm. "Send Amos for the doctor."

"Please," Grace said, as she tried to sit up again.

Her father touched her shoulder, his eyes showed a mixture of concern and hardness.

"I can sit up," Grace insisted.

"You're sure?" Phillip's eyes searched her face. "Your color seems to be coming back."

A servant stood next to him with a glass of water. Phillip took the cool glass and offered it to Grace, his hand shaking.

She felt like a spectacle as she sipped the cool water, sitting before five pairs of eyes peering down at her. Heat crept up her neck and onto her cheeks. "I believe I'm feeling much better, thank you." She glanced up and cleared her throat.

"Leave us," Phillip said.

The three servants left the room. The mysterious, dark woman with the blue eyes stood at a distance.

Grace saw weariness in her father's eyes. She remembered telling him her mother died before she fainted.

"I'm sorry about mother."

"I had no idea," he said, as he peered at her skeptically.

"She had tuberculosis. She had been battling the illness for a long time. Near the end she spent much of her time in bed. Doctor Newton did everything he could for her. Then one day, she died." Grace gazed at her father. "For the first time in my life, I was all alone. No mother or father."

"But you had other family, your aunt and grandparents."

"It's not the same." She bristled and went on. "After the funeral I spent a good deal of time getting mother's affairs in order. That's when I found the bundle of letters." She gazed at him. "Letters you started sending twenty years ago."

Grace eyed the dark woman standing by the window. She stood rigid and glared at them. It was clear she resented Grace.

Grace pulled her eyes from the ebony woman to her father and said, "That is when I learned you were not dead."

"Dead?" Phillip stood to his feet. "Of course I'm not dead." He shook his head in disbelief. "Is that what your mother would have you believe?" He walked to the drawing room window where a stand of tropical trees sat close to the house. Grace noticed his back stiffen as he stood looking out the window for a while. She wished the woman standing across the room would leave them alone. Tension grew as she waited for her father to come back to where she sat.

"I've heard enough," he said as he turned toward her. His eyes seemed tired. "I'm not convinced you are my daughter, though there is no question you belong to Olivia. One only has to look at you to know that to be true." He ran a tired hand over his rough face. "But Olivia never said a word about you. As much as she wanted to go back to the states, I cannot believe she would have withheld information about you from me. You are mistaken. You thought I was your father. But I'm not. I will have my coachman give you a ride back to town after the doctor has tended to your arm." With that he left the room.

Grace sat stunned. Did he believe she was an imposter after his money? She fingered the locket at her throat as her thoughts ran rampant. She tried to imagine how she would think in his position. If she were her father, she'd not be bamboozled either by a young woman showing up claiming to be his child. Had she come all the way across the Atlantic Ocean for nothing? She swallowed hard. What now?

An hour later, a sling draped over her shoulder and her left arm resting in its hold, Grace sat in a fine coach with the Cooper seal on each side of the doors. She felt numb as the carriage bounced over the rutted roads back to Riverbend. She reached her hand to where her necklace once hung. She'd left it on the mahogany table by the sofa and told one of the servants to give it to her father. Maybe he'd realize the child he had sent away was indeed his daughter. By then, it would be too late. She would have purchased passage back to America.

Tears stung her eyes as the pram bounced over the road. She swallowed the lump in her throat and gazed through blurred eyes out the window. It all had ended far too quickly. She'd spent months planning and traveling to the ends of the earth to find her father. Only to be swept out the door of his Great House as if she were a waif begging for his riches. She wiped at the tear that trailed down her cheek, and sniffed.

As the coach rolled down Main Street, Grace reached for her black, stringed purse. It didn't lie on the gold velvet seat. She reached under her flounced skirt and searched the floor. The purse lay nowhere. For the first time, she realized she did not have it with her. Had she left it at the Great House?

She swallowed as tears threatened to spill once more. Not only had she lost the privilege of being with her father, but also she didn't have a cent to her name. She had no way to pay passage back to America. Nor could she purchase a room at the hotel. The jostling of the coach matched the jarring of her heart. What would she do now?

Moments later, the carriage pulled up in front of the only hotel on Main Street. Grace stood on the wooden walk in front of the building feeling much like an orphan. Without a word, the coachman went into the hotel. Grace glanced up and down the street. What does a person do who doesn't have a cent to her name?

"Your room is waiting for you, Miss," said a male voice behind her.

Grace whirled around to face the coachman. "I don't understand."

"Mastah Coopah will be paying for your stay." He left her side and pulled the two carpetbags from behind the carriage. "I'll get some help to bring your trunk up to your room." He carried the two bags into the lounge and set them down. "The porter will carry your bags for you."

"I left my purse at the Great House. I will need it to pay passage back to America."

"I sure be telling him, Miss."

Grace went to the hotel desk. "I'm Grace Cooper. I understand you have a room reserved for me."

The man behind the desk glanced at the sling holding her injured arm and signaled the porter. "Take Miss Cooper's bags to room four." Grace followed him up a flight of stairs. Once in her room, she gazed out the window. She didn't have a home to go to when she got back to the states. She'd have to take Aunt Katy up on her offer to stay with them.

She fell onto the bed and wanted to sob herself dry. She'd waited six months to make this trip, yet after being on the island less than twenty-four hours, she'd have to turn around and sail back. At least she'd gotten to see her father. Never mind that he'd sent her away.

The following morning, Phillip Cooper sat across his desk from Captain Drew Harding. He fingered the locket while he listened to the captain's story. "You've seen documents proving Grace Cooper is my daughter? Where are they?"

"I gave them to Grace."

"If what you say is true, why didn't she show them to me?"

"She was supposed to."

Phillip eyed the captain. "You've never given me reason to doubt your word." He frowned. "I wouldn't have sent her away with documented proof that she is my child. He opened his hand and stared down at the locket again.

The captain leaned forward. "Isn't that the necklace Grace was wearing?"

"Yes it is. She left it when I sent her away." He grimaced. His fingers shook while he opened the clasp and peered down at the young couple inside. He glanced up at Drew and snapped the locket shut. "I gave this to Olivia as a wedding gift. I'm an old fool. I must send my coachman after the girl. If she's a Cooper, she belongs here."

Mid morning, Grace heard a rap at the door. She opened it. A young man handed her a note.

"Thank you." She shut the door and sat on the edge of the bed. She glanced at the envelope addressed to *Grace Cooper*, in eloquent handwriting. Grace broke the seal and unfolded the fine stationary paper, with the Cooper Coat of Arms at the left, and her father's name, Phillip Cooper, in the center. *Be ready to leave within the hour. My coachman will bring you back to the Landing.* Had he seen the locket?

Grace didn't know whether to laugh or cry. Either would suffice. She was on her way to her father's house at his command. Her stomach knotted. Was the worst of it over?

SEVENTEEN

TWO HOURS LATER, Grace tried to still the fluttering of her heart as she stood before her father. "My aunt said I should have written to you before I sailed to Jamaica. Sometimes I act before I think it through. I sent the letter last minute." She bit her bottom lip. "I don't always listen to sound advice."

"It should have come by now." Phillip turned to Tia, who stood at a distance, "Have you seen the letter?"

Tia stiffened, yet her eyes did not flinch. "No, Sir."

"Let's have no more talk of this for now." Phillip gently opened Grace's hand and let the locket fall into her palm. "Are you all right, dear?"

"Yes."

He turned to Tia, "Show my daughter to the room at the end of the hall upstairs.

Grace popped her head up. Had she heard him right?

"Across the hall from the nursery, sir?" Tia asked, and glided across the floor toward Grace.

"No." He raised his broad shoulders. "The blue room across the hall from my chamber."

Tia flashed him a hard look. "Sir?"

"Do as I ask." His hand rested on Tia's waist, briefly. "And fetch Hedy. Have her see to Grace's bath."

Tia moved out of the drawing room, her shoulders rigid.

Grace caught a slight flinch in the woman's eyes, but she moved gracefully into the foyer. She turned angry eyes at the rest of the servants who waited with curiosity. "Back to work, all of you!" she snapped.

In an instant, the small group parted and spread throughout the Great House.

"Fools! All of them!" Tia hissed under her breath, but loud enough Grace caught every word. Their eyes met and held. "Follow me."

Grace spied her two carpetbags sitting on the marble floor in the foyer. Wrapped in muslin and lying out of sight near the bottom of one bag was a bundle of personal letters written in her father's hand, tied together with a stout length of twine. She reached down to pick up a bag with her good arm.

"Leave them," Phillip said. "Zeek will take them to your room."

"Sir," Zeek said. "There be a large trunk on the front porch as well."

Phillip turned to Gemma, who stood in the dining room, keeping her distance from Tia's stormy eyes.

"Gemma, send for Amos. Tell him to bring the trunk up to my daughter's room."

Twice Phillip had referred to Grace as 'my daughter' in the space of a short time. A warm glow filled Grace's heart, and for the first time, she smiled. With light steps she followed Tia up the stairs.

Phillip stood at the base of the stairs and watched Grace climb the stairs with all the grace of a princess. Her hair flowed in auburn curls down her back. She lifted her dark green skirts and ascended the stairs.

He walked back to his study and shut the door. He crossed the room to his desk and sat down, weary. "I have a daughter . . . the spitting image of my beloved Olivia. Olivia," he whispered. "How could you have kept my daughter from me all these years?"

Anger welled up in him. And grief. A mixture of feelings balled up inside. Olivia had not only deceived his daughter, she had deceived him. He should have shared in the upbringing of this child. She had kept the prize of a lifetime to herself. All these years he'd waited for Olivia's return. Instead, a daughter he never knew existed walked into his life.

Grace followed Tia down the hall. When they reached the last door on the left, Tia opened the door and stood back, her mouth grim.

"This room used to belong to your mother. No one has slept here since she left." Tia glanced about the room with indignation. "I've never cared for the room."

Grace entered. Tia immediately stepped out and closed the door.

Bright and airy, the room and everything about it reminded Grace of her mother. A lump rose in her throat as she moved about the bedchamber. When her mother had last stood there, she wasn't much older than Grace.

The room had been partitioned into two sections, the decor in both done in china-blue roses on cream-colored fabric. The four-poster bed sat in front of slate-blue draperies. A vanity table and double wardrobe were the only other pieces of furniture in the bedchamber. The north side of the room, lined with French doors, led out to the balcony.

An opening from the bedchamber led to an exquisite sitting room. Three windows faced out over the balcony. Before them stood a sofa and two stuffed chairs. A round, oak table stood in the middle of the room with a vase of fresh flowers. Another door led from the sitting room.

Curious, Grace opened the door and peered into the smaller bedchamber she'd slept in earlier. Once back in the bedchamber, she opened another door that led to a private bathroom with a clawfoot tub and necessity chair with a pail beneath it. An ornate mirror hung on the wall over a washstand.

Grace walked back into the bedchamber. She loved her new accommodations. Her trunk would be brought up soon, and she would be able to unpack.

Her eyes rested on the bed. She could imagine Smitty curled up on the coverlet. She missed him. She wished there'd been a way to bring him with her.

Her emotions had taken a toll. Though it was nearly noon, she longed to crawl into the large bed and let herself fall into an abyss of sleep.

Just about to give in to the temptation, she heard a polite tap at her door. A young colored girl entered the room, followed by two men with large pails of steaming water in each hand.

"I'm Hedy, Miss. Mastah Coopah said I was to draw your bath." Hedy crossed the room to the bathtub. The men followed her into the bathroom, glancing curiously about the room, their eyes falling on Grace.

She heard the water slosh into the clawfoot tub. They came out one at a time and left as quickly as they'd come.

"May I ask where you get the hot water?"

"There be a bath house beyond the outer kitchen, Miss. Mastah Coopah keep a large boiler of water burning all the time."

"Thank you, Hedy." Grace eyed the girl who appeared to be around 16, maybe 17.

"We'll be returnin' with more water." Hedy said, and left the room.

Grace gazed at the bed. It would have to wait.

The hot water felt soothing to her arm. When Grace stepped out of the steamy bathroom draped in a robe, she found the room empty. At last, she climbed into the soft bed, wanting nothing more than to fall into a deep slumber.

Images of a dark woman with crystal-blue eyes filled Grace's mind when she closed her eyes. She sensed the woman disliked her vehemently. Who was she? Why did Grace's coming upset this woman so?

EIGHTEEN

HEDY TAPPED ON the door late in the afternoon. Her eyes grew round as Grace struggled to button the back of her gown with one hand.

"That's my job, Miss Coopah." She turned Grace around. "Miss Tia be having my skin if she knew you be helpin' yourself like this." She went to work buttoning up the back of Grace's dress and made sure there were no wrinkles in her gown.

"When you be ready to get dressed, you pull this chord in the corner." Hedy crossed the room and grabbed hold of a thick, gold-braided chord hanging from the ceiling. She pulled it once and a clear bell tone rang through the room. "When I hear the bell I come right away."

"I see. Then you're my personal chambermaid?"

"That's right. I draw your bath, comb your hair, and see you be put together proper like before you leave your room." Hedy beamed, proud of her position.

Grace smiled at the dark girl standing behind her as she inspected herself in the mirror.

"Does that mean you make my bed and clean the room, too?"

"Oh, no." Hedy shook her head. "I only tend to you." She grinned. "Minerva be cleanin' your room."

"I see," Grace said again.

"Now if you'll sit down on this stool, I'll fix your hair."

Hedy had a natural flair for combing hair into a stylish fashion. Her nimble fingers tucked and pinned Grace's hair until the result was more than satisfactory.

Another rap sounded at the door. Hedy opened it a crack.

"Mastah Coopah be saying he ready for Miss Coopah to meet the staff before they sit down for suppah."

"She just about ready."

"How do I look?" Grace asked, admiring the pale orange, taffeta gown. The gathered bands of the puffed sleeves and skirt were trimmed in tobacco-brown appliqué. Her hair was pulled back in long ringlets and tied with a bow at the back of her neck in the same pale orange as the gown. Her auburn curls glistened in the late afternoon sunlight shining through the doors. Grace turned away from the mirror, pleased to have an efficient chambermaid.

Her fingers clenched and unclenched the pale orange fan embroidered with the same tobacco color.

The humidity was thick, and the fan would be an absolute necessity for cooling herself this evening. Besides, it helped to keep her hands busy.

"Lawdy, Miss Coopah. You look just fine." Hedy smiled. "That sling don't take away from your fancy dress at all."

Grace glanced at the makeshift sling over her lovely dress. She would have given anything to not have to wear it.

"Mastah Coopah's gathered all the staff in the drawing room. We best be gettin' down there real soon." It was plain to see Hedy didn't like to keep the Master of the Great House waiting.

"Shall we go then?"

Hedy opened the door and held it aside for Grace as she passed through with her yards of ruffled skirts. She made her way down the hall to the top landing where she paused.

"Go ahead," the young girl whispered. "They be waitin' for you."

Grace gazed down at the butler. He stepped over to the drawing room and nodded his head. A moment later Phillip appeared.

Grace descended the stairs, aware her father watched her. She saw pride in his eyes and felt a glow of warmth in her heart.

Phillip met her at the bottom of the landing and gently pulled her right hand through the crook of his arm. "You look quite refreshed, my dear. I must say the resemblance between you and your mother is startling." He squeezed her hand.

"I've been told as much." She smiled warmly.

He led her toward the drawing room, where the servants waited. Her eyes swept over the lineup, and stopped. Behind the group stood the stranger who'd rescued her the day before, his eyes glinting with amusement. *What is he doing here?*

Heat tinged her cheeks as she glanced at the tall, handsome man with the chiseled jaw, who towered over the servants in the room. As he observed her, one eyebrow quirked upward. Before averting her gaze from his taunting eyes, she caught one more thing—the undeniable surprise as he looked from Phillip to Grace. His smoky gray eyes held her for one long moment.

Grace dragged her eyes from his and turned to her father.

"Today is a glorious day. Most of you know a most wonderful surprise walked into the house." Phillip glanced down at Grace. "When my wife, Olivia, left Cooper's Landing twenty years ago, she took with her a treasured secret." He draped his arm over Grace's shoulder. "She was with child, with my daughter, now grown to be a young woman herself.

"I haven't had the privilege of sitting down to get acquainted with her. All that in due time. For now I want you to welcome my daughter, Miss Grace Cooper."

The room full of servants murmured, smiled and viewed her with curiosity. Yet one pair of eyes sent an unsettling chill down Grace's spine. Tia glared at her, her arm draped over the shoulders of a beautiful mulatto woman.

The young woman was not dark like the rest of the servants. Her skin had a honey glow. Nor were her eyes a dark, liquid brown, but green like emeralds. Grace recognized her as the young woman who'd sat in the wagon at the wharf. Again she was attired in a formal dress. Grace raised her chin in disdain at the boldness of this servant. At that moment those eyes searched hers.

Tia's cold and steely eyes scanned Grace, and the uneasy feeling remained. Grace tried to shake it off. Why would this woman, whom Grace assumed was a servant, be so bent on animosity toward her? How dare she act this way toward a woman in the company of her father? She turned away and tried to listen as Phillip continued to speak.

"There are many others on the plantation whom you will meet over time, but the people in this room are those you'll need to know. They are the house staff. As the days progress you will eventually meet the servants in the outer kitchen, stables, sugar mill, and maybe even the fields."

Grace nodded, unable to find her tongue.

His hand stretched to the right. "You've met Tia." Phillip's eyes shone, as he nodded toward the tall, graceful woman. "She is the headmistress of the house. Her duties stretch from directing the staff to planning the balls we hold at least once a year."

Her father smiled at the woman. An intimate look passed between them. Grace didn't miss the look of endearment between her father and the tigress. She cringed. Must he be so open about his affection toward this woman in the company of others?

Phillip turned back to Grace. "The young woman standing next to Tia is Kindra. She is Tia's daughter." He cleared his throat and moved his gaze to the rest of the group, who shuffled uneasily as they glanced at Kindra and back to Grace.

Kindra's eyes fell as he moved on to the next servant.

Phillip continued, "Next is Dinah. She is the cook."

Dinah moved forward ever so slightly and nodded. "Ma'am" was all she said.

"Gemma the downstairs maid."

Gemma smiled. "Pleased to be meeting you."

There was something calming in Gemma's mannerism and voice. Grace liked her immediately.

"You've met your personal lady's maid, Hedy."

"Yes." Grace glanced at the shy girl.

"Next is Laulie. She's the nanny here at the Great House, and is now midwife to many of the women here at the plantation. She's been with us from the beginning." Phillip smiled in Laulie's direction.

"Have there been children in the Great House?" Grace glanced up at her father.

"Yes. Two."

Grace noticed the stranger's wide smile as he stood behind Laulie, his hand laid affectionately on her shoulder.

"Cameron was nine when he joined us at Cooper's Landing. It is a story I'll save for later. Laulie was his nanny."

Grace was forced to acknowledge the gentleman known as Cameron. Their eyes held for the space of a moment. She fanned herself, glad she had the instrument to keep her hands busy.

Her father went on. "Cameron Bartholomew, Camp to most of us here, is like a son to me. He's the foreman of Cooper's Landing."

Cameron tipped his dark head toward her, "We meet again, Miss Cooper." The glint in his eyes goaded her.

Grace hadn't missed her father's declaration. *He is like a son to me.*

"You've met?" Phillip's eyes jumped from Cameron to his daughter.

Grace cleared her throat and moved her fan faster, hoping to quell the blasted heat creeping up her face once more. "On the road to Cooper's Landing." She peered at Cameron. Her eyes pleaded that he not disclose the awful details of the accident yesterday.

Cameron's baritone voice filled the room. "Jimmy Downs had a problem with his horse pulling the cart with your engaging young daughter. The cart spilled your daughter and her trunk into the ditch. It was my gentlemanly duty to assist them." He arched a dark brow at her and sent a comical grin to her father.

Grace could tell this stranger . . . foreman . . . whoever he was, enjoyed making sport of her. Dare he exploit the matter of her pantaloons dangling from a tree limb as well? Her eyes narrowed.

Phillip raised his brow. "You said you fell, but I had no idea your cart spilled on the road." He frowned and eyed the sling holding her arm. "Thank goodness Camp came on the scene when he did."

"As your foreman said, he quickly took care of the situation. We were able to be on our way without too much fuss." Grace tipped her head at Cameron. "A gentleman to be sure, and you have my heartfelt appreciation, Mr. Bartholomew."

"You can call me Cameron. And you are welcome."

Watching the beautiful woman standing next to Pip, Cameron admired the girl's spirit. *We could use some spark around here at Cooper's Landing.*

But questions reeled through his mind. Why was she here? And why in tarnation had she traveled alone without an escort? Didn't anyone educate the young lady that it was dangerous to cross the ocean with barbarians alone? She was lucky she hadn't been abducted, or worse, killed on the way.

She couldn't weigh more than a hundred pounds soaking wet. She looked dainty as a pearl. Should've been protected as one, too. He pulled his gaze away from Grace and glanced down the line of servants. Tia surveyed him with a cool gaze.

Grace observed the scowl on Cameron's face. A moment ago he'd had fun at her expense. Now he looked as if a storm brewed in his mind.

"Let's move on," her father said. "Minerva is the upstairs maid. As you can see, the house is quite large. There are twenty-three rooms. We had to divide the work load into separate areas and duties."

Minerva's black eyes leered coldly at Grace. She did not step forward as the other's had. Neither did she acknowledge the introduction. Instead, she glanced quickly at Tia, then folded her arms over her chest and lifted her chin.

Tia acknowledged Minerva ever so slightly before looking back at Phillip.

So that's how it is, thought Grace. *Minerva needed Tia's permission to acknowledge me.*

Grace eyed the young woman next to Minerva. Their eyes held. A hint of a smile touched her lips. "And you are?" Grace deliberately dismissed the belligerent servant and stepped toward the young colored girl.

"Penny, Ma'am."

Grace recognized her from the morning she'd rode in the wagon with Kindra to the docks landing.

Phillip turned to the small group. "That will be all."

The servants dispersed from the room. Cameron followed the entourage to the foyer.

"Supper will be served shortly," Phillip said. Grace stood beside her father as the two of them watched Camp slip out the screen door. "Although Camp is in charge of the field hands and outdoor duties, he takes all his meals in the house."

The drawing room now empty, Phillip crooked his elbow and Grace slipped her hand through his arm. He led her to the grand dining room.

Try as she might, she could not get the foreman off her mind.

Phillip moved to the head of the table and seated Grace at his right hand. Tia and Kindra moved to the end of the table and sat down. The hairs on the back of Grace's neck rose as they did. Dare they sit at the master's table?

Grace hadn't missed the fact that most of the female servants wore black dresses with white aprons. Tia and Kindra, however, wore lovely, flowing gowns in bright colors. Why didn't they wear parlor maid's uniforms? Her father said Tia was the headmistress. Shouldn't she be dressed as one? He failed to say what title Kindra held in the house. Grace wished she understood what was going on. But this was her father's house. She held her tongue and waited.

Just as the three cooks carried bowls of food to the table, Cameron strode into the dining room. He pulled out the chair opposite Grace and smiled. "Smells good."

"We be baking this chicken for nigh two hours. You be helpin' yourself before the food gits cold." Dinah placed a large platter in front of him and Dinah peered at Grace across the table. "We keep him well fed." She laid a hand on his shoulder as she leaned over to place the potatoes on the table.

The cooks continued to bring in delectable dishes of green beans with bits of bacon and onions, applesauce, and biscuits and jams.

Grace glanced at her father. She saw the warm look he gave Cameron. No doubt they shared a bond that went beyond plantation owner and foreman. She wondered at this while Penny placed a bowl of sweet potatoes in front of her.

Seven empty chairs divided the two ends of the table. Was there a significant reason for this? Why were slaves sitting at the Master's table? Her jaw worked as she tried not to look their way. She'd never shared a meal with a slave. She wasn't up to doing so now. She caught a glimpse of Kindra's face. Hurt? Betrayal?

Grace didn't know what to make of it all. She bent her head for a moment of silent prayer. She gave thanks for the food set before them, and then she gave thanks for the privilege to sit at the same table with her father. It would be a moment she'd never forget.

NINETEEN

GRACE ROLLED OVER in the soft bed. She noticed the sharp throbbing in her left arm had ebbed to a dull ache. She peeked one eye open. For a moment she didn't remember where she was. She sat up and glanced around the cozy, blue-and-white room. *It's morning and I'm at Cooper's Landing.* She smiled.

She quickly slipped out of bed and heard slaves working beyond the balcony. She threw on her bathrobe and pushed open the French doors to the veranda. A gentle breeze brushed against her face and she squinted up at the bright morning sun. Her cheeks flamed as the activity below relayed the late hour. *What must my father think of my sleeping the morning away?*

Grace could see workers in the kitchen garden beyond. Then shanties. And cane fields, where a line of slaves hacked down the tall stalks with machetes. Far to the left, beyond the stables and outbuildings, the cattle grazed.

She went back to the bedchamber and opened her wardrobe. If she dressed in a hurry, she might have breakfast with her father. She selected the blue day dress that once belonged to her mother. When she laid the dress on the bed, a light tap sounded at the door.

"Come in, Hedy."

The girl came into the room. "I be in several times. You be sleepin' like a baby." She eyed the day dress on the bed. "I see you done picked out a dress for yourself."

"I did. Has my father gone down for breakfast yet?"

"He been down to breakfest hours ago, Missy. He and Mastah Camp be gettin' up in the wee hours of the mornin' and be out to the fields at the crack 'o dawn."

"Oh." Grace frowned. "Am I the last one up?"

"I be thinkin' so, Missy."

"Well then, let's get me dressed. I want to explore the plantation today. If I hurry, maybe I can catch up with my father."

"Morning, Miss Grace." Dinah moved into the dining room with a plate of scrambled eggs and bacon. "Your father said he'd be back later this morning to give you a tour of the Landing. You best eat your fill as there be lots to see." She smiled and set the dish before Grace.

Grace sat in the same chair as the night before. The table seemed to stretch extra long with only her in the room. She glanced around, then remembered seeing her mother's portrait above the sideboard the day before. She rose to have a closer look.

"I remember when your father had that painting done of your mother," Dinah said.

Grace moved back to her chair. "You've been here a long time, haven't you?"

"I be here before your mother come to the Landing. I remember how your father be beside himself doing all he could to make everything perfect for her. When your mother stepped through those doors she done lit up this old house like something we never seen before. She done lit up your father's eyes, too." Dinah laughed, jiggling her plump belly. "Nothing ever made your father as happy as your mother." Then her smile turned to a scowl. She headed for the kitchen door. "Then she done left and broke your father's heart."

"I'm sorry."

"What you be sorry for, you can't help what your Mamma done."

Dinah started to leave and turned back. "Course, there be some speculation that you're gonna do the same thing to Master Cooper."

"I'll do no such thing!" Grace straightened in her chair.

"And again, there be some folks who don't believe you be Master Cooper's daughter.""Who would say that?"

"Tia and Minerva, and most the slaves out in the shanties."

"That's nonsense." Grace stared at Dinah. How could she blame the people here at the plantation for being skeptical? "And you?"

"You sure be your mother's chile."

"I'm my father's daughter, too. I'm sure it will take time for the others to come around. I'm not leaving. I'm here to stay."

"Time will tell, Missy."

Dinah disappeared into the kitchen. Grace stared at the closed door.

She bowed her head and prayed for her food with a lump in her throat. Then she added, *"Lord, it sure seems Mother hurt a lot of people when she left, especially Father. I can't undo what Mother did, but please help me shed your light on these people. And again, thank you for making a way where there seemed to be no way to be here with my father. Amen."*

She snapped her napkin open, laid it on her lap, and took a bite of cinnamon toast. If she hurried, she'd be ready when her father returned for her.

An hour later, Grace stood on the front porch and peered out over the long drive. Graceful trees and flowering bushes appeared in every direction. The air was filled with a fragrance that could only be described as tropical. A giddy feeling rushed through her, and she wanted nothing more than to explore the Landing.

She skipped down the porch steps with her white umbrella and moved out toward the sugar mill. She stood beside a fenced yard and watched the workers. A lane led from the cane fields to the buildings. Slaves guided donkey carts full of chopped cane stalks to the mill house. Men and women grabbed arm loads of the thick, green grass and carried them to the side of the long structure, where they dropped their load on top of the growing pile of stalks.

Another set of workers shoved the sugar cane through a chute on the side of the building. A loud grinding sounded from inside the mill house. Behind the building a windmill loomed high overhead with paddles that turned round and round. She observed the workers, while curious eyes glanced her way.

With her umbrella held high, she walked down a narrow dirt road that led toward the slave shanties. She'd never seen such a sight—rows and rows of small, wooden houses, fenced in with dirt walkways leading to each one. No vegetation or green lawns grew near the houses. Instead, wooden chairs and tables sat outside the small shacks. Barrels and tubs of water sat near the doors.

Some of the doors stood open. An old woman sat in a doorway with a metal bowl on her lap while she snapped peas. She squinted and watched Grace move quickly down the lane. Grace waved at the old woman. The slave just stared.

The sound of horse's hooves loomed from behind her.

"Whoa." Phillip reined in his black Arabian. He slid off the saddle and walked over to Grace, a lead rope in hand.

"Good morning." He grinned. "I see you've taken it upon yourself to tour the plantation."

"Yes. I woke up late. I had no idea I'd slept in."

"To be expected, my dear. You had quite a time the last couple of days, what with the trip from the shipyards to the Landing, and an accident on the way as well." He glanced at her as if eyeing her heavy dress layered with petticoats.

"Are you warm?" he squinted at her in the bright morning light.

"A little."

"We must see that you have a new wardrobe for our tropical

weather."

"That won't be necessary. I'm fine. Really."

"Have it your way." He pointed ahead of them. "Come with me. I have something to show you."

The lane circled around beyond the blacksmith shop, barns, stables, and a number of wooden buildings. Phillip's sleek Arabian horse followed them as he held the lead rope loosely. Before long they came to the stables. He opened the wooden gate to let them through.

"Have you ever ridden a horse?"

"Yes. Grandfather Unruh has horses. He taught me how to ride when I was twelve. I straddled the horse, rather than ride the traditional side-saddle." Grace lifted her chin guessing her father would find this scandalous.

His brows rose as he glanced down at her. "Hmm."

"What is that supposed to mean?" Grace asked.

"Your mother didn't object to your brazen ways?"

"Brazen?"

"It's not proper for a young lady to expose her ankles." He cleared his throat.

"I wore knee boots and long skirts. I was quite respectable." Grace flushed.

They went through the stable doors and moved down the row of stalls. A stableman popped his head up from a cubicle.

"You done ridin'?" asked the man.

"For now, Nate. I want to introduce you to my daughter, Grace."

Nate dusted his hands on the sides of his pants and walked up to her. "Glad to be meetin' you." He shook his salt and peppered head. "My Gemma be right. She be sayin' you look just like your mothah."

"I've been told as much."

"I just finished groomin' this little lady." Nate walked back to the stall where a chestnut-colored mare stomped her hooves.

Grace followed him. The horse's coat was a rich reddish-brown, the mane and tail black with a white diamond shape on her forehead.

She nudged Grace's hand with her soft, velvet nose.

"She's beautiful."

"She's yours," her father said.

Grace stopped petting the horse and turned to gape at her father. "Mine?"

"Yes. A fine Arabian mare. She needs to be ridden. That's why I asked if you knew how to handle a horse."

Grace looked down at her day dress. "Not in this, and I don't have a riding skirt."

"I can arrange for a riding skirt to be made for you."

"Thank you, Father. What is her name?"

"Dandy. She's got spirit. The name fits her, as you will see."

Grace went back to the stall to run her hand over Dandy's soft, velvet nose. "Well, little lady, I think you and I are going to get along just fine."

Phillip cleared his throat. "Since you haven't ridden a horse in a while, I suggest Camp ride along with you the first couple of times you take her out."

Grace became rigid. "That won't be necessary. I'm sure I can handle Dandy just fine."

"I won't take any chances, my dear. Let me have my way on this."

"All right." Grace didn't look her father in the eye for fear he'd correctly read her thoughts. It was true she hadn't ridden in a while. She wasn't sure she could pull it off with Cameron chiding her with his mocking eyes.

Amos came through the stable doors. "Mastah Coopah!"

"Yes, Amos?"

"Captain Harding be up at the house waitin' for you. He brung the rest of Miss Coopah's trunks." His eyes round, he continued, "Sure be a wagon fulla them."

Phillip glanced down at his daughter. "How many trunks did you bring?"

Grace winced. "Seven."

Phillip whistled and laughed. "Let's head back to the house."

Grace gave Dandy one last pat. "I'll be back."

"This be the last trunk," Amos said as he and Denzel placed the trunks in Grace's room. Grace remembered she hadn't seen her black stringed purse since she'd arrived back at the Great House.

"Need anything else?" Denzel asked.

"No. Thank you."

"Then we be leaving."

"Yes, of course." Grace looked around the room. *Where had she laid her purse?*

Hedy's eyes swept the room. "Lawdy, Miss Coopah. You sure have a lotta trunks."

"Hedy?"

"Yes, Missy."

"Have you seen my purse anywhere?"

"I sure don't remember seeing it." She set to searching around the trunks, drawers and wardrobe.

"Maybe I left it in the foyer or the drawing room." Grace bit her bottom lip. She'd probably find her purse downstairs. "Start unpacking the trunks. I'm going down to the drawing room to find my purse."

"I do that."

When Grace entered the drawing room, she found Captain Harding, her father, and Cameron in a deep discussion. At her appearance, the three men stood.

With a broad grin Captain Harding tipped his head. "We meet again, Miss Cooper." He smiled. "I heard you took a spill on the way to the Landing."

"Yes, I did." She glanced past Cameron to the table next to his armchair. She bobbed her head this way and that, peering behind the table, to the floor. *Where could my purse be?* She picked up a pillow on the sofa and dropped it back. She planted her right fist on her hip and glanced around the room.

The room grew silent. Grace continued to look around the sofa, the floor, and the other tables. After a moment, the silence grew loud. She stared at the three men who gawked at her.

"What are you looking for?" Phillip asked.

"My purse. A black-stringed purse." She peered up at them. "I've not seen it since I've arrived. It must be here somewhere."

The three men helped search the room. They moved the sofa back and replaced it. The same with the two stuffed chairs. They picked up pillows and tossed them back on the sofa. After a thorough search, the four stood in the center of the room puzzled.

"Where could it have gone?" Grace asked.

"Did you have it after the cart accident?" Cameron asked.

"I don't remember. You don't think it's lying in the ditch, do you?"

"It's possible."

"Do you have anything of value in your purse?" Phillip asked.

Grace looked at Captain Harding. "All my money is in my purse."

The three men groaned.

"I will look for it tomorrow. I have a trip to make into town," Cameron said.

"Tomorrow?" Her heart sank.

"It's not likely to be out in the open. We would have seen it."

"That's true," she said.

With the matter settled, Phillip said, "Have a seat, dear."

Grace sat with the three men and turned to the captain. "How long will you be in port?" She kept her eyes from straying to the handsome foreman who sat across the room. His smoky grey eyes watched her. Her heart thumped wildly. Why did Cameron have this effect on her?

After a moment, Captain Harding drummed his fingers on the side table. "If you don't mind, I'd like to visit the Borjeaux." He stood and scooped up his hat.

"Of course," Phillip answered, a twinkle in his eyes.

The captain tipped his hat toward Grace and quickly took his leave.

"I've work to attend to in the study." Phillip stood. "I'll leave you two to visit." He nodded his head toward Cameron. "I'll meet up with you later."

Grace looked at everything except Cameron. She'd never seen a man who could unsettle her as this foreman did. To sit alone with him felt awkward. Aware of the racing of her heart, she wondered what must be going through the foreman's mind. She wanted nothing more than to escape to her bedchamber and supervise the unpacking of her trunks.

Time seemed to drag.

"If you don't mind, I've unfinished business to attend to." Cameron scooped up his wide-brimmed hat and made a fast exit out the front door. Grace stood in the drawing room and watched through the wide doorway as the foreman took the steps two at a time.

Outside, Cameron chastised himself for being tongue-tied. He didn't know what to make of it. One moment he had no trouble talking to Grace, then the next, he couldn't find his tongue. He brushed his hat against his pant legs and sauntered out to the sugar mill, determined to get a certain green-eyed woman off his mind.

Grace picked up her skirts and headed for the stairs. The honey-skinned servant appeared from the dining room. The two women nearly collided.

"Oh. I didn't see you, Miss Cooper."

Grace's eyes flicked over the colored girl's attire. Today, she wore an emerald-colored gown of light and airy material. It complimented her. Still, why would a slave wear such fine attire? The servant had the audacity to pose as if she were as polished as the English. Grace had never seen such a thing. And what was she doing in the Great House? Grace had a million questions to ask her father when the time seemed right.

"What's your name again?" Grace asked, her voice crisp.

"Kindra, Ma'am."

"I don't recall what position you hold here at the house. I know father must have said, but somehow it bypassed me," Grace said a might stiffly and tapped her foot.

Kindra stepped back, her eyes searching the floor. "I'm sorry. I must go." She turned and fled up the stairs.

Grace watched, bewildered. Then she started up the stairs after Kindra. When Grace reached the top, a door closed. She glanced down the dim hallway to the west wing. She'd missed which room belonged to Kindra.

Giggles drifted from her own bedchamber on the east wing. When Grace opened the door, her mouth dropped open.

"Oh, Missy!" Hedy stood stalk still before the mirror, clothed in one of Grace's finest gowns. She wore Grace's satin white boots and held her peacock-feathered fan. Hedy shrank back. She laid the fan on the vanity table and bent to pull the satin boots off, until she stood barefooted before Grace.

"I don't know what to say." Grace rubbed her forehead. "If you will be so good as to take off my gown and put these clothes away, I shall pretend I didn't see anything."

"Yessum, Missy." Hedy proceeded to slip out of Grace's fine gown and moved about the room like a rabbit, all the while clothed in her muslin slip. She hung the fine gown in the double wardrobe and at last stood before Grace, her eyes pinned to the floor.

"Hedy."

"Yes, Missy."

"I'm disappointed in you. You're not to touch my clothes except to lay them out or put them away. I won't tolerate this kind of behavior a second time. Do you understand?"

"Yes, Ma'am. I surely do. I won't be doin' anything like that again, Miss Coopah. I don't know what be gettin' into me. I'm real sorry."

"I think you've learned your lesson. Get dressed. You may go."

"Miss Coopah?" Hedy pulled her smock dress over her head and slipped on her work boots. "Will you be reportin' my misbehavior to Tia?"

Grace eyed the girl trembling before her.

"No." She took hold of Hedy's shoulders. "I believe this will never happen again. You may go."

"Yes, Missy. Thank you, Missy."

When the door closed, Grace leaned against it. *What a day. I didn't find my purse, and now Hedy is taking liberties with my wardrobe.*

She crossed the floor and slumped on the bed. *Maybe I should crawl back into bed and start this day all over again.*

TWENTY

CAMERON'S HORSE TROTTED to the place past the bridge where he'd first found Grace and Jimmy in the ditch. He slid off the stallion, tied the reins to the nearest tree, and then searched for Grace's purse. He searched the edge of the wagon road. The dirt had grooves where the wagon wheels had dug into the ground.

He walked down the slope and looked under the large leaves of the palm bushes. He squinted upward at the branch above the spot where he'd found Grace sitting against a large rock, the same branch where the pair of pantaloons and white umbrella had hung near the clearing, and grinned. He thoroughly searched the area, but the purse was nowhere to be found.

When he climbed the slope, his eye caught something white near the base of one leafy plant. He crossed the ground to inspect the object. A lone glove. It was small in his broad hand. He slipped the glove into his shirt pocket. With one last glance around the clearing, he shrugged and moved up the slope where Scimitar waited for him.

Three days later, Grace's arm was back to normal. Every day the rain drizzled in the early morning hours, and by the time the household arose, the sun had warmed the ground. In late afternoons, a light rain drizzled again, but within the hour it stopped. Then steam rose from the ground with a tropical fragrance.

This morning, wanting to learn the layout of the house, Grace roamed from room to room. She found a large ballroom. It echoed with the sound of her shoes clicking the floor. She twirled around, imagining a ball in full swing. She left the ballroom and found a narrow hallway lined with portraits. Many were ancestors she didn't know. The hallway led to a morning room. Tall plants sat in the corners, and two doors led out to a garden. From there, a cobbled path led to a garden room with a fountain in the middle. Water dribbled down a small cascade of rocks into a pool. Goldfish swam in and around crevices. Grace dipped her hand in the water. A goldfish swam behind a rock.

Grace found the library and stepped inside the room. One wall was lined with books from floor to ceiling. She searched authors' names and picked up one book after another, fanning the pages.

On the wall over the fireplace, a wall mount held two rapiers. Grace smiled. She stood on tiptoe and lifted a foil down. Flicking the handle this way and that, she skirted the library table as if fighting an opposing enemy. Delighted, she replaced the foil and left the library. Her father's home seemed lavish, and yet it was not overpowering in its richness.

Grace fingered the locket that hung around her neck. She missed her mother. The gold piece not only brought comfort, it was also a reminder of who she was. She was the daughter of Phillip and Olivia Cooper.

Dinah had said, "Tia, Minerva, and the slaves out in the shanties have their doubts you're Phillip's daughter." It was enough for her to know her father believed her. The corners of her mouth lifted. She would prove to him she was a true Cooper. She would dig her roots in these grounds and do whatever he expected of her.

Grace walked out to the front porch and watched the Arabian horses in the distance. She heard footsteps and turned.

"Father, good morning."

"Good morning to you. I hope you're finding plenty to do around here."

"I've just finished looking through the rooms downstairs."

"I'm pleased. I want you to feel comfortable here," Phillip said.

"Thank you, Father." Grace leaned against a tall pillar. "I've taken walks around the north side of the house and familiarized myself with some of the outbuildings. Yesterday I ventured out to the sugar mill and the boiling house. You have quite an operation going here. I was surprised to find a small hospital behind the two buildings. It's nicely equipped."

"It's common for plantations in Jamaica to have hospitals on their estates. We've too many slaves and too many accidents. The boiling houses alone pose many problems for the slaves."

"We don't have hospitals on our plantations in Charleston. Some things are quite different here. But I fear I've only touched on a small portion of the Landing. I could see more if I could ride my horse."

"There'll be time for that. Camp's had his hands full the past couple of days. I'll bring it up to him. If you're not busy, I'd like to have a word with you in my study."

"Of course." She followed her father down the hallway.

"Have a seat, dear." Phillip motioned to a chair in front of his desk.

Grace lifted her skirts and sat down. She eyed the cluttered office. Phillip lit his pipe and gazed at Grace for a moment. "Captain Harding told me an interesting story while he was here."

Phillip leaned back in his leather chair. "He said your aunt gave him a document confirming you were my child."

Grace lowered her eyes. "Yes, she did. Unfortunately I can't produce the document. It is lost at sea."

A wry smile curved his lips. "When you first arrived, I would have wanted to see such papers."

"And now?" Grace asked, her heart pounding.

"You're a Cooper. I see it in the way you walk, and in the way you talk. You've an adventurous side to you, like your father."

148

Relief washed over Grace as she peered up into the warm eyes of her father. If he'd had any doubts, it was plain to see they were gone.

"Aunt Katy promised mother she'd look after me."

"Your aunt's a clever woman. She was never one to let circumstances get in her way. If your mother asked her to look out for you, which I'm sure she did, Katy did what any responsible person would have done. She made sure you were not misrepresented. For that, I'm grateful."

"Even though you've not seen the document?"

"Yes."

Grace grew thoughtful. "Aunt Katy had a difficult time letting me come to Jamaica."

"You didn't have a problem leaving your family to cross the seas to Jamaica?" He squinted as he puffed his pipe.

Grace glanced past him to a picture on the wall. Then her eyes moved to his. "No. I didn't. I wanted to meet my father more than anything in the world." Her eyes grew moist. She shifted to meet her father's weathered face and then looked down at her hands in her lap. "I wish you could have seen mother one more time."

Phillip circled around the desk to where she sat. He reached out and smoothed her long, silken hair. "How I wish your mother were with us, too."

"It is difficult being without her. At first, I couldn't imagine a day going by, without sobbing my life away. But through prayer and perseverance, God has seen me through my tough times."

"I've seen you reading the Bible on occasion. You take after your mother. She was a godly woman. Like you, she chose to spend time with her daily devotions." Phillip looked past her, a faraway look in his eyes. "I fear I stumbled in her eyes on more than one occasion."

Grace glanced up. "Do you keep the faith?"

Phillip stiffened and moved back. The leather chair groaned when he sat down. "I've no time for such things, Grace. I've been a busy man all these years. I've seen a lot of things that make me wonder if there is a God. I don't know. I don't care to know."

Grace leaned forward. "You can't mean that. Surely you believe there is a God."

"I will never stand in the way of your belief, Grace. It just isn't for me."

She gazed at her father, heartbroken. A tear slid down her face.

"Don't shed tears for me. I'm a happy man. I have everything a man could want and more. And now I have the most beautiful daughter in the world sitting across from me in my home. My life is complete."

She cleared her throat. "You may think you have it all, Father. But what does it profit a man to gain the world, only to lose his own soul? Until you have the peace of God in your heart, you *don't* have it all." Grace looked everywhere, but her father. She missed her mother, but she knew where she was. She couldn't stand it if her father were to leave this life, lost in sin. Her chin shot up and she swallowed. "I'll pray you change you mind, Father."

"You do that, Grace. I'll have no quarrel with your praying for my soul. Just don't expect me to change. I'm happy with the way things are."

The words in her mother's diary came rushing to her mind. Before she could take her words back, she spit out, "How can you say you're happy with the way things are? You drove mother away because you made money your god."

Blood rushed to his worn face. "I tried to provide for your mother to give her everything she could ever want or need."

"Is that why she never cashed the checks you sent? She didn't want the money. She wanted you. Just you!" Tears stung her eyes as she got out of her chair. "But you didn't come!" Grace didn't wait for a response. She turned and fled up the stairs. Safe in her room, she threw herself on her bed. She sobbed until she fell asleep.

TWENTY-ONE

AN HOUR LATER, Grace sat on the side of her bed. Sleep had cleared her mind, and she thought back to the words she'd flung at her father. It wasn't a Christian way to act after preaching to her father. Guilt plagued her as she freshened up. Somehow she would have to make amends.

She skipped lunch. Instead, she searched for her purse again. As she did so, she came across her sketchpad and colored pencils. She carried them to the sitting room and sat down on the sofa. She thumbed through the sketches she'd drawn on her trip and tried to think where she could have put her purse.

Too distressed to concentrate, she set the sketchpad aside and decided to take another walk. She left the house and worked her way to the stable. She found Dandy in the corral and pulled herself up on the fence to pet the mare's silky nose. Grace leaned over the barrier, her hand outstretched. "It's okay, Dandy."

"Give her an apple and she'll be your friend for life," came a deep voice from behind her.

Startled, Grace turned to see Cameron walk up beside her. He hooked a thumb in his pants pocket and glanced up at her. "Your father wants me to give you riding lessons."

She glanced sideways at him. "I can ride a horse. It's just been a while."

"Dandy's got some spirit in her. Best to be sure you can handle her."

"Shall we give it a try?" she challenged him.

"In that?" He pointed a finger at her dress with its wide flounced skirt.

"I'll change."

"I'll saddle her up then. Meet me out front. I'll have the horses ready."

Grace hurried to the Great House. She was expected to come and go through the front door, but she preferred to go through the kitchen. A trio of heads turned when she flew into the room.

"Afternoon," Dinah said.

Fresh-baked cookies lay on the wooden table cooling. They smelled wonderful.

"What brings you in here with your eyes all lit up?" Dinah asked.

"I'm changing clothes. Cameron's going to give me a brush-up course on horseback riding."

The trio glanced at each other. Gemma said, "You be liking that horse Mastah Coopah give you?"

"Now don't you be going on about her horse, Gemma." Dinah raised a hand as if batting a fly away. "Old Nate, he be telling everything going on." She rolled her eyes to the ceiling.

"Now go on and git yourself changed. Camp, he be good with the horses. Best there ever was."

Grace eyed the table of cookies and raised a brow.

"Have one before you hurry on up them stairs." Gemma laughed.

Grace took the cookie with her through the dining room and up the marbled staircase. Once in her room, she opened the double wardrobe. All she could see were long dresses, not one suitable for riding. She shoved the dresses from one side to the other. "Goodness, surely there's at least one dress I could wear."

She eyed the cinnamon-colored traveling dress. If she didn't wear all the petticoats, it might do. She pulled it out of the wardrobe and threw it across the bed, then rang the bell. Moments later Hedy poked her head into the room.

"Yes, Missy?"

"Unbutton me quickly."

"You changin' clothes in the middle of the day?"

"Yes. I'm going horseback riding with Cameron. Now get my boots before he changes his mind."

Cameron held Dandy's reins when Grace stepped out on the front porch. She watched him rake the length of her with an approving look. She'd pulled her hair up and tucked it under a cinnamon-colored top hat. She knew the dress appeared formal, but it would have to do. Her kid boots peeked out from under the hem.

Cameron helped her onto the sidesaddle. Dandy snorted and stepped back. "Whoa, girl," he said, his deep voice soothing. "Easy there."

Grace stiffened and waited as Cameron mounted his black stallion. Feeling awkward with both legs dangling to one side. She wasn't used to riding sidesaddle.

"Let's take the main road to the bridge. It's a nice ride and will give you a feel for the horse."

Grace gave the reins some slack and nudged Dandy with her heel. She braced herself for the ride. They rode up the carriage drive. She tried to relax with the rhythm of the horse. So far, so good.

Cameron glanced back. "You all right?"

"Yes. We're doing fine."

He picked up the pace to a canter, reining Scimitar onto the main road as Grace moved alongside. They rode in easy silence for the first quarter mile.

Then Dandy snorted and pinned back her ears. Before long, the mare picked up speed. Grace bounced precariously, trying to hold on. The faster the horse went, the harder she worked to keep her balance.

All at once, Dandy lunged forward, kicking up dirt as she pulled ahead of Cameron's horse.

"Hold on there!" Cameron shouted.

Grace bounced on the saddle and held on with everything she had. The mare began to run in long strides and Grace bent low to keep her balance. Her hat flew off and her hair tangled in the wind as they neared the bridge.

Cameron put his horse into a full run. Scimitar's nostrils flared and his eyes grew wide as they sped across the wooden planks.

"Rein in your horse!" Cameron shouted, when he was near enough for Grace to hear him.

"I can't! She won't let me!" Grace barely turned her head, but when she did, his heart sank. Her face was pale, her eyes wide with fear.

Dandy ran on, kicking up dirt as she went. Grace bounced dangerously on the saddle. How she stayed on the saddle he didn't know. His mind raced for a strategy to slow Dandy down. He needed to get ahead and grab the reins.

Cameron nudged the stallion faster until they were even with Grace and Dandy once again. Dandy snorted, breathing hard as she ran toward the curve in the road. Up ahead, a line of trees bordered the bend. He had to make a decision.

"Jump onto my horse!" He held out his hand toward her.

"No! I can't!"

"Yes, you can! Give me your hand! Jump!" The two rode side by side as the horses drew closer to the bend.

Grace could see Dandy wasn't going to make the turn and

154

frantically grabbed Cameron's strong arm. He pulled her off the runaway horse. She swung behind him straddling Scimitar, leaning her head on his shoulders and clamping her arms around his waist.

Dandy veered into the field before the bend. "Whoa boy!" Scimitar pulled his head back with Cameron's tug on the reins and slowed to a canter. When the horse stood still, his sides heaved.

Grace slid off the stallion and stumbled to the ground.

"What in tarnation happened?" Cameron climbed down and came around the horse to stand before Grace.

"I don't ride sidesaddle. That's what happened." She stormed over to the chestnut mare.

"You don't ride side-saddle? Then how do you ride?" Cameron removed his wide-brimmed hat, shoved back a thick thatch of black hair, and replaced his hat in one angry gesture.

"I ride like you do. I straddle the horse." Grace reached for Dandy's reins and brought her alongside Scimitar. "I had no control over the horse in that silly position."

"Well, why didn't you say so in the first place?"

"Because I didn't want to look like I didn't know how to ride like a lady, that's why."

His dark brows lifted.

"Can we ride back to the house now?" She shoved her long ringlets over her shoulders. His eyes glared down at her in disbelief. "You can't handle the horse."

"Yes I can." Grace unbuckled the cinch and pulled the sidesaddle off the horse. It fell to the ground with a thud. She mounted Dandy with Cameron's help. Her wide skirts fanned out around the horse revealing high kid boots. She clicked her tongue and pulled the reins so that Dandy walked up onto the main road.

"Lord, have mercy," Cameron groaned.

"If you're worried about me, you're wasting time. I'll be all right now."

"You lead."

"Beat you to the house!" Grace heeled into Dandy's side. She shot out onto the road and flew down the lane.

"No, you don't!" Cameron yelled.

The two of them ran through the lane. Before long they crossed the bridge. Grace circled Dandy back to the side of the road and slowed the mare to a stop. She slid off the horse and scooped up her top hat.

Cameron reined in Scimitar. By the time he approached the clearing, she was already on the horse again.

Lord, help me keep my temper. That blasted woman is going to show off, if it's the last thing she does. He spurred Scimitar until they came up beside Grace and her chestnut mare.

She glanced over her shoulder and gave him her winning smile, hair flying in the wind.

He couldn't help but grin. "Okay, Grace. To the house." His horse jumped out ahead of Dandy.

"Oh, no you don't." She lifted herself from the saddle and bent low, her face near the chestnut's mane. The two raced down the road in synchronized rhythm.

Up ahead, tall palms came into view. Down the lane, through the circle drive, one horse led by a head.

In front of the house, Cameron reined in to stop and jumped off his horse. He looked up with a broad grin on his face. He bowed low as she peered down at him.

"You bested me this time, Cameron. We'll give it a try on another day."

He strode over to her horse and circled her waist with his broad hands. He pulled her down to stand before him, holding her close. She looked up, heart pounding. She could feel his warm breath on her face as he gazed down at her.

"You ever do a thing like that again and I'll turn you over my knee and give you the spanking of your life!"

"You touch me and you'll wish you hadn't!" She pulled free from his hold.

He reached out and crushed her to him again. Their eyes held for what seemed a thousand moments. Then he let her go. She turned and stomped into the house.

TWENTY-TWO

When Grace retired to her room that evening, she thought back to the afternoon's ride with Cameron. She grinned, then scowled. He was a good horseman, but she'd shown him she knew how to handle a horse. She'd given him a good run in the race and nearly bested him. She wouldn't need his watchful eye anymore. A tinge of regret crept into her heart. She had to admit, she enjoyed his company.

Grace recalled his masculine scent as he held her against his hard chest that heaved from the fierce race. His heart had pounded against her own. Had it hammered from the adrenaline of the race, or because he held her in his arms? Heat rose from her neck to her scalp. Grace shook her head as if to shake off thoughts of Cameron. She bent to loosen the shoelaces of her kid boots.

A hot bath would ease her tense nerves.

Hedy popped her head into the bedchamber. "Are you getting ready for bed, Miss Coopah?"

"Yes, I am."

The girl turned Grace around to unbutton the long line of tiny buttons down her back.

"I'm going to take a hot bath before I retire. Unhook the locket, too."

"I best be gettin' Amos and Cato to bring up hot water," she said, handing the locket to Grace.

"Please do." Grace set the gold piece on top of her vanity and let the dress slip to the floor. Wearing only her light-gauze slip, she moved to the sitting room where her Bible lay on a table next to the sofa. She lit the oil lamp and pulled her Bible onto her lap, then thumbed through the Scriptures. Before long, her eyes slid closed.

"Miss Coopah." Hedy shook Grace's shoulders jostling her head as she did. "Wake up, Missy. Your bath water be gettin' cold."

Grace struggled out of grogginess. "Humm?"

"Come on, Missy. Wake up."

Grace sat up straight and groaned, "Every bone in my body aches."

"Your bath water be waitin' for you." Hedy put both fists on her slim hips and frowned.

"I'm awake." Grace glanced toward her bed. " Did you lay out my robe and nightgown?"

"Yessum, Missy, I sure did."

"Ouch!" Grace took a couple of steps and straightened.

"Somethin' wrong?" Hedy's brows knit together.

"I'm sore from riding today."

Hedy followed Grace into the bathroom and took the garments as Grace undressed.

Grace slid down into the perfumed water letting the heat soothe her sore muscles, glad the water was still hot. "You may go. I'll be awhile."

"You be ringin' the bell if you need me, you hear."

"Thank you, Hedy. Goodnight."

Grace heard the door close and knew she had the room all to herself. As she lay in the steamy water, her thoughts raced back to when Cameron had slid his strong hands around her waist and pulled her close to him. Her cheeks burned, not only because he had held her close, but because truth be told, she didn't want him to let her go.

The next morning Hedy's hands flew as she buttoned the cream-colored day dress sprinkled with tiny blue flowers and brushed Grace's long hair. Before long, Grace joined the others for breakfast.

Crewmen from the *Savannah Rose* stood at the entrance to the dining room. All eyes turned toward her.

"Good morning, gentlemen." Grace swept past them and entered the dining room.

Captain Harding sat at the table with a mug of coffee in his hand. She sat next to her father, but turned to the captain, "It's good to see you again."

Only moments earlier, the crewmen stood by the door, casually waiting. Now they all stood at attention, slicking back their hair with sun-bronzed hands. Jesse Simmons, the sailor who'd assaulted her on the ship, raked her with penetrating eyes. She diverted her gaze. Why had the sailors joined the captain this trip?

Jesse licked his lips and straightened. Cameron walked in and smirked at the sailors. "Men, you're excused. You'll find your breakfast in the kitchen."

"I was just telling the captain we are going to throw a party in your honor," Phillip told Grace.

"My honor? Whatever are you talking about?"

"It's time the community met my daughter who has sailed across the seas to find her father. I mean to invite all of Jamaica and my cronies from the high seas for a grand celebration." He banged the table as if for emphases and smiled at Grace.

She jumped. The men laughed.

"I don't think that's necessary." Her eyes grew wide at the absurd idea.

"There'll be no talking me out of this one, my dear. I've made up my mind."

The captain said, "Mrs. Cavendish sends her regards."

Grace lifted her brows. "You've seen her?"

"No, but a friend of mine has and passed the message along."

"You've met Mrs. Cavendish?" Phillip broke in.

"Yes. We traveled together on the *Savannah Rose*. We got along superbly."

"I've known the old gal a good many years. She is a grand woman."

"I agree," Grace said. "She invited me to visit her plantation. I hope that can be arranged sometime." She turned to the captain. "If you see her, tell her I send my regards as well."

Phillip glanced at the captain. "Would you do me the honor of delivering a note to the Borjeaux? I've invited them for supper tonight. I would like to introduce Grace to them before the ball."

Captain Harding's eyes lit up. "You haven't met Camille?"

"No, but I'm looking forward to meeting her." Grace took the coffee cup Gemma handed her and took a small sip. She leaned her elbows on the table and glanced at the three men before her.

Cameron's smoky gaze pinned her to where she sat. She adjusted herself in her chair and cleared her throat. "Good morning, Cameron. Did you sleep well last night?"

"I did." He smiled and speared a bite of salt fish. "And you?"

"It took a while to fall asleep, to be honest. It's been a while since I've gone horseback riding."

The men chuckled.

"I planned an easy ride, but things took a different turn." Cameron's eyes lit as he spoke.

"That was partly Dandy's fault." She leaned back as Dinah placed a plate of scrambled eggs and salt fish before her.

"I think she wanted to show off." He quirked a smile her way.

"Well she accomplished that just fine." Grace smiled.

"I meant you, not the horse." Now his eyes took on an amused glint and held her gaze.

The room grew quiet.

Phillip broke the silence and turned his attention to Captain Harding.

"I gave the chestnut mare to Grace. She took the horse out for the first time yesterday. Apparently, Dandy showed Grace her spirit." His eyes twinkled.

"Or the other way around," Cameron said.

The men laughed. Grace pretended to pout.

"Did you find your purse, dear?" Phillip asked.

"No, I didn't." She frowned.

Cameron cleared his throat before his deep voice reverberated through the room. "I searched for it yesterday morning." He scooted his chair back and reached into his pants pocket. He pulled out a small white glove and extended it to her. "I found this under a bush. But no purse."

Grace took the soiled glove. "I didn't know I'd lost it." Her brows puckered together. "But no purse?"

"I checked from the top of the road to the bottom of the ditch." He shook his head, " No purse." He wiped his mouth with his napkin. "I'm an optimist. It's there. We just haven't found it yet."

Grace glanced at his mouth as he dropped the napkin on his plate. *What would it be like to be kissed by him?* she mused, and then blushed at the thought. His gray eyes seemed kind. She dropped her gaze.

Grace forked her food around her plate. She wondered that her father planned a celebration in her honor. Apparently he hadn't taken offense to the accusations she'd flung at him the day before. She was still in his good graces.

After breakfast, the men dispersed. A light rain drizzled. Grace popped open her umbrella and moved off the front porch while the captain's men unloaded crates from the wagon onto the dirt road. She waved at Corky, who leaned his head out the side of the wagon.

Apparently the women in the slave shanties had grown accustomed to seeing Grace walk past their houses with her umbrella shading her face. They waved at her. She viewed the children playing in the dirt.

Big brown eyes stared up at her. She walked over to the wooden fence and glanced down at a small African boy. He put his finger in his mouth and gawked at her.

"What's your name, little fella?"

The toddler turned and ran to the front stoop of the shanty. An old woman sat on the wooden steps and smiled a toothless grin. The drizzle stopped as quickly as it had started.

Grace was about to turn away when she saw Laulie, the Landing's midwife rounding one of the shanties and coming toward the front gate. She carried a hamper full of blood-soaked linens. Laulie gazed at Grace, weary-eyed.

"Mornin', Miss Coopah," she said.

Grace gawked at the hamper.

"Lettice done had her baby boy this morning." She glanced back at the shanties. "Poor woman liked to died in the wee hours of the morning."

"Mercy, Laulie. Is she all right?"

"Yessum." She gave Grace a weary grin, her teeth white and straight.

"And the baby?"

"He be a healthy one. Mastah Phillip, he sure like the baby boys when they be born. Best be getting these rags to the wash room." She nodded to Grace and walked around the bend in the road.

I wonder if it would be possible to see the new infant. Grace would bring it up to her father this afternoon.

She moved away from the fence and glanced at the servants weeding the kitchen garden. They stopped and squinted at her. Some spoke to each other before they went back to hoeing the ground, throwing weeds into the large baskets.

Grace walked to the stable. An apple lay ripe and plump in her skirt pocket. She planned to take Cameron's advice and make friends with her horse. She stepped quietly into the dim stable. The smell of hay mingled with horseflesh assailed her. Expecting to find Nate tending the horses or cleaning stalls, she was surprised instead to find Tia and Jesse at the far end of the building, their heads bent together. Their voices carried to where Grace stood.

"Everyone will be occupied this evening with that wench who claims to be Pip's daughter. No one will be paying attention to us. When you're done eating, come out to the stable," Tia said.

The horses stomped and snorted.

"Meet me here at 9:00 tonight. Blissmore is expecting us."

Jesse moved close to the black woman and drew her to him. "When are we leaving this island, Tia?"

She gave him a wry grin and moved out of his hold. "When you take ownership of that piece of junk you made a down payment on. Then we'll talk about getting out of here with our flesh intact."

Scimitar snorted and raised his head over the stall. The two looked back. Grace stood with an apple in her hand. They stared at her.

"What are you doing here?" Tia's brash voice asked.

"I've come to give Dandy an apple." Grace swallowed the lump in her throat. Did they know she'd heard their scheme?

Tia and Jesse covered the distance between them. Crystal eyes bore into her as the two brushed passed.

"Do you think she heard?" Jesse whispered loudly.

"Shhh! You fool!"

Grace glanced back as she moved to Dandy's stall. The chestnut bobbed her head out and took the extended apple. Grace ran her hand over the horse's head and spoke in soft, low tones. "What is that tigress up to, Dandy?" The chestnut responded by pushing her nose into her hand. "I'll be back, pretty girl." She patted the top of Dandy's neck and left the stable.

Her mind whirled as she tried to process the conversation between Jesse and the headmistress. Why the secret talk in the stable, and who was Blissmore? She hadn't heard that name before. She would tell her father or Cameron that a conspiracy was in the making. What it entailed she didn't know, but if Tia was intent on causing trouble, her father should be warned.

When she reached the Great House a wagon was parked between the side door of the kitchen and the bricked building known as the outer kitchen. Grace could hear the murmurs of the cooks as they worked.

Penny and Kindra came out of the side kitchen door, bearing empty baskets. They placed them in the back of the wagon, chattering away until they saw Grace.

"Afternoon, Miss Coopah," Penny said.

"Same to you."

Grace turned to Kindra. "You're going to town? Maybe I'll join you the next time you go for supplies." She shaded her eyes from the sun. "I've not been to Riverbend since I've arrived."

Kindra lowered her eyes. "If you want to go to town, Zeek would be happy to take you in the carriage. It wouldn't be fitting for you to go with the likes of us."

"I'd prefer female companionship." Grace glanced at Kindra's dress. She still wondered why the young woman dressed so. Penny held the reins as if escorting Kindra into town.

"Your father wouldn't approve of your traveling with the likes of us, unless of course, we rode in the back of the wagon."

"Dinah's going to have our necks if we don't git to town and back before dark." Penny glanced down from the wagon seat. "If you're ridin' with me, you best git on up here."

Kindra picked up her blue skirts, put one foot on the wagon wheel and hoisted herself into the seat next to Penny. She glanced back at Grace. "Thank you just the same, Miss Cooper."

Penny snapped the reins and the wagon jerked out onto the drive.

Grace stood in the empty lane and looked after them. She hadn't asked to accompany them as a friend. She only wanted to go to town. She wanted to see what it was like to go without a man. Was that the rebellious side of her? She didn't know and didn't care. This was all new to her. If traveling into town without a man was acceptable, she wanted to give it a try.

Grace didn't understand the mulatto woman's position around here. She certainly must be a servant or slave. But she dressed too fine. Kindra seemed to have free reign on the estate. Was she given favor because she was Tia's daughter? Grace had seen Kindra's haunted looks in the company of the rest of the household, as if she were out of place.

Her father should be admonished for letting Tia and Kindra have free reign, but then how did one do that when he owned this dynasty? It was all she could do to keep her mouth shut and keep her opinions to herself.

Still, as Grace climbed the stairs, Tia's sneaking around and talking to that no-good Jesse Simmons troubled her. Whatever was brewing in the woman's mind involved Jesse. Grace didn't trust him. She'd talk to Cameron when he came in that evening.

When she reached the top landing, she headed for her room. At the end of the hall, she found her father's chamber door ajar. She knew he'd be out in the fields. She meant to close the door, but instead, pushed it open further. Inside, Grace circled the room, curious.

A low set of drawers sat against the east wall. On it lay a sword enclosed in its sheath of royal-blue metal. The Cooper coat of arms decorated the sheath. Grace picked up the heavy sword, admiring its beauty. Nearly four feet in length, its weight was bearable, the brass hilt a fine piece of art.

Grace pulled the sword from its case and swung the blade in the air, arching it this way and that, the way she'd seen Mr. Laws handle a sword at fencing lessons.

Both hands holding the sword, she held it out in front of her and smiled, then returned it to the table.

A door led to a personal bath, and another door in the sitting room led to where? Grace glanced behind her, then turned the knob. It was locked. She stood back. Her father's bedchamber was laid out like her own. Having already been to the small room from her own sitting room, she realized the door must lead to Tia's room. Grace frowned as she gaped at the locked door. Then a realization came to her that made her stomach rile. Tia was the true mistress of the house, not just the headmistress to the servants.

A wave of nausea settled in her stomach, Grace moved away from the door and walked back to her father's bedchamber. Thoughts reeled in her mind. She wanted to stop them, to leave the room as innocently as she entered it. But it was too late for that. All the years her father waited for her mother's return, there had been another woman in his life. A woman with a child.

Grace sank into a chair near the bed. Another horrific thought flew into her mind. That child was near her age. Not dark like her mother. Her skin was honey-colored, as if she had an English father. Her nose was straight, her face heart-shaped, and her long, black hair was silky and straight.

Until now, she didn't understand why Kindra appeared familiar. Kindra had the likeness of her father and herself—the Cooper eyes, emerald green.

All of it made sense. Tia in her fine gowns. Her arrogant behavior.

Grace's hands flew to her head as she moved to the door and into the hallway. With one last glance into her father's chamber, Grace shut the door and crossed to her room on tiptoes. Moments later, she heard another door close across the hallway. It closed softly, as if someone didn't want to be heard. Was that Tia? Did the woman know Grace had been to her father's room?

The house was full of dark secrets. Jesse and Tia. Kindra and her father. Grace had questions she wanted answered. Why was Kindra's true identity kept a secret? Did her father think so lowly of the mulatto girl? He saw to Kindra's every need and she lived in the Great House. He even let her eat at the family table, rather than in the kitchen with the servants. Other than that, Kindra rarely showed her face around her father.

And rightly so! Grace thought. She was a slave, wasn't she?

Everything she'd learned about slaves in South Carolina seemed just and right. She didn't agree with the free reign given these two women.

No wonder Kindra's eyes appeared vacant and sad. She, too, was Phillip's daughter. All the sullen looks now made sense. She remembered the hurt in Kindra's eyes when she stood among the house servants. She remembered, too, how the servants shuffled their feet during introductions. All of it showed clearly now, as if she were looking through a glass window. How could her father do this to Kindra?

And yet, could she embrace Kindra as her half sister? Could she overlook their difference, their skin color?

Grace had longed for a sibling. Being an only child had been lonely. The knowledge that she had a sister all these years made her head spin. It was shear fate that her sister was a black slave. Grace sat down and leaned her head on the sofa. All of this was too much to bear.

Lord, my heart is hardened against this woman. But you knew all along I would come to this house. You knew I'd find out I had a sister, albeit estranged from our father. Help me. I don't know how to go about making things right. But I want to try.

"Be still, and know that I am God." The words from the Psalms came back to her in a rush and calmed her. A reminder from her Lord.

Grace stared at the ceiling. She'd asked and He answered. Be still? Say nothing?

TWENTY-THREE

GRACE SHOVED GOWNS from one side of her wardrobe to the other as Hedy watched.

"I don't know which one would be most fitting for tonight's dinner." Grace's brows pulled together as she chose one gown, scrutinized the design of the dress and put it back. After repeating this process a number of times, she lifted out a pale pink tea gown, brocaded in silks, and smiled. "This will do." She held it against her. "What do you think?"

Hedy rolled her eyes. "Lawdy, Missy, you look good in alla these fancy gowns."

Grace handed the gown to Hedy and sat down at the vanity table. It was all she could do to keep her spirits up. She'd pledged obedience to her maker to keep silent regarding her newfound secret about Kindra and her father. She'd have to act as if she didn't know.

Hedy brushed Grace's hair into a silky sheen. Then she brought out the heated iron to make long ringlets that cascaded down her back.

An hour later, Grace met her father in the foyer.

"You look absolutely charming, my dear."

"Thank you, Father." She lowered her eyes. The secret changed everything. Could she pull off the masquerade that she was oblivious to the dark matters in the Great House?

Cameron appeared from the drawing room, dressed in a royal-blue waistcoat, breeches, and white shirt. She looked up into his dark eyes.

Was that a glint of amusement he shot her way?

She turned away, shoulders rigid. She wasn't in the mood for whatever tease he had in mind. She just wanted to get through this evening.

Cameron couldn't hide his smile. Grace had awakened a keen sense of awareness of her. She piqued his appreciation of her character, and tonight, she was quite lovely to look at. She stood in the foyer in a gown of soft pink that shimmered a white haze from the brilliant lights of the chandeliers. A thick ruffle of lace enveloped her neck and fanned out over her shoulders. Auburn ringlets flowed down her back. In the palm of her hand, she held a pink fan.

"I see the Borjeaux have arrived." He walked to the screen door.

"Yes, Zeek has gone out to help them from the carriage," Phillip said.

"And Camille?" Grace asked.

"The captain will be along with Camille and her brother shortly. They went on a picnic this afternoon."

Phillip put his hand on Grace's back. "Come, my dear." He pushed the screen door open and led her onto the front porch. Mr. and Mrs. Borjeau climbed the steps toward them.

"Good evening." Mr. Borjeau shook Phillip's hand and glanced down at Grace. His smile broadened as he stretched out his hand to her. "My name's John Borjeau." He turned to his wife. "And this is my lovely wife, Claudia."

Grace took Claudia's hand. "I've heard so much about you."

Phillip grinned. "My daughter, Grace Cooper."

Phillip kissed Claudia's cheek. "You look enchanting as ever."

John Borjeau was a tall man with snow-white hair, deep-blue eyes and a ready smile on his angular face. Claudia's white hair was streaked with silver. Peacefulness emanated around her. The two complimented each other.

Zeek stood at attendance while the party entered the house. He took Claudia's shawl and John's hat and hung them on the hall tree near the front door.

Gemma had just finished lighting the oil lamps when Grace and Claudia swept into the drawing room. The men pulled out their pipes and lit them. Soon the room buzzed with conversation. Grace liked the Borjeaux immediately. Before long, she had answered questions about Charleston, South Carolina, and her trip across the sea.

"I remember your mother," Claudia said. "We were friends while she was here."

"It must have been difficult to see her go," Grace said.

"More than you know." She patted Grace's hand. "I heard she passed. I'm sorry for your loss."

"Thank you. We were very close." Grace looked down at her hands in her lap, gathering strength to keep tears at bay.

"You must come to Yarabee Hall and have lunch with us some afternoon."

Grace looked up. "I'd like that."

The screen door squeaked open and all eyes turned to the entryway. Captain Harding came in with a lovely brunette in tow, a gleam in his eyes.

The three men stood as Camille crossed the floor to where her mother sat. Grace stood to meet Camille.

"This," the captain said with a smile he couldn't hide, "is Camille Borjeau."

Camille reached a slender hand toward Grace. "You're right, Drew darling. She's beautiful." Her deep-blue eyes scanned the room and she waved to the men. "Be seated gentlemen."

A tall young man stood at the entrance to the drawing room.

"This is Camille's brother, George," Drew said.

He nodded their way.

Grace knew immediately she and Camille would get along just

fine. Her straightforwardness reminded her of Josie. Camille's long hair cascaded down the front of her shoulders, not in ringlets like the day's fashion, but straight, long, and silky. Her silver gown flowed over her slender hips.

Gemma appeared. "Mastah Coopah, supper is served."

"Thank you, Gemma." He glanced at the room full of guests, "We'll resume our conversation in the dining room."

The party crossed the foyer into the dining room. Grace held back. "After you," Cameron said, glancing over her shoulder at the party being seated.

Tia appeared at the foot of the stairs. She stared at them before she walked down the hallway and out the back door. Night air brushed into the room and curled around their feet. Grace glanced down the empty hall.

Was Tia going to meet Jesse? She had yet to tell Cameron about Tia and Jesse's secret meeting out in the stable.

Kindra lifted her shimmering, green gown as she tiptoed out to the garden behind the Great House. Light from the house shone across the ground. The yellow haze helped her make her way across the damp lawn.

She searched the shadows beyond. A pathway led to a small stone bench on the bricked patio. Behind the bench, a tall Spanish oak hovered overhead. She neared the bench and waited, hands clung to the sides of her gown.

A shadow moved from behind the tree. She watched a tall figure loom into the pale moonlight.

"Denzel!" She flew into his arms.

"What took you so long? I've been waiting nearly an hour!" He held her close.

"Mother. She's in such a state of uncertainty tonight. She kept glancing out my balcony to the yard below. I feared she knew you were out here waiting for me."

"Do you think she knows?"

"I don't know. She wanted to take a walk in the night air. Did you see her?"

"She didn't come this way. I've been here a while."

Kindra drew away from Denzel's arms and paced. "After all the work she went through

to get me dressed for tonight's company, at the last moment, she told me not to join them. She

didn't bother to change either. She's been acting strange lately. I wish she would confide in me."

Denzel pulled Kindra under the shadow of the Spanish Oak. "Forget about your mother tonight." He bent his head to claim her lips.

"Umm." Kindra came up for air. Their eyes clung to each other for the breath of a moment. Then she pulled his head down to hers again.

Crickets made a chorus of noise. Frogs croaked under the lush, tropical foliage. A lone parrot cawed in the darkness. Two lovers hid behind the Spanish oak, wishing for all the world they didn't have to hide. Denzel's work at the sugar mill and her mother's watchful eye made it nearly impossible to find time together. What moments they stole, they made the most of. Kindra leaned into Denzel. "Don't ever let me go," she whispered.

Servants came and went through the swinging door, laden with bowls and dishes. On one side of the table sat plates of curried chicken, mango coleslaw, sweet and sour cabbage soup, and sweet potato fritters. On the other side of the table, sat bowls of mango chutney, dumplings, sugar peas, rice, and a platter of Johnnycakes. Food was passed around while conversation filled the room.

Drew and Camille sat opposite Cameron and Grace. Grace kept her gaze stayed on their guest. The slave revolt was the main topic throughout the dinner hour. Soon the servants cleared away their plates and returned with desert plates filled with mango cobbler.

"I've been watching the price of sugar fall with the new contraptions the Americans have invented. Their sugar process seems more efficient," Phillip said.

"I wonder," John said, "Do the Americans have the same problems with slaves on their plantations as we are experiencing in Jamaica?"

"The newspapers have indicated that more and more plantations are experiencing uprisings. Discontent is growing. We've more slaves than plantation owners," Phillip said, he puffed his pipe and blew a billow of white smoke over the table.

"How long before the Africans overthrow the plantations and flee?" John frowned.

An hour later, the dinner party moved to the drawing room again. The men smoked their pipes and talked about the slave uprising. The women sat on the rose-printed sofa with small talk and soft laughter. Grace couldn't remember having ever spent such a delightful time. The drone of insects could be heard through the window screens on the porch, as they swarmed the oil lamps. The fragrant scent of tropical flowers wafted in on the evening breeze.

The air felt thick with the smell of rain in the distance. Out in the shanties, the slaves sang their soulful songs. The plantation sounds came alive. She understood what her mother meant when she said, *"Everything grows so much faster there than at home. There's a sort of steamy smell coming up from the earth, like a hot damp blanket."*

"Grace?" Her father said, across the room.

Grace smiled. "Please forgive me. I just remembered something mother said when I was a child."

"What was it?" Her father asked.

"That the air is like a hot, damp blanket in Jamaica." She peered at her father. "She was right."

"Yes." His eyes took on a dreamy look. "She was right."

The room hushed as father and daughter stared at each other.

John stood and reached out a hand to Phillip. "Thank you for a pleasant evening. We must do this again soon."

The rest of the company stood and moved toward the front porch.

"You'll receive an invitation to the ball in a few days," Phillip said, and turned to Claudia. "May I ask a favor of you?"

"Certainly. What can I do for you?"

"I'd appreciate it if you'd escort my daughter to a seamstress shop in Riverbend. She needs an appropriate gown for the ball." He grinned at Grace and pulled her next to him.

Camille came to Claudia's side. "Let's take her tomorrow. Mrs. Kramer is the finest seamstress on the island."

"I'll put her in your charge, Claudia. I trust your good judgment."

"You won't be disappointed." The Borjeaux climbed into their carriage. It rumbled out of the drive toward Yarabee Hall.

Drew escorted Camille to his waiting buggy. George sat in the back. He waved goodbye. Cameron and Grace stood by and waved at all of them. The buggy lurched forward as the horse trotted into the dark night.

Grace whirled around. "Thank you for a beautiful evening, Father." She glanced at Cameron who stood in the driveway. "Good night." She lifted her silk skirts and crossed the wooden floor to the screen door and stopped. The muffled sounds of servants talking and cleaning up trailed out to the porch.

Grace looked back with the screen door in her hand. "Will Kindra be coming to the ball?"

Phillip's eyes jumped to Cameron and then to her. "I hadn't planned on it, dear. Why?"

"Just curious." Grace went in without looking back.

Phillip and Cameron exchanged looks.

"Do you think she knows?" Phillip asked.

"It's hard to say. She hasn't said."

Phillip nodded and moved into the house. He took the stairs at a slow pace. The top of the landing looked a mile away. At the landing, he panted. Sweat clung to his brow. He wiped his forehead with the back of his sleeve. His head swam. Phillip gripped the banister and closed his eyes. He worked his way to his chamber.

Moments later, Zeek tapped at his door.

Phillip panted, "Come in."

Zeek stopped. "You need me to go for the doctor?" He took a handkerchief and patted Phillip's forehead.

"No. I'll be fine. Let me lie here a moment."

"Anything I can do, Mastah?"

"Sit with me."

"I sure be doin' that. I be right here," he said. Zeek sat next to Phillip's bed.

Zeek's a good man, Phillip thought. They'd been together a good many years. The clock ticked loudly. He didn't open his eyes but heard the creaking of Zeek's chair. He let himself fall into a slumber. He was in good hands.

The woman crept into Grace's room and slipped over to the dressing table. The moon shone through the window, revealing Grace's jewelry box. Dark fingers shuffled through bracelets, necklaces and rings. Nothing of importance there. Then she eyed the locket lying on the vanity table. She picked it up and opened it. There stood Phillip with his Missus. She needed something tangible that belonged to Grace. This was perfect for her voodoo magic. The woman slipped the locket in her pocket and patted it. She heard the sound of footsteps in the hall, and waited. Again, a second set of footsteps. She must escape before she was found out. The woman peeked through the slit in the door. It was Zeek. He closed Phillip's door behind him. She must go.

She stood outside the master's door. The hallway was clear. She tiptoed down the stairs and out the door.

Grace entered her room. Horse's hooves sounded beyond the balcony. Curious, she stepped out onto the veranda. The moon shone bright as she gazed over the wooden rails. Grace could see the horse stable from where she stood. A wagon stopped in front of it. Jesse helped Tia step down and pulled her to him. She kissed him and then moved toward the house with the feet of a panther. When she neared the house, she glanced up toward the east wing.

Mosquitoes hummed around her face, but Grace dared not swat them for fear Tia would see her. She stepped back into the shadows, and Tia disappeared below.

The fragrance of the honeysuckle vines wafted up to the second story balcony, the evening air fresh on her face. She waited before she moved to the wooden rail and leaned over to look below. Someone lit a cigarette beside the stable, his form obscure. Was it Jesse?

Graced peered below the balcony, she saw nothing but the thick, crawling honeysuckle vines. She shuttered and moved back into the safety of her dimly lit room.

Cameron strode toward the outbuildings. Across the road from the stable, the barn was lit up. He moved into the building, where Corky and Erik relaxed in a game of cards. Cameron looked around for Jesse. He was nowhere to be seen.

"Good evening, fellas. Are you about ready to call it a night?"

"Yes, sir." Erik folded his hand and laid it face down on the table.

"Where's Jesse?"

"He's been out most of the evening."

"By himself?"

"As best we know."

Cameron nodded. "Have you seen Tia this evening?"

"No, sir."

"Goodnight then."

"Yes, sir. Goodnight."

Cameron walked out of the barn toward the horse stable. Lightning bugs flitted about him, their twinkling in the evening air a welcome sight. One flew close enough he could have caught it if he'd wanted to. He recalled his summers as a boy. He used to catch the fireflies and put them in a glass jar and watch them flit around with their orange-yellow glow. He'd later let them loose. He sometime referred to them as, 'Peenie Wallies' as the Jamaican's did.

He neared the stable and saw a movement in the shadows. A second later a tiny red glow flicked through the darkness. Was that a lightning bug, or the remains of a cigarette?

Cameron crept toward the stable and crouched behind the wagon. He waited in the deepening shadows. He suspected Jesse would be lurking close by. Cameron eased himself around the side of the stable and came out on the opposite side. Moonlight lit up the grounds. Jesse wouldn't be hiding in the spotlight. A twig snapped. Cameron's head jerked to look toward the opposite side of the building. When he came back to the main road, no one was there.

He took off his hat and shoved his hair from his forehead. "Dad burn dingit!"

In the morning, Grace called Hedy to her vanity table. "Have you seen my locket?"

"No, Missy. It be lying on your table last night."

"It's not here." She bent to search the floor. "I meant to wear it for the party, but I forgot to put it on."

Hedy got on her knees and searched behind the table. Moments later, her head popped up, "It sure not here, Miss Coopah."

"Well, keep your eyes open for it."

"Yessum I do that."

First my purse and now my locket, Grace mused. *Was there any connection to the two disappearances?* She reached a hand to her throat, bare without the gold piece. It must turn up soon. She couldn't bear to lose it.

There was a rap at the door. "Come in," Grace said, as she moved to the wardrobe.

Minerva entered the room with a pile of bedclothes in her arms. "Sorry, Miss Cooper. I thought you'd be downstairs for breakfast. I can come back later." Minerva turned to leave.

"Wait." Grace eyed the servant woman. "Have you seen my gold locket?"

"No, Ma'am, I haven't. Is it missing?"

"Yes. It was on my vanity last night. When I woke up this morning, it was gone."

"I'll sure be looking for it while I clean your room."

"All right." Grace watched Minerva leave the room. "I hope she finds it."

"Let's get you dressed." Hedy went to work, fussing over Grace's hair and buttoning her gown. "You just wait and see, Missy. Your locket be showin' up."

A half hour later Grace sat down at the table, miffed. She glanced at Cameron and took her seat.

"Good morning."

"What's good about it?"

Phillip cleared his throat, "Is something wrong, dear?"

"My locket's missing."

"Are you sure?" Concern showed on his weathered face.

"Yes, I'm sure. I've spent the better part of the morning searching for it."

"First your purse and now your locket," Cameron said. "Do we have a thief in the house?"

"It seems that way." She frowned and snapped her napkin open.

"We've not had that problem before. It must be a coincidence," Phillip said.

"Some coincidence." Grace focused first on her father, then Cameron. She started to say more, thought better of it, and clamped her mouth shut.

"I'm headed out to the fields." Cameron scooped up his wide-brimmed hat and stepped out onto the porch. The screen door slammed behind him.

Phillip eyed his daughter warily. "I've got work to do in the study." He made his exit as well.

Grace glanced about the empty room. *Well, fiddle!*

An hour later, Cameron walked out to the drive where Grace sat in the Borjeaux's yellow pram with Claudia and Camille. "Did your necklace turn up?"

"No." Her chin rose.

Cameron hid the smile that threatened to take over his stern look. He lifted his straw hat and brushed back his hair. He slapped his hat against the side of his pant legs before returning it to his head. He glanced at the pretty little lady who seemed to think she didn't need anyone's help.

"You ladies try to be back before dark. It's not safe on the road these days. Heard tell some ruffians attacked a wagon the other day."

Claudia glanced down at Cameron. "We'll return before dark. Thank you for the warning."

The driver flicked the reins and the carriage lurched out the drive. Cameron watched them leave, then glanced back at the Great House. Did Grace misplace her purse somewhere in the house? Had someone stolen it before they took the locket? He wiped his brow with the sleeve of his shirt and turned back toward the sugar mill. These days he didn't know whom to trust.

TWENTY-FOUR

GRACE LOOKED FORWARD to the outing to Riverbend. She hadn't ventured off the Landing since she'd arrived. Pools of shade dotted the long carriage lane hedged with palm trees. The breezes rattling the palm branches gave small relief from last nights rain as the buggy moved out toward the main road. The heat rising from the wet earth only added to the day's sultriness. The air reeked of tropical scents and nettlesome insects were thick. Grace swatted at a mosquito and was grateful for the thin veil on her wide-brimmed hat that helped protect her face. The carriage jostled the women as it rolled over the deep-rutted, one-lane road. Up ahead, a black buggy coming toward them swerved to the left and stopped.

"The Moore women," Camille said. She gave Grace a sidelong glance. "Jacqueline must be on her way to pay Cameron a visit."

When their carriage came even with the buggy, Jacqueline and Grace exchanged glances. Jacqueline's red hair showed hues of gold in the morning sunlight. Violet waved with her free hand. She held a parasol over Jacqueline and herself with the other hand.

Grace's party moved past the buggy and continued on as the horse's hooves pounded a rhythm on the hard, dirt road. Against her better judgment, Grace glanced back at the buggy while it moved out onto the lane again. Jacqueline had turned to glance at the yellow carriage that swiftly rolled toward town. Even at the growing distance between them, Grace caught the haughty look of the redhead.

"The Moore women come to Riverbend quite often. They live on the north side of Blue Mountain." Camille brushed at a mosquito. "Jacqueline is the older of the two sisters. She has her sights on Cameron. Violet only comes along for the ride and to chaperone."

"I met them on the *Savannah Rose,*" Grace said. A taut feeling jumped into her stomach.

"They're a couple then," Grace mused aloud.

Camille brushed her hair away from her shoulder. "Frankly, I think Jacqueline is a prude. Cameron deserves better."

Grace raised her brows. "You sound as if they're practically engaged."

"Truth to tell, most of us from Riverbend have been expecting an announcement any day now."

They rounded a bend in the road that looked familiar. Grace gazed down a ravine and recognized the spot where the cart had spilled into the ditch.

She recalled how her heart had nearly stopped, when Cameron scooped her up and carried her to the waiting cart. He may have his sights on the prudish Jacqueline Moore, but there was no denying he had an attraction for Grace. She'd seen the depths of his eyes light up when he looked at her and felt his heart pound close to hers when he'd pulled her off the horse. But she couldn't think about that now. If Cameron and Jacqueline were a couple, she'd best put all thoughts of him aside.

Late that afternoon, Phillip waited for Grace as she climbed the steps of the front porch. Her cheeks were flushed as she came through the front door.

"Father! We had a wonderful time today. Claudia has impeccable taste and I do believe you'll approve of the gown I'll wear to the ball."

Phillip didn't miss the light in Grace's emerald eyes. "The outing was good for you. You must do it more often." He held a dark blue, velvet box in his hand. "I have something for you." He opened the lid and pulled out a diamond solitaire necklace.

"It's beautiful!" Grace looked up at him, her cheeks tinged. "You shouldn't have."

"It belonged to your mother. She left it here when she returned to Charleston. I've kept it all these years. I want you to have it."

Tears brimmed in Grace's eyes as she fingered the diamond jewel. "Thank you, Father. I'll wear it proudly." She stood on tiptoes to kiss his cheek.

Tears stung Phillip's eyes as he brushed a kiss on her forehead. Now go on up and get ready for supper, little one. The meal will be ready soon.

He watched his daughter sail up the stairs, and his heart lurched. Who could have known a certain auburn-haired young woman would light up his life?

The day of the party arrived. While the September trade winds blew in, warm and balmy, the grandfather clock struck three long bell tones.

"You mustn't keep your father waitin', Missy," Hedy said.

"You're the reason I'm late," Grace snapped, her nerves in a ball.

"You'll be thankin' me later when all the fellas can't git their eyes off of you."

"Won't be a soul who gives a wit how I look."

Grace spun around and swayed. The gown flared out. She imagined dancing in the arms of a certain black-haired gentleman. Her cheeks flamed at the prospect. Jacqueline Moore and her family would be at the ball. The chances of dancing with the handsome foreman of Cooper's Landing were nil, unless of course, he danced with her out of respect for her father.

"I hear music. Are we late?" Grace glanced in the mirror one last time. Half her curls were piled on top of her head, pinned with tiny white jasmines. The other half hung down her back in long ringlets.

"That be your cue, Miss Coopah. You best git on out there."

Grace took a deep breath. With the slightest hint of a nod, she followed Hedy out the door and into the hall. She tried not to feel nervous. In fact, she tried not to feel anything at all, but it didn't work. Her heart pounded in her ears as she moved toward the top landing. She feared she'd kept her father waiting far too long.

She glanced down the wide, marble staircase and saw him looking up. Grace descended the stairs. Would he approve of her dress? The glossy burnt-orange, taffeta gown formed three flounces, all trimmed with black shirring. The form-fitting jacket was trimmed similarly. A pale lace blouse was visible beneath the jacket; its delicate bows burnt orange to match the dress. Grace wore a fringed shawl of a dramatically different color scheme, reminiscent of Japanese textiles, yet part of the ensemble. When she looked at her father, she saw his approval.

Cameron appeared next to Phillip, his hands folded behind his back. His dark eyes met hers when she neared the bottom step.

As her foot hit the marbled floor, her father's warm, approving eyes offered all she'd hoped to find in them. He loved her. If she had any doubt before, those fears were put to rest. He glanced over her exquisite dress in satisfaction and crooked his right arm. "You look absolutely stunning, my dear."

"I couldn't have said it better." Cameron half bowed, his eyes staying on her as he did.

"We mustn't keep the guests waiting. They're eager to meet you." Phillip's smile remained as he escorted Grace down the hallway accented with a dozen candles lighting the way to the ballroom.

She smelled Cameron's cologne behind them. He too, was attired quite exquisitely. She couldn't help but notice how handsome he looked.

But Jacqueline Moore was here, or would be soon. Cameron would likely spend the evening attending to the redhead. Grace didn't give much thought to his token compliment. Her father expected a kind word, and he'd complied. She expected nothing more.

Tonight was her night. She'd make the most of it. She'd brush all thoughts of Cameron from her mind, if such a thing were possible.

The music stopped when Phillip Cooper stood at the entrance to the ballroom. All eyes settled on Grace and her father.

Phillip cleared his throat and gave his daughter a proud look. "May I introduce my lovely daughter, Grace Cooper."

A round of applause resounded through the spacious ballroom, then quieted. He stood slightly away from her, his eyes shining. "I have invited all of you to share in the joy of her arrival at Cooper's Landing. Please take the time to get to know her."

He hooked an arm around her waist and pulled her close. The room thundered with applause again. When the noise abated, Phillip continued, "There are tables on the lawns with a bounty of food. Please join us outside. Tonight, when the sun goes down, the band will strike up festive music and we will resume the party in the ballroom. Now come, let's eat!"

Kindra escaped from the milling crowd to her room. She stood before the mirror, turning this way and that, and bent toward the glass and looked closely for the hundredth time. Ever since Grace Cooper had arrived, she was aware of two things. One . . . she and Grace could pass for sisters, save the color of their skin. They did not share the same mother. But Kindra was certain they shared the same father. She and Grace had his eyes, emerald green, and his dimples. But more than that, they had his unbending nature, headstrong and challenging.

Yet the resemblance between Olivia and her daughter, Grace, was strong. That she knew from the oval picture of Grace's mother hanging in the dining room. Grace had strong qualities of both parents.

Secondly . . . Kindra couldn't help but notice her father's obsession with Grace. He showered her with attention, something Kindra had wished and waited for all of her nineteen years.

No one, not even her mother had told Kindra, Pip was her father. She just knew. She saw how he was with Tia, her mother, and knew why her own skin was soft and honey-brown like molasses, not dark like the slaves' on Cooper's Landing. She continued to gaze at her reflection, taking note of her petite nose, slender lips and long, silky, black hair.

While most of the slave women on the plantation wore muslin blouses and dark, loose skirts, Kindra wore the silks and satins of high society. She'd done so all her life. Pip allowed her mother to spend money lavishly on Kindra's wardrobe. She was accustomed to living an elegant lifestyle equal to any white woman on the island.

Yet when she tried to mingle at Pip's parties, people avoided her like the plague. She couldn't contain her disappointment. It wasn't her imagination. When she asked her mother about it, Tia waved her away as if Kindra were making too much out of it. Tia had no wish to mingle with their company. She usually stayed confined to her room until the last carriage drove away.

Finding no answer, Kindra had approached one of the help. She remembered when she found Penny, the youngest servant in the kitchen, and came straight to the point with her question.

"What's wrong with me?"

Penny had been her friend as far back as she could recall. Kindra remembered that day. Penny had looked at her with creased brows. "What you be talkin' about, Sissy?"

"When we have company, they avoid me. It's as if they feel uncomfortable around me."

Penny shook her head and backed away with a hand stretched out toward her. "I can't be havin' this conversation with you, Miss Kindra. I be straight out of line. You best be askin' Mastah Camp or someone else, but you sure don't be askin' me."

"I'll do no such thing, Penny. I'm asking you and I want you to be truthful with me. Please?"

She remembered how miserable Penny looked. The girl had glanced around the kitchen as if she was sure someone was listening to their conversation. "You didn't heah it from me!"

"No, I didn't, so tell me."

"Well . . . um . . . I sure don't feel good about this, Miss Kindra."

"Go ahead. I don't want to spend the rest of my life wondering what's wrong with me."

"Well . . . you . . . um . . . know who your mothah is."

"Of course."

"But do you know who your fathah is?"

Kindra felt struck by lightning. She stood frozen to the floor and stared at Penny. "I . . . I think I do, Penny. Truth is, Mother's never said."

"Well that be your problem, Miss Kindra." Penny paused and glanced about her, then lowered her voice to a near whisper. "You be considered what the white men call an illegitimate child. You be born out of wedlock. Society find it difficult to befriend you cause of that." Penny hung her head and tears formed in her eyes. "I don't think of you that way, Miss Kindra. And most folks heah at the Landin' don't neither. It just be those white folks."

Kindra had swallowed then lifted her friend's face, her hand held softly under her chin. "Don't cry, Penny. It isn't your fault I asked."

Penny shook her head and looked away.

So the white folks don't think I'm fit for them. It all makes perfect sense now. Kindra lifted her full skirt and left the young cook in a state of despair. All this was new to her, and she needed to digest this new information.

She was caught between two worlds. That of the Great House, where she was expected to carry on as if she were nobility, and the world where she wished she could stay. She belonged in the fields with the people who worked the plantation. She longed to spend time with the women and children.

Kindra waited until most of the people had left the ballroom before she walked out onto the lawn. She knew her crimson gown with the modest ivy pattern in black on both the overskirt and underskirt brought out the warm tones of her honey-brown skin. Double layers of black embroidery set off the low, dropped-shoulder neckline. A ruby necklace lay against her chest. It matched the crimson hues of her gown.

Brows rose from the upper class as she moved boldly across the grass. Their eyes appeared to ask, "How dare she dress as one of us?"

Kindra felt the arrogant stares as she moved away from the sounds of the party. She searched the crowd for Denzel. She'd heard he was to attend the coaches as the guests arrived. After the party was under way, he'd keep an eye on the slaves who dressed in fine, white pants and shirts and served the guests.

Jacqueline Moore, her hand hooked possessively through the crook of Cameron's arm, sent Kindra a condescending glance. But Camp nodded his recognition, a slight smile on his lips.

Kindra simmered. *I won't run,* she told herself. *I'll stay and eat if I choke. There isn't one person who had a right to be here more than me, especially that Moore woman!* She lifted her chin and walked on, searching for Denzel in the thick crowd.

Grace listened to the hum of voices, and the tinkle of glasses that filled the hot afternoon air while she and her father meandered through the crowd. Many of the guests introduced themselves to Grace. She observed the house servants who carried silver and china vessels from the back kitchen to the dozens of tables shaded by umbrellas made of woven cane and bright canvas.

Phillip handed Grace over to the Borjeau women and joined a group of gentleman who stood talking while they smoked their finely carved pipes.

Cameron broke away from Jacqueline momentarily. He sauntered over to Grace, who stood with Claudia and Camille. He gestured to the white-linen-covered tables where a rich assortment of food waited. "Help yourselves, ladies. There's plenty of food here."

"Thank you, Cameron. We will," Grace said.

They approached one of the long tables. A roasted pig with an apple in its mouth sat in its center. There was so much food it would be impossible to taste it all. Camille and Claudia followed close behind Grace and commented on the variety of food.

Grace said. "I mustn't eat too much, or I'll never fit into my new evening gown."

As the afternoon wore on and the guests milled about the lawn, she cast a quick glance toward the Great House in time to see Jacqueline come out and move to join a circle of young women.

Camille hooked her hand through Grace's slender arm and they walked leisurely through the crowd. The rolling lawn thronged with groups of stylish men and women, but Cameron was nowhere in sight. Her mind halted. She'd allowed herself thoughts of the foreman far too often. Without thinking, she sought his whereabouts. This had to stop. He was already taken.

A coach rolled into the circular drive and stopped. Curious eyes turned to see who had arrived. The coachman opened the door and a familiar face looked out over the milling crowd.

"Mrs. Cavendish." Grace smiled. "Come Camille, I want you to meet a good friend of mine." The two women crossed the lawn to where the coach waited. Agnes Cavendish peered out into the bright sun and smiled.

"Dear girl, how are you?" She stretched out her veined hands to

Grace.

"Mrs. Cavendish, I am well. What a delightful surprise to find you here at my party. Father never said a word about sending you an invitation." She gathered the elderly woman in her arms and gave her a warm hug.

"Camille, this is my good friend, Mrs. Agnes Cavendish. I met her on the *Savannah Rose*." She turned to Mrs. Cavendish. "And this is my new friend, Camille Borjeau. Her father owns a plantation next to Cooper's Landing."

"I'm pleased to meet you, Mrs. Cavendish. Your name sounds so familiar," Camille said.

"And I, too, am pleased to meet you. I know your father."

"Let's find a table where you can sit down. Are you hungry? Would you like something to eat?" They walked toward a table with a canvas umbrella shading it. Grace waved Dinah to her side.

"Mrs. Cavendish has just arrived. Please put a plate of food together for her."

"Yes, Miss Cooper. Right away." Dinah turned to Agnes. "Is there anything you favor? Pork, Chicken, Beef?"

"Oh, a slice of pork and a vegetable will suffice for me, thank you."

"Right away, Ma'am."

Grace turned her attention to Mrs. Cavendish. "Will you be staying with us a few days?"

"I hadn't given any thought to staying at the Landing. I've made arrangements to stay at the hotel in town."

"Nonsense. You'll stay here at the Landing with us. We'd love to have you. I have so much to tell you."

Grace and Agnes spent the next half hour explaining to Camille how they'd met and how Grace and the Moore women spent the afternoon on Mrs. Cavendish's tobacco plantation in Barbados.

"I had to give Grace lessons on bartering with the native market people. They would have taken every last schilling she possessed if I hadn't intervened." She chuckled at the memory.

Grace blushed. "I have a lot to learn." She cocked her head to Mrs. Cavendish. "You haven't been on your plantation long. Are you leaving for Charleston so soon?"

"As a matter of fact I am. I'm sailing on the *Savannah Rose* in three days."

"If the ship leaves in three days, I hope the captain will be here tonight." Camille tinged a shade darker. "I had hoped to dance with him at the ball."

"If I know the captain as well as I think I do, he's in town at the boarding house getting all decked out for the ball." Mrs. Cavendish's weary eyes twinkled at Camille.

The afternoon sun baked down on the milling crowd and Grace wilted under the layers of material. She needed a break from the heat. The Great House would be cool inside.

"I'm going to powder my nose," Grace said. "Would you care to join me?"

"I'll wait for you here," Camille said.

"And since I've just arrived, I believe I'll stay and enjoy the company of your new friend," Agnes chimed in.

"If you'll excuse me ladies, I'll return shortly." Grace stood and walked across the lawn. Jacqueline raked her with a wry grin and then turned back to the women in her party. A harsh giggle filled the air. Then her voice muted. The others laughed as well.

Grace hurried up the marble stairs. The first bedchambers on each side of the hall had been designated as powder rooms for the women. The doors stood open and women came and went, using the mirrors to assess their garments and powder their noses. The hall to her bedchamber was crowded. Hedy appeared at her door and swiftly made an assessment of Grace's hair and clothes. After making a few adjustments, she declared Grace fit to return.

Grace made her way past the women who congregated in the upstairs hallway. As more women came up the stairs, she moved to the right as she descended again.

She hadn't seen Tia since the party began. Curious, she glanced about for the headmistress. She searched the first floor rooms and moved out the back door. Few guest roamed the tropical garden, and Grace moved out to the side lane toward the stable. A man's voice came from its interior. Tia exited the barn, glanced at Grace, then pushed past her and disappeared.

Grace watched as Tia hurriedly walked back to the Great House and entered through the back door.

Grace peered into the barn. She didn't know whom she expected to find. Perhaps her father. Not Jesse Simmons. Her expression must have told him so, for he frowned and his eyes swept her with a crude glance.

"Nice of you to join me." His eyes flicked over her appreciatively.

Grace stood still. He was far bolder than when she'd last seen him on the ship.

"What brings you out to the stable, rather than the guests who await your presence." He moved toward Grace and licked his lips. "Lookin' for me?"

Grace shivered. She would not give him the satisfaction of knowing how he affected her. "If you'll excuse me, I thought no one was here. I just wanted a moment of peace alone with my horse." She gathered her skirts. "I've guests to attend to."

She turned to leave, but swift as a snake he came between her and the stable doors. "There be plenty of time for your guests."

Fowl whiskey breath permeated the space between them. She dug her nails into her palms and glanced past him, wishing she'd not chosen to wander out of range of her father or Cameron. She tried to appear as if his antics didn't frighten her. Voices floated their way. "I believe we have company."

A dark brow arched. "We'll send them away."

"Why are you here? Aren't you supposed to be on the ship?" She raised thin brows and tried to brush past him.

"I rode in with the captain. I've work to do while the party goes on." He caught her wrist. "No use pretending offense. We both know what you be. It's time, darlin', you discard that masquerade you be playin'."

"Masquerade? What are you implying?"

"You fool no one here at the Landin', Missy. Tia said you be nothing but a waif looking for a fortune." He leaned his stubby-bearded face close to hers, eyes jeering. "You'll stoop to anything, darlin, includin' stealin' an inheritance that ain't rightfully yours."

He poked his face close and clenched his teeth. "We both know you ain't nothin' but a wily wench in disguise. Admit it."

Stung, Grace drew her hand back and slapped his face. "You're despicable! I'll hear no more of this nonsense." She turned to escape his advances.

"Oh no you don't." He grabbed her waist and jerked her back. "I ain't through with you." Strong arms pinned her to him. He bent his foul face to hers. Grace struggled, turning her head as he tried to kiss her, his stubby beard scratching the side of her cheek.

"I'll tell no one of your secret if you give yourself to me."

"Let go of me or I'll scream!"

Footsteps sounded beyond the stable doors. His grip loosened enough for Grace to twist free. She rushed out into the corral and collided into Cameron.

He steadied her, studied her face.

"Someone needs to put that rat behind bars!"

His expression hardened as he looked toward the stable. "Wait for me out front."

"I—I must talk to you," she said with a rush. "About Tia."

"I'll only be a moment," he growled.

"Yes, of course." With relief, she turned toward the garden, wanting nothing more than to get away from the wretched scoundrel who'd insulted her.

Grace hoped Cameron would put an end to Jesse's incessant harassments. She moved passed the side patio and out toward the lawn.

She looked at her palm, still stinging from the slap. At least she'd given Jesse something to think about. She wasn't a pushover. She wouldn't take his guff without a fight.

TWENTY-FIVE

CAMERON MOVED TOWARD the barn door with a deliberate calm, belying the cold rage that ran through him. When he turned toward the crewman, his mind raced. The sailor needed to be taught a lesson for slandering Phillip Cooper's daughter, and for his hand in stealing slaves off of Cooper's Landing.

Jesse stood at the door. "The stables becoming a popular place," he said.

"Let's go inside, sailor. I want a word with you." Cameron said.

"The Missy, she left in a huff." Jesse rubbed his scruffy jaw.

"So it appears. Her hand has left quite a stain on your cheek."

Jesse dropped his hand and he flashed a wry grin. "She come askin' for attention, and when I give it to her, she done changed her mind. That be a female for ya." Jesse stepped back.

"You dream, Jesse." Cameron worked his jaw. "Grace has better taste than to flaunt herself on the likes of you. Only a woman of squalor would lower herself to your standard."

Cameron hoped Simmons would become angry and fly at him. Nothing would give him more pleasure than to flatten Jesse right here, right now. He'd pay for dishonoring Grace, but not before Cameron got the information he'd come for. Jesse had information on the suspicious antics of Tia, and Cameron intended to get it out of him.

Jesse's brown eyes measured Cameron warily. "I don't know what you're hinting at. I've not wronged the wench if that be what you're suggesting."

"I'd say the *lady* will have the last word on that. Your reputation hinders your credibility."

"What are you talkin' about, Camp?"

"Aren't you a smuggler. A traitor to the *Savannah Rose*? A spy for Tia?"

Cameron watched Jesse draw himself up to his full height. "What gives you the right to hurl such accusations against me?"

"We've been watching you, Jesse."

A quick flush darkened Jesse's face, and his jaw tightened. "By the saints of the sea. I don't have to take any of your lip. I'll flatten you out right here. Should of done it long ago when I found ya' in the hold."

"You never did know how to pick on someone your own size. You bully women, but I've never seen you take on a real man." Cameron said, deliberately goading him.

Jesse's eyes blazed. "You be thinkin' 'cause you're half-owner to the Landin', you be the most powerful landowner in the West Indies, and that be givin' you more honor, do you?"

"More than I can say for you. Heard you put a down payment on the *Caribbean Dragon,* that miserable piece of vessel you call a ship."

Cameron saw what he'd waited for–Jesse's momentary flinch.

"I owe you no explainin' of my comin's or goin's. Everything I do is done with respectability." Jesse leered at Cameron.

"I beg to differ. Most folks don't think too kindly of you stealing their slaves in Jamaica and along the Caribbean Coasts."

"Such lies."

"It's true, is it not, you've been smuggling slaves off the plantations and selling them for a fine profit these past few months?"

Jesse's mouth twisted, and changed the subject, "Perhaps it be you who have designs for Mr. Cooper's daughter, eh?"

"I haven't come to discuss who occupies my thoughts. Your illegal trade allowed you to acquire money to buy a ship. Now *that*, interests me, Jesse."

"Have you come to harp about African slaves? How hypocritical when Cooper's Landing has more than its share. Besides, if we're involved in slave trading, what be that to you? Hundreds of upstanding gentlemen in England and the West Indies be involved in slave trading. Where do you think they git their money? Why worry yourself about my profits?"

"It's not slave trade, Jesse. It's stealing. Slaves from each of the plantations have come up missing. A little here, a little there. Who would know something was amiss? Except that a few of our own slaves have come up missing as well. I'm not too fond of slave thievery here at Cooper's Landing."

Jesse paled. "Lies," he said. "I have nothing to do with that."

Cameron folded his arms. "Where do you sell those miserable wretches you've abducted? To Blissmore?"

"I swear I don't know."

"You lie." Cameron said.

Cameron's jaw shot out and the cords in his neck strained. "We've been watching you. I have men staked out around the ship yards. The smugglers you do business with sold the slaves. Slaves from the revolt. Men who believed they'd find freedom. Many of them have been treated far better here on the plantations in Riverbend than they'll ever be treated by their new owners."

Jesse's eyes narrowed and his stance changed. He looked like a man cornered by a pack of hyenas. "You have no proof."

"I could come up with enough evidence to see your neck in a noose where it belongs."

"This is absurd. I'd not knowingly sell slaves that belonged to other planters. I only deliver the slaves she– " Jesse stopped. His eyes searched the grounds beyond the barn door.

"Tia? We'll get to her in a moment. The man who runs your smuggling outfit. What's his name?"

Jesse's lips went white. "Why should I be tellin' you?"

Cameron grabbed the front of Jesse's shirt and pulled him close. "I know our slave Cuffee's been smuggled with the lot of them. The man's name. I want it."

"You harp like a woman, Bartholomew."

Cameron grabbed Jesse by the throat and slammed him against the stall. "His name!"

Jesse's face turned a deep red, but he shook his head.

Cameron increased pressure on his jugular vein.

Jesse started squirming, his eyes bulged.

"Give me his name and you live you filthy rat."

Jesse's knees weakened. "It be Morgan Blissmore."

"That's more like it." Cameron released his hold, then shoved Jesse backward.

Jesse buckled to the floor. He scrambled to his feet, eyes ablaze and his mouth twitched. "If anyone be askin' if I told you so, I'll deny it to my grave!"

"Morgan will be hanged. You know that."

"Still, he be the man."

"In cahoots with Tia?"

"That remains to be seen."

"If you are lying, I'll find out sooner or later, and I'll call you out, Jesse. You'll hang."

"I be speakin' the truth." For a moment all the fight went out of him. "I've not engaged in the business of my own doin'. I swear it. It's the merchant ship I be wantin'. I've a chance for respectability. Why plague me?"

Jesse paused and straightened as if he had the upper hand. He leaned toward Cameron. "You best be lookin' the other way, Cameron. Phillip won't be too pleased if you be diggin' up dirt on his woman." His eyes mocked. "Or the mother of his child, even if he don't recognize her as his own." He gestured with his chin. "It wouldn't do to tarnish the name of Cooper's Landin', now would it?"

Cameron straightened. "I'm needed elsewhere right now. But make no mistake. I'm watching you and that woman. It won't be me who'll tarnish Pip's good name here at the Landing. It'll be Tia."

Jesse's eyes narrowed and he licked his lips.

Cameron shoved a forefinger against Jesse's chest. "And another thing, Jesse Simmons. Keep your filthy hands off Pip's daughter. If I even so much as see you looking at her, so help me, I'll hang you myself!"

Jesse stepped backward and scowled.

Cameron scooped up his black wide-brimmed hat and left the stable, eating up the ground toward the front lawn.

He glanced over the crowd on the lawn and thought of the scene he'd walked into only moments earlier. He looked for Grace and found her near the circular drive talking with Camille.

"Excuse me, Camille. May I have a moment with Grace?"

"Certainly." She turned to Grace. "Lovely party."

Cameron took Grace's elbow and walked along beside her. For a moment they said nothing. Waiters walked slowly about, carrying gleaming trays filled with refreshments. He took a glass of punch and offered it to her.

"Are you all right?" He broke the silence.

"Yes." She fidgeted with the fan in her hand.

"I've warned Jesse to keep his hands off of you. Should he touch you again, I'll take stronger measures."

"Thank you." She glanced up at his features, dark and menacing. "Jesse said something that is quite troubling."

"How so?"

"Apparently some people here are under the presumption I'm masquerading as my father's daughter."

"And you were not prepared for this?"

"Honestly, I had hoped it wouldn't come up."

"There are some who will want more proof."

"And you?"

Cameron glanced out over the crowd of people who gathered on the lawn, then back to Grace. "Your father believes you are indeed his daughter. That's good enough for me."

"But you have your doubts."

"You appeared out of the blue."

Grace's temper rose. She changed the direction of their conversation.

"I overheard Tia talking to Jesse a few days ago."

Cameron stopped. "What did she say?"

"She told him to meet her that night at the stables."

"Did she say why?"

"They saw me. They gave each other a conspiratorial look and parted ways."

His hand closed tightly about her arm as his eyes searched hers. "Have you mentioned this to anyone else?"

"Of course not. You're hurting my arm."

He dropped his hand. "You mustn't mention this to anyone."

"I won't speak of it. Now if you'll excuse me, I want to speak with Mrs. Cavendish."

"Be careful, Grace."

She turned back. "Have you any idea what they're up to?"

"It's better not to say anything at the moment. But like I said, be careful."

Grace walked toward Mrs. Cavendish and noticed Jacqueline excuse herself from a small party. She crossed the lawn to where Cameron stood. He crooked his arm and the two went to stand in line at one of the refreshment tables.

The sight of Jacqueline on Cameron's arm irked Grace. But why should she care? Grace sensed eyes on her back. She glanced back to find Tia speaking with Minerva. They pinned their gazes on her and then turned and walked away.

Violet came toward Grace with arms outstretched. "You look marvelous." She embraced Grace and laughed softly as they examined each other's party gowns. Grace glanced back at the two servants. Though they'd walked away, Grace believed they gauged her every move.

Phillip excused himself and worked his way to his study. His chest tightened. Sweat beaded his brow. He shut the door and slumped into his chair, trying to breathe regularly. A heavy weight crushed his chest. Never before had he felt so consumed with pain. Was his heart getting worse? *Lean back in the chair*, he told himself. *Just rest. It'll pass.*

Grace left the small party at her table to change into her evening gown. When she lifted her foot to climb the marble stairs, she heard a familiar voice behind her.

"Is that you Grace?"

Grace stopped and turned around.

"Darling, you look absolutely stunning." Ruby Moore swept across the room with hands extended and sparkling with diamonds. Her skirts of brocaded emerald and satin shimmered in the light of the chandeliers. "How marvelous to see you."

"Mrs. Moore, how nice to see you again."

"Indeed." The older woman scrutinized her up and down. "You sly thing, I hadn't realized you were Cooper's daughter. How wonderful to meet again." She studied Grace's elegant gown with a direct stare.

"I'm happy you could make the party."

Mrs. Moore took Grace's arm as they proceeded up the stairs. When they neared the top, Grace looked over the banister to where

Cameron stood below. She let her eyes play over his features, chiseled in their perfection.

"Come along, dear," Mrs. More said as she directed Grace to the top of the landing.

Grace dragged her eyes off the handsome foreman and followed the older woman into the guest chamber.

A black-haired woman swept across the floor toward them. Her probing eyes studied Grace's features as though searching. "Ruby, how charming she looks. I never realized Phillip had a daughter." But the woman's eyebrows rose as she spoke, and she pursed her lips.

"You look just like Olivia, my dear. You are an eyeful. Best watch her tonight, Ruby. She'll have every man in Riverbend after her, including Cameron."

Ruby rolled her eyes toward the ceiling. "Grace, dear, this is Cecilia, my brother's wife, the lady of Briton Hall. Don't mind her. She does go on sometimes."

"Like I said," Cecilia skimmed her eyes over Grace. "She's already got the gents talking."

"I'm quite able to take care of myself, thank you," Grace said. *Was it true the gents were talking about her?* She flushed at the thought.

"Mother," came an exasperated voice across the room. Grace turned to find Jacqueline in the corner adding finishing touches to her hair. She seemed to fairly bristle.

Across the chamber, Claudia Borjeau stood near the French doors, alone. Their eyes met, and a knowing smile reached her mouth.

"There you are, dear." She claimed Grace from the hovering women. They moved out to the balcony. Alone with Claudia, Grace felt relief from the chamber full of curious eyes.

"You looked like you could use a rescue from the crocodiles in there." Kind eyes looked over her.

"You're very observant, Claudia. Truth to tell, I was at my wits end. Do I truly look incapable of looking out for myself?"

"Some of the ladies here in Riverbend have no couth and they'll go to any measure to start tongues flying. You handled yourself well. I'm here if you need me." She placed a soft hand on Grace's arm. "Shall we get you dressed for the evening ball?"

Grace and Claudia left the stuffy room for Grace's own chamber. Hedy went into full swing as she helped Grace out of the burnt-orange gown and into the pale blue crinoline. A half hour later the women stepped back into the guest rooms.

As soon as they entered, Jacqueline slapped her fan on the vanity. "How well do you know Mr. Bartholomew?"

Grace stopped. Remembering Claudia's warning, she chose her words cautiously. "Why hardly at all—"

"No matter," interrupted Jacqueline and turned her back. "I shouldn't be surprised if he spends a reasonable amount of time with you tonight. You're practically brother and sister."

Grace stiffened and her jaw tensed. The suggestion that she and Cameron were remotely related was absurd. Annoyed, she changed the subject. "When will you be sailing back to Charleston?"

Suddenly the room quieted. Kindra, dressed in the lavish, crimson-colored gown stood at the doorway. Her eyes met Grace's. Her dress shimmered as she moved into the room. Grace smiled. Kindra smiled back, shyly. It took a moment before Grace realized all eyes gaped at them. Not a sound, not a rustle.

"Your father would like you to join him in the ballroom." Kindra's eyes stayed on Grace.

For the first time since Grace had arrived at the Landing, she felt sorry for Kindra. They were sisters. They had the same blood. She felt as if an iron rod rammed down her back. It was one thing if she believed her sister looked scandalous in her fine clothes. But she'd not stand by and watch Kindra be humiliated among these women.

Grace laid her hand on Kindra's slender arm. "Tell him I'll only be a minute."

Kindra left the room. The whispers resumed. Grace swept out of the room, her temper rising. If no one else would champion her sister, she would.

TWENTY-SIX

GRACE NEARED THE alcove at the bottom of the stairs when a voice interrupted her thoughts.

"There you are," said a deep voice.

She glanced up inquisitively into the stranger's face. The man was clearly a sea captain, she observed from his attire.

The captain gave a slight bow. "I shall be highly disappointed if you deny me the first waltz." He was a handsome man with a thin mustache above his smiling lips.

"I'm sorry. Have we met, Captain?"

"I'm Captain Billy Picoult. My ship is *The Intrepid Sea Baron*. I work for your father." He peered down at her. "And you are the mysterious Grace Cooper. The missing link turned up?"

"I'd be pleased to oblige, Captain, but I believe I will save the first dance for my father."

Phillip walked up and stood between the captain and Grace. "If you don't mind, Billy, I will escort my daughter to the ballroom."

"By all means." He bowed low.

Grace took her father's arm and entered the ballroom where an orchestra filled the far corner of the room on a makeshift stand. They struck up a waltz. Phillip led Grace onto the floor in time to the music. A moment later, others joined them.

"You're right," Phillip said. "Claudia has impeccable taste. Your gown is beautiful."

"Thank you, Father She smiled, remembering her appearance in the mirror. The bell shape of her crinoline expanded toward the back, creating a floating train effect. The pale-blue gown made of satin-striped sheer lay over a silk taffeta underskirt. The overskirt was in the same satin-striped sheer. The scooped neckline revealed her porcelain skin and the single diamond solitaire necklace given to her by her father. She carried a fan in white-gloved hands.

For the first time that evening, Grace thought of her mother. If only Olivia could see how grand the Great House had been decorated in her daughter's honor. Phillip had the servants in a dither all week while they prepared the house for the ball. He wanted everything perfect for the grand occasion.

Grace twirled about the floor on her father's arm, glad to see the Borjeaux take to the floor. They soon disappeared among the throng of people. Grace concentrated again on her father, wishing her mother were with them.

"What are you thinking about, Grace?"

"Mother. I'd give anything if she could watch me dance with you. I missed getting to dance on your shoes on my tippy-toes when I was a child."

"And dance on my shoes you would have, had I known you existed, my dear. You look so very much like her. When I look at you in the soft lighting of the evening, I could swear . . ." " He paused. Tears touched the corner of his eye. "She told me she would love me forever."

His words brought bitter resentment she'd tried to bury inside of her. *How could you have betrayed her with Tia?* Grace looked away.

Cameron led Jacqueline onto the floor, near the polished edge. When Grace saw him swing Jacqueline in a graceful waltz, her eyes pooled, and the room blurred.

"Pardon me." A familiar voice cut in. "I'm late, and I've not danced with the guest of honor."

"Of course." Phillip handed Grace to Captain Harding.

"I hope you don't mind my cutting in," Drew said, keeping pace with the music.

"Not at all, Captain." Grace smiled. "You rescued me."

"Are you all right?" Drew asked. "You seem somewhat sullen."

"Yes, I'm fine. I'd just experienced a moment of melancholy. I have such mixed emotions."

Grace cast a glance at those not dancing. Camille held a glass of punch in her hand. Violet stood next to her chatting away.

Captain Harding led her through the waltz. No words were needed. Instead her ears filled with the pleasant din of voices and laughter, the tinkle of glasses, the music playing in the background, and the swish of gowns as beautiful women danced about the floor.

He waltzed well, and Grace was careful to follow his lead. "How is it going with your father?"

"On one hand, it is more than I wished for," Grace said. "On the other hand, it has been a bitter cup to swallow."

"Kindra?"

"Yes. And Tia."

"I thought as much." He tipped her chin up. "I warned you."

"You did. And I've only recently discovered what you were trying to tell me. Father doesn't know I know. I've not brought it up to him."

"You're angry and hurt, are you?" Drew swung Grace to the edge of the floor.

"I understand my father's keeping silent. I've only been here a short while."

"Are you going to tell him you know?"

"No, and I would appreciate it if you'd keep this to yourself."

"You have my word."

Grace glanced over Drew's shoulder and noticed Cameron standing apart from the merrymakers. He watched the dancers. Or was he watching *her*?

She couldn't be certain. He was a commanding figure, and she was not the only woman to notice him. A few heads turned, perhaps hoping he'd favor them with a waltz. Cameron glanced around the room with an austere air. *Where is Jacqueline?*

The music ended, and the captain led Grace to a chair.

The band struck up a new waltz.

"Excuse me, Miss Cooper. Would you give me the honor of the next dance?"

Grace peered up at the captain she'd met earlier. "I'd be obliged." She reached out her free hand and Captain Picoult led her onto the dance floor. He swept her away in a glorious waltz. The other dancers twirled around them.

"I'm one of twelve captains who work for your father."

"You said as much. I'm pleased to meet you, Captain."

"I count it a pleasure to dance with the belle of the ball."

"You're too kind, sir."

He guided her through a series of steps.

"Enough hoarding of the fair damsel, Billy," said a bold voice as the music ended and a third waltz began.

Grace recognized Jesse's voice. He swept her away before she could reply. "Why are you at the ball? Who let you in?" Grace looked around for help, her heart thumping.

"No offense, sweetheart, but you be owing me an apology since we were so rudely interrupted in the barn," he said with cantankerous smile.

"Jesse Simmons!" she breathed. "You'd best leave me alone."

He threw back his head and laughed heartily. "I be a determined man."

Grace stopped waltzing. "I'll not be dancing with the likes of you!"

Lifting her skirts and turning around, she collided into Cameron for the second time that day.

"Oh!" she cried, looking up in surprise.

"You have a habit of rushing into my arms, Grace. Are you trying to tell me something?" He gave her a cheeky grin.

"Of all the nerve!" She glared into his dark gray eyes. "I've done no such thing."

"Oh, but you have." He touched her lower back with his hand and led her off the dance floor. When he delivered her to an empty chair, his eyes smouldered. "I have an appointment with Jesse Simmons. Do me a favor and stay out of trouble. I can't be on hand every time you need rescuing."

"Why you—" She was at a loss for words and bit her bottom lip. "I do not need rescuing, and I'd be obliged if you'd find someone else to entertain you."

As elegantly as she could, she swept out of the ballroom and escaped up the marble stairs. When she reached her room, she slammed the door shut and paced the floor. How dare that old snake, Jesse Simmons, be so bold as to walk into the ballroom and presume to dance with her! And Cameron, how dare he presume she needed *his* assistance. She stopped. She needed to calm down. Grace opened the French doors and gazed out at the pale moonlight. It looked so peaceful. She let the stillness quiet her jangled nerves.

A knock came at her door. Was it Cameron? She stayed on the balcony and ignored it. The rap came again. Grace looked back and shook her head defiantly. She'd be glad when this evening was over. A third rap. Grace stood quietly, willing herself to stay put. She'd not give Cameron the upper hand. If she waited, he'd leave.

"Grace?" Camille's soft voice.

"Out here." Her shoulders slumped.

Camille joined her on the balcony. A few moments passed. Grace reached out to take Camille's soft hand.

"Are you all right?" Camille asked.

"I'm fine."

"Want to talk?"

Grace turned to the brunette. Their friendship helped more than Camille could know. "No."

Camille nodded. "Sometimes words are not needed."

Crickets sounded below and locusts made a chorus in the trees.

The night was alive with a harvest of noise, each creature making its own distinctive sound. And though they blended, Grace could pick out each one.

The moon shown down on them, and Grace thanked God for giving her a friend like Camille. "I feel better now. Thank you. We'd better go down to the ballroom."

As the guests cleared the floor and a soothing refrain filled the ballroom, Grace curtsied to the gentleman who had danced with her. She was leaving the floor when a strong hand reached for her.

"Permit me." Cameron held Grace's arm.

"If you'll excuse me, Cameron—" He did not release her.

"The guests are staring at us. I think it best if you honor me with a dance."

She looked away from the potent dark eyes and gave a curtsy. "As you wish."

Don't think about how this feels, she told herself as his arms encircled her.

If only she could get lost in the music and the shimmering chandeliers lighting the ballroom, but the look on his face made that impossible. For all the world she had no way of knowing what went through his mind.

Grace was aware of guarded glances as they waltzed.

"I expected Jackson Gifford to come to your rescue," Cameron said.

"Why is that?"

"He's had his eye on you all evening."

"I wasn't aware of it."

"I was."

Grace said nothing, concentrating on her steps.

"As for my intervention with Jesse Simmons," he said lightly, "I couldn't endure seeing you cast into the lion's den."

"I appreciate your concern for my safety, Cameron, but I'll not allow myself to be trapped by him, nor by an arrogant gentleman who'd make sport of my folly."

He laughed quietly. "You certainly are Pip's daughter. You're much like him, you know."

She stiffened.

"That was a compliment. I happen to think well of your father."

She struggled to keep her poise. More than anything she wanted to be with Cameron, yet her instincts told her to run. Wasn't he practically engaged to Jacqueline?

His fingers tightened around her waist.

"Would you like a breath of air? Don't refuse," he said, "I need it." He steered Grace through the watching guests, out onto the portico and down a flight of steps.

Holding her skirts to keep from tripping, Grace cast a frantic glance ahead into the fragrant shadows. "Cameron, I can't disappear with you into the gardens. What will the guests say? It isn't proper."

"You're quite safe."

"From you or gossipy tongues?"

He gave her an amused smile. "I knew if we stayed in the ballroom another moment, Jacqueline would have interrupted. I wanted to have a word with you."

"What could you possibly need to say to me out here that you couldn't say inside?"

"Just for once, Grace, be still." He cupped her chin toward him.

Her heart hammered in her ears. The hand that tilted her face was warm. She wanted this. She wanted to feel his lips on hers.

He bent his head toward her. Their lips brushed. But before he could fully claim her lips, she moved out of his hold, her face aflame, her eyes wide.

"Are you out of your mind?" She stepped back.

"What you say is true. I'm out of my mind in love with you." He encircled his arms around her tiny waist. "I believe you've cast a spell on me." She could feel his breath on her cheek.

It seemed an eternity that time stood still. She waited motionless in his embrace. She felt his arms grow stiff. He let her go and stepped back. "I can see you don't share the same feelings as I do. My apology." He bowed ever so slightly.

She shook her head. "You're wrong. I do share the same feelings. It's just that—"

"My mistake." He took another step back, regret showing in his eyes.

"Cameron—"

"I'll escort you back to the ballroom."

The glow of the ballroom lit the garden. As they moved toward that light now, disappointment washed over Grace. She wanted to deny his accusation that she didn't care. She wanted to turn back to the privacy of the garden, where the fragrance of night flowers encompassed them in their luscious scent. But she didn't resist when he moved her forward.

They returned in silence. Feeling a lump in her throat and confusion flood over her, Grace relented. When they entered the ballroom, his strong hand guided the small of her back, his mouth grim.

Jacqueline and Violet met them at the doors. Jacqueline's eyes narrowed. "Cameron! Grace!"

"Hold your tongue, Jackie. It's not what you think."

Grace tore herself from Cameron, pushing between the Moore sisters. She wove through the throng of dancers to the hallway outside of the ballroom. Once away from the music, the people, and the noise of laughter, she leaned against the wall and took a deep breath. Tears smarted her eyes.

He'd only wanted one simple kiss. Why had she resisted? Deep down, she wanted him to kiss her. She'd fought that wild desire to be near him. Would he try again? Probably not. She gave a desolate groan and pushed away from the wall. She wanted nothing more than to be alone. To sink into bed in her misery. How much longer before the ball was over?

"Grace?" The voice was her father's.

She looked away.

"Grace?" He turned her tear-streaked face to him.

"Are you all right, honey?"

She nodded as he shoved a white handkerchief into her hand. She dabbed the tears from her face.

"Oh, Father," she sighed. "This is the most beautiful ball I have ever attended."

"But?"

"Cameron . . . he . . . I." Her lips quivered. She couldn't go on. "I'm not sure what I want."

"There's plenty of time to figure out what you want, dear. There's no hurry. Now go upstairs and freshen up." Tenderness showed in his eyes. "You'll be all right by morning." He kissed her forehead.

All at once she clung to him and said, "Father, I'm so glad I found you."

"So am I, my daughter. So am I."

TWENTY-SEVEN

THE DAYS TOOK on a pattern at Cooper's Landing. Early mornings were spent on Bible devotions. After breakfast, Grace took her daily walk around the plantation. She loved these walks, for each day had its own unexpected event. While some slaves had grown accustomed to seeing Grace and waved at her, others still gawked in curiosity. Numerous rumors had gone around about the white woman. Grace hoped that by now they understood she was indeed the plantation owner's daughter.

She spent the afternoons riding Dandy out to the cane fields or to the river. Cameron had warned her about the boa constrictors. They were prevalent in the cane fields, as they fed on rodents who burrowed underground, and ran rampant through the thick cane stalks.

Often she carried her sketch pad and drew scenery that appealed to her. The world was full of color here in Jamaica. Parrots splashed with an array of reds, yellows, and blues flew overhead and landed on branches to watch her tread through the tropical brush on the chestnut mare.

Grace found her own paradise near the bank of the river, secluded among the tropical plants. A large boulder sat some ten feet away from the rushing water. Small boulders protruded into the river. The flat rock was a perfect platform for sitting and drawing the afternoon away.

She delighted at the sound of the water splashing down between the wide expanse of banks. If she was lucky, a ground squirrel would stop a short distance away to watch her with curiosity, it's tail flitting and feet ready to flee. She'd quickly sketch the creature. Her pad overflowed with drawings of scenes here in her secret hideaway. Bullfrogs, dragonflies, and birds of every description crossed her path. Her sketch pad became her visual diary of the days spent on the Landing.

Some mornings, Grace brought the rapier from the library to her sitting room. Not sure how the others would take to her sport of fencing, she hid the foil in the folds of her day dress and hurried to her bedchamber. Once inside, she brought out the rapier and swiped the air, flicking her wrist, making the blade hiss. She liked the feel of the rapier's long, thin, flexible blade. If only Josie were here, they'd spend the afternoon practicing the skill of sword fighting.

Late afternoons were not so easily spent. After a nap she would, on some days, write a letter to her Aunt Katy or cousin Josie. In time, she took up needlepoint to keep her hands busy.

On several occasions Phillip called Grace into the library, where he smoked his pipe and told her stories of how he came to own Cooper's Landing. She learned of his adventures across the seas and asked many questions. What were the islands like? How did he come to know Agnes Cavendish? She cherished the hours they spent alone, he in the leather chair, and she in the overstuffed settee.

Grace hadn't seen much of Cameron in the days following the ball. Was he avoiding her? Had he regretted their rendezvous in the garden? It was time for harvesting the sugar on a greater scale. The field hands moved feverishly to get the cane stalks into the sugar mill, while the slaves in the boiling houses worked nonstop to get the hogshead filled with the crude sugar. Grace hoped Cameron's involvement with the sugar process was the reason she hadn't seen him of late.

Before the ball, Cameron had told her, "Hurricane season is on its way. The winds alone can be harsh. We've got to get the field hands to bring in the end-of-the-year crops to transport to the wharf's warehouses." He'd hoped to sell the crop at a good price. They only had a month or two at best to speed up the sugar process. Cameron left the house before the sun rose and often didn't return until after the dinner hour.

One afternoon Zeek appeared while Grace sat in the drawing room, needle in hand, working on an embroidery design for a pillowcase. He held a silver tray with an envelope on it.

"The courier arrived with two letters, Miss Coopah."

She lifted the envelopes from the silver tray. "Thank you."

He left as silently as he appeared. She glanced at the return address of the first letter. "Aunt Katy!" She quickly slit the envelope open and pored over the letter.

> My Dearest Grace,
>
> Your letters have brought solace to my soul. For the first two weeks after you sailed away, I could hardly sleep a wink. I prayed every day for your safety and finally had to put your sweet soul in the hands of the Master.
>
> We were thrilled to read that your adventure on the ship was grand. We enjoyed every detail you wrote in your letters. And to think, you actually got to take the wheel at the helm. You're a brave girl. Josie and I had wondered how you felt when you set foot on Jamaican soil. Your description of the multitudes of colors in the marketplace sounds fascinating.
>
> I apologize for taking so long to respond. We've been helping your grandfather tend the store and have been taking applications for a new clerk for the apothecary shop. At long last, Mr. Perry has been hired. He's been educated as a pharmacist and seems a trustworthy man. If need be, I could trust him to work

the shop should I have to leave for any length of time.

Grace smiled. *Is that a hint?*

Have you found your purse and locket? We're concerned someone in the house is stealing your personal items. Be watchful, Grace. You haven't been at Cooper's Landing long enough to truly trust those people in the Great House. I dearly wish I were there to watch out for you.

Me, too.

You said you've learned disturbing news. I was disappointed that you chose not to disclose it in the letter. Please let us know in your next post.

All is well here. Your grandparents send their love. Josie is going to send her own letter. Look for it to come soon.

I sorely miss you and your smiling face,

Yours lovingly,

Aunt Katy

Grace wiped tears from her face. She missed Aunt Katy and Josie fiercely. She folded the letter and put it back in the envelope. She picked up the second letter. The return address was from Ethan Boyd.

She hesitated before she slit open the envelope. The note was short, but the message was clear. He insisted she return to Charleston. If she didn't, he'd come for her. He implied she had plenty of time to adjust to her mother's passing. It was time for them to get on with their lives. The last line read, "I won't take no for an answer," and it was signed, "Yours forever, Ethan Boyd."

Grace glared at the letter before placing it back in the envelope. Would he never give up? She wouldn't reply. That should send a clear message to Ethan that she was not interested in returning to Charleston.

Two days later after supper, Phillip summoned Cameron, Grace, and the household staff. One by one, members of the Great House filed into the drawing room.

Grace sat on the end of the sofa, curious. Why had she and Cameron been summoned for what seemed an official meeting? She glanced at Cameron, his profile somber. She willed him to look her way. When he did, his expression was indifferent. She leaned against the sofa and waited, for what, she didn't know.

Tia sat in the overstuffed chair next to Phillip, her thin brows arched as she waited. Kindra stood with Penny and the rest of the servants, her hands folded before her.

"I've gathered you all together to make an announcement," Phillip said. "As you may already know, Grace has agreed to live here at Cooper's Landing."

Nods and murmurs answered him.

"From this day forward, Grace will relieve Tia as headmistress of this house. She'll also take on some of the duties Camp has been assigned, chiefly the bookkeeping. If you've questions or need counsel, it is Grace from whom you'll seek advice. She will confer with Cameron or myself until she is familiar with all the goings-on here at the plantation.

"As most of you know, my health has been a great concern in the past months. I don't know how much longer I have with you. It will take a great burden off my mind knowing my daughter is here to take over." His look was firm. "She'll hold this duty whether I'm home or abroad."

Grace's mind raced. What did he mean by health issues? Why

would he declare this proclamation before he'd spoken to her? Furthermore, if his health was bad, why would he risk going out to sea? Grace glanced at her father, then at Cameron, then back to her father. She dared not look at Tia. Thoughts continued to reel in her head. She wanted to halt the meeting. She wanted to ask her father what illness ailed him that he didn't have long to live?

An ominous silence prevailed. Grace stole a glance at Tia, whose eyes bored into hers. Anger penetrated from the tigress as Tia sat like stone in her chair. Minerva's mouth formed a thin line as she stared fiercely at Grace.

Cameron's expression revealed nothing. Grace held her composure and waited.

Phillip dismissed everyone except Cameron and Grace. The servants left quietly, their curious eyes glancing back at Grace.

Tia left the room with her back straight and her head held high. She didn't look at Grace, but Grace sensed dark tension emanating throughout the room.

Moments later, she and Cameron sat alone with Phillip.

He glanced at Cameron. "I want you to show Grace the accounting books. I don't know of any better way for her to get the feel of running things around here than to see the checks and balances of this operation. "

"Yes, sir," Cameron said, sullen.

Grace watched Cameron's eyes smoulder.

"You're still in charge of the field and outbuilding ledgers for accountability of the crops and sugar processing, Camp."

Cameron nodded, his lips a thin line.

Phillip turned to Grace. "I don't think you need anyone to show you how to run a house."

Grace squirmed inwardly, but outwardly she held her composure. "Honestly, Father, I wasn't the one who ran our home. I am, however, a quick learner."

"I'm sure you are. You're a Cooper."

Grace smiled. "I'll speak with each of the servants. I'm sure it won't be a problem."

"Good. With these matters settled, I can rest."

Grace wanted to ask him about his illness, but waited.

"And Grace," he interrupted her thoughts. "Come see me in the morning. I've another matter to discuss with you in private."

"Yes, Father. I will."

Phillip rang the bell and the butler appeared. "I'm ready to retire to my room."

Zeek stood next to the chair as he rose. Phillip nodded to the butler. "I can make it up the stairs, but I need you to come along and prepare my room."

"Of course."

Grace wanted to vacate the room as well. She needed to think, to rationalize her father's decision for giving her all this responsibility.

Phillip stopped midway in his tracks, as if he read their thoughts. "Fate has brought you here, my dear. At first I didn't know why you'd come." His green eyes lit up. "But now I do. You're a Cooper. Your heart belongs here."

Cameron opened the screen door, shedding light across the wooden floorboards of the front porch, and out to the circular drive. Grace stood near the rail, looking over the lawn where a full moon cast shadows beyond the tropical foliage. She appeared out of sorts.

"Nice evening, isn't it?" Cameron kept his voice strong, deep timbered.

"Yes, it is." She leaned against the white pillar behind her.

Cameron glanced at the moon, then at Grace. Her auburn curls caught the rays of the hazy light. He didn't know when it happened, but she'd worked her way into his every waking moment. He'd tried to will her out of his mind, but it didn't work. Up till now, he'd known what he wanted. Now he wasn't sure.

"A good deal has happened in a short time, has it not?"

"Yes, it has. I've a mind to talk to my father about that. I believe he's moving too fast for my peace of mind."

"Mine too." Cameron cleared his throat as he walked to the opposite side of the porch and leaned against the pillar facing her. "We have some things we need to clear up."

"Such as?"

"How you plan to run things around here, given half of the estate is mine." He waited for her reaction. "Your father and I are partners here at Cooper's Landing. As a rule, we usually discuss changes that need to be made. Now that you've arrived, he's forgotten protocol."

Grace darted a look at him and frowned.

Cameron mused. "Can't say that I blame him for being overzealous since you've showed up." He pushed away from the pillar and rubbed a rough hand over his face. "It appears he's trying to make up for twenty years in a short time." He glanced over at Grace. Her expression had blanched. Had she heard a thing he'd said at all?

For a stunned moment, Grace grew silent. Then she echoed, "My father's partner?"

"Ahhh." Amusement tugged at the corner of Cameron's mouth. "I can see there are more surprises in store for you. Yes, your father offered to sell me half interest in the estate four years ago. I accepted. It's been a satisfactory arrangement for both of us."

"I see." Grace suddenly saw more than he'd related to her. She saw how foolish she'd been to abandon the life she'd known in Charleston on the strength of a bundle of old letters. How could she plan a future here if her father had sold half-interest of the Landing to Cameron? She knew nothing about running a sugar plantation. Could she trust this man to be transparent with her? Surely it'd never work for the two of them to share the land some day.

She bit her bottom lip until she tasted blood. Her eyes jumped to his. "And you plan to stay at Cooper's Landing indefinitely?"

"Yes." He stood to full height. "Up till now there's never been any thought of anyone else running the Landing. It was just your father and I."

"My coming has changed all that."

"Was that the plan?"

Grace bristled. "No, Cameron. My goal was to meet my father. I accomplished that."

"And now?"

"I'll sail back to Charleston."

"Good. You won't be sorry." He let down his guard.

"I'm not so sure," Grace bristled. "It seems to me, you're in an awful hurry to get rid of me."

"You have keen insight, Miss Cooper. I plead guilty to your accusation." Cameron held up his hands as if a gun were pointed at his chest.

Grace lifted her chin, her heart pounding wildly. She clutched her skirt and stepped up to him at arm's length. "At least you've the decency to admit it." She looked out over the lawn, then back to him. "I said I'm going home, but I didn't say when. Goodnight, Mr. Bartholomew."

She grabbed her skirt with one hand and opened the screen door with the other. As she stepped over the threshold, she heard Cameron's last reply.

"The name's Cameron, Miss Cooper. Call me, Cameron."

Out of the corner of her eye, she watched her father enter his study. Had he been listening to their conversation? No matter. She'd had just about all she could put up with. Grace wanted nothing more than to put the day behind her. In the morning, she'd prepare for her journey back to Charleston, where she didn't have to look over her shoulder and stay one step ahead.

When she looked back, Cameron hadn't moved. He watched her with a steady gaze. "By the way, I'm just as surprised about my father's rash announcement as everyone else, Cameron." She shrugged. "If I stayed, I have a feeling I'd get the hang of things around here really soon."

"I don't doubt that." Cameron tipped his wide straw hat and turned toward the porch steps. He took the steps two at a time and disappeared into the night.

Later that night, Grace lay in her bed and stared at the ceiling. The weight of her father's decision seemed monumental. Did he believe she had the ability to help run this plantation? She'd never run anything in her life, much less a sugar estate. She kicked her blankets off and pulled the cool sheet up to her chin. If her father thought he could depend on her, she wouldn't let him down. Charleston could wait.

That settled, she turned on her side facing the French doors, where the tall palm trees cast long shadows across the floor. Sometime in the night she heard Cameron's bedchamber door close.

Life had a way of dealing out a new hand, like a deck of cards. Before you picked up the hand and viewed its contents, you were already destined to win or lose. She'd know in a few days how this would affect her. Either way, she would face it head on.

TWENTY-EIGHT

IN THE MORNING, Phillip summoned Grace to his sitting room. Before he could get to why he sent for her, she pummeled him with questions.

"Father," Grace paced the floor. "I don't know where you got the idea I'm capable of running this house or any part of Cooper's Landing. I've only worked in my grandfather's general store stocking shelves and bookkeeping. And furthermore, I've only been here a mere few weeks. I know nothing about sugar farms."

Phillip looked as if he was anxious to settle this aggravation with Grace.

After wearing a path on the floor, Grace finally sat down on the plush sofa.

"My dear, I've had several warnings that my heart is not good. Each time, I think it will be the last. But truth to tell, I can't deny I've a life-threatening problem. My surgeon has warned me that there's nothing he can do."

Grace gazed at her father, her throat thick. "I've only just found you. I can't lose you now." She flew across the room, laid her head on his lap, and wept.

"I didn't choose to be ill, my dear. I, too, want many more years with you. You've become such a delight to me." He patted Grace's shoulder and brushed his hand across her curls. "We must make the most of the time we have left. And we will indeed."

Grace could not control her weeping.

"Please don't cry. I've made the decision to put you in control of the house, because one day this will all be yours. You must learn how to handle things here at the Landing. I'm doing you a service, dear." He lifted her head and cupped her tear-stained face in his hands. "I believe I have time left for us to have a good many days, weeks, maybe months together. I want to see you smile, dear."

She flung her arms around his neck. "Promise me you won't leave me. Promise me."

Grace took the white handkerchief her father thrust into her shaking hand and blew her nose. She sat on the sofa. With a quivering voice she said, "I will do whatever you ask."

"Now that's my girl. Let's get a few things understood." For the next forty-five minutes, Phillip instructed his daughter in what he desired for her to do.

Pip spent the next hour with Cameron. They discussed his decision to move Grace into authority at the Landing. "I want her to learn how to handle this operation. We'll start slowly. As partner, you own fifty percent of the operation. It's only reasonable to give her a fair shake. I need your word you'll help me in this."

"Of course, Pip," Cameron said, his face flushed. He paused before he said, "You haven't played fair with me. I understood your health had improved."

"I thought that as well. I wanted to believe it. But I had another attack before the ball." He cleared his throat. "I'm trying to make the transition easy for you two."

"And Tia?"

"I don't have to tell you she'll make things difficult." He paused. "I've known for some time she's up to something. I don't know what it is. She has distanced herself from me these past months, long before

Grace arrived."

"And Kindra?"

"I don't have an answer to that." He frowned. "I'll think of something. Let it be for now."

Cameron nodded. When it came to Kindra, Phillip was always at a loss for words. Cameron rubbed his knees with his calloused palms and stood. "Is that all?"

Pip gave Cameron a hard look. "I'm counting on you, Cameron. Don't let me down."

Cameron stood and looked at Phillip. "I've been avoiding this, but we must talk," Cameron said.

"How so?"

"Tia. You have your suspicions about her."

"Yes, I do."

"Well, Sir, they well founded."

"What is it, Cameron, speak up."

Cameron spent the next half hour telling Phillip all he knew. He could no longer protect Phillip from the devious ploys of the tigress. When he finished, he watched Phillip's face strain. He looked worn out.

"I'm sorry, Pip. But I thought you should know."

"That blasted Morgan Blissmore! How did he and Tia become comrades in this evil display of thievery?"

"I don't know, Pip. I'm still trying to get to the bottom of this myself. We can't prove anything yet. We've got to catch them red-handed."

"When you do, I want to be the first to know."

"You've got it, Pip."

Phillip walked into his study the next morning and shut the door. What with the sugar estate and the merchant shipping business, bookkeeping was the mainstay of it all. It desperately needed his attention. From the time his heart began giving him trouble, much of the accounting had gone neglected. His mind wasn't working right. When his newfound daughter arrived at the house, it had changed his routine.

Piles of papers lay on every surface. Cameron kept the logs on the sugar processing, then turned those figures over to him. His reports were figured for profit and loss statements.

There was also the matter of the tobacco industry in Barbados, the venture he hadn't disclosed to Cameron. He spent the last five years experimenting in tobacco. The last two years had yielded high returns on this island's investments, which now held a full-fledged plantation with hired hands running it. On his last venture out to sea, he'd spent much-needed time in Barbados observing the operation.

Yes, it was time Grace took over the bookkeeping. She had a level head on her shoulders. She had the ability to handle the work. He would insist, however, on keeping the books on the tobacco investment himself. He wasn't ready to disclose this project at the moment. With this in mind, he pushed aside the paperwork dealing with the sugar estate and concentrated on the tobacco ventures.

The following afternoon, Grace and her father sat in his study.

"You said you handled the books for your grandfather," Phillip said.

"Yes, I did. Not to be prideful, but I'm good with numbers and accounting."

"Who's doing the books for your grandfather now, may I ask?"

"My cousin Josie. I trained her before I left Charleston."

"Cameron and I leave for Barbados in a week. We'll be gone five to six weeks. I'd like to show you the books before we leave. Then you can file these papers . . ." He waved his hand over the conglomeration .

. . "and continue the books while we're gone."

"You're leaving me in charge of the Landing alone?"

"Yes, dear. You can do it."

Grace glanced at the office that was in shambles. Her brows lifted.

"You have complete control of putting this office back in order. Use your own discretion." He gave a wary grin.

Grace saw she was not the only one who had her doubts. Was this a test?

"The files are in order. That'll help to some degree. If I have trouble finding papers when I get back, you'll be able to show me where you've put them. Agreed?"

Grace reluctantly nodded her head. She never dreamed her father's study would be turned over to her so quickly.

"You can do this, my dear. I'm counting on you."

"I'll do my best." She swallowed.

"I'm sure you will."

An hour later a velvet haze settled in the office. Pip sat in the leather chair, in front of the desk talking to Cameron. "I've read in the newspaper there's going to be a convention in Barbados regarding the sugar industry. I want to be there. I want you there, too. I expect we'll be gone five weeks, maybe six." He puffed on his pipe and squinted at Cameron.

This was the first time Pip had offered to take Cameron on a business trip. Usually one of them needed to be on the plantation to keep things running smoothly.

"Who'll keep an eye on the estate?" Cameron's dark eyebrows lifted, and then it dawned on him. "You don't think your daughter is up to it, do you?" He frowned.

"As a matter of fact, I do." Pip smiled. "Denzel will be here. We'll put him in charge of the field hands and outbuilding operations. It'll be good for Grace to have the experience of watching the place without us."

Cameron frowned. "I don't know, Pip. She's young. You said we'd be there to help Grace learn."

"That was before I learned about this convention. Sales are down in the sugar industry. We both need to be at that meeting. Whatever news we attain to up our sales will benefit us all."

"Why don't you stay, Pip. I'll go and bring back what I learn?"

"I want to go, Son."

"You're being a stubborn old mule. Your heart is not good. And she needs you. Besides, the servants may take advantage of her, especially Tia."

"I've already thought of that. I'll talk to Tia before we leave. Grace will do fine." He set his pipe in the ashtray. "I've already talked to her about doing the books. It won't be too soon for me to turn this over to her."

Cameron stood. "I disagree. I don't think she's ready."

It had been three days since her father and Cameron sailed for Barbados. The weight of the plantation was now on her shoulders. Grace was relieved to know Denzel was in charge of the field hands and the outdoor operations. There was added relief in knowing she could call on Denzel, if need be.

Grace rolled up her sleeves and walked into the study. Her father's office was a clutter of papers—ship's specifications, merchant orders, letters, invoices, correspondence, pamphlets, broad sheets, sailing manifests, notes, and contracts. She held her breath as she looked at the menagerie of stacked papers.

He knows where everything is without looking, thought Grace, *but how am I to make sense of all of this?* She bent over the first stack of papers.

It took Grace the better part of a week to organize the office, stopping only for brief meals and a few words with Dinah.

"I don't see how you be wantin' to do this," Dinah said, as she brought in a small plate of cold cheese and fruit to Grace, who'd not left the study since the first break of dawn.

"I want to help my father, Dinah. And besides, no one else could be concerned with the Landing's holdings." She held a slim stack of papers and aligned them by tapping them on the desktop. "I want to give Father peace of mind that his office is in order."

"What you be needing is a breath of fresh air. You be cooped up in this study too many hours."

Grace smiled, and returned to the stack of correspondence dealing with the latest voyage of the *Mindingo*.

"Thank you for lunch," she said as Dinah prepared to leave the room. "I'll be fine."

The following morning Grace entered the library, intending to return a few books to the shelves. She noted the room needed dusting. Were the servants lenient with housework because the men were away?

She found the servants in the kitchen standing in a circle talking. They jumped when she entered the kitchen. "Good Morning, Miss Cooper," Dinah said. The other servants glanced at her and shuffled.

Grace pointed to Gemma and Penny. "I want you two to follow me. And the rest of you best get to your assigned post and back to work."

The servants glanced at each other.

"Now!"

In a matter of seconds, the cooks turned to kneading bread and placing biscuits in the oven. Minerva went upstairs, her face hard. Penny and Gemma followed Grace down the center hall to the library.

Grace ran her forefinger along a bookshelf. She turned it up for them to see the film of dust covering her fingertip. She arched an eyebrow. "Do you want Master Cooper to find his library in this condition?"

"No, Missy. We sure don't."

"Then I suggest you do something about it." She gave them a stern look.

Gemma and Penny set to work with dusters and mops cleaning the floor, dusting the shelves, and polishing the brass handles of the elegant cabinet in the corner. As Grace filed correspondence and made neat stacks of the shipping manifests, she stepped out to the hallway and peered into the library. The two servants glanced at her as they shined the windows of the French doors.

At noon, Dinah poked her head into the study to inquire if Grace would be stopping work for a midday meal.

Grace pushed away a wisp of hair that escaped from the emerald ribbon at her neck and tucked the strand behind her ear. She fanned her face with a contract for a new shipment of sugar bound for the Americas. She noticed the ink stains on her writing finger. Maybe she had spent too much time in the office.

"How long you gonna sit in this stuffy room, honey chile? You should git out into the countryside with that sketchpad of yours." Dinah wagged a finger at her.

Grace sat back in her father's leather chair and steeped her fingers. "I have a house to run."

"Alla this be sittin' right here for you when you git back. Now you best find some other means to fill your day," Dinah urged. "You be wastin' away."

Grace sighed. "All right. I've one more sheet of paper to file and then I'll take your advice."

"Bout time, Missy." Dinah walked out of the study with her shoulders straight and her head held high.

Grace knew Dinah had genuine concern for her. Their affection had grown in the past few weeks. She shook her head and filed the last sheet of paper. Then she glanced at the room and smiled. "Well done."

Grace slipped out of the office with a feeling of accomplishment. She stopped in the library. The servants were nowhere to be seen, but the room smelled of fresh polish and the library fairly shone. Sounds from the kitchen meant busy hands.

Well you've met your first challenge, and you handled it just fine.

Grace headed toward the kitchen and nearly collided into Minerva. The house servant held an armload of towels and glared. Neither moved. Grace stood her ground, appalled that Minerva held her ground as well. Grace's heart thundered in her chest.

"Step aside, Minerva."

Minerva stepped back and started around her. Her elbow brushed against Grace's arm as she did. Grace took a step back and the hackles on her neck raised. "Minerva!"

The dark woman having nearly set foot on the first step of the stairway, turned, brows raised.

"Have you nothing to say?" Grace pursed her lips.

"Oh. Excuse me, Ma'am." She turned and walked briskly up the stairs.

Grace frowned. It was time for a reckoning day with that feline.

TWENTY-NINE

THE WEEKS DRAGGED by. Grace wished for her father's return. But more than that, she missed seeing Cameron's face at the Landing. How long before the two men returned?

Clad in her riding dress with sketchbook tucked firmly under her arm, Grace descended the marble stairs. Kindra reached the front door ahead of her. She peered back. Grace lifted a hand to wave before Kindra slipped out the door and closed it behind her.

Grace hummed a tune when she breezed into the dining room and over to the sideboard. A large bowl sat centered on its polished surface, filled with an assortment of fruit. She found a juicy, red apple and polished it with her sleeve.

Still humming, she slipped into the kitchen where a trio of heads looked up. "Now that be what I'm talkin' about, Missy. You headin' out to that fine horse of yours." Dinah chuckled in her deep tone, sweet as molasses.

Grace held up an apple in one hand and her sketch pad in the other. "I'm riding out to the river if anyone needs me."

The three cooks smiled. "About time you crawled outta that office." Gemma spoke for the group.

Grace shaded her eyes from the bright sun and noticed Kindra standing at the entrance to the sugar mill house. Denzel strode up and pulled her into the shadows. Grace squinted her eyes and saw Denzel take Kindra into his arms and embrace her with a long kiss. Grace frowned. She hadn't noticed the two were lovers. Just when she began to think of Kindra as a sister, reality struck her. Kindra's world was black. She loved a black man. In irritation she continued toward the stable where the chestnut mare waited for her.

A baby wailed somewhere in the distance. Grace walked down the lane and strained her ears to listen. It came again, the frantic wailing of an infant. She neared the gate to the shanties and listened to the incessant cry.

Curious, Grace opened the gate and stepped for the first time into the slave district. She had been by the shanties, but never had she stepped into their territory before. A worn path led to each of the homes. Ten huts stood in each row, eight rows deep.

She walked past a row of shanties toward the sound of the distressed infant. The wails grew louder when she neared the fourth row. Grace rounded the corner, aware of the curious African women who watched her. Having found the small hut where the baby howled, Grace lifted a hand to knock. The door suddenly flew open. Tia glared down at her.

"What business do you have with my niece?"

"I heard the baby crying . . ."

"Leave my people alone. Go back to the house where you belong. You're not wanted here."

Grace nearly faltered, yet she stood her ground. "You've forgotten. My father has put me in charge while he is gone. If one of our people is having a problem or is endangered, I have every right to intervene." Grace glared back at the black tigress.

Tia brushed past. "No white woman belongs near these shanties, with or without the Master's permission." Chin set hard and her mouth clamped shut, Tia stormed away from the small hut.

Grace drew in a deep breath, lifted her skirts and stepped into the shanty. The dimness blinded her, and for a moment she stood without moving, waiting for her eyes to adjust. The smell of hemp and cane filled the hut. Grace turned to see the mother who shrank back holding her infant against her bosom.

Grace reached out and touched the infant's forehead. The baby's body felt hot. She looked around the small room. An oval wash pan filled with water sat on a long board at the side of the room. She pulled the baby out of the fearful mother's arms, all the while crooning softly. "It's all right, little one."

The mother cried, chanting words Grace couldn't understand. She pulled on Grace's arm reaching for the infant, but Grace elbowed her back and laid the baby on the table in the middle of the room. She pulled the swaddling clothes from the screaming child and lifted her to her shoulder. "Now, now," she crooned. "Please don't cry. We're going to try to get your fever down."

She carried the naked infant to the pan and carefully submerged it into the lukewarm water, first one tiny foot, then the other. The baby wailed as she scooped water over its belly and thin legs. She remembered her mother doing this to a neighbor's baby when she was a child. It brought the fever down.

Grace gazed out the door to see a group of women standing by as she crooned to the baby while cooling the infant's fever. Minutes went by as the infant girl kicked and squalled in the tepid water. The mother stopped tugging on Grace's arm, and the wailing subsided as the infant shuddered.

The shanty grew quiet. The infant kicked the water, seeming to enjoy the soothing coolness. The mother stood beside Grace, tears streaming down her cheeks, leaving a light trail.

"Send someone for the doctor." Grace continued to gently pour water over the infant.

"The doctor no see baby."

"He'll see *this* baby." Grace went to the door of the shanty and looked over the curious crowd of women and children. "Someone go after the doctor. Tell him the planter's daughter sent for him."

A young black boy broke away from the crowd and set off at a run. Ten minutes later, a tall African man stood in the doorway, his immense frame shutting out the afternoon sunlight. "I'm Doctor Moab, Miss."

"Thank God you came." Grace finished wrapping a large cloth around the baby. "This baby is burning up. She needs your attention."

"I don't be working with the infants, Missy." He shook his head adamantly.

"Why not?"

"It not what I do. I care for cuts and wounds. No babies."

"Well, you *will* care for this infant. Surely there is something you can do."

She could see the muscles in his jaw working. "I try." He glanced warily about him. "Bring baby to the hospital."

Grace glanced at the mother. "Do as he says."

The mother nodded, her black eyes shining.

Grace picked up her sketch pad and turned to leave.

The mother timidly tugged on Grace's shoulder. When she turned around the mother held up a woven doll made out of the cane grass. "I make. You keep."

Grace put a hand up. "No thank you." She'd heard many of these people believed in witchcraft and voodoo magic.

"You keep," the mother persisted. Grace accepted the gift against her better judgment. She smiled again at the grateful mother.

The crowd backed away as the doctor, mother, and baby moved into the dirt yard. The small crowd followed them to the front gate and watched as the infant was carried toward the plantation's hospital behind the sugar mill.

Grace spun around to face the women standing near the fence. "The baby will be all right."

Bright teeth shown as the slave women smiled at Grace. "Be all right," one of the women said.

As Grace glanced back toward the mother and infant following the doctor, she stopped. Tia slipped into the sugar mill. "Good Lord, have mercy. What now?"

Grace headed for the stable and gave Dandy the apple. She thought about the mother and baby she had just left. She wanted to know why the doctor wouldn't see infants. "Saddle my horse," she told Nate. "I'll be back."

She walked back toward the hospital that stood next to the sugar mill. She listened for Tia. She heard nothing. As Grace stepped into the white clapboard hospital she looked around at its surroundings. The walls were whitewashed. The mother stood next to the doctor as he bathed the baby in a pan of water. Her brows rose as Grace approached the doctor.

"Well?"

"The baby is teething. It be normal for the infant's temperature to rise during this time. She'll be fine. I show the mother what to do."

"Then she's not sick?"

"No. I check her throat. Everything normal there."

"Why don't you see infants?"

"My hands are full with the people who work the fields and the boiling house. Not enough hands to care for so many." He nodded toward the beds.

Grace counted eight beds with men lying in them.

"They get overheated from the sun in the fields. Men spend too many hours in the boiling houses. Sometimes they don't make it. They die of heat stroke. I do what I can."

Grace nodded. "You need another doctor to help you."

"Mastah don't see no need for another doctor. We do what we can with what we have. He get us the medicine. No more."

It made sense that the plantation owners built hospitals on their grounds. A city doctor would have his hands full caring for the sick on the plantations and the town folks too. Things were different here. She didn't recall ever seeing a hospital on the plantations in Charleston.

One doctor was not enough. But then, she was sure her father already knew that. Grace left the hospital, determined to talk to her father and rectify the situation.

Half an hour later Grace and Dandy picked their way through the tropical brush toward her favorite spot beside the river. She tied the mare to a bush near the running water before perching on her boulder. She pulled the voodoo doll out of her pocket and laid it on the rock. For the better part of an hour, Grace drank in the rays of the warm sun and sketched the scene before her. A hummingbird flitted into view.

The bird's wings fluttered so fast they blurred. It darted from tree to flower, to honeysuckle bush to tree again. Grace slowly lowered her sketch pad on her lap. She must capture this magnificent creature on paper.

The hummingbird sat on a thin branch not ten feet away, its charcoal head and red bill hovering about nervously. The back of the bird was interspersed with emerald-and-black feathers. Two thin tail feathers draped down, trailing below him, nearly ten inches long in pure black. Under the hummingbird's bill and down its belly were tiny feathers the color of emeralds.

She had never seen a humming bird with long tail feathers. But then, many of the birds in Jamaica were different from those back home in Charleston. Grace delighted in this new creature and thanked God for the gift he gave her this day.

Very slowly she lifted the sketch pad and turned the page. Within minutes, she'd captured every detail of the hummingbird. After she had completed the last stroke with her charcoal pencil, the bird flew away. She waited to see if it would return. The water danced over the stones and ran down the wide gorge toward the bridge. Before leaving the tranquil river, she picked a few flowers and tucked them in her sketch pad. Then her gaze landed on the voodoo doll. Should she throw it into the river?

Instead, she picked it up and eased onto the saddle, the tiny doll in her hand. She and Dandy trotted back to Cooper's Landing. The Great House came into view, along with the narrow road that led east toward the miles of cane fields. She reined Dandy onto the wagon road.

A red-gold twilight painted the far-reaching horizon. It bled into the paler sky above the miles of sugar cane stretching toward the road. The Jamaican sun had saturated the brown earth of Cooper's Landing, and now the trade winds came in cooling the air, as they did each evening, bringing sweet relief.

She heard the wind rushing through the tall stalks and saw their green leafy heads bend, swaying in the wind. She nudged Dandy on in the lengthening shadows, the red sky turning purple as she rode. Up ahead, four black crows circled over the cane fields. One crow sat on a post at the side of the road. All at once, Dandy reared her head, her eyes wild as she stomped and snorted. She sidestepped and reversed. Grace squinted in the dusk.

Dandy's sides heaved as she breathed hard. Grace bent down, leaning over the black mane to inspect the road before them. A boa constrictor slithered across the narrow road.

Dandy whinnied and reared straight up. Grace thudded to the ground. She scrambled to her knees and crawled to the side of the road as the chestnut mare lowered its hooves onto the boa as it tried to slither across the lane. Dandy jumped forward again, raising her front legs and snorting, her nostrils flaring wide, her head bobbing up and down. The boa raised its head, mouth opened wide as it tried to make contact with the horse's leg. The horse came down and pounded the dirt. In bolting speed the constrictor threw its long body around Dandy's front left leg. The horse reared, whinnying fearfully, pulling its hoof out of the intense grip of the constrictor. Her hooves came down again and again, eyes white with fear.

Grace jumped to her feet and stumbled back into the tall dark cane stalks and watched helplessly. She shivered as her horse fought back.

The boa was strong and resilient. Its head flew forward in defense of the attack and tried to clamp its large mouth onto the mare's legs.

The crows cackled and swarmed overhead, swooshing low to the ground, hopping on the dirt road, then lifting off into the darkening sky to caw at the horse and snake. The narrow road filled with raucous sounds.

Hovering in the shadows of the rustling cane, Grace thought she heard running feet behind her. *It's the wind,* she reasoned. *I'm imagining things.* Still, the sound sent prickles up her spine. Her horse stepped away from the advancing snake, it's withers trembling.

Then horse's hooves pounded the darkening road. Grace peered out from the cane stalks. Denzel raced toward Dandy. Grace ran out to the edge of the road. Again she heard running feet behind her. This time she knew it was not the wind or her imagination. She caught a glimpse of a form darting from the rows of cane. She stopped, fear rippling up her spine. Denzel slid off his horse and charged toward the boa with a machete. He raised the long knife over his black head, the muscles in his back bulging, and swung down with full force, slashing the boa's head from its body.

Bile forced its way into Grace's throat. She turned back toward the dark cane stalks. A slave stood before her with a machete raised above his head.

She froze.

Bare-chested, wearing white, cropped pants, his black eyes rested on her trembling form. Slowly, he lowered the machete to his side. His jaw clenched. He turned on bare feet and disappeared into the jungle of cane stalks. The light of the moon rose above the cane. Denzel whirled her around.

"You all right, Miss Cooper?"

"Y . . . yes, I'm all right." She shivered.

"What you doing out here on this dark road by yourself?"

"I was just taking a ride, I didn't—"

"It is never safe to ride alone out here. You could have gotten yourself killed."

Dandy trotted down the dark road. "You wait." Denzel jumped on his horse and nudged it into a full run. Grace stood alone, hugging herself, while the ominous cane stalks rippled in the trade winds.

She still held the image of the black slave with the machete held high over his head ready to strike her dead. What Denzel said was true. But by the grace of God the field hand had turned and run, leaving her shaken in the twilight. She crossed the road to wait for Denzel, knees weak. Moments later he appeared, holding Dandy's lead rope.

Grace eased herself onto the back of the chestnut. Together they rode back to the Great House. In the lengthening shadows, she turned back to see the boa's body laying limp on the dirt road, its head lying some feet away. Crows circled around the leftover debris and tore at its flesh. The voodoo doll lay off to the side of the road, a reminder that she shouldn't have kept it.

THIRTY

SHAKY LEGS CARRIED Grace toward the Great House. In only a matter of minutes the heavens would be dark and filled with a million stars, twinkling above. She entered the kitchen and tried to ignore the wide stares of the three cooks.

"Lawdy, Miss Coopah. What happened to you?" Dinah rushed over to inspect Grace. Her right arm was skinned, her skirt was smudged, and her hair was disheveled. "You sit right here while I fetch something to put on that arm."

Gemma hollered out the kitchen door for Amos and Cato to fetch hot water for Miss Coopah's bath. While they made several trips to Grace's bedchamber, carrying buckets of steaming hot water, Dinah dressed Grace's wound.

"Now before you go thinking about soaking in that bath water, you sit down and eat a bite of supper."

Rather than sit alone in the dining room at the long table, Grace remained in the kitchen. Penny placed a plate of pork roast and sweet potatoes before her.

"Now what happen out there?" Dinah placed plump fists on her hips.

"You lookin' like you been drug through the cane fields, Missy." Gemma fanned herself with the hem of her apron.

Warmth flowed through Grace as she observed their concerned faces. For the first time since her arrival at the Great House, she felt a genuine part of the household. It heartened her to know they cared.

Grace told her story between bites of the tender roast pork and potatoes. She told them about the wailing infant and the gift with the grass-woven voodoo doll. Their dark eyes grew wider as Grace told them about the boa constrictor, and being thrown from the chestnut mare.

"You shouldn't have taken that voodoo doll. Don't you know that be witchcraft a working in that doll?" Dinah hovered over her. "That's why you be having that evil snake finding you on the road." She rolled her eyes toward the ceiling.

"What you do with that doll, Miss Coopah?" Gemma fanned herself as if the house were on fire.

"I dropped it on the road." Grace wrinkled her brows. "Come to think of it, I don't have my sketchpad either."

"Don't worry about that sketchpad. We'll send Amos out for it in the morning, heah?"

Hours had gone into the sketches in her picture journal. The thought of it lying on the road disturbed her. Yet she'd not make a fuss about it. "If you'll excuse me, I'd like to go upstairs and soak in the tub."

"You do that," Dinah said.

At the base of the stairs, Grace heard shouting from above. She climbed the marble stairs. The voices came from the west wing. She glanced back and tiptoed closer to the bedchamber. She listened to determine whose voices were beyond the doors.

"You can't tell me what to do anymore." Kindra's voice rose. "I'm nearly twenty years old. I'm a woman. I have the right to choose who I want to be with."

"You'll not be alone with him again," Tia said, with a deadly voice, "or I'll take measures to get rid of him."

"You wouldn't."

"I would."

"I hate you!"

"You won't hate me when you're sitting pretty in a respectable home of your own."

"I don't want anyone else. I want Denzel."

"You'll never find respectability with a slave."

"Some day he'll be free, and when he is, he'll buy our own land. He'll build us a house."

"Your head is in the clouds, Kindra! It'll never happen. A black man cannot buy land here in Jamaica. And besides, what makes you think Denzel will become a free man?"

"I don't want to talk about it!"

"You listen to me and you listen good." Tia's voice grew quiet, closer to a growl. "If I ever catch his hands on you again, you'll never see his face again. You hear?"

A door at the end of the hall opened and closed. Grace fled behind the wall before the stairs. Tia stepped out and stopped.

Kindra's choked voice yelled on the other side of the closed door, "I'll have Father . . . Master Cooper send me away!" Then she sobbed. Grace imagined her sister's body shuddering, racked with anger and pain.

Tia stood at the door and whispered loudly. "Hush. You'll be heard throughout the house."

Grace froze where she stood in the shadows. Tia moved down the hall and looked back where Grace hovered. Her eyes pinned Grace to where she stood, then raked over her disheveled hair and clothes. "You must have something more to do than stand here listening to other people's business, Miss Cooper!" She whirled down the stairs on swift feet.

Grace stepped out. Near the bottom of the stairs, Tia gazed up at Grace with hatred in her eyes. She jerked the front door open and swept out into the darkness.

Shaken, Grace went to her room. Hedy had lit the hurricane lamps, and a bathrobe lay across Grace's bed.

"Let me help you out of your rumpled clothes." Hedy ran around to

Grace's back and unbuttoned the tiny buttons from her neck to waist. "You best git in that tub while it's still hot."

Grace let her body slip down into the steamy water, perfumed with lavender oil. She leaned her head back and closed her eyes. She let the heat of the water soothe her weary mind and body. *What a day,* she mused. First the incident with the fevered infant, then the boa constrictor. Grace agreed with Dinah, she shouldn't have accepted the voodoo doll. If Amos brought the doll back with her sketchpad, she'd burn it.

Grace lay immersed in the bath water so long, it cooled. She pulled herself up and stood, the water dripping down her body. When she reached for a towel, she heard a sound in her room. "Hedy?" Grace stopped and gazed at the closed door. She silently lifted the towel off the hook and wrapped herself in it.

A drawer scraped open. It sounded as though someone shuffled through her things. Then the muffled sounds stopped. Grace carefully stepped out of the tub onto the soft rug. She gripped the towel close around her, and bent her head toward the door to listen. The drawer scraped shut.

"Hedy?"

The chamber door shut softly. Grace waited. Slowly, she opened the bathroom door and peered into her chamber. She glanced around the room and settled on the tall dresser. The top drawer stood ajar. She crossed the floor, the towel held tightly about her, and stared at the white camisole partially hanging out of the drawer.

The smell of jasmine permeated the air. She glanced down. A small cluster of white jasmines lay on the floor. Grace picked up the spray of flowers and sniffed the tangy-sweet scent. *Tia?* She had jasmines tucked in her hair earlier today. Grace glanced at the door. Was Tia out in the hallway waiting?

Standing with the towel draped around her damp body, she shivered.

A tap sounded on the door. Grace jumped. The door opened a

crack and Hedy peeked in. She dropped the sketchpad on the table. "Goodness, Miss Coopah. I be comin' to tell you, Amos done found you drawin' paper. And here I find you standin' here just a shiverin'. You be catchin' a cold standin' there like that." She rushed to the side of the bed and lifted a white cotton nightgown toward her. "Let's git you into this, Missy."

Grace let the towel drop to the floor as Hedy slipped the nightgown over her head.

"You be shakin' like a leaf. Are you all right?"

"Did you come into my room a few minutes ago?" Grace's voice shook.

"No, Missy. I be down in the kitchen with Penny." Her liquid eyes grew round. "Why you be askin'?"

Grace went to the tall dresser and pulled open the drawer with the white camisole. "Someone was just here." She picked up the jasmines and held them toward Hedy. "Whoever it was dropped these."

"I sure don't know nothing about that." She glanced at the door to the hall and back to Grace, her eyes wide.

"Say nothing about this to anyone," Grace said.

"Yessum, Miss Coopah."

"You may go."

The girl slipped out the door. Weary, Grace blew out the lamp beside her bed and climbed under the cool sheet. She lay there, her mind racing over the events of the day. What was Tia looking for? Her eyes wandered to the white jasmines on her night stand. The moon cast a pale haze into her room, the shadow from the palm trees looming ominously across the wall. Her eyes slid shut. The house felt eerie with Cameron and her father gone. Grace tried to ignore the feeling that something evil, something overshadowing, threatened her life.

Heavenly Father, I need your peace that passes all understanding. I need your strength while I am weak. With that, she punched her pillow and rolled over. She refused to give into the ominous silence that prevailed.

Thirty

In the shadows, outside Grace's door, a woman opened her hand. The diamond solitaire sparkled in the dim light. A nice exchange for the spray of jasmines she'd left in the room.

Grace's eyes snapped open. She waited. A long time later, she heard the sound of horse's hooves outside her window. Grace kicked off the sheet, hurried to the French doors, and leaned over the rail to peer out toward the stable. Tia sat alone in the wagon seat as it moved slowly toward the front drive. She held the reins and drove out of view.

Where is she going?

Grace shut the French doors. She opened her bedchamber door and peered down the dark hallway. At the far end of the west wing, Kindra stood outside her door in her nightgown. Grace pattered barefoot down the hall. Kindra met her halfway. On the upper landing, both girls peered out the long window where the east wing divided from the west. Grace slipped her hand into Kindra's as the wagon rolled out of sight.

"Where is she going?" Grace whispered.

"I don't know," Kindra said.

"This isn't the first time she's left in the late hours of the night."

"I'm aware of that. I fear my mother's up to no good," Kindra's dark eyebrows furrowed.

"I fear the same." Grace paused. "I'm sorry, Kindra, but I must tell Father when he returns."

Kindra nodded. "I understand. What with the apprehension of a slave revolt, and some of our own slaves missing here at the Landing, I somehow believe she's caught up in the rebellion."

Grace recalled the half-naked slave she encountered in the cane field and shuddered.

Kindra looked fearfully into Grace's eyes, the moonlight casting shadows about them. "I'd hoped her night capers would come to an end. I fear for her." She paused and frowned. "She *is* my mother."

Grace placed her hand on Kindra's shoulder. "I know, my sister."

Kindra's eyes snapped open. "So you know?" she whispered.

"Yes, I figured it out a few weeks ago. The house is full of secrets. This is one of them."

"And Father?"

"He doesn't know I know." Grace studied Kindra's eyes. "Don't let on that I know. When the time is right, I'll tell him."

"I'll say nothing to Mother, then." Hope seemed to grow in Kindra's countenance.

"No matter what happens at the Landing, we have each other," Grace said softly.

Kindra's eyes glistened in the moonlight. "I'm glad you came," she said in a choked voice.

"Me, too." Grace clung to her sister.

A sound came from below. A creak . . . then light footsteps. The girls released each other.

"Go to bed," Grace whispered. She touched Kindra's shoulder. "Say nothing."

Kindra backed away, toward her bedchamber. Grace did the same. She watched Kindra disappear behind her door, then shut her own. Moments later, the floor creaked outside her door.

A chill crept up her spine. Grace searched the room for anything that could serve as a weapon. Too dark. She waited. Then softly, the footsteps faded and all was quiet.

Grace thought back to when she stood in the center hall with Kindra. Why had she claimed her hand? Why had she told Kindra her secret, that she knew they were sisters? What had come over her? Grace shook her head. Nothing good could come of it. Society would look down their nose at her. So why? *Because they needed each other, that's why.* Grace mused.

The voice in her head spoke the truth. She needed someone to talk to, someone who'd understand her. What's done is done. She couldn't take it back.

Grace slipped out of bed and stood on the balcony. The moon hung high overhead. Her eyes traveled over each of the buildings, then stopped. A light burned in the barn across from the stable. Smoke billowed out the barn doors. Fire!

Grace ran into her room and pulled the gold-braided bell chord hanging from the ceiling. She stepped out into the hallway and cried, "Fire!" She ran down the stairs and out the front door. The grounds were lit by the light of the moon. No one stirred. Grace ran around to the kitchen door and rang the dinner bell. She pulled the rope again and again. The loud clanging pierced the silent night.

She heard footsteps running through the dark. Soon Denzel and some of the field slaves congregated behind the house.

"Fire!" Grace pointed toward the barn. "We need water!"

"Wake up the other men!" Denzel shouted orders to Amos.

The Landing came to life. Lines grew long as the slaves waited for full buckets of water. Three wells were not enough. The barn became fully ablaze. Small animals were led to safety. Buckets were passed to the last man, who threw the pittance of water on the large flames. Grace joined the water lines, lifting the sloshing buckets to the next person. It wasn't long before her arms ached and her body wilted. She didn't stop. She accepted the buckets, and though she nearly dropped them, she passed them to the next man in line.

All at once, one slave ran from the flames, his clothes ablaze. Several men ran to douse water on him. The water sizzled his skin. He screamed in pain.

"Get him to the hospital!" Grace called, as she left the line. She turned from the singed man, who shuddered in pain, to the towering inferno that blazed out of control.

The booming of combustion rang through the air. Smoke billowed in the sky. It seemed they were fighting a losing battle. "More water!"

Grace raised her voice over the noise around her.

The slaves kept a steady pace. The intensity of the flames grew unbearable. As Grace ran to the edge of the road, she saw Kindra had joined the forces to put out the flames. She stood in her nightgown hauling buckets to the next person.

The roof caved in and sparks flew into the air. Red embers carried to the building beside the barn. Slaves doused water on the small building, but the roof burst into flames. The men concentrated on the small building, seeing they were losing the battle with the barn. Weary tears blurred Grace's vision. She lifted the hem of her nightgown and wiped her eyes. Soot blackened the white gown. Grace peered out at the grounds. People ran every which way, some carrying buckets, some emptying out buildings in the line of fire. Some stood, exhausted, eyes pinned to the flames. Her feet, like lead, moved to the line of buckets being passed.

As she swung a heavy bucket to the next person, she saw Minerva down the drive in a long line of slaves at the next well. She passed sloshing water to the next man, still dressed in her day clothes. It was past midnight. Bewilderment surged through her. Had Minerva been up all night?

Grace slipped and fell and spilled the precious water on the ground.

Denzel came to her side and pulled her up. "You best get on up to the house, Miss Cooper. We'll fight the fire."

Grace glanced over the long driveway behind the house. It looked like Hades. She collapsed onto the back steps of the Great House. She bent her head and cried. "Please, God! We need your help. There aren't enough men to fight this blaze."

She sobbed and watched through blurred vision as the slaves continued to fight the fire. She looked at her hands, black with soot.

The world felt black, smelled black. The acrid smoke permeated everything around them.

The sky grew dark. The moon hid behind black clouds. In the distance, lightning flashed. Moments later she heard thunder boom overhead. Then rain began to soak the land around them. Slaves dropped their buckets and fell to their knees. The barn continued to burn. It was gutted now, the skeleton in cinders. The small building next to it had a large gaping hole at the top with flames licking the dry boards.

Thunder crashed through the air, and Grace starting laughing. She twirled with her palms open wide, and she lifted her face to the rain washing over her. Then she stopped. Kindra walked up and stood next to her while Grace gazed out over the devastation.

"I've failed Father," Grace said, as she looked at the damage the fire had caused. "This wouldn't have happened if he had been here."

"This was no accident, Grace. Someone is responsible for this."

"But who?"

Out of the darkness, Tia walked up to the two women. She eyed her daughter. "Go into the house, Kindra, and get cleaned up." Tia turned her daughter toward the back door.

Kindra glanced back at Grace before she disappeared into the house. They'd held each other's gaze with a kindred spirit.

"Go in!" Denzel called to Grace, as the rain continued to fall at a steady pace.

"No! I'm not going in until I see the last flame is put out."

"That won't be long with this rain."

"Just the same, I'll wait."

Denzel pushed off the porch and walked around the buildings.

At long last, the final flame flickered out.

"What of the man who got burned?" Grace asked Denzel.

"He's dead."

"Oh, no." Grace leaned against the back porch railing.

"Go in now." Denzel pushed Grace into the back hallway. "Ain't nothing we can do till morning."

Dazed, Grace stared up at the marble staircase. She'd always credited herself that no hill was too hard to climb. But she had failed her father miserably. She crept up the stairs in defeat.

THIRTY-ONE

THREE DAYS LATER, Grace bolted into the kitchen from the side door. "Is it true? Is my father on his way to the Landing?" She glanced at the cooks, then to Kindra.

A smile played on Kindra's lips, and her eyes shone. "We expect them in the next hour or two."

"Or two?" Grace winced.

"They may have business to attend to at the dock's landing."

"Oh." Grace clutched her skirts. "I'm going to change."

An hour later the Cooper carriage rolled into the circular drive.

Grace stood on the front porch. Cameron stepped out of the carriage first. She held her breath. A smile split his face as he waved at her. She nodded.

Phillip stepped out next. He squinted as he glanced up. A smile spread across his face. "It's good to be home, I'd say."

"Father!" Grace flew down the steps and ran into his arms. "I've missed you."

"You look good to my eyes, my dear." He held her at arm's length and stopped. "What is it, Grace? You look frazzled."

"Come into the house. I've terrible news to tell you."

They hooked arms and went up the porch steps. Zeek stood at attention, his dark eyes beaming. "Welcome home, Mastah Coopah."

Phillip laid a hand on the butler's shoulder. "Thank you, Zeek."

The coachman brought their baggage to the porch steps. Zeek carried them into the house.

Kindra watched her father greet the house servants. His gaze swung briefly to her. His eyes held hers momentarily but then looked away. She held her breath, her heart pounding in her chest.

All she wanted was his acknowledgment that he was glad to see her, too. He glanced back at her, lifted a brow, then turned to Cameron, who instructed Nate to get the wagon and give the hired coachman a ride back to town.

Moments later, Grace and her father sat in his study. "Before you tell me this terrible news you speak of, I brought you something," Phillip said, a gleam in his eye.

"What is it?" she asked as he handed a bulky package to her.

"Open it," Phillip said.

Grace accepted the brown-wrapped package, but with little joy. She dreaded the news she had for her father. She tore at the paper and, involuntarily, her eyes opened wide. She lifted a navy-blue, split riding skirt, a beautifully starched, white blouse, and a navy-blue, velour vest. She looked at her father with gratitude.

"I thought you might like a proper riding skirt when you ride Dandy."

"Thank you, Father. You shouldn't have."

"Of course I should. I'm your father. Now what is it you wanted to tell me?"

When she'd finished telling him about the fire, they walked out to assess the damage. They stood before the mound of ashes that had been the barn. Grace swallowed. "You left me in charge of the Landing, and I failed miserably."

Phillip's brow furrowed and his green eyes blazed. "This is something you could have no control over. I fear this was a deliberate attack."

"But who would do this? A man lost his life."

"There has been much talk about the slave revolt. I fear some of our own slaves have become discontent. Come; let's go into the house. Camp and I have work to do. We must put a stop to this."

A week passed before Phillip and Cameron formed a meeting with the slaves and the field hands. Grace had never seen all the workers in one place. They were scattered about the drive behind the house. Phillip stood on a wooden wagon, as to be seen over the crowd. Cameron stood beside him, and Denzel stood on the ground, before the wagon.

"I brought you all together because I'm concerned about the rumors I've been hearing," Phillip began. "As a plantation owner, I hear what is going on at other plantations. Word has it, slaves have been disappearing from all parts of the island. We've lost a few of our own." Phillip's voice carried over the crowd. His eyes narrowed as he looked into the eyes of the men closest to him. "I'll not put up with any rebellion on my plantation. I've been a good task-master, a fair man. But don't misjudge me. I'll hang the first man caught running away."

Grace moved away from the crowd and into the house. Things were changing. She could feel it in the air. She glanced out the window to see Tia standing at the edge of the group. Some of the slaves watched her, then Phillip. The slaves seemed restless. Was Tia behind any of this? Where did she go late at night? Tia had made her presence known. Grace watched her walk away, smooth as a panther. Did the slaves feel threatened by her presence?

A few days later, as Grace walked from the dim stable into the sunlight, she nearly collided into Cameron.

"Afternoon. I'm glad I caught you before you returned to the house." Cameron smiled down at her.

"I just finished taking Dandy out for a run." She let her gaze run over his face, taking in his chin, with its slightly dimpled cleft, and admiring the physical strength indelibly stamped in his broad shoulders and muscled arms. Gratitude, admiration, respect—she tasted all those things . . . as well as a trace of resentment.

He'd been home three days and had hardly spoken a word to her. But he'd ridden out to the Moore plantation to see Jacqueline. That alone spoke volumes of his true interest. The garden scene at the ball had only been a momentary play on her emotions. She stepped back and folded her arms across her chest.

"I was headed to the house to rest," she said.

"Too bad. I'm going to have Nate hitch the horses to the wagon and make a trip into town." He glanced down at her. "Want to ride along?"

Her head jerked up. "I'd love to. Do I have time to change?" It had been weeks since she'd been to Riverbend. She had a few errands she wanted to attend to on her own.

"Sure. I'll bring the wagon out front. See you in ten minutes?"

Grace nodded and raced toward the house. She knew he merely desired company while he made the hour-long ride into town. She fought the fantasy that there was any more to it. Whatever happened in the garden on the night of the ball he'd dismissed. He showed no hint of interest now. If anything, he seemed to prefer time away from her. What could have been was lost, thanks to her hesitation to show how she truly felt. He would never know that everything within her desired his touch, to feel his lips on hers.

Changed, she stepped out on the front porch. Cameron grinned and helped her into the wagon. Minutes later they traveled down the narrow, rutted road.

Grace wished they hadn't grown apart. She'd give anything to have things the way they were before. She tried her hand at breaking the silence. "How's it going in the fields?"

"Great. We have a load of hogsheads ready to deliver to the wharf." He glanced down at her. "There's a good shipment ready to go out, more barrels than usual."

They rode in silence again. Twice she gazed up to see him staring at her. Her cheeks burned. His elbow brushed hers as he flapped the reins. Was that deliberate?

An hour later, they rode into the crude town. Rough buildings squatted by the wharves. She remembered the first day she'd arrived at the wharf a couple of months ago. It all seemed different coming from the Landing. They rode to the heart of town. The board walks and streets crawled with people as the wagon jostled toward the last building on Main Street.

"Whoa!" Cameron pulled on the reins and set the brake. "Wait here," he said as he climbed down. "We ordered supplies for the head coopers at the plantation. We're running low."

A sign hung from a wooden post outside a barn-like building. "Wainwright Supplies."

Her thin eyebrows lifted. "Coopers?"

"Coopers make the barrels and casks needed to haul the hogsheads of sugar." He paused and gazed at her with smoky-gray eyes. "We do most of our own work at the Landing. But it's necessary to give them supplies to work with." He touched the edge of his wide-brimmed hat and squinted. "I won't be long."

Grace took advantage of the time alone to glance about the busy street. The buildings pressed close together along the waterside of the wharf. They were tall and narrow, some similar to those in Charleston. The shops included taverns, public houses, and a hotel, as well as a blacksmith and stable.

Across the street sat a building with two narrow windows in front. An ornate sign hung in front of the building inscribed with the words, "Law Office of Desmond Rothschild." A few doors down, a primitive building stood apart from the row of shops. A metal sign hung from a pole outside the structure. "Knives, Swords, and all things Metal." She'd heard that metal continually corrodes in the damp, salt air of the tropical islands. There would be a need for new metal supplies for the planters and townspeople alike.

She grew restless, glancing at her list of supplies for the second time. All at once she heard a man shout, "Move along. Hey! No sampling the goods!" She turned in time to see a shaggy-haired boy darting through the throng of people on the wooden walk, an apple clutched between his small hands. The lad swerved between a water barrel and the corner of a building and disappeared down the alley, leaving a ruckus behind. The store owner fumed as he retrieved the apples that had tumbled down the wooden walk.

Grace discerned that eyes were watching her. She chided herself. After all, she sat in the wagon on a busy street. Still, the hairs pricked the back of her neck as she adjusted herself on the wagon seat. She glanced back at the noise of men laughing at the store owner.

Then she saw her. Tia stood near the entrance of the general store, her head bent toward a stocky man. His hair was long and greasy, his beard and mustache unkempt. He wore a thick triangular black hat with a plume of feathers rising above. They shook hands and he nodded his head. He removed a stubby cigar clamped between his yellow teeth and tossed it out onto the dirt.

"The blasted son-of-a gun better stay outta the way, before I blow his head off," he yelled.

Tia seemed unruffled. She handed him a slip of paper, and glanced back at Grace. Tia glared, then picked up the hem of her scarlet cape and stepped into the road.

What was Tia up to?

To her surprise, Tia stepped into the back seat of a waiting buggy. Nate sat erect on the driver's seat, eyes darting about. Minerva sat in the seat beside Tia, eyes shining. Tia spoke to Nate and he flicked the reins. With grim lips, he moved the buggy out into traffic. He nodded his head at Grace as they passed by.

Grace sat dumbfounded. Then she spied Tia's gruff man, who nabbed an apple, shoved it in his pants pocket, and strode up the walk. Grace tapped her foot on the wooden floorboard and waited for Cameron to come out of the store. She wouldn't wait any longer. She had errands too. Maybe she'd run into Tia's friend. Find out who he was.

Grace climbed down and headed for the general store. What she needed would only take a minute. When she stepped inside the building, she grinned. There were rows and rows of goods. The shelves were stocked with every imaginable piece of merchandise. She checked her list, determined to buy the few items she needed. She glanced out the open door. Cameron hadn't come back to the wagon yet. She had more time. After finding embroidery thread and personal items, she paid for her purchases and walked out to the wagon.

Minutes ticked by. The sky darkened. Thunder rumbled in the distance. People hurried off the streets. Cameron emerged, two men trailing behind him carrying long, thin boards. Another man carried an armload of thin metal. They placed the material in the back of the wagon. They repeated the process several times.

The tropical air took on a dampness that grew unbearable. She was going to wilt. *How much longer?* she wondered. A raindrop splashed on her arm.

"Oh, no." She glanced toward the building while Cameron came out, folding a sheet of paper. He quickly tucked it inside his breast pocket before climbing into the wagon.

"We've got a storm rolling in."

Before the words were out of his mouth, big raindrops plopped onto her parasol. Cameron snapped the reins, and the wagon jerked out onto the road.

An hour later, the torrent of rain continued ferociously, soaking the ground and everything in sight. She could hardly make out Cameron's frame, only a few feet away, as he struggled to guide them to the stable at the Landing. A large tree limb stretched across the ground, blocking the stable doors. Grace saw someone in the mud beneath the heavy branch.

Cameron raised a hand for her to stay back as he rushed forward.

"It's Pip." Cameron's hoarse voice rose above the rain. "Your father's trapped!" He knelt by the still form on the ground.

A low moan escaped her father, and his eyes fluttered open.

"Grace, run to the shanties and get Denzel! Hurry!" Cameron shouted.

Cameron moved branches while Grace set out at a run for the slave quarters. The driving rain deepened the mud. Her boots sank into the mire making it difficult to run, but she managed to pass the back side of the stable, the blackened remains of the barn, and the livery stable. Finally, she found the gate to the shanties.

"Denzel!" Grace cried while she ran down the narrow row. "Denzel!"

A door opened, spilling light from within. Denzel stepped into the rain. "What is it, Miss Cooper?"

"Come with me, quick!" She grabbed his arm and tugged at him to follow. "My father's trapped under a fallen tree limb. Cameron's with him now."

The two bent their heads as they ran through the mud and sloshed their way back to where Phillip lay with his head on Cameron's shirt. Pellets of rain pummeled Cameron's bare chest and ran down his tanned skin.

"How is my father?" Grace panted.

"Soaked to the bone. Heaven knows how long he's been lying here." Cameron's brow creased with a scowl. "Denzel, help me get him up. I think he may have broken his left leg. Let's take it easy in case he's hurt anywhere else."

"Wait!" Grace bent down and stroked her father's brow. "Father, can you hear me?"

Phillip's response was inaudible.

"Let's get him into the house."

The two men worked for the next half hour getting Pip into the house and upstairs to his room.

"Send Nate for the doctor," Tia told Gemma as she stood at the base of the stairs. "Tell him to be quick about it!"

Grace stood back and watched Cameron gently maneuver her father into a comfortable position, then she moved to a chair next to the bed. She took hold of her father's hand and silently prayed. She shook from the sight of finding him helpless under the fallen branch. She couldn't lose her father now. She had just found him. Her brow creased as she searched his face for signs of relief from the pain.

"Is there anything we can do for you while we wait for the doctor?" Grace asked in a gentle voice.

Phillip pulled his calloused hand away and patted her knee. Pain showed in his eyes, yet he smiled bravely. "Don't fret so, my little one." He took a deep breath. "I'm a tough old badger. I'll be back on my feet in no time."

Cameron watched Pip, his gaze intent, his jaw tense.

Tia stood at the foot of the bed, her eyes like cold stones. Phillip tried to smile, but the ice in Tia's eyes remained.

"I believe I'll have Dinah bring some hot tea." Tia left the room stealthily as a cat.

Cameron glanced at Grace. Did he feel the tension too? He gave no indication of what he thought. His face a mask.

Grace dragged her gaze away, feeling chilled. This house held more secrets than she cared to admit. She searched her father's face. He closed his eyes. It seemed the pain had eased for the moment.

The door opened once more. Kindra slipped in and walked to the foot of the bed. She didn't look at Grace or Cameron. Her eyes stayed on her father. She reached a hand to the raised portion of the cool sheet and touched it. Then she turned to leave.

"Kindra," Grace whispered.

She stopped at the door, her back to the room.

"Come sit with us," Grace said.

Cameron's head snapped up. After an intense look at Grace, he turned to Kindra, stood, and stepped aside. "Sit here." He pointed to his chair.

Kindra pushed her hair behind her ears and took Cameron's seat. She glanced warily at Grace.

"I think I'll go see how things are downstairs." His eyes questioned Grace, but she turned away. He closed the door without a sound.

For the first time, it was only Grace and Kindra alone with their father. He appeared to be asleep. She studied him, acutely aware they both had wanted to know him as a father all their lives. Grace glanced at Kindra. Her sister's eyes were stayed on their father. For the next hour she and Kindra sat on either side of the bed, neither speaking, deep in thought.

Gemma popped her head into the chamber an hour later. "The doctor is here."

Kindra stood and brushed her skirt. "I'll see what I can do to help downstairs." She smiled at Grace and glanced one more time at her father, then left the room.

Phillip opened his eyes the moment the door closed. Had her father known Kindra was in the room? Did he sense her presence? His brow creased once more as a low moan escaped him.

THIRTY-TWO

THE OCTOBER DAYS grew still in the Great House. Phillip complained of severe headaches. Yet there was no indication that he'd injured his head. Grace had an inkling something wasn't right. She couldn't put her finger on it. But there were secrets in the house. Was someone trying to silence him?

Cameron invited Grace to join him for a ride into Riverbend. Grace climbed into the buggy and straightened the wrinkles from her skirts. Cameron stepped in beside her and shook the reins. The mare raised her head and started out of the circular drive.

They rode in silence, lost in their own thoughts. Cameron gave Grace a sidelong glance. They'd grown accustomed to each other and she realized she wouldn't want it any other way.

As the two rode through the thick, tropical wagon lane, she felt his gaze on her. When she looked over, their eyes caught and held for the breadth of a moment. This seemed a good time to ask him the question she had wanted to ask for a good while.

"Father said you came to the Landing when you were a child. I'm curious how this came to be." She scrutinized him and waited.

Cameron smiled, deepening the crease in his face. "Your father was on his way back from a trip to the states when I met him on the *Savannah Rose.* I was nine years old."

Grace tilted her face toward him. "You were nine years old when you met my father? How is it you were on his ship at such a young age?"

"I was a stowaway." He looked straight ahead, giving her a view of his sun-lined, bronze profile.

"You ran away from your mother and father?"

"No, just my father. My mother passed that year." His jaw tightened.

"And then?" she leaned forward, eager to hear the rest of the story.

Cameron spent the next few moments relaying how desolate his childhood had become after his mother's passing and how he'd spent his days at the docks, wishing to sail away from all the hurt and sorrow.

"One day I walked onto your father's ship with a family. No one noticed I didn't belong to them. I hid in the belly of the ship and was found below deck in the cannon room. Jesse hauled me up to the captain's deck to be punished. Instead, your father took me under his wing."

Grace listened to his story. Her shoulders grew stiff. She tried not to care that her father took Cameron on as a child, but she did.

Cameron laughed. "It made Jesse hotter than a pistol. That son of a gun wanted to see me whipped and thrown overboard." Cameron's eyes gleamed at the memory. "Your father brought me to Cooper's Landing. I had to work like everyone else to earn my keep." He tipped his hat off his forehead and ran a sleeve across his brow. "I've spent the last twenty-four years learning everything there is to know about growing and harvesting sugar cane, not to mention working with the stock and his prized Arabian horses.

Grace stared ahead. She studied the potholes in the road and frowned.

"When I was young, I worked alongside the slaves in the fields. That's when I met Denzel. We used to play in the fields and the barns. Your father knew I needed a friend. We became like brothers. Over the years, Denzel picked up a lot of what I'd learned about the crops. The field hands have a different kind of respect for him, as he is one of their own. Your father eventually made him overseer. Now he answers to me, and I answer to your father."

"It seems the two of you had quite an arrangement," she clipped.

He casually flapped the reins. "Pip was like a father to me. Over time he gave me more responsibilities. One day he announced to the field hands and those at the Great House that I was the new foreman of Cooper's Landing, just like he announced you were in charge of the Great House and some of the duties beyond. I was twenty years old. I've been the foreman ever since."

The buggy pulled up in front of a row of town buildings and stopped in front of Desmond Rothschild's office. He tied the reins around the brake post, then jumped down and went around to help Grace to the ground.

Grace shook her skirt to loosen the wrinkles. She couldn't look Cameron in the eyes just now. She couldn't explain the pain she felt at all the years she'd lost with her father. It wasn't Cameron's fault, nor her father's. If only her mother had been able to stay at the Landing, she wouldn't have lost the years she'd so desperately desired to spend with him.

Just the same, she couldn't shake the envy hanging heavily on her heart. She couldn't shake the anger toward her mother for not allowing her the right to be with her father. It was hard to let it go. Her mother deceived her, and for that, she resented her.

Cameron, on the other hand, had been adopted into her father's heart and taken in like a son. He shared many close years with her father. He had memories she'd never know.

Cameron hadn't missed the look of disappointment on her face. He tipped her chin up. "Grace?"

Her eyes met his, brimming with unshed tears.

Cameron reached out to wipe her tears with his thumb, his mouth grim, and his demeanor apologetic. "I'm sorry the subject was brought up. I didn't mean to hurt you."

"I asked and you answered. I don't want to talk about it."

"All right." He hesitated, concern on his face. "Let's go in then." He led her to a door that read: "Desmond Rothschild Attorney at Law."

She didn't know they had come to town to see an attorney. The two walked into his office.

"Good afternoon, Cameron, Miss Cooper. What brings you into town?" asked Desmond.

Cameron took off his straw hat and reached out to shake the attorney's hand. "We're here on business, Mr. Rothschild."

"Have a seat." He pulled out a chair for Grace.

Cameron moved into a chair next to Desmond's desk and told the story about Pip's accident. "We thought he'd only broken his leg." Cameron paused for effect. "He's been mighty sick. He was supposed to be up on crutches and getting around not long after Doc put his leg in a splint. Now Doc's wondering if maybe there's some internal injury from the mishap."

"You don't say," Desmond said, and frowned. He removed his spectacles and cleaned the wire-rimmed glasses with a white cloth.

"Pip's convinced he won't be around much longer and asked me to come into town to see if you'll come out to Cooper's Landing and work out a new will."

Cameron looked at Grace, then Desmond. "Things have changed since his daughter has shown up."

Grace shifted in her chair and concentrated on Cameron's explanation for the visit. She didn't know her father wanted a new document drawn up. Her mood sobered. She wasn't here for her father's money or his property.

"Of course that changes things," Desmond said. "Tell Phillip I'll be out to the Landing tomorrow morning." He stood to his feet and shook hands with Cameron. He gave Grace a nod, then waved the pair out of his office.

Desmond sat in a chair, while Phillip sat propped up against a pile of pillows.

"I don't know what's happening to me, Des. I've had an excruciating headache for the past few weeks. I can't keep food down. I feel like my days are numbered." He glanced at the attorney. "You ever feel like you're living in a tunnel and can't get out?"

"No, can't say that I have."

"Well, that's how I feel. I feel like darkness is at the edge, ready to swallow me up."

"I'm sorry to hear that, Phillip." Desmond cleared his throat. "Cameron said you wanted to make adjustments to your will. Are you up to talking about that now, or would you like me to come back another day?"

"The sooner we write up the new will, the better."

"I sent your last document to your accountant in London. I'm headed for England in a few days. Let's start by listing your requirements. I'll write it up and have you sign it. In the meantime, I'll bring back the previous documents. How's that?"

"That's fine." Phillip closed his eyes.

"I'm ready when you are . . ."

An hour later, Minerva came into Phillip's room. "Tia said to bring you a cup of hot tea, sir. Maybe this will help you feel better." She leaned over and held the cup to his lips. He sipped the hot liquid and then fell asleep.

Kindra moved into the room and relieved Zeek from his post. She sat patiently as she watched her father's chest rise and fall in a slow rhythm. For the first time in her life, she had the upper hand. She had something to say. And she wanted her father to listen.

The Great House grew quiet as the doctor went in to see Phillip. He'd been in the room several minutes when he came out and shook his head. "There's nothing I can do. He doesn't have long. I'm sorry."

Grace turned to Cameron. "We can't let him die!"

He pulled her into his arms. She clung to him, fear gripping her heart. "I'll not lose father! There must be something we can do!"

"Grace, there's nothing we can do." He stroked her hair as she leaned into him. "If you want to say goodbye, you need to go in and say it now."

She raised her head and stood back, wiping the tears as she did. "Where's Kindra?"

"I'm here." Kindra stood a few paces away, fear etched into her pale face.

Grace pulled her into an embrace. "Father's waiting for us." She led Cameron and Kindra into the room and shut the door. The three stood at the foot of the bed. Cameron touched Grace's back and she moved to her father's side. Phillip seemed oblivious to the three in the room. "Father . . . can you hear me?" Grace held his hand and gazed down at him.

Phillip stirred. Kindra and Cameron moved up closer to the other side of the bed. Cameron kneeled and stroked Phillip's head, while a tear slipped down his face. Grace sank to her knees, her skirts rustling. She laid her cheek on Phillip's rough hand. "Father, it's me, Grace," she choked. "Don't you die. I can't bear it." She put her head down beside his and wept the way she had as a child.

A feeble hand reached out to try to pat her head. She looked at him through tears. His eyes flickered open, but she saw they didn't see her. Death was approaching.

"I love you so much, Father. I finally got to know you. You'll remain in my heart forever." Her voice caught as a sob choked her. Tears fell relentlessly as she kissed his hand, then stood and kissed his forehead.

Behind her, Kindra wept softly. Cameron moved back to let Kindra near her father. She knelt and touched his cheek as a tear slid down her face. "I love you, Father. I always have."

Thirty—Two

Phillip stirred and let out his last breath.

The evening air hung heavy as Grace returned from the river. Her soul was full of misery, her world torn apart. She couldn't bear it, knowing her father had slipped away from this life into an eternity destined for eternal darkness. She'd prayed he'd make his peace with God, but God seemed to have turned a deaf ear to her prayers.

She nudged Dandy into the long drive. In the faint shadows of the night the slaves stood outside the Great House, singing a soul-searching song. Each held a small candle, flames flickering as they did. It was their tribute to the Master they'd loved a good many years.

Her eyes glistened as she glanced toward an upper window in the tall house.

Kindra gazed through the window of her father's bedchamber, her finely featured face, the color of honey, pressed against the pane. Her reflection faded into the evening shadows that fell forebodingly across the glass. Kindra loved these people, who in turn loved her.

The slaves nodded at Grace and then moved toward the side of the drive, and back to the shanties. She sat tall in the saddle, for her father's sake, as one by one they turned and walked away. They continued to sing and move down the lane behind the Great House.

Nate stayed behind. He took the reins of the horse, and Grace slipped to the ground. His dark eyes appeared sorrowful.

"Sorry for your loss, Missy. If you like, I be takin' this fine horse 'o yours to the stable."

Grace laid a hand on his arm. "Thank you, Nate. You've lost a good master, too. I hope to live up to my father's legacy." She picked up her skirt and moved up the steps into the Great House.

She still had a house to run. Now that her father was gone, she had more responsibilities. She would throw herself into this land. She'd prove she was a Cooper, through and through.

THIRTY-THREE

GRACE HAD WEPT when her mother died. She'd sensed her mother's presence in every corner of her consciousness. But in the clear morning air at her father's graveside behind a grove of papayas, she felt numb. No tears came. There was only a void where grief should have been. She had come to find her father, and now that he was lost, so was she.

Grace turned her attention to the people around the graveside. Planters and laborers, men from the sea and men from the land. They came from all over the island to pay their final respects to Phillip Cooper. Because of the heat, the funeral had to be held almost immediately, yet all had stopped what they were doing to be here.

Grace shook hands with each of the guests as they filed by. Kindra sat beside her, silently watching. Grace insisted Kindra sit up front as a daughter. They were sisters, after all. Camille filed by and touched Grace's hand. She bent and whispered, "I'll come by in a few days to see how you're doing, dear friend." They hugged briefly. Camille touched Kindra's hand and gave her a warm smile.

Tia stood to the right, watching them. Above her long, black gown she wore a wide, black hat draped by a long, black veil over her face. Only the crystal blue of her eyes showed through the veil. She viewed the crowd as they passed by her daughter, as a panther would her cub.

When the long line of people had gone, Grace lifted her skirt of black crinoline and stepped precariously through the clumps of wet grass, steam rising from the ground. The Jamaican rains were followed by intense heat. Grace could hear Kindra's skirt swish in the tall grass behind her as the two girls walked to the Great House in silence.

Their father's death had thrown them together. They'd held each other and cried and turned to each other for solace. Would this be the beginning of a new relationship for them? Would the wall of black and white that divided them be torn down? Grace glanced at her sister and smiled. *The Lord giveth and the Lord taketh away.* Her father was gone, but he'd given her a precious gift in her sister.

"You look entirely undone," Drew said. "You must come and sit down." He led Grace to a chair on the long porch.

In the next instant Cameron thrust a glass of juice into her hand. "Drink it," he commanded.

Cameron returned to the house to attend the guests. She was grateful she didn't have to deal with the company alone.

Jacqueline was somewhere on the premises. She hadn't given her condolences yet, and truth to tell, Grace wasn't in the mood for pretense. She'd already had a trying day. Jacqueline wasn't here for her anyway. She'd come to pay her respects to Cameron.

When Cameron returned a few moments later, he pulled a chair over and sat down, facing her. "I'm sure nothing is as you expected it to be," he said. "Losing your father has left you in shock; so if you're trying to find any sense to the situation, it's likely to elude you."

The sympathy in his voice touched a chord in Grace. The numbing fog lifted. "I came to Riverbend to find my father. But instead, I got half of his sugar farm. What good is it to me?" Her words were not bitter but marked by deep grief. "I don't know the first thing about raising sugar cane."

Cameron clenched his jaw before speaking. "The first thing about sugar cane," Cameron said, with a hint of a smile, "is that it is grown not raised. And we generally refer to the land as a plantation, not a farm. Beyond that, it isn't necessary for you to know anything. You have a partner on the premises who will protect your interests. I can assure you that your affairs will be in safe hands. You can go home as soon as you are ready."

Grace looked up. " I can't go home. I have no home to go to."

"You said you had a townhouse in Charleston."

"I let it go back to the bank before I came. After my mother died I meant to start a new life with Father."

A low whistle escaped Cameron's lips. "You don't do things by half measure, do you?" he asked, as if in amazement and admiration. "Didn't your family caution you against letting the house go before you found your father?"

"Yes, they did." Grace stiffened. "I didn't tell them until after I'd done it." She dropped her gaze when Cameron stared at her in disbelief. Heat flooded her face. Exhausted, she wasn't up to explaining her situation back in Charleston. Not today.

"It's been a long day," he said, rising. "I imagine you must be on the brink of collapse." He touched her elbow, lifting her to her feet.

"I suggest you take a nap. You should postpone any decisions about staying until you've had a few days to think it over."

"We have a house full of guests. I can't leave them without a hostess."

"Most of the guests have gone. Those remaining will understand, Grace. I'm here, too, don't forget." Cameron glanced out to the lawn. Drew Harding stood with a few of his crewmen. He gazed at Grace, brow raised.

"I suppose a short nap won't hurt."

"Good." He walked inside the house with her. "And by the way," he ran a calloused hand over his chin. "Should you decide to stay on at Cooper's Landing, you might take into consideration that you don't have an appropriate chaperone. I hadn't wanted to bring that up, but it has to be considered, Grace.

She hadn't given their living arrangements any thought. But of course, he was right. Slaves were not considered *proper* chaperones. They had a house full of people who could not save her reputation. Her cheeks burned.

Grace turned to flee up the stairs. As she pivoted, her foot slipped. She flailed, but Cameron's arm went around her waist, catching her in midair. His arm remained and held her near.

Her heart raced as she looked into Cameron's dark, gray eyes with their fringe of lashes. His mouth descended. Her eyes fluttered closed as his lips covered hers in a lingering kiss.

For a single moment nothing existed. She was lost in the warmth of his embrace. She wouldn't resist. As much as she wanted to remain in his arms, she realized the impropriety of their actions, and twisted out of Cameron's arms.

"Stop!" she lashed out. "Isn't this what we're trying to avoid?"

Cameron looked stunned. "What? Grace wait."

"No, she choked. "It isn't right. We can't do this."

"It's a bit too late to tell me."

"For your information, Cameron Bartholomew, everything has come *a bit too late* for me. Just when I *want* to be in your arms . . . we've no chaperone."

Heat rose up her face. "I . . . I don't want to talk about it." She turned for the stairs. This time she didn't stop.

"You can't deny you enjoyed the kiss," he called after her.

She stormed into her bedchamber and slammed the door. No, she couldn't deny she enjoyed the kiss.

Cameron turned in time to see Jacqueline standing in the hallway. She looked stunned. "So this is the reason you rode out to my father's plantation to have a talk." Her face contorted. "I've waited a year for a marriage proposal. But that wasn't the purpose of your visit. You couldn't commit to a relationship." Jacqueline glanced up the stairs. "Now I know why."

"I'm needed outside." Cameron turned and opened the screen door in time to be rescued by Captain Harding. The two men walked out to the lawn. When he turned back, Jacqueline stormed across the lawn.

Kindra crossed the lawn just then, a fruit drink in hand. Jacqueline caught up with her, hooked her hand in the crook of Kindra's arm and led her away from the crowd.

"Tell me Kindra, how does Grace intend to save her reputation now that she and Cameron will be sharing the Great House without a chaperone?"

Kindra pulled free and stared at her. "If you think I'm going to go along with your ploy to destroy my sister, you're wrong."

"Your sister?" Jacqueline laughed. "Has she blinded your eyes as well?"

"Good day, Miss Moore. I'm needed up at the house. I've no intention of entertaining wagging tongues." Kindra lifted her chin and swept away toward the Great House.

THIRTY-FOUR

GRACE AWOKE IN the late afternoon. She kicked off the sheet and propped herself against the pillows to think. Even though she'd prayed and tried to let the peace of God consume her, she still felt lost. Tears threatened to spill over once more. She'd been cheated. She and her father should have had years of memories. He should have seen her marry, seen his first grandchild. All of that had been snatched from them. Now she had no one.

She missed Smitty. He would have sat with her and purred his sentiments. She didn't even have him to console her. Grace reached for a handkerchief from the night stand and blew her nose, listening to the sounds below. Life went on as usual. How could that be?

She turned her thoughts to her predicament. Living in the Great House without a chaperone wouldn't do. She didn't want to leave Cooper's Landing, but under the circumstances she couldn't stay. Her heart twisted with indecision.

Aunt Katy would have had the answers Grace needed. She always did. Grace sat up straight. *That's it. Why not have Aunt Katy and Josie come to Cooper's Landing?* Her aunt had fussed and fumed before Grace left Charleston because of her pledge to keep an eye on her niece. "I'll write a letter posthaste. Knowing my situation, she'll come." Grace could stay after all.

The answer to her problem took shape in her mind. How Cameron would accept the solution remained to be seen. He couldn't expect to

275

sleep in the house until a chaperone arrived. She remembered seeing a set of bunk beds at the far end of the stables. A few hooks on one wall served as a place to hang clothes. He'd have to sleep in the bunkhouse.

Aunt Katy could have the chamber adjoining her sitting room. She loved adventure. Aunt Katy would welcome the excuse to travel to save her niece's reputation.

Grace went to the sitting room and pulled a piece of paper from the small desk.

> Dear Aunt Katy,
>
> It is with sad news that I send this post. My father recently had an accident and has this week passed away. This has left me alone in the Great House with the foreman of the plantation, Cameron Bartholomew. With no chaperone, my reputation is at risk. Although the reasonable thing to do would be to return to Charleston, I hesitate to do so. My home is here now. It is with the intent to stay that I request you and Josie come until I can make other arrangements.
>
> There is much to share, but I must keep this letter short. Please Come. I miss you and Josie terribly.
>
> Your loving niece,
Grace Cooper
>
> P.S. Bring Smitty.

Satisfied, she rang for Hedy. The girl helped Grace into her black crinoline gown and combed her hair. Grace left the bedchamber in search of Cameron. The front door leading out to the porch stood open. Lingering guests sat on chairs lined up against the house. Grace expected to find Cameron there. A few men stood on the lawn, but Cameron was not among them.

As she looked for him, she thought of his kiss before she'd gone up to rest. Her face heated. She had reacted to his kiss with fervor. *I shouldn't have been so harsh with Cameron, especially when I wanted that kiss as much as he did.* So much so, in truth, she wasn't willing to leave Cooper's Landing. It wasn't only her father's house she didn't want to leave. She didn't want to leave the man who'd claimed her every waking moment, who'd captured her attention in ways no other man could. Just looking at him sent her pulse racing. She'd stay. Nothing could change her mind on this matter.

She went into the dining room.

Gemma looked up when Grace came in. "Can I git you anything?" The black woman carried a silver tray with four glasses of fruit punch.

"Not just now, Gemma. Have you seen Cameron?"

"He been outside talkin' with the men folk." Gemma squinted through the dining room window out beyond the porch. Another group of men gathered out there. Cameron was not one of them.

"Shall I tell him you be lookin' for him?"

"No, I'll look for him later. I'll see if there's anything left from lunch in the kitchen."

"You do that, Miss Coopah." Gemma smiled. "You be needin' your strength."

Grace slipped into the spacious and airy kitchen. Dinah set glasses on the long, open shelf. Seeing Grace, she smiled, her white teeth seeming whiter against her dark skin. "Afternoon, Miss Coopah," she said. "You look a sight better now."

"Thank you, Dinah. Are there any patties left from lunch?"

"Yes, Missy, there is. You sit yourself down at the table right here and I'll fetch you a plate."

The heavy-set woman pulled a plate from the shelf. She filled the patty with spicy meat and diced vegetables. She added a few pineapple slices to the side.

Grace sat at the small, comfortable table. Dinah made it feel homey.

"I feel right sorry you lost your father." Dinah set the plate of food in front of Grace.

"Thank you, Dinah. The truth is, I feel lost at the moment."

"Well sure you feel lost," Dinah crooned. "But don't you be feeling like you can't come talking to ole Dinah," she said, pointing to herself. "I got all the time in the world to listen to you, chile. I'm good at keeping my mouth shut, too." She clamped her hand over her mouth. "That's a sight more than I can say for some folks in this house."

Grace's eyes smarted while she watched Dinah's animated gestures. "I'm glad I came down for lunch." Grace dabbed at the corners of her eyes with a napkin. All at once it all seemed too much. The loss of her father and her mother in one year was more than she could bear. Tears fell relentlessly, and she didn't try to stop them.

"I sure don't want to be stepping outta line here, but I be thinking you sure do need a hug." Dinah leaned down and held Grace, crooning as Grace shook with tears. After a while, Grace pulled back and dabbed her eyes again.

"Missy, you ever need a shoulder to cry on, you come cry on these big ole shoulders. You won't be the first." Dinah's voice was slow and husky, lilting in the Jamaican way. "Now you get some of that food into your stomach. It'll make you feel a heap better."

Grace did feel better. That night she watched Cameron disappear out the front door with an armload of bedding. That settled, she went to bed.

The next morning as Cameron stood among the workers in the sugar fields, he saw Grace coming down the road and suppressed a smile. She wore a green gauze dress layered with petticoats. He eyed the white gloves, bonnet, and the lacy parasol. He shook his shirt away from his sweat-soaked back.

"Good morning, Miss Cooper," he said. "Lovely day for a walk, though the heat wave is still with us." He turned toward the field hands who ripped at the tall cane grass.

"It's hotter than I anticipated." She fanned herself.

He watched her eyes fall to where his loose, white shirt revealed his chest. Then her gaze moved to the leather whip in his hand. "Have you ever had to use that?" She pointed at the whip.

"Rarely. It keeps the slaves in line just seeing it. They're not too fond of the prospect of the leather across their backs."

Grace winced.

"What brings you a long, hot mile from the house, Miss Cooper?"

Grace straightened her shoulders, angling her parasol. "I've thought of the perfect solution to our problem, Cameron."

"I'm sure you have," he said.

"I'm quite certain you don't want to continue sleeping in the stable, and of course you can't sleep in the Great House. I've sent for my Aunt Katy, from Charleston. I'm sure she'll come. She loves to travel, not to mention it would put her at ease to keep an eye on me." Grace's eyes shone.

Cameron removed his straw hat and raked his fingers through his hair. He focused on something in the distance.

"Cameron?"

His eyes came to rest on her cheeks, rosy from the long walk. Her delicate eyebrows rose, waiting for his reply.

"I hoped you'd give more thought to returning to Charleston, maybe stay with your aunt until you could find better accommodations."

"Why?" Her brows creased in irritation. "Why is it so hard to accept my staying on at the plantation?"

"Things aren't as they seem here, Grace." His voice rose. "But I can't talk about it."

"Such as?"

"Like I said, I can't talk about it. It's not safe for you to be here at Cooper's Landing. Not today anyway, nor tomorrow." He looked out over the green fields of sugar cane. "I can't worry how you're doing up at the Great House while I'm working out here in the fields."

"I can take care of myself."

"I'm sure you think you can." Cameron clenched his jaw. "You don't have any idea what you're talking about. Some of the people here at Cooper's Landing are suspicious of you. They think your story of being Pip's child is contrived."

"I know that." She raised her chin a shade higher. "You don't think I see the stares, the suspicion? I know I'm not accepted by some."

"You're not accepted by most of these people, Miss Cooper." He slapped his hat against his pant leg and replaced it on his head. "You don't hear the talk that goes on outdoors."

"That's not true. I've made friends with several of the slave women in the shanties."

"Maybe so. But the men have the last word." He glanced at the field hands who listened to their exchange. Their eyes showed curiosity.

"They'll learn to accept me, Cameron. I'll earn their respect." She squared her shoulders and glanced at the men in the fields.

"I admire your determination. But it isn't the laborers I'm worried about."

"You mean, Tia?" Fire danced like hot coals in the depth of her eyes.

"That's exactly who I mean," he said. "I wasn't sure if you had a clue about her."

"I have my suspicions."

"Such as?" Cameron asked.

"That Tia was my father's mistress."

"And?"

"Kindra is my half sister." She stopped and looked up at him. "I've wanted to say that since the day I found out."

Cameron stood at attention. "When did you find out?"

"About a month before my father died. I happened into his room and realized it was arranged the same as mine. Tia's room is attached to his. Kindra is Tia's daughter."

"Pip never came right out and claimed Kindra. When you showed up, it answered everybody's question here at Cooper's Landing."

"What question is that?"

"You and Kindra have a striking resemblance to your father. Kindra's not dark like the rest of the slaves on the plantation."

Grace nodded. "I felt I'd seen her somewhere before. It took awhile to figure out why she seemed so familiar. Now I know. Seeing her was like looking at myself in the mirror."

"Exactly."

"But everyone says I look like my mother."

"You do. But there's no mistaking you're your father's daughter. You share some of his features as well."

"But the people are still suspicious that I'm not my father's daughter?"

"They choose to ignore the resemblance between you and Kindra. Slaves have always shown disdain for the planters taking their women and having them at will. Kindra is a reminder that Pip had his way with one of their own."

Cameron pulled a handkerchief from his back pocket and wiped his brow, erasing the beads of sweat that formed on his forehead. Then he shoved the cloth into his pocket again.

"She was born the year after your mother left Cooper's Landing." Cameron shuffled.

"You were here then?"

"That's right. I was eleven years old when your mother left. I thought she was the most beautiful woman I'd ever seen." He traced the dirt with the whip. "She broke your father's heart. It took a long time before Pip started acting like himself again. A year after your mother left, Pip brought Tia and her baby into the Great House."

"Father said he loved Mother." Her brows furrowed.

"He always thought your mother would return to Cooper's Landing."

"But Tia?"

"He was a man, Grace." He cleared his throat. "Tia started flaunting herself in front of your father after your mother left. Pip resisted her for a short time. But before long, he'd given in. Soon after, Tia was with child."

"He moved her into the Great House right away?" Grace asked.

"No. It wasn't until Tia had the baby. Word came from the slave quarters that a white baby had been born to Tia. When Pip saw the baby, he moved her into the house and had a nursery set up."

"Kindra got what I've wished for all my life," Grace whispered.

"It wasn't as you suppose." Cameron tipped her chin up with his forefinger and gazed into her green eyes. He noted the color in her cheeks had grown a deeper red. He steered her back toward the Great House. "Thanks for coming out to talk to me. I'll give what you've said some thought."

"What is there to think about, Cameron? I've come up with a perfect solution." She darted a look at him. "I'm not asking your permission. I'm simply informing you of my plans." A pout formed on her lovely, red lips. "You can't possibly have any objection."

His hands shot up in defense and his jaw clenched as he worked to control his temper. Once again, in her enthusiasm, she'd overlooked a pertinent fact: It could take weeks before the letter arrived to her aunt's home. Then the wait for a response. What would he do in the meantime? He'd not sleep out in the bunkhouse that long. Not when he had a comfortable bed upstairs in the Great House, the same bed he'd slept in for the past 21 years before she'd come.

But glancing into her stubborn eyes, he supposed the stable a better choice than losing Grace forever. But he said, "You can't stay, Grace."

Grace stared at him. "The letter will be sent first thing in the morning. I'm not leaving."

She frowned. "Good afternoon."

"Grace."

She stopped and looked at him.

"You do beat all." He flipped the whip in her direction. "Do me a favor and send one of the women from the shanties out here with water, would you?"

"Yes, I can do that." She tipped her pert nose in the air and walked back toward the house.

THIRTY-FIVE

AFTER GRACE'S FATHER died, she found living at Cooper's Landing sufficiently satisfying. It didn't take long, however, before she found herself gazing out at the fields, wondering how the operation worked. Although she'd cast a curious eye at the activity around the sugar mill, she understood little of the process.

"I want to help with the harvest," Grace told Cameron at dinner. "I own half interest in the estate. I want to share in half of the responsibilities." She had no idea what that role would entail, but she wanted to learn.

Cameron's eyes grew dark, clearly not eager to have her participate. "It's only been a couple of weeks since your father passed. If you want to help with the plantation," he said, "keep doing what you're doing here in the house. You're already doing your part. The bookkeeping *is* half of the responsibilities. By the way, how's that coming along?"

"I've managed to keep the books up just fine. I plan to go through the drawers in the office and straighten them. I've only touched the surface with the basic work. But back to my request, I'm not saying I want to *work* in the fields. I do, however, want to learn what it's all about. I want to *know* so that all the numbers in the books mean something." She picked up her napkin beside her plate.

He cleared his throat. "I'm relieved to hear that." He glanced at her attire. "It's not advisable for you to wear your fine clothes out in the fields. They'll be ruined in no time."

"I already thought of that. I'll work on finding something appropriate to wear." She nibbled a bite of sweet potatoes.

A glint of amusement played in his eyes. "We have a seamstress on the property who can make you something suitable."

"Thank you for reminding me. I'll look into it."

"We are self-sufficient on the plantation. Much of what we need we can find right here," Cameron said.

"There's so much to learn, which is why I brought this up. I feel I'm not doing my share."

"You'll learn, all in good time." He winked. "By the way, have you heard from your aunt?"

"Aunt Katy? No, I haven't. I'm expecting a letter any day now."

"Think she'll come?" He forked a bite.

"I don't think horses could keep her away." Grace flushed under his gaze. He'd warmed to her in the days that followed her father's passing. She welcomed his gentle attentions. It was best, however, to keep their distance until her aunt arrived. She worked at keeping topics geared to the plantation. She also tried to keep herself busy. How one man could fill a woman's mind the majority of the day disturbed her. She pushed her food around her plate, absorbed in thoughts.

Cameron took another bite of chicken.

Grace waited, as she sensed he had something more on his mind. With the table to themselves, she was aware of his strength, his muscular arms leaning on the table while he ate, the way his dark, wavy hair fell forward on his forehead. He appeared starkly rugged, a man of the outdoors.

Her face grew warm as she waited.

Cameron put his fork down and leaned forward. "You've taken a load off of my work schedule by keeping the books. I've been meaning to thank you. It hasn't gone unnoticed. You've also done a superb job of handling the staff in the house. It has freed me to concentrate on the much-needed work out in the fields. Your father had more insight than

I'd given him credit for."

"I'm glad I can help." That she and Cameron worked well as a team gave Grace a keen sense of accomplishment.

Grateful, she smiled. "I think I'll take a walk before I settle in for the evening."

Cameron's dark eyes settled on her. "Don't go far. I'm not sure it's safe for you to be alone at night."

She dropped her napkin on her plate and rose. "I'll only be out in front of the house."

Cameron heard the screen door close softly behind her. He hadn't missed the glow on her cheeks and in her eyes. For the first time he could remember, the dining room felt empty without her presence. He hadn't felt like this before. It wasn't as if he wasn't used to dining alone. Since Grace's arrival the house had taken on a more pleasant atmosphere. At least for himself. Then he thought of Tia.

Is Grace safe here? Tia showed discontent every time they crossed paths. He'd seen hatred in the tigress's eyes. It was his mission to keep Grace unscathed from the cats claws. He glanced at the entryway. A part of him wanted to go after Grace, to be near her. Instead he went down the hall to the study.

To Cameron's surprise, Grace maintained both attendance and interest out in the fields and in the sugar houses over the following weeks. She attacked all tasks with equal earnestness. The more she learned, the more she wanted to know, and the more information she took in, the more suggestions she put out. A development, Cameron told himself ruefully, he should have foreseen. He had to admit some of her ideas were excellent.

One Sunday afternoon, shortly after the noonday meal, Grace

tracked down Cameron in the office. She stood before the desk with her arms folded across her chest. She had a plan and was eager to share it with him.

Cameron looked up, askance. "Do you have something on your mind?"

"I think the slave children need to be schooled," she began. "I want to teach the children how to read and write . . ."

Cameron's hands flew up. "Not so fast, little lady." He came around to sit on the edge of the oak desk. "What makes you think these children need to be schooled? They don't need to read and write to work here at the Landing. The little girls are going to grow up to clean houses, and the boys will work the fields." He lifted an eyebrow at her.

Both hands on her hips, Grace said, "Of all the nincompoop things to say." She paced the length of the small office and came back to stand in front of him. "They have a right to know how to read and how to count. It will open up a whole new world to them."

"That's exactly my point. They *don't* need to know how to read or count. Once they learn about the outside world they'll become discontent. They'll learn there's more for them than we have to offer. We don't want the workers wishing to be somewhere else, Grace. The answer's no."

"Don't you think these people feel loyal to us? Where would they go? I overheard you and Drew talking about the slave revolt the other day. Some of the slaves on other plantations are rebelling. We don't have that happening here, but if we did . . . wouldn't you feel better knowing they'd have a better chance of making it out in the world than they do now?"

"We have had our share of the slaves revolting here on the Landing. A few have come up missing, just so you know."

Grace thought back to the slave who'd threatened her with a machete in the cane fields. She didn't tell him she'd come face to face with one of the slaves in rebellion. It would be counterproductive to her cause.

"I don't know, Grace." He paused, watching her. "I know you want this, but it's a bad idea. Besides, we can't build a schoolhouse for the children. This is our rainy season."

"I've already thought of that. I was out looking around the buildings the other day. You have a big shed that is nearly empty of supplies. It would be the perfect place to hold a school. I'd only need a few benches made for the children to sit on. And old Nate could paint some small squares of flat wood with black paint, for slates."

"You've thought this through, haven't you?" He stood and leaned against the desk and tapped a pencil against his thumb. "We don't have black paint. We'd have to go into town and buy some the next time we go in for supplies."

Grace flew at Cameron and threw her arms around his neck. "Thank you. I'll make a list of the supplies I'll need. When do you go into town again?" She moved to pull out of his arms, but Cameron held her in a firm grip.

"Not so fast. It's not often I have the pleasure of your throwing yourself at me." Amusement played in his dark eyes.

"Let go of me, Cameron." Her heart hammered in her chest.

"Not till I get a proper thank you," he said huskily.

"Well, of all the—"

Cameron brought his head down close to hers, his warm lips grazing hers.

Grace tried to pull back. "Cameron."

"Yes, my darling?"

He claimed her lips, pulling her close. She couldn't resist any longer. She'd wanted this far too long. She clung to him, needing to feel his strength holding her. The kiss seemed to last a lifetime. Grace pushed on his chest, needing to take in a breath of air. Her cheeks burned and her head swam.

Cameron smiled. "Sweet Grace," he said, holding her close. "You've captured my heart, my soul, every living part of me."

"And you have done that to me." She wriggled out of his arms.

"And if we don't put an end to this, we'll send tongues wagging. We can't do this, Cameron, not until we are properly chaperoned. And even then my aunt would have you thrashed if she saw how forward you are with me."

Cameron reached out to her, a lazy smile on his lips. Grace took another step back. "Please listen to reasoning." She didn't want to resist his touch, but if she didn't go now, she'd run right back into his arms. Grace turned and purposefully walked out of the study and down the hall.

"You do beat all, Grace."

She heard his exasperated response to her hasty exit. She also heard his footsteps as he sauntered out of the house.

One evening in late autumn, Cameron, now accustomed to speaking about the business at supper, announced that he needed to go to town the next day. "I usually have the contract for the year's crop at this point in the season, but the sugar agent hasn't been around to see me yet. I want to sign an agreement before the market gets overloaded and the price drops."

Grace came to attention. "I want to go along with you."

Cameron raised a hand to halt her speech. He was used to her eagerness to learn every aspect of the business and was prepared before he broached the subject. "I figured you'd want to be involved in the marketing end of things. Be ready by nine in the morning."

As soon as they entered the sugar agent's office, a cluttered corner of a large shack on the harbor, Grace felt uneasy. Allen Campbell, a tall, middle-aged man, leered at her.

"Well," he said, twining long fingers over his chest. "Nice of you to drop by with your purty lady, Bartholomew."

"Miss Cooper's her name and I'm here to sell the Landing's sugar," Cameron said, his eyes cool. "We've come to draw up a contract for this year's crop."

"Have a seat." Mr. Campbell gestured to the chairs next to his cluttered desk. "Let me pull your file."

They spent the next forty-five minutes haggling over sums until they came to an agreement. When they'd finished, Mr. Campbell scooted his chair back and reached out to shake Cameron's hand. "We have a deal. Good day, sir."

Outside the shack, Grace glanced at Cameron's solemn face. "Did we do well?" she asked.

They waited for a donkey cart loaded with bananas to pass them before they crossed the road. "Not as well as we have in the past. It's getting harder to sell sugar from these parts. Problem is, new equipment in the states has made the process faster and easier. They don't need as many laborers to process the cane, so they can lower their price. We can't compete with them." He reached a hand behind her back and steered her across the dusty road to the hotel. "Let's eat before we shop for supplies. I've worked up an appetite."

Having spent the better part of the afternoon in town buying goods, they'd loaded the wagon down with crates of supplies, barrels of food, and gunnysacks full of rice. Rice was the one provision not grown on the plantation, and one that seemed to make it to the table most often. On the wooden floorboards behind Grace sat a box with the items needed to teach the children at Cooper's Landing.

As they traveled back to the plantation, Cameron pulled the horse off the main road onto a narrow path, heading north. Trees grew densely there, making it difficult to see ahead. After some moments of ducking and dodging the long branches that reached out over the road, they came to a clearing with a waterfall, its mist spraying deliciously over the ground, cooling the air.

Immediately, Grace's eyes grew round and she laughed in delight. "Cameron! What a wonderful sight!" She jumped out of the wagon and walked to the edge of the pond. First standing on one foot, then the other, she pulled off her shoes and let them lie where they'd landed. Then she lifted her skirt just enough to let her stockinged feet tread timidly to the water's edge. "Ahhh," she breathed. The water made little ripples over her feet.

Cameron was elated at her response. Now it was his serious intent that her attention stay focused on the scenery before her. He tethered the horse and then stripped off his outer clothes. Once he was down to his underclothes he hollered, "Don't look now, Grace," as he whizzed past her.

Grace glanced over her shoulder, then turned quickly forward, clamping her eyes shut. She imagined her face glowed as a splash sounded from the pond. Cameron came up with water streaming down his face and waded past her, waist deep, then headed for the waterfall. She stared at his bare chest, hard and muscular. She diverted her gaze quickly so as not to see more than she ought.

"This water is cold!" He swam further out to the middle of the pond, nearing the waterfall. "Come on, Grace, get in."

"No!" she cried back, wiggling her stockinged toes in the shallow water. "I can't swim."

"Then at least get your legs wet," he called out as he approached the waterfall and worked his way behind it. "I won't look."

She envied his venturous spirit. The heat was intense, and the misty spray from the waterfall invited her, too. She grabbed her gauze skirts and raised them a tad and glanced out toward Cameron. "Don't look!"

"I won't." His back turned, he swam to the far side of the pond. He dipped under the water and disappeared.

This gave Grace the courage she needed to timidly step out a little further into the water. She stepped precariously, as she had never learned to swim. She waded through the cool, shallow water and delighted at the refreshing relief from the intense heat of the day.

Water spilled over a crest of rocks down into the large pond that served as a holding pond. To the left she could see the water spilling into another pool, much smaller, where it broke out into an expansive stream.

She could see fish swimming against the current. A mist sprayed over the area, cooling the stagnant air and her skin. She spied a brown turtle, which crawled to the edge of the pond and plopped into the pool.

She cast a glance toward Cameron. True to his word, he wasn't looking. She saw his head bobbing up and down, the water up to his neck. He kept his face toward the opposite bank.

Grace giggled and kicked the cool water with her toes. The hem of her skirt was dangerously close to the soft lap of water. She bent to lift her skirt a bit higher. As she did, she stepped off the ledge of sand, lost her footing, and fell back into the water with a splash. Her feet could not find any sand beneath her.

"Help!" She cried out and then swallowed a mouthful of water. She coughed and spurted water at the same time, kicking frantically to keep afloat.

Cameron heard the splash, and turned in time to see Grace's head disappear under water. His heart lurched. He dove under water and stroked against the currents in wide circular movements. He came up once only to see her sputtering, coughing, and screaming, "Help me!" then disappear again.

He plunged under water again and swam past the strong current. He neared her floundering form. He reached for her waist and pushed her up and out of the water. He heard her take in a deep gulp of air. Then she started coughing again.

"G . . . get me . . . out . . . of here!" She turned and clung to his neck.

As Cameron moved closer to the shore, he reassured her, "You're all right, Grace. I've got you." He soothed her as he held her in the cool water.

Grace shook. "Please get m . . . me out of this water."

"I want to." He paused and glanced at his clothes lying on the sandy shore.

Grace followed his gaze behind her. Seeing his clothes lying in a heap on the hot sand, her eyes flashed with apprehension. She pealed her hands from Cameron's neck, and pushed against his chest. She kicked her feet to stay afloat.

"Wait." Cameron grabbed Grace's wrist and held her up out of the water. "Let me help you to shore."

"You can't help me." She struggled against his grip.

"Stop just a minute. I'm not going to come out of the water until I know you have your footing." His loose arm was already making circular movements to move them in the direction of the shore.

Grace turned her head so as to not look at him. Cameron dipped under the water to his shoulders. With a leap, she stumbled forward to solid ground.

Grace stood shivering on the hot sand with her back turned to Cameron. She held her hand over her eyes and listened to the sounds of Cameron pulling on his clothes. He reached for her hand and pulled it away from her face. "You can look now," he said sheepishly.

Look she did, but not at him. Her mouth dropped in horror. Her white gauze dress was soaked to a now-opaque hue. She looked up in time to see Cameron glance down the length of her with a grin of appreciation.

"Give me your shirt!" She pointed to the green shirt in his hand.

Cameron thrust the shirt toward her and turned his head. Color rose up his neck and over his ears. She hadn't missed the look on his face. It was obvious he enjoyed seeing more than he had a right to.

Grace's fingers flew as she buttoned up the baggy shirt that turned a dark green from the dampness of her soaked dress underneath.

"You can turn around now."

Their eyes met and held, her cheeks crimson from shame. He stood bare-chested and awkward. Shared intimacy hung in the air, a moment they both knew could ruin their reputations.

But their eyes held and she felt a fluttery heat in her belly.

"You're soaking wet. Let's get you home," Cameron said in a husky tone.

They went dripping along the path through the tall grass to the waiting wagon. The horse's head bobbed up and he whinnied when they came to the clearing.

Neither spoke on the rutted road back to Cooper's Landing. Cameron hoped no one would cross their path. They were both wet, and he with no shirt. A lump filled Cameron's throat with a raw ache. He hadn't realized until now that he truly loved this woman sitting beside him, more than he loved his life. He didn't know when it happened, but somehow she'd worked her way into his heart. He wouldn't have done anything to harm her. Yet, he'd put her in a delicate situation. He swore under his breath for his carelessness.

By now the shirt she wore had become completely soaked. The dark color hid her rigid body underneath. Aware of the dampness of her auburn-colored hair, of her emerald eyes staring straight ahead, and the haughty way she held herself, he chastised himself. But if she sat any further to the edge of the wagon seat, he feared she'd be jostled overboard. He couldn't blame her. Her anger penetrated the air around them. She looked everywhere except toward him, her jaw set grim and taut.

Cameron clicked his tongue, "Get along, Sunny," he called to the blonde mare.

It was almost sunset when they arrived at Cooper's Landing. When their wagon neared the Great House, they saw a carriage parked in front of the lawn. They turned to each other with dread and then back to the carriage. "Who could that possibly be?" Grace moaned.

"Maybe it's your Aunt Katy," Cameron said. He pulled the reins to stop the wagon at the end of the lane. He climbed down. "You best take the reins from here. I'll wait." He nodded toward the house. "It won't do for the two of us to enter the house soaking wet." He pointed at his soaked shirt over her dress, then down at his bare chest and wet khakis.

Grace nodded, her eyes blazing with green anger. She left him standing in the lane.

Stunned at the probability of her aunt coming at this most inopportune time, Grace's brows knit together as she tried with difficulty to walk toward the house in a waterlogged dress that weighed her down. She feared the servants would see her. Their gossipy tongues could ruin her, especially Tia. She walked past the handsome carriage and tiptoed up the steps to the porch. Leave it to Cameron to let her be gawked at in this awkward moment!

THIRTY-SIX

GRACE'S FOOTSTEPS SOUNDED loud to her ears when she crossed the wooden floorboards of the front porch. She stopped at the entrance and pulled off her kid boots and wet stockings. She listened for sounds in the house.

Maybe I can slip in unnoticed. The door creaked and Grace winced. She peered warily into the foyer. She saw no one. Good. With shoes in hand, she crossed the marble floor on tiptoes. When she passed the entrance to the drawing room, she glanced to her left.

Two men dressed in suits, vests, and bow ties—looking as if they'd just attended a state dinner—gawked at her. Grace bobbed her head back and fled up the stairs.

She ran to her chamber at the end of the hall. She'd barely entered the room, dripping water from the hem of her skirt, when she heard a tap on the door.

"Come in, Hedy."

Hedy entered and shut the door. "Miss Coopah, what happened to you?" She crossed the floor and unbuttoned the long, baggy shirt. "I'd tell you to sit down while I draw your bath, but I thinks you better stay standin'."

"Draw my bath. I can get these wretched clothes off while you do."

The girl disappeared to find Amos. After many trips, he and Cato filled the tub. Grace sat in a chair, clothed in a light blue night robe. The wet clothes lay piled on the floor in a heap.

"You git to soakin' in the tub while I run your clothes to the clothesline."

"Thank you, Hedy." Grace crossed the floor to the bathroom and eyed the tub full of hot water. "*Water*. By the time I get out I may look like a prune."

Grace stepped over the porcelain side and sank into the perfumed water. She leaned back and closed her eyes. "Hedy?"

"Yes, Missy?" The black girl appeared at the door holding the sopping wet clothes.

"Who are those men in the drawing room?"

"Why they be your relatives, Miss Coopah."

"Relatives?" Grace sat up in surprise, sloshing water as she did.

"They be your fathah's brothers," she said. "Only seen 'em a few times over the years. But they be your uncles."

Grace leaned back and closed her eyes again. She waved Hedy away from the door.

She didn't remember hearing anything about uncles from her father. Why hadn't they come to the funeral, and why were they here now? Thoughts of the two men sitting downstairs in the drawing room tumbled through her mind as she closed her eyes and let the warm water quiet her shivering body. She heard the chamber door close and knew Hedy had left the room, burdened with her wet clothes.

"Well," Grace sighed, "They came unannounced. They can wait until I'm suitably put together before I make an appearance."

Visions of herself looking like a wet mop danced in her mind as she sank lower into the water. She'd learned that first impressions made for lasting impressions. So much for first impressions.

A wry grin crossed her mouth as she recalled the foreman who'd mischievously put her in this horrid predicament. Cameron appeared miserable on the trip home. It served him right. He had soiled her honor. When her uncles were gone, she'd give him a piece of her mind.

She thought of how handsome he was, when he stood on the sandy soil with no shirt on. She did like seeing his bare chest. Color rose to her cheeks as she sank beneath the water.

An hour later, Grace appeared at the drawing room entrance looking refreshed and dressed like a lady. Hedy had taken extra measures to pile Grace's hair on top of her head in a most delightful style. Tendrils curled over her forehead and down the back of her neck. Grace had chosen a tea gown of pale blue-and-white, brocaded silk, with lace and velvet. She carried a matching fan, which she held loosely in her left hand. As she crossed the floor, three pairs of eyes followed her.

The two men, austere and dour, seemed older than her father.

The third man she'd left at the end of the lane only an hour earlier. He stood tall and dashing in his dark-blue jacket. His white shirt, casually open at the top, revealed tanned skin. A thrill went through her as their eyes held. She felt a catch in her throat.

Cameron smiled broadly and strode across the floor toward her. "Miss Cooper." He put his hand under her elbow. "May I introduce you to your uncles?"

Reluctantly, she let Cameron take the lead. She took his cue and put on her most gracious manner. "Please do." She pasted a smile on her face as the charade continued.

"This," Cameron said as he gestured to an elderly man on his left, "is Mr. Richard Cooper."

Grace dipped slightly, extending her hand. Her uncle gave a limp shake before he kissed her hand. Grace stilled herself. Nothing irked her more than to shake a man's hand that felt like wilted lettuce leaves. She preferred a good sound shake. She withdrew her hand and faced the other man who scowled at her with what—contempt?

"And this is the eldest of the three brothers, Mr. Henry Cooper."

Grace extended her hand, trying to gauge what kind of man Henry would prove to be. His grip, strong and firm, scared her. Grace quickly withdrew her hand.

Gemma appeared at the drawing room entrance. "Suppah is served."

As the four entered the dining room, Grace glanced at the door that swung into the kitchen. She'd much rather sit in there with the servants. Yet she remembered the first impression she'd made with her uncles. She resigned herself to remedy that.

Cameron pulled out her chair. She flashed him a wary glance. "Thank you, Cameron."

"So what brings you to Cooper's Landing?" Cameron asked, coming right to the point. He sat next to Grace and opposite the dour gents.

Henry took the lead. "We've been traveling abroad on business when we heard that our brother, Phillip, had passed. We deemed it necessary to come and pay our respects." He glanced at Richard. "After supper we'll convey our business. For now, let's enjoy the meal."

Cameron glanced at Grace, eyebrows raised. For the next half hour, only the sound of utensils against bone china broke the silence.

When they returned to the drawing room, Gemma followed with a tray of iced lemonade and papaya thumbprint cookies. Each of the men took a cold glass from the tray. Gemma set the plate of cookies on a table and exited the room.

"Have a seat," Cameron said, as he gestured to the guests.

Richard cleared his throat as he took his place on the sofa. Henry, however, remained standing in the center of the drawing room.

"I must say, young lady, we were not aware Phillip had a daughter. He never mentioned you in his contracts." Henry raised a brow and stepped forward. "There must be some certificate or document showing you are indeed his child?"

"Yes, of course, Uncle. My mother kept good records." Grace sizzled. She took a step back to put distance between them.

"As Mr. Bartholomew announced earlier, we are your father's brothers. As such we are also our father's heirs."

Henry paced one way, then the other. "We received word of our brother's demise several weeks ago," he said. "It seems the appropriate time to set past accounts straight. I suspect you're not aware that Phillip purchased this estate using a loan from our father. That loan has not been paid."

Grace darted a glance to Cameron. His countenance was stern.

"Isn't my father an heir to Grandfather, as well?" she asked.

"No, he's not," Henry said. "Your grandfather disowned your father when he married your mother."

Grace felt shot through the heart.

Her uncle showed no emotion. "As heirs to our father's entire holdings, we inherited all properties, including our brother's outstanding loan. Now that Phillip has passed on, however, with no mention of this debt paid in our father's will, I can see no point in delaying the proceedings any further. We've come to foreclose on Cooper's Landing."

For a long moment, Grace tried to grasp the scope of what he'd said. As it registered, she turned cold with shock.

"If that is the sole purpose of your visit," Cameron said dryly, "You've wasted your passage. Cooper's Landing carries no foreclosable mortgage."

"I beg your pardon?" Henry said in contempt. "My business is with Miss Cooper."

It was a look of hauteur Cameron had seen before, the type of impression that had given him his disdain for the English upper class. He was more than equal to dealing with it. "If your business concerns Cooper's Landing," Cameron said, "you'll speak to me as well. I'm half-owner of this plantation."

Henry's eyebrows shot up again. "Bartholomew? Ah, yes, I believe your name has come up in connection with the property."

"As well it should," Cameron returned. "It is on the deed. And in view of the straightforward nature of the document, I'd say any claims you may have about ownership are baseless. Pip had a new will drawn up. Our attorney is in England as we speak, putting together all of Pip's information regarding his assets. He should be returning any day now. When he does, he'll set the record straight."

"Has there been a reading of the will?" Henry asked.

"No," Cameron said. "The attorney will read the will when he returns.

"It's unusual to wait so long for the reading of a will." Henry looked skeptical.

"Pip died quickly. Mr. Rothschild is in London collecting documented material he'll need before he reads the will."

Grace listened to the banter between the two men. For the first time since she'd arrived on the plantation, she was grateful that Cameron owned half of the Landing. She was deemed utterly speechless with the news her uncles were here to foreclose on her beloved father's estate. Moreover, she was encouraged by every word that came out of Cameron's mouth. It gave her hope as she listened to his reasoning.

"You say your name is on the deed." Henry raked Cameron with doubt in his eyes. "We want to see those papers, young man. Since our brother's will has yet to be read, my solicitors are, of course, prepared to establish the legitimacy of all claims."

Grace shot Cameron a look. She had heard enough and was ready to send them packing.

Richard broke in. "Perhaps we should discontinue the discussion of the estate for now. It's been a long journey, and jolting news for you. We've spent half of the afternoon waiting for our niece, Grace, to return from town." He gave Grace a wry grin. "I'm sure we'll all benefit from a good night's sleep." He rose from the sofa and stood next to Henry. "It's a long ride back to town. Could you afford a room for your uncles for the night?"

Grace felt mentally dislocated. She didn't want to harbor these two men in her home, even if they were her father's brothers. Against her better judgment, she picked up a bell from the table and shook it twice. Gemma appeared at the entrance. "Yes, Miss Coopah?"

"Please escort my uncles to the guest rooms down the hall."

"Yes, Miss Coopah." She prepared to leave with the two gents in tow, but turned back. "Will that be all for the evening?"

"Yes, Gemma. You may retire for the evening."

"Good night."

"Good night, Gemma."

The two men followed the servant woman down the hall.

Grace stayed behind with Cameron. "Of all the nerve!" she spat.

Cameron's jaw worked before he spoke. "I'll find the document proving this land is paid for in full in the morning."

"You're sure you have such a document?" Grace asked, with a sickening rush of fear in her stomach.

"Pip worked on a new will before he died. What I don't know is if he accomplished what he'd set out to do before he passed." Cameron sank into the overstuffed chair.

"Your father seemed unsettled for several days after Desmond had come. I was under the impression he hadn't finished the details on the new will. Something Des said led me to believe that the trip to London was necessary, even though they spent a good many hours in seclusion while your father was ill."

"I remember the attorney came out to the house." Grace thumped the delicate fan in her hand. "As a matter of fact, I was concerned father wasn't getting the privacy he desired while conferring with the attorney."

"Why is that?"

"Tia found several excuses to come and go from his bedchamber during the time Mr. Rothschild was here."

"I wasn't aware of that." Cameron frowned. "That could account for the reason he couldn't finish the will. And as far as I know, Desmond Rothschild hasn't returned from his trip. Until then, there'll be no reading of the will."

"So now what do we do?"

"We have the original document disclosing the land is cleared of debt. He filed it away before you came."

"Are you sure?" Grace paced the floor. "I didn't see it."

"I'm sure. He showed it to me. He wanted me to know where he kept the document." Cameron hoisted himself out of the chair. Restless, he joined Grace in pacing the floor.

"And the document is legal?"

"No doubt about it. Pip had it notarized." Cameron's brows creased. "It's in the credenza in the office."

"Thank goodness," Grace said. After all that happened that day, she couldn't stay up another moment.

"Let's forget about this for now." Cameron slipped his arm around her waist and guided her to the entrance of the drawing room.

All resentment toward Cameron evaporated with their new circumstances. She gazed up into his dark eyes. He cupped her chin and lifted her face to his. "Go to bed." He kissed her forehead. "This will all go away in the morning," he said huskily, then kissed the top of her nose.

"Aren't you going to bed?" she asked, while he gave her a small push toward the foyer.

"Not just yet." He hesitated. "But you go along."

When Grace reached the top landing, she turned to peer down the stairs. Light spilled out from the drawing room across the marble floor in the foyer. The house was quiet.

But as she stood there, something told her she wasn't alone. Shadows lurked everywhere. She glanced down each end of the hallway from where she stood. No one. The hairs on her neck rose.

Tia's bedchamber door was to the left of where she stood. Had she been listening to the conversation below? Not once did the woman make an appearance that evening. Tia could usually be found lurking near, as if she had a right to know all that went on at the Great House. Had she known the intent of the uncle's visit?

Grace didn't fall asleep. She watched the door through the dark shadows and lay awake thinking about the evening's events. For the first time, she realized just how much the plantation meant to her. Here she'd gone from a state of timid dependence to one of self-confidence. Here she found direction and purpose. Here she found love; that of her father, Kindra, and Cameron.

Grace kicked off the quilt and pulled the cool sheet up to her neck. She'd not turn Cooper's Landing over to her uncles. If they thought they had a meek little niece who'd be easily persuaded to listen to their foolish ideas, they were wrong. She punched her pillow and sank her head into its softness.

Her father plunged through darkness, his arms flailing through nothingness. She heard his desolate scream as he fell, fell, fell, deeper into the abyss of utter darkness.

Something in her spirit wanted to rescue him, to pull him back, but he fell at such a speed, no one could save him.

"Why didn't you listen to me while you still had the chance, Father?" she whispered into the dark night. Heaviness weighed in her soul. "Why God? Why did you let him die before he made his peace with you?"

Grace's eyes snapped open. She slipped out of bed and walked to the doors of the balcony. Her damp nightgown clung to her. She ran her hand over her clammy face and stared out the windowpanes of the French doors. Shadows swayed from the palm trees. For the third time since her father had died, she'd awakened from the same terrifying dream.

Moonlight filled her room, as if a tunnel of light from heaven shown down on her. She gazed into the light and closed her eyes. "If there is any chance of redeeming his soul, Lord, please have mercy on him." She wiped her eyes and lay down again, finding sleep in the still of the night.

THIRTY-SEVEN

GRACE AWOKE TO the sun shining into her bedchamber. She slipped out of bed and swung the French doors open. The trade winds blew in from the bay and billowed her gown. She stood for a moment, letting the breeze calm her.

A rap sounded at her door. "Come in, Hedy."

Grace stepped back into the bedroom. "Is Cameron downstairs with my uncles?"

"No, Missy. He done left for the provisional fields at dawn."

"And my uncles?"

"They be sitting in the dining room."

He left me alone to deal with my uncles? "Get me dressed, Hedy."

Grace entered the dining room to find Henry seated at the head of the table and Richard at the other end. She moved to the sideboard and dished up a plate of scrambled eggs and salt fish. Penny pulled out a chair in the center of the table. "Will you be havin' tea, Miss Coopah?"

"Please." Grace eyed the two men who studied her in brooding silence. "Good morning, Uncles." She snapped her napkin open and laid it upon her lap. "Did you sleep well?"

"We did." Eyes dark, Henry flicked his wrist and looked at his watch.

"Your tea." Penny sat a cup and saucer in front of Grace's plate.

"When Cameron comes in from the fields, he'll clear up the matter of the deed. He can prove that my father purchased Cooper's Landing before Grandfather Granville disowned him." She glared at the two dour gents at the table.

"I believe you have your information misconstrued, Grace. I recall your grandfather loaned Phillip a large sum of money. Generally speaking," Henry said, with a coldness that shriveled Grace's sense of victory, "one expects an attorney present to vouch for documents. Should you have such a document, we'll want our attorney to review it." He took a sip of coffee. "Which means the document will need to be sent to our attorney's office in London."

Her heart sank, but she put on a bold front. "I'll not send the document anywhere without conferring first with my attorney here in Riverbend. Mr. Rothschild is a highly respectable lawyer. He has the credentials to verify my father's deed to the plantation. His word will have to do."

The two men glanced at each other.

"I don't see how we can waive the need to send the documents to London," Richard chimed in. "Supposing you truly have such a document."

Henry scowled and scooted his chair back. "We'll continue this conversation after we've had a look at the papers." He brushed crumbs off his dark jacket and checked his watch again. "It's 8:30. I want to have a look at the grounds before we sail. We have a ship to catch before noon."

Grace's spirits soared one instant and plummeted the next. She'd not seen the document Cameron had spoken of. Did such a deed exist?

An hour later, Grace stood at the entrance to the office to find every drawer open and papers haphazardly strewn on the tabletops. Cameron stood with his back to the door, talking to himself, while he opened and shut each drawer of the low chest in front of him. "Dad burn dingit! It should've been right here." He turned and opened the top drawer of a tall oak chest next to the credenza and shuffled papers.

Grace cleared her throat. Cameron whirled around, and threw her a look of mild exasperation. "I can't understand it." He ran a frustrated hand through his hair. "The paper should have been in the top drawer of this chest." He pointed to the low credenza and shook his head. He glanced around the room that now looked like it had been struck by a hurricane. "I've combed through every drawer. I don't know how, but the deed is gone." He folded himself in the leather chair behind the desk with a look of defeat.

"Oh, no," Grace groaned. She moved a pile of papers off the chair in front of the desk and slipped into it. "Now what are we going to do?"

"We're going to keep looking, that's what we're going to do." The two of them searched every drawer, every table and behind the furniture to no avail. The deed was gone.

"I'm going to search Father's bedroom. Maybe he hid it there," Grace said, as she backed out of the office.

"Good idea. He could have shown it to Mr. Rothschild and not returned it."

Grace held up her hand and crossed her fingers. "Wish me luck."

An hour later, Grace returned from her father's bedchamber with no deed. She had set to work straightening papers, when Gemma popped her head into the office. "Lunch be served, Miss Coopah."

"Has anyone seen Cameron?"

"He said to tell you he be headin' out to the fields."

"Are my uncles still here?"

"They be putting their baggage in the carriage." Footsteps sounded in the hall, and Gemma stepped away. Grace poked her head out of the office door.

"There you are, Grace. We're leaving," Henry said. "It appears you don't have the deed to Cooper's Landing. We don't intend to spend another minute waiting for such nonsense. You should be warned that you'll be hearing from our attorney with the foreclosure notice in the very near future." He pursed his lips. "Be prepared to vacate the premises within the next couple of months."

Grace snapped her head up. "You forget Cameron owns half of this estate."

"We'll need to see the deed, young lady. Without it, you have no proof. We will return in two months." With that, Henry Cooper walked out the door. Moments later the carriage moved out of the long drive.

Gemma stared wide-eyed. "Don't mean no disrespect, Ma'am. But I be thinkin' good riddance!"

Grace shook her head at the servant. "I'm glad they're gone. That'll give us some time to find the missing deed."

"You best git to eaten' your lunch."

"Thank you, Gemma. I'm famished."

Cameron loped Scimitar toward Riverbend. Needing time alone to think, he led the stallion out onto the dirt road. Before long he found himself beside the road where Jimmy's cart had spilled Grace and her belongings. He slipped off the stallion and tied the reins to a tree limb.

Once more, he searched the grounds for the black-stringed purse. This time he moved beyond the clearing and waded through the brush. He shoved large leaves aside and poked around the bushes. Nothing. Just when he'd decided to go back to the main road, his peripheral vision caught site of a dark object lying below a bush.

Cameron brushed back the low-hanging leaves. There lay the purse, wedged behind a small boulder. It lay precariously to the side, it's handle draped over the tall stone.

He pulled the purse out from behind the rock and held it up. It had a snag on one side and felt wet. He glanced inside the bag. Soggy velvet and miscellaneous items met his gaze. He grinned.

"Grace sure is going to be happy to see this."

Cameron stepped into the study while Grace bent over the account books. She looked up. He held something behind his back, looking as if he had a secret.

"You've found the deed?"

He shook his head.

"What are you hiding behind your back?" She stood and poked her head to one side.

He jerked away, his eyebrows raised. "You must first guess what I've found."

"My purse?" She lurched forward, threw both arms around him, and fingered the soft material. Then she jumped back. "You've found my purse?"

He stretched his arm forward, the black purse in his hand. "After several attempts, my persistence paid off." He grinned.

She took the purse and threw her arms around him again. "I can't believe you found it." She stepped back and fingered the damp material. "Oh, no," she groaned. "It's wet."

"It's been raining for weeks."

"I know." She glanced inside the barely intact bag, digging her fingers into the moist purse. She found the velvet pouch with the British coins the captain had refunded her, but the material had begun to disintegrate from mildew. Miscellaneous items of no importance lay ruined in the bottom of the bag. She pulled out her mother's handkerchief and smelled it. The smell of mold assailed her senses. Grace jerked her head back. "I don't know how to thank you for not giving up." She smiled.

"You just did." He kissed her forehead.

"I was sure someone had stolen my purse along with the locket. I must be imagining things."

"You may be right. I hope your locket does turn up. It would put my mind at ease." He replaced his hat. "I haven't thought too kindly of the idea that we have a thief in the house. The carriage is gone. I assume your uncles have left?"

"They have. They're still threatening to foreclose on Cooper's Landing. They're to return in a couple of months."

"That'll give us time to find the missing deed." His eyes grew dark. "We'll find it before the hounds return."

THIRTY-EIGHT

GRACE WATCHED THE workers pound dowels into the wood frame for the new barn. Charred lumber had been hauled away. It seemed only yesterday her father had arrived home from the long trip. Now he was gone.

She entered the wooden building where she wanted to start the new slave school. Setting her box of supplies on the dirt floor, she mentally pictured where the teacher's desk should go. From there, she determined how many benches the building would hold. Then she went in search of Cameron.

"I'll need a table and chair for the teacher's desk and ten small tables and stools for the students. Would you mind making arrangements with a carpenter to build them for the school?"

Cameron sighed. "I'll see what I can do. How soon do you need them?"

"I'd like to begin classes before next month." She squinted up at him with her hand shading her eyes. "Is that asking too much?"

"No, Grace. I'll see to it."

Back in the schoolhouse, Grace visualized the room full of children ready to learn their ABC's. She hummed a cheerful tune, eager to get it started. A half hour later, Grace peeked out of the dingy window. Kindra stood near the pane watching her. A grin tugged at Grace's mouth as she stepped out into the sunlight.

"I heard about the school," Kindra said. "When will it open?"

Grace didn't miss the wistful look in Kindra's eyes. "Have you an interest in the school?"

"It's been a dream of mine for quite some time. I never had the courage to bring it up to Father."

"Did you go to school?"

"No. Cameron taught me how to read and write when I was a child."

"He did?" Grace thought back to his reluctance to let her start the school. A smile tugged at her lips.

"I could use your help, Kindra. I don't know how to approach the children's parents about the school."

"I do."

"You may be the one to teach the little ones. I've had visions of the children showing reluctance to a white teacher." Grace folded her arms across her chest. "They'll respond to you."

"May I see the room?"

"Of course." Grace opened the door and the two stepped inside. In the next half hour, Grace shared her ideas. "I believe Nate could paint a blackboard and hang it up front right here." She moved to the front of the room and looked back at Kindra. "There's a world globe in the office and one in the library. I'll bring one out to the school. The children can learn about other countries, as well as Jamaica."

Before long, Kindra had a number of tips of her own. "The children should have small slate boards. Then they could practice their letters at night. I know a couple of the children are artistic. They could help us make picture books for the younger ones." The smile on Kindra's face was contagious. Grace brimmed with excitement as the two went back to the Great House talking and laughing as they went.

That night Grace lay in bed and thanked God for his love and mercy. This would be the first venture she and her sister would share on the Landing. Her heart light, she drifted off to sleep.

As the days added up to weeks, Grace found plenty to do on the Landing. One morning she descended the stairs with plans to look for the missing deed. A niggling in the back of her mind told her if she didn't find it, it was time to confront Tia. Did her father's mistress have a hand in the deed's disappearance? Grace neared the bottom step and heard horses in the circular drive. She followed Zeek to the front door and peered out. A carriage pulled up. Grace held her breath. Had her uncles returned?

When the driver opened the coach door, Josie stepped down, smiling.

"Josie!" Grace rushed to embrace her cousin. "You're here!"

They laughed as they turned toward the carriage.

"Aunt Katy!" Grace fell into her open arms.

"Why, let me have a look at you." Aunt Katy held Grace at arms length and smiled. "You don't look like life has given you a day of trouble since you've been out of my sight." She turned toward the coach driver. "Hand me that carrier."

The coachman reached inside the carriage and pulled out an oblong, wicker cage. He set the carrier on the ground at Katy's feet.

Grace opened the leather-strapped door. "Smitty!" She lifted out her orange-and-white, furry cat. "Oh, you poor dear, you look like you're all out of sorts." She glanced at her aunt. "Was the trip hard on him?"

"Oh, he showed his disdain all right. If the truth will have it, he got better treatment than the rest of us." She grinned and scratched the top of Smitty's head.

While they talked, the coachman set their bags on the ground. "Is that all you fine ladies need?" he asked.

"That will be all," Katy said. "The rest will be delivered in the morning." She paid the driver his fee and turned to the girls.

Grace signaled Zeek. "Take these bags upstairs and leave them on the upper landing."

"Right away, Missy." He reached for the first two bags and disappeared into the house.

When Grace glanced up, she found Kindra standing on the porch watching all the excitement.

Aunt Katy's brows raised and she turned to Grace. "Who might this be?"

Graced held out her hand, inviting Kindra to join them. "I want to introduce you to my sister, Kindra Cooper."

Aunt Katy and Josie gawked. They turned to Grace and back to Kindra. Aunt Katy found her tongue first. "There's a close resemblance between you two girls. There's no mistaking that." She elbowed Josie. "I'm Aunt Katy. Katy Johnson." She reached out and shook Kindra's hand.

Josie came forward and smiled timidly. "And I'm Josie Johnson." Her blue eyes glinted. "I do believe we're in for a few surprises, cousin."

"You're right, but all in good time. Let's go into the house. You must be weary from the long drive." Grace slipped her free hand in the crook of Kindra's arm and held her back, in order to let her aunt and cousin walk up the steps before them.

Grace spent the next half hour showing her aunt and cousin their rooms. Once done, they entered the dining room.

"I want to hear all about your trip on the *Savannah Rose*. Did the captain put you up in the luxury cabin?" Grace asked.

"Yes, he did." Aunt Katy filled Grace in on all the details of the trip.

"So much has happened since I left Charleston." Grace told them about the cart accident and then sobered. "I'm glad I had time with my father. I'll never regret having made the choice to come here." Her eyes grew moist. She glanced over to Kindra. "But God filled that void. He knew I'd be lost without both of my parents, so He gave me more family here."

Kindra squeezed Grace's hand. "It is I who have been given the surprise of my life. When Grace appeared, I was angry and hurt. I wanted her to leave, to go back to where she came from." She glanced at Grace with love in her eyes. "Now my life has taken on a whole new meaning."

Tia stood at the base of the stairs, listening. Hate filled every nook and cranny of her being. First Grace stole Phillip's heart. His days took on a whole new direction as he focused on the brat. Now, she cast her spell on Kindra, stealing her daughter's heart, too. The two were inseparable. But this wasn't Grace's home. Tia seethed. She'd find a way to get rid of her. She'd move slowly. The spirits would tell her when the timing was right.

Later that evening, after the women settled in the drawing room, Aunt Katy asked, "Now where's that foreman you've got sleeping in the barn?"

Grace jerked her head up. "You mean Cameron."

No sooner were the words out of her mouth than Cameron strode in. His brows quirked up.

"Did I hear someone call my name?" Cameron walked into the drawing room and removed his wide-brimmed hat. "Cato said company had arrived." He glanced at the women in the room.

Grace stood and went to his side. "Aunt Katy has arrived." She slipped her arm through his and led him to her aunt. "This is Cameron Bartholomew. He's the foreman of Cooper's Landing."

"Good to meet you, son." Aunt Katy put her hand behind Josie's back, and this is my daughter, Josie."

Josie blushed and gave Grace a slight smile.

"My pleasure." He gave a nod Josie's way.

Grace turned to Cameron, "You missed supper. Is anything wrong?"

"We've got a problem in the boiling house. A piece of machinery has broken down."

"Really. What is it?"

"The pipe that circulates the heat for the sludge. It's worn out. We may need to cut a new one."

"Will this cause a setback?" Grace's thin brows rose.

"Hope not. I have one of the men taking a look at it now. I'm heading back out to see how it's going." Cameron touched the brim of his hat and said, "Ladies."

"This is quite an operation you have going here," Aunt Katy said.

"Yes. There's never a dull moment." Grace cleared her throat.

While Grace talked about the things she'd learned in the past couple of months, Smitty lay curled in her lap, purring.

"I'm amazed at the change in you," Aunt Katy said. "You've matured in ways you never would have, had you stayed in Charleston. I had hoped to convince you to return to South Carolina. But it's clear you've given your heart to this land."

"I have, Aunt Katy. I love it here."

"It's been a long day." Aunt Katy turned to Josie. "Are you ready to retire?"

Contentment settled in Grace's soul as she carried Smitty to her room and shut the door. She smiled as the cat circled the room with curiosity. He poked his head under the bed and then came out to walk stealthily to the other side, his tail resembling a cane as he swished it. Satisfied he'd seen enough, he jumped up on the bed, curled up, and observed her with lazy, green eyes.

Grace hugged herself as she peered out over the balcony at the starry night. A tropical breeze blew gently around her. The sky was dark and clear, and she could see beyond the cane fields to the dark waters of the Caribbean Sea. Stars twinkled in the rippling waves, like millions of diamonds glittering over each lap that bobbed in the sea. Glad to have Aunt Katy and Josie here, she imagined life could return to normal. At least Cameron wouldn't have to sleep in the stable any longer.

In the still of the night she heard the familiar sound of Cameron's chamber door open and close softly. She smiled. He was out of the bunkhouse. For this alone, he'd welcome her aunt's arrival at the house.

The next morning, shortly after breakfast, Drew Harding and a couple of crewmen pulled into the circular drive with the rest of Aunt Katy's luggage. When her aunt came down the stairs, Grace was in easy conversation with the captain.

"Aunt Katy," said Grace, "I was telling the captain to bring the Borjeau women over for tea tomorrow."

"And who might the Borjeau women be?"

"They're our neighbors. Camille is a good friend of mine." Grace glanced at Drew, who'd come to attention at mention of the young woman's name. "Claudia is Camille's mother."

"I guess that answers my next question," Aunt Katy said.

"What's that?"

"I wondered if there were womenfolk around here besides us. Don't get me wrong, I do love having you girls to talk to, but it's a breath of fresh air to talk to someone my own age."

"Then it's settled, Captain. I'll have Dinah put together a nice luncheon for tomorrow and we'll introduce our neighbors to my family."

"I'm headed over there right now. I'll pass the word along."

"If you don't mind, I'd like to jot down an invitation to them. Do you have a moment?"

"I do."

"I shan't be long." Grace disappeared to the study and penned a note on a piece of parchment paper. She found the captain on the front porch sitting on a cane chair waiting for her.

"I'm looking forward to introducing my aunt to Claudia."

"I believe the Borjeau women will be delighted as well." He stood, scooped up his hat and disappeared down the steps.

While Aunt Katy napped, Grace and Josie walked around the grounds behind the house. Pride in her father's accomplishments welled within her as she filled Josie in on the ways of the plantation.

"It's beyond me how much detail you've absorbed in the past few months." Josie smiled. "Do the slaves always watch you so?" She glanced at the curious eyes of the workers, as if intimidated by their wide stares.

"Don't mind them. You're new here and they're curious. Many of them have been here all of their lives. They've put their life's blood into this land. They are protective over Cameron and myself."

Grace learned this was true since the death of her father. They'd seen her kindness. In turn, they guarded her as a hen would her chicks.

As they rounded the lane, they came upon Kindra teaching a handful of African children in the new school. They came to the open door and stepped inside as Kindra pointed to the blackboard and repeated the first three letters of the alphabet. She carefully wrote the letter 'A' on the board and instructed the children to follow her example. Innocent eyes followed Grace and Josie as they observed the classroom.

When the two women came out into the bright sunlight, Josie said, "The plantation is like a community in itself."

"It is. And you've only seen a small portion of Cooper's Landing. In time, you'll learn to appreciate the hard work and devotion it takes to keep this place running."

"I've not been here a full two days and I believe I already have." Josie stopped and put a hand on Grace's arm. "When does the captain return to the Landing again?"

"Why?"

"I left my blue-printed dress in the cabin on the ship. The next time the captain comes out to the Landing, I need to ask him to look for it."

"He left this morning. He won't be back for another week," Grace said. "I'll try to help you remember to tell him."

"I bought it specifically for this trip."

"Did you bring your fencing uniform? I'd hoped we could pick up where we left off. I practiced some on the ship. But I'm afraid Erik was too easy on me."

"Do you have foils here at the Landing?" Josie asked.

"We do. I usually bring the blade to my room and practice alone. It'll be good to go a round with you."

That evening after everyone retired, Tia approached Grace in the dimly lit hallway.

"I was not aware you'd invited your family to the Great House. How long will they be staying?" she asked, her jaw tense.

"It could be indefinitely." Grace leveled her gaze with Tia's.

"Too much has changed in too short of time. I suggest you slow down."

"Every change I've made has been for the betterment of this house and operation. And I'll thank you to keep your opinions to yourself, Tia." Grace turned to walk down the hallway to her room.

"If I were you, I'd be more careful. All kinds of accidents can happen around here."

Grace whirled around. "Are you threatening me?"

"Not I. However, there are those on this plantation who'd like to see you gone." Her eyes showed brightly in the dim light.

Grace waited until Tia disappeared into her bedchamber. Then she stepped inside her own room and closed her door. She sat on the bed next to Smitty, stroking his back and smiling. He flopped over for a belly rub. "Well, you've not a care in the world, have you?"

A moment later Aunt Katy crept into her room, wide-eyed. "I overheard the interchange in the hallway. You'd better take Tia's warning to heart."

Grace patted the bed for her aunt to sit down. "You mustn't worry, Aunt Katy."

"I've seen the way she looks at you. And that upstairs cleaning woman makes my skin crawl. What is her name? Minerva?"

"All is well, Aunt Katy. Remember, God never sleeps. He is watching over us." She leaned over and hugged her aunt. "Now give it no more thought."

THIRTY-NINE

GRACE WALKED INTO the kitchen at the break of dawn, expecting to find Cameron at the dining room table. He wasn't there. She lifted a mug and held it out while Dinah filled it with coffee.

Smitty trailed behind her, then rubbed himself against Grace's ankles and purred.

"What brings you down so early?" Dinah asked, as she set the coffee pot on the burner.

"I couldn't sleep. I've had nightmares three nights in a row. I don't know what to do."

She picked up the orange-and-white tabby, scratched behind his ears, and stroked his fine, soft fur.

"We'll fix that problem starting tonight." Dinah picked up a metal sheet of biscuits and brought it to the center worktable.

"How can you fix my problem?" Grace set Smitty on the polished floor.

"I make a special tea that'll help you sleep like a baby. I've made this concoction for myself many times." She placed her fists on her hips. "Why you be having these annoying dreams?"

"Because Father died before he made his peace with God. It's the hardest thing I'll ever endure, knowing he's in eternal darkness."

"You best put that kind of thinkin' behind you, honey chile. Ain't nothing you can do about that now."

"I've tried to, but the dreams don't stop." She sipped the hot coffee and watched Dinah put together a delicious meal of bammy, saltfish, and ackee. She cooked the red, pear-shaped tropical fruit, which looked and tasted much like scrambled eggs. Maybe her tea could help. Grace knew if something didn't change soon, she'd be worth nothing in the next few days.

That afternoon, Grace, Josie, and Aunt Katy went for a drive in the buggy. When they returned to the Great House, Claudia and Camille had arrived. They spent a leisurely afternoon sitting around the table on the front porch, eating sandwiches and drinking the island punch. A servant woman brought out a dish of dainty cookies. "Is there anything else you need, Miss Coopah?"

"We're fine, thank you." Grace turned to the women. "This is a first for me. I've not had the occasion to picnic on the front porch. I believe we should do this more often."

As the hours passed, clouds rolled in, threatening rain. The Borjeau women left quickly, and the rest of the women proceeded into the house at the first flash of lightning.

Darkness settled over the land. Grace glanced out the screen door before she led the women into the drawing room. "Cameron and Denzel will have to round up the workers and send them back to their shanties. They can't work in the rain."

She looked over to see Aunt Katy watching her. "You have settled into this way of life nicely, Grace. If one didn't know better, they'd think you'd been here all your life."

"Sometimes it feels that way. Father gave me responsibilities for the business soon after I arrived. The more I learned, the more I wanted to know." She sighed. "I love it here."

"We know," Josie said. "Mother and I thought we might talk you into returning to Charleston. Now that we've come, we wouldn't think of asking you to leave. You belong here."

"I'm glad you came." Grace smiled. "There was no way I could have explained what it's like in a letter. You had to see it for yourself."

For the next three nights, Dinah brought tea to Grace's room. Grace finally found the rest she so desperately needed. "It has been pure heaven getting a full night's sleep, Dinah. I'm grateful you had a remedy for my dilemma."

Days went by and the women found plenty to keep them busy. In between bookkeeping and the school, the days took on a pattern that left Grace feeling contented.

One morning Grace awoke with a splitting headache. Her stomach roiled and she ran to the bathroom. She sank to the floor and leaned her head over the necessary chair. Her head pounded while her stomach wretched. *Oh Lord, why am I so sick?* Sweat beads formed on her brow. After a moment, Grace stood on wobbly legs. She splashed cool water over her face, dried it, and peered into the mirror at her pale reflection. "I'd better go back to bed." Grace spent the day with her head in her hands, grateful for Aunt Katy, who took over the tasks that needed tending.

By nightfall, Grace felt no better. "I believe I'll retire early tonight. My head feels like it's going to split. Please forgive me," she said to her aunt and cousin.

"Don't you dare apologize, young lady. You get to bed and stay there," Aunt Katy admonished her. "In the morning, we'll send for the doctor."

Grace moved from the sofa in the drawing room to her bed. Smitty followed close behind. He jumped up onto her bed and circled three times before lying down, lifting a hind leg for a foot wash.

Minerva knocked on the door and slipped into the room. "Here's your tea, Miss Coopah. Dinah says to drink it all." She set the cup on the night stand and asked, "Are you feeling any better, Missy?"

"No. I'm feeling worse." She groaned. "Thank you for the tea. Maybe it'll help me sleep tonight."

"Drink it all. It should help you sleep." Minerva's brows drew together.

Grace thought about the change in the cleaning maid's behavior. It seemed Minerva couldn't do enough to make life easier for Grace. It had started shortly after her father's death. Not one to hold a grudge, Grace wanted to believe Minerva had had a change of heart.

Grace awoke to a thumping sound outside her room. She was surprised she had awakened, having drunk Dinah's special tea.

Now, however, she sat up and listened. The floor creaked outside her door. She held her breath, then slipped out of bed. She nearly stumbled, her brain in a fog, and her stomach roiling. She opened the door and peeked out into the hallway. No one. She peeked across the hall to Tia's chamber door. It was closed.

Outside her chamber, Grace closed her door until she heard the latch close tight. She did not remember closing many doors back home, but here, it seemed necessary. As the latch clicked, Grace stood on wobbly legs. The silence of the house seemed almost ominous as it closed in around her.

With tentative steps she walked to the stairway at the end of the hall. She leaned over, listening for sounds in the dark below.

Rain beat on the window behind her. She swayed and held onto the rail. Fear clawed at her throat. She knew she ought to go back to bed, but something told her someone was down there. The room swam. She took the first step down the stairs.

Again, the creaking sound. Grace held onto the banister as she descended and glanced around, the hairs tingling the back of her neck. She moved into the dining room. Her mother's portrait peered down at her in the dark. Her mind felt embroiled as if she were in a distant place. In her muddled state, she tried to see her mother's eyes. But in the dark, they evaded her. Then Grace peered out the window. The rain made puddles in the circular drive.

She tiptoed to the foyer, then the drawing room. She heard the creaking again. She paused, her back to the fireplace. She reached for the fireplace poker. Only silence. Grace crept back to the foyer. *Where had the sound come from?*

A sharp clanging resounded beyond the dark hallway. Grace jumped. The morning room? She shook her head as she crept down the narrow hallway. Shadows lurked all around. Large portraits of people she didn't know hung on the wall. The ancient eyes seemed to watch her, their smiles mocking her. A chill worked its way up her back.

Grace quietly tiptoed into the morning room. Tall leafy plants stood in the corners. They seemed ominous, as if dark figures stood by. She reminded herself they were only plants.

Lightning illuminated the room and the luscious tropical garden that lay beyond the doors. A breeze prickled her skin. The familiar scent of rain wafted in. Then it dawned on her, the doors stood ajar. Why else would she feel the breeze around her bare feet? She padded to the morning room doors and peeked out. *Who's out there?*

Grace crept out onto the narrow, cobbled walkway. Rain pelted her as she ran to the round, glassed greenhouse. The door was open. She hesitated, then slipped inside and softly closed the door.

In the center of the garden house, water trickled from the tall fountain down a number of boulders to the six-foot-round pool below. A breeze wrapped around her bare feet. *Who opened the doors?*

The familiar scent of jasmines wafted in from the garden.

Mesmerized by the scents in her foggy state, Grace pushed away from the water fountain and hid behind a large leafy tropical plant. Tia moved into the clearing beyond the fountain, not ten feet from where Grace stood. She waited, afraid to move.

Tia chanted in a singsong manner as she moved about the garden, oblivious to Grace's presence. She held a long sword while she sang. A flash of lightning lit the blade. Grace listened, enchanted, yet fearful. All at once the tigress stopped. Her gaze jumped to the massive plants where Grace hid.

She held her breath. Did Tia know she was there? Slowly, Grace inched her way toward the doors. As she shrank away, the humming and chanting began again. *Was she singing to her gods?*

Grace slipped through the morning room doors and locked them. She proceeded to the safety of her room. Once inside, she locked her door and went to the balcony. Could she see the garden room from here? Her eyes searched the ground until they focused on the greenhouse near the tropical garden where Tia sang her native song. The sky lit up and the greenhouse illuminated. As she suspected, Tia was gone.

An object gleamed on the ground outside the garden house. From here, Grace couldn't make out the object. She had to know what it was. Tia had been acting strange lately. What was she hiding? Somehow Grace knew that object would help her find the answer. She had to go back to the garden and retrieve it.

Once again, she descended the stairs, this time motivated to move swiftly through the rooms. But in the morning room, she stopped. Was someone there? Grace shook her head as if to clear her vision. A breeze barely touched her. The doors she'd locked, now stood ajar. No matter. She'd have to hurry.

Grace advanced to the patio. She wove in and out through the tropical plants until she came to the clearing beyond the garden house. Only moments ago, Tia had stood inside the greenhouse, smooth and sleek like a panther, holding a sword as if caressing it. Now, on the ground lay a long metal sheath with the Cooper coat of arms. Her father's sheath. Why had Tia taken it? It lay empty. Where was the sword?

Grace learned the slaves had hundreds of rituals and superstitions. Tia had used the sword while she chanted. Sheet-like illumination lit up the grounds. Grace quickly grasped the cold metal sheath and hid it in the folds of her gown. Ignoring the fear that gripped her, she entered the morning room. She took the stairs two at a time. In her room, she shut the door and leaned against it.

The scent of jasmine filled the room. Grace closed her eyes and shook her head. Her knees were weak, her head light.

The sheath clashed to the floor. Then utter darkness.

"Grace. Wake up."

The voice sounded far away, beyond the darkness that shrouded her. A masculine voice. She couldn't reach the world that seemed only a finger's tip away.

"Grace, darling . . ."

That voice . . . calm and soothing.

"Grace, wake up, honey."

It was Cameron. She wanted to reach out to him. He'd never spoken words of endearment

to her. Now she couldn't respond.

Something else filled the room. Jasmines. She smelled the fragrance, ever so faintly. Was Tia here, too? Is she standing next to Cameron? Grace struggled with the inner darkness.

Her eyes fluttered open. Cameron stood beside her, tall and commanding. She saw relief in his eyes.

"What happened, darling?" he asked.

"I . . . I don't know. I came into the room and shut the door. I brought Father's sheath to the room." Grace bolted upright and glanced toward the door. "Where's the sheath?"

Aunt Katy stood on the opposite side of the bed, her eyes wide as she listened.

"The sheath?" Cameron left her side and glanced about the room.

"It's on the floor by the door."

"Lie down, honey," Aunt Katy said. " We'll worry about it in the morning."

Cameron stepped back to Grace's side and gently forced her to lean back against the soft pillow.

"Tia's been to my room. Do you smell the jasmines?"

"The French doors are open. The fragrance from the garden has filled your chamber."

"No! Tia's been here!" She looked at Cameron, then her aunt.

"We don't doubt your suspicion that she's been to your room," Cameron said, his deep voice gentle. "But you'll wake up the rest of the house if you don't keep your voice down. Go back to sleep. We'll talk about this in the morning." Cameron kissed her forehead. Then he strode to the door, glanced back looking uncertain, and left the room.

Aunt Katy said, "Go to sleep, dear."

Grace closed her eyes. Where was Tia? *Is she waiting in the shadows?*

When Grace woke up again, the candle had been snuffed out and the room was dark. Only a silver streak of moonbeams lit the room. Someone had changed her wet clothes. She now wore a cotton, rose-printed nightgown, cool in the humid room. Then she remembered. Aunt Katy and Cameron had come to her room. Where was the sheath? Had Tia retrieved it? She'd look for the sword in the morning. If it wasn't there, she'd search Tia's chamber. She had to know where it was.

A woman standing in the shadows held the cool sheath against her chest and listened. The house had quieted once again. One thing was certain. She had the upper hand. Sounds in the house scared Miss Coopah, as well they should. Grace best go back to where she came from. If not, extra measures would be required.

FORTY

GRACE AWOKE TO Dinah carrying in a breakfast tray. Aunt Katy took the tray and set it down on the night stand. "I'll see that she eats."

Dinah glanced at Grace with soulful eyes and slipped out of the room.

"You gave us quite a scare, young lady." Aunt Katy plumped the pillows behind Grace as she spoke. "What happened last night? We heard a loud crash, and Cameron and I came running."

Grace stared out of the French doors to see the rain still coming down. "I heard noises. I wanted to see who was up."

"Good Lord, child, I'm never going to find sleep if you plan on turning into a sleuth. Are you trying to get yourself killed?"

A rap sounded at the door, and Cameron peeked his head in. "Is she awake?"

"She's awake. Come in."

Cameron's brows lifted as he glanced down at Grace. "How do you feel?"

"I'm fine." Grace eyed Cameron. "Tia was down in the garden room last night with Father's sword. I found her dancing and chanting in her native tongue. I watched her for a while and then returned to my room. The next thing I knew, you woke me up."

Cameron paused before he spoke. "Dinah said you've been having nightmares. Could you have dreamed this?" He touched her hand gently.

330

Grace raised up. "It wasn't a nightmare, Camp. It was real. I was there."

He looked at Aunt Katy with apprehension, then back to Grace. "I want you to rest today. You've been working too hard lately."

Grace fell against the pillows and closed her eyes. A single tear slipped down her cheek. Her lip quivered. "You don't believe me."

"Grace, honey, I don't know what to believe, but I do know I don't want you padding about the house in the middle of the night. It's not safe."

Her eyes snapped open. "Then you do believe me."

"I told you before it wasn't safe to be here. Promise me you won't go traipsing around the house in the middle of the night." His eyes pierced hers.

"I promise."

Cameron let out a deep sigh. He bent and kissed the top of her head. "After the fierce storm we had last night, I'm not sure how the crops have fared. I'm going out to make my rounds. Stay in and rest . . . for me?"

"I will."

Cameron turned to Aunt Katy. "I'll be back after I check on the fields and the shanties. Sometimes these rains wreak havoc on their roofs. Keep her lying down, will you?"

"You don't need to give me orders, young man. I'm keeping her in bed all right."

He looked at Grace. "I'll be back after lunch."

"I'll be watching for you." Grace smiled.

When the door closed, Aunt Katy pulled a chair up to the bed and said, "I think we should return to Charleston. This place makes my skin crawl."

Grace slept the best part of the day away. A sunset lined the horizon when Grace rolled out of bed and rang the bell. Hedy popped her head into the room.

"Run my bath. I'm going downstairs for supper tonight." Grace walked over to her vanity. Her locket lay embedded in a small spray of jasmine flowers. She turned to Hedy. "Did you find my necklace?" She held it up.

"No, Missy. This be the first time I seen it since you lost it."

"I didn't lose it. Someone took it." She picked up the spray of jasmines and tossed them in the wastebasket, then opened the clasp. The picture of her parents was embedded in the heart-shaped locket. "Good." She spun around. "Forget the bath. Get me dressed. I've had enough of this nonsense. It's going to stop, once and for all."

An hour later, Grace entered the dining room, where everyone sat except for Tia. Grace took her usual seat as the servants brought her a plate and beverage. All eyes were pinned on her.

"It looks like you've been sitting on a pincushion, Grace. Is something wrong?" Aunt Katy asked.

"As a matter of fact there is." She patted the locket at her throat. "My locket has been missing for weeks. It showed up this evening on my vanity."

"You should be glad, but I suspect there's more to it." Aunt Katy's eyes widened.

"There is." Grace glanced at Kindra. "But I'll deal with it later."

"Mother?" Kindra asked.

"That would be my first guess. And come to think of it, my last guess, too."

In the days following, the weather remained warm, but with the trade winds blowing the rains becoming more frequent. Grace had never seen so much rain in her life. She relished the day when the sun would come out and stay out. She returned to her bookkeeping and helped Kindra with the school. The nights had calmed, and she found she didn't need Dinah's special tea to help her sleep.

Her uncles would be back soon. They had still to find the deed. Grace stood at the entrance of the study, fists on hips, and decided today was the day to look for the missing deed. With Tia in town, Kindra out at the schoolhouse, and Aunt Katy and Josie off to the Borjeaux's, she had the house to herself.

She thumbed through the files in the filing cabinet. No luck. She turned to the high chest. Papers were haphazardly stashed inside from when Cameron had searched the drawers. Grace rolled up her sleeves and pulled all the papers out. She went through them, one by one. Before long, Grace had immersed herself in paperwork.

Smitty marched into the room. When Grace crossed to the oak desk, the cat hopped onto the tabletop and lay down, wrapping his long tail across his feet like an orange cloak.

Grace gazed down at him and pursed her lips. "Now how am I to work with you lying in the middle of the desk?" She picked him up and sat him on the floor. He moved to the door and began cleaning himself, disdain showing in his green eyes.

The temperature had dropped. Tia pulled the hood of her scarlet cloak over her head. She flapped the reins of the wagon while she rode into Riverbend. The skies filled with dark clouds. It looked like it could pour within the hour.

She had to see Mr. Cranston again. It had only taken a little persuasion to talk the attorney into drawing up a new will for Phillip Cooper. His fee was outrageous, but when the Landing was hers, the cost would be worth it.

A flat, black case lay under the wagon seat with the deed to Cooper's Landing. With the threat of rain, she needed to hurry. It wouldn't do to have the paper get soaked.

Moments later, Tia pulled up to Cranston's office. She sat in the outer room while he talked with another client. She laid the black case on a chair and paced.

Mr. Cranston stood and shook hands with his client. Soon he strode over to where Tia stood. "Good to see you again."

"Have you drawn up the new papers for the will?" She sat down before his desk and drew the deed out of the flat case. She placed it on his desk and waited.

"I've been swamped with clients lately, but I did get your papers drawn up. It's a good thing you brought the deed. It took some time to get his signature to look legitimate." He opened his side drawer and searched through some files. "Here it is." He examined Phillip's signature on the deed against his forged copy, then nodded. He laid the papers on the desk for her inspection.

Tia leaned in as if reading the words. She wouldn't let on she couldn't read. After several moments, she sat back. "Perfect. And you're sure no one will dispute the terms in the document?"

"I don't know how anyone could. This is much the same as the original will, except for the changes in names and date. You are designated as the main heir of Cooper's Landing and his fleet of ships. Your daughter will have a handsome income once the funds are transferred to your account."

Tia scooped up the papers and unlatched the black case she'd borrowed from the office at the Landing. She slid the papers in and patted it.

Mr. Cranston cleared his throat. "And now the fee for my services?"

"Yes, I have the money right here." Tia opened her scarlet bag and drew out a thick envelope. She slid it across the desk to the attorney, and stood.

Mr. Cranston walked ahead to open the door for her. "Good day Tia, and good luck."

Grace bent over the drawer and placed the last sheet of paper on top of the orderly stack. One more folder to search and she'd be done. The folder had no heading. When Grace opened it, she gaped at a letter that appeared to be a legal document. She sat down and read through it slowly.

> To whom it may concern. I, Granville Henry Cooper, in my own handwriting, let it be known this day, 5 February 1806, I give my son, Phillip Thomas Cooper, fifty thousand pounds to be used at his discretion, free of debt. Let it also be known, all monies given him prior to this date are declared free of payment. In the same token, however, as long as he is married to Olivia Grace Cooper, he will no longer receive funds from my account. Moreover, Phillip will no longer be considered my son.

The document, notarized by an attorney in Bath, England bore the signature of Granville H. Cooper.

The corners of her mouth turned up. She tucked the document in the folder and filed it in the cabinet. As soon as Cameron came in from the fields, they would celebrate this news. Her uncles couldn't touch Cooper's Landing now.

The next morning Grace awoke with a severe headache again. She had tea before she'd gone to bed, but not Dinah's special remedy. She had sipped the steamy brew while reading her Bible and fell asleep. But now in the early morning hour, her head wanted to split open.

When Hedy arrived to get her dressed, Grace asked her to tell the others she wouldn't be down till later. She lay against her pillow and rocked her head. Sometimes she felt like she was fading into a dark tunnel—she stopped rocking and her eyes snapped open. Her father had described feeling the same way. He used those same words . . . *fading into a tunnel?* Was it the tea? Had someone poisoned her father and now wanted her gone as well?

Grace didn't believe for a minute Dinah would harm her father. Yet the next time someone brought tea to her room, she wouldn't drink it.

Angry, Grace sat up in bed, determined not to give in to the massive headache. She stumbled to her wardrobe and found a dress. Soon she was ready to go downstairs.

The sound of wagon wheels sailed up to her room. Grace leaned over the balcony rail and saw Tia sitting in the wagon veiled in her red cloak, Jesse beside her.

Grace stormed out of the bedchamber and down the stairs. She took the back hallway that led to the yard and marched out to the stables. Grace wanted to have a word with Tia, and now.

When she was halfway to the stable it started to rain again. The thunder rolled. She sloshed through the mud as she neared the barn. The wagon was parked outside. She bolted into the stable and looked around. Jesse and Tia were nowhere to be seen. Grace moved farther into the building. Other than the sounds of the horses munching their grain, it was quiet.

Where did they go? Grace whirled around and ran out through the double doors. The rain had not let up. Before she could take another step, a sharp pain pierced her head. She opened her mouth to cry for help, but fell into utter darkness.

"Out of my way!" Cameron shouted as he carried Grace into the drawing room. Aunt Katy, Josie, and the servants all followed as he laid Grace on the sofa.

Kindra peered over Josie's shoulder. "I'll go get a blanket."

"She's soaking wet," Aunt Katy said. "Can't we get her up to her room where we can change her clothes?"

Cameron looked down at Grace. She was unconscious, but she let out a low moan. What had she been doing out in the rain?

"She's waking up. Let's do as you say. I'll take her up to her room." He scooped Grace into his arms. Aunt Katy, Josie, and Kindra followed close behind. The servants stood at the base of the stairs and looked on, concern on their faces.

"Miss Coopah done had too many of these spells lately. There be somethin' mighty wrong heah," Gemma said.

Aunt Katy parked herself next to Grace's bed like an eagle watching her young. "I'm taking Grace back home," she grumbled, a resolute look on her face.

"This is home to Grace now." Cameron eyed Aunt Katy with a wry look.

"Not anymore. It isn't safe for her here."

"We'll have to let Grace decide on that." Cameron stood and stared at the sleeping form, coal smoldering in his gray eyes.

Grace's eyes fluttered open. She first saw Aunt Katy, though she sensed someone else in the room. She turned to see Kindra in the other chair, praying softly.

Grace moaned. Aunt Katy leaned over her. "How are you feeling, honey?"

"My head feels like it's about to split wide open," she whispered.

"Do you want Dinah to fix you her special tea?"

"No." Grace tried to roll onto her elbows but lay back, too weak to move.

"You know you'll feel much better if Dinah fixes her concoction,"

Aunt Katy crooned.

"I have a bad feeling about the tea," Grace whispered.

"What did you say?" Kindra leaned over her this time.

"I think someone is putting poison in my tea," Grace said a little louder.

Aunt Katy glanced at Kindra. "My Lord, don't let that be true." She told Kindra how Grace had been having nightmares, and Dinah had been fixing a special tea to help her sleep.

"What kind of nightmares?" Kindra asked.

"Her father never made his peace with God. It's upset her something terrible." Aunt Katy shook her head and straightened the blanket under Grace's chin.

"That's not true," Kindra said.

"What's not true?" Aunt Katy asked.

"Father did make his peace with God."

Grace looked over at Kindra. "How do you know?" she asked, barely above a whisper.

"Before the doctor came, I went in to speak to him. I wanted to let him know that even though he couldn't show his love for me, I'd always loved him. Then I forgave him." Her eyes grew moist.

"He said he'd always loved me. He didn't know how to show it. He worried what people would say about his having a black child." Kindra held her sister's hand. "He apologized. Then I asked him if he had ever made his peace with God. When he said he hadn't, I asked him if he wanted to."

Grace found the strength to lean on her elbow and she turned toward Kindra. "And what did he say?"

"He said, yes." The light from the candle flickering in the kerosene lamp made the tears on Kindra's cheeks glisten.

Grace let herself fall back against the pillows and sobs racked her body. She covered her face with both hands and let all the pent-up tension flow as she cried, "He said yes. He isn't in utter darkness. He's with Mother in heaven. They're finally together again."

Kindra threw her arms around Grace and rocked her sister, while they cried tears of joy for their father. After a long while, Kindra sat back in her chair and dried her tears. Aunt Katy gave Grace a hanky and she blew her nose.

With puffy eyes and nose, Grace smiled at the two women in the room. "I had no idea you were a Christian. It never occurred to me to ask if you shared the faith."

"Laulie taught me and Camp from the Good Book. We never went to church on Sundays, but it didn't matter. Laulie taught us all we needed to know."

"Laulie can read?"

"The Good Book is hidden in her heart."

When Cameron came into the room an hour later, Grace, Kindra and Aunt Katy all smiled at him.

"What's everyone so happy about?" he asked.

"Have a seat. We have good news."

FORTY-ONE

CAMERON READ THE document before him. Tia sat on the opposite side of the desk and watched his expression. He examined the signature at the bottom of the page. "If you don't mind, I'd like to keep this and show it to Grace."

"Certainly." Tia rose to exit the office, then turned around. "I understand you already own half of the Landing. However, I want Grace gone from this house. You can tell her or I'll tell her myself. It makes no difference to me." She turned and left the office.

An hour later, Grace sat before Cameron. He leaned back in the leather chair with a look of heated frustration.

"Tia has no idea how much trouble she's stirred up with this counterfeit document. Pip has never dealt with this unscrupulous lawyer, Beauford Cranston." He pointed at the paper in her hand. "It's not even notarized."

"Are you certain the document is a hoax?" Grace's brows furrowed while she read the official-sounding jargon.

"Yes, I'm sure. It doesn't have your father's full signature. Pip always signed his middle name. You'll note it's missing. And there's no witness. Tia meant to trick us into believing the validity of this document, but the joke is on her."

He swivelled the chair and leaned forward. "I wonder how much she paid that attorney to draw up this will." He frowned. "He should be prosecuted. I'll show it to Des when he gets back. "What about Tia?"

"We can't let this go. There's a price to pay for fraud. She'll soon learn her attempt at trying to take over the Landing has failed. To think she asked me to convey to you that she wants you out of the house."

"She said that? Of all the nerve." Grace jumped from her seat and paced the floor. "I've had it up to here." Grace sliced the air above her head with the wave of her hand. "Well, no matter. I found the notarized letter from my grandfather, Granville Cooper. Father *is* free and clear of any debt to him. We should take his letter and Tia's forged document to Mr. Rothschild."

"Sounds good. Desmond returned from his trip yesterday. Let's take care of it right now."

"What are you going to tell Tia in the meantime?" Grace folded her arms across her chest, and tapped her foot.

"That we are getting legal advice."

Cameron and Grace sat before Desmond's desk and watched while he read both documents. When he was done, he looked up. "To my knowledge, Phillip Cooper never did business with Beauford Cranston. Even if he did, it is highly unethical for an attorney to give the will to the beneficiary before it has been read to all parties involved. The document is fraudulent." He pointed to the bottom of the page. "There's no date and it's not notarized." He tapped his quill pen on the desk. "That could have been intentional. At any rate, I have a legally signed, dated, and notarized statement. It supercedes this piece of work."

He leaned across the desk. "You could implicate Mr. Cranston for writing up this will, if indeed he forged Pip's signature. If he didn't, you might want to get to the bottom of who did. There's a high price to pay for forgery."

He lifted the document Granville Cooper signed and read it again. "If you don't mind, I'd like to keep the letter from your grandfather with your records. I'll return it to you when I read the will. I see you have the deed to the property."

Grace leaned forward seeing the deed for the first time. She glanced at Cameron. "When did you find this?"

"I didn't. Tia said your father gave it to her. She gave it to me along with the bogus document."

"Would my father have given her the deed?"

"No. I don't believe he would have. I suspect she stole the deed when no one was looking."

Grace turned red. "It's high time Mr. Rothschild read the true will." She leaned back in a huff. "When we're through with all of this, we'll need to decide what we're going to do with Tia. To think she wanted me out of the house. She's the one who'll go, Cameron."

"I'm in full agreement." He turned to Desmond. "I hope Pip didn't give her rights to stay on at Cooper's Landing."

"I can see this is a major concern to both of you, but until I read the will, I can't disclose that information."

"When will you be coming out to the Landing?" Cameron asked.

"Is Captain Harding in port?"

"No. He won't be back for another week."

"Let me know when he's back. Then I'll come out to read the will."

Cameron stood and stretched out his hand, "Thank you, Mr. Rothschild. Glad to have you back." With that, he and Grace left the office.

Grace stepped out of the drawing room at the sound of horses' hooves. She looked out the screen door. Captain Harding sat in the wagon. Beside him sat a distinguished-looking gentleman. In the back were Jesse and Corky. The captain climbed down and strode up the steps. He came through the door Zeek held open for him. But Grace's eyes strayed to the gentleman behind him. She stared at his light-brown hair, brushed off his forehead. Then she looked into his almond-brown eyes. Their eyes locked.

"Ethan" she said, barely over a whisper. Then she found her voice. "What are you doing here?"

"I've come to take you home."

Grace gaped at him, then turned to Cameron, who stood behind her.

He stood at attention at Ethan's announcement, a hard glint in his eyes. "Who is this man?"

"I'm . . ." Ethan began.

"This is Doctor Ethan Boyd. He's a friend of mine from Charleston." She turned back to Ethan. "I had no idea you were coming."

"Didn't you receive my letter? I said I was coming for you."

"I didn't think you meant it." Grace swallowed.

"I did, Grace." He took a step toward her. "I had no idea you'd left until I received your letter." His eyes pierced hers.

"And you didn't understand the intent of the letter?" She frowned.

"You were distressed with the death of your mother. I knew you wouldn't come home until you'd had time with your father. But now I've come to take you back to South Carolina."Zeek held Ethan's bag as if he wasn't sure whether to take it to the guest room or throw it out the door.

"Can we discuss this in private?" Ethan asked.

Grace dug her fingers in her palms. "Zeek, show Ethan to the guest room, and Drew your room is ready."

As Grace watched Ethan follow Zeek down the hall, her face heated.

Grace turned to Cameron. "I didn't know . . ."

Cameron brushed past her and stormed out the door and down the steps.

Grace ran to the screen door and pushed it open. She watched

Cameron stride toward the mill house, eating up the ground as he went.

"Look's like I brought a bucket of worms," Drew said.

"Yes, you did. But I'll handle it. You *will* be taking Ethan Boyd back to town with you when you go."

"I can do that." He tipped his hat. "I think I'll go find Cameron." He stepped out the door and turned in the direction of the mill house.

Grace returned to the drawing room where her aunt sat knitting and her cousin worked on a needlepoint. Grace paced the floor. "What is he doing here?"

"Why the surprise?" Aunt Katy asked. She pointed her knitting needle toward Grace. "You two had the town thinking there'd be a wedding announcement before you left. I expect we all wondered how the doctor would handle your leaving." She rolled her eyes. "Now we know."

Grace walked to the window and back to the sofa a number of times, sighing as she did.

A moment later, Ethan entered the drawing room. "May I have a word with you?"

"Certainly," she replied crisply. "We can talk on the porch." Aunt Katy's knitting needles clicked faster as they left the room. Grace could well imagine Aunt Katy and Josie would listen through the open window.

"I've brought you something," Ethan said. He pulled out a small velvet box and opened the soft lid.

A beautiful emerald necklace, encircled with tiny diamonds, glimmered at Grace. Her eyes jumped to Ethan. "You shouldn't have."

"Of course I should." He pulled the necklace out of the box and stood behind Grace's chair. He reached around her neck and clasped the jewels in place. "This is a gift for our engagement." He kissed her cheek, then sat down. "A matching ring will follow at the wedding."

"There'll be no wedding, Ethan. I told you in the letter I'm not going to marry you. I meant what I said. You shouldn't have come." She reached to unclasp the emerald jewels. "I can't keep the necklace."

Ethan's hand went up to pull her hand down. "You've been distraught since your mother's passing, and I know my coming has caught you by surprise. Keep the necklace and think about it a few days." His eyes grew hard. "I'd like us to wed by Christmas. That's why I chose the color of emerald. It seemed most fitting."

"Things have changed since I've come to Cooper's Landing. I'm not the same woman I was when I left."

"You're stronger. I can see that. Most becoming, I'd say."

She fingered the beautiful necklace. "I have bookkeeping that needs to be done. I can't think about this right now."

"What am I to do while you work?"

"I haven't the foggiest idea," Grace answered, her voice clipped.

"Maybe I'll take a walk." He glanced beyond the porch. "There should be plenty to see. I'd like to learn about the plantation while I'm at it."

They both stood. "The captain's going to be here a few days. When he leaves, so do you."

"Fair enough. I believe you'll come around." He touched her shoulder and went down the steps.

Grace returned to the drawing room. Aunt Katy and Josie both dropped their eyes to the necklace around her neck.

"Are you keeping that thing?" Aunt Katy asked.

"Of course not, but it is quite beautiful."

At the side of the mill house, Cameron scrutinized the slaves who pushed the cane stalks through the opening at the side of the building. Rage ran through him. That and humiliation.

Drew appeared and removed his wide-brimmed hat and slapped it against his pant leg. They stood in awkward silence.

"I had no idea who the man was, Camp. He could have been her brother for all I knew." Drew scratched the back of his neck.

"Don't lose any sleep over it. Like you said, you didn't know." Cameron kicked a clump of loose grass. "Grace never talked about suitors back home. Like a fool, I assumed she was free to see whomever she liked."

"Grace said she wants to send him packing."

They heard footsteps coming from behind them and turned. Ethan walked up. "I hope I'm not interrupting anything."

Cameron shrugged. "I was just showing the captain our new machinery."

Drew gave Cameron a wry look, but Cameron shook his head.

"My men are waiting. I've crates to unload. I'll meet up with you later," Drew said as he backed away and turned toward the wagon.

Cameron watched Drew go and then turned to Ethan. "I spend the majority of my time out in the fields with the gang teams. Come along if you wish." He raked the polished-looking gent with a glint in his eyes. *The longer he's out in the field, the less time he has to spend with Grace.*

An hour later Cameron held the field ledger. He penciled in some figures and closed the book. "I'm going to ride out to check some stock." He looked at the ledger in his hand.

"I'm headed back to the house," Ethan said. "I can return the ledger."

Cameron stared at Ethan, his jaw working. "That won't be necessary." He set the ledger on a table in the mill house.

"Suit yourself." Ethan said, and watched as Cameron headed for the stables. He eyed the ledger and picked it up. He walked to the Great House, the field book tucked under his arm.

Grace spent the morning on the account book, but her mind refused to settle long enough to think straight. She shut the book and stood. She told Ethan she'd no intention of marrying him while in Charleston.

Ethan meant nothing more to her than a friend. And what of Cameron? She wrung her hands. She wanted to run to him.

Weary, Grace leaned her palms on the desk, her back to the door. Someone came in and stopped. Grace turned in time to see Ethan place the field ledger on the credenza. He walked over to Grace and held her arms.

"I've thought of nothing but coming to escort you back to Charleston, Grace. Please come home," Ethan said. He appeared miserable.

"Ethan, I told you in the letter, I'm not going back. There's nothing for us. Don't you see?"

"I thought you ran from the pain of losing your mother, not from me."

Grace looked away. "I wasn't running from anything, Ethan. I left Charleston for a life I've wanted for a long time."

He tightened his hold, and pulled her to him, burying his face in her hair. "Grace . . ."

"Ethan . . . no . . . please don't!" She pushed on his chest.

Above her voice she heard the screen door close and footsteps in the hallway.

Ethan's mouth covered hers. Grace squirmed. And then the door opened. Over Ethan's shoulder, she saw Cameron, his cool gaze taking them in from head to toe.

"Cameron!" she gasped.

Ethan spun around. Grace tried to move away, but his hard fingers grasped her waist, holding her tightly, as though he possessed her.

"We weren't expecting you," Ethan said.

"Evidently not." Cameron turned to Grace. A derisive smile touched his mouth. "My apology for interrupting."

She flushed, unable to speak.

"Had I intruded a moment later, I'd have expected to hear a ringing slap." Cameron gave Ethan a terrifying glare.

His words pierced Grace's heart. She clutched her chest. "It's not what you think."

"Spare me." Smoky gray eyes bored into hers.

"You may as well know that Grace and I are engaged," Ethan said coolly. "The wedding is to be held here at Cooper's Landing. We intend to sail back to Charleston together after the holidays." He bent his head toward Grace. "Show him the emerald and diamond necklace, darling. I bought it for our engagement."

Grace whirled away. Her hand grasped the necklace. Cameron's gaze fixed upon the sparkling jewels.

"My mistake. I should have known." He looked around the small room avoiding her eyes. His jaw clamped. "Actually, I came for the ledger." His eyes pierced Ethan. "I left it in the mill house, but it wasn't there when I got back." He walked past them to the credenza and picked up the book.

Grace's heart hammered, and she clutched her skirts. She hated Ethan for boldly continuing his charade. She had a mind to make good the ringing slap of which Cameron suggested. Speechless, she couldn't move. How could she prove to Cameron what Ethan said wasn't true?

Cameron's cold eyes met hers. "I'll be out in the field." He stepped out of the office. A moment later, the screen door opened and closed with a sharp bang. Her heart flinched. He was gone.

Didn't he care? Would he leave her with Ethan without a fight?

But of course he would. According to Camille, he'd planned to marry that Jacqueline Moore.

Grace ripped off the necklace, and caught up her skirts. She fled from the study, stepping into the afternoon sunlight. Cameron stood by the boiling house, mounting his horse, Denzel on horseback beside him.

"Grace!" Ethan called, and followed her out the door.

"Don't!" she pointed at him.

Grace thrust aside her pride and ran down the steps. Coals smoldered in Cameron's eyes as he reined in Scimitar and turned in the saddle to look down at her. "Miss Cooper?"

His voice was steady, his eyes cool. Grace's throat tightened at the emotional distance she saw in his gaze. She wouldn't flaunt herself at him. If she went to him it would be with dignity.

She stifled a sob. "Let me explain."

"What's to explain? Actions speak louder than words, Grace." He glanced down at the jeweled necklace sparkling in her grip. "I'll thank you not to make me out more of a fool than I already am."

She searched his face. How could she make him understand that what he saw was only a lie.

He peered down at her with eyes cold and hard.

Grace knew she must save what dignity she had left. With as much decorum as she could manage, she said, "See you tonight."

He tipped his wide-brimmed hat. "Till tonight.

Grace returned to the house with a heavy heart. She met Ethan in the foyer. He scathed her with malice. Grace said nothing. She simply mounted the stairs to her room.

Cameron watched Grace leave. The sight of Grace in Ethan's arms had left him raw and reserved. His eyes narrowed.

"Come on, Denzel. The field hands are waiting for us."

The two rode to the cane fields. Denzel, usually talkative, rode quietly. He looked as if he wanted to say something, but his lips were clamped together as if to lock his thoughts away.

Cameron turned sideways. "You got something to say, say it. Otherwise, quit stewing over there."

"You're gonna let her go, just like that?" Denzel asked.

Cameron gave him a cold glance. "I don't want to hear it."

"And Cameron says he knows women." Denzel whistled, ignoring his boss. Cameron stared out at the cane stalks waving in the trade winds. "It's my belief that if you let a woman like Grace escape, you've got your head buried in the sand."

Cameron grew more irritated by the moment.

"You know and I know that Grace could be had by you if you wanted her. Yet you let her fall into the hands of that fool man." Denzel shook his head as if in disbelief. "You should fight for her."

"You dream. She's going to marry Ethan."

"Yet she comes running after you. It's you she wants. You're too busy pretending not to feel. I saw her eyes, Cameron. I saw something worth fighting for."

"Your tongue wags too much. We've got work to do." Cameron nudged his horse into a trot. He left Denzel and his horse standing in the road.

Cameron wanted to believe his friend. Seeing Grace in Ethan's arms wrenched his heart like steel smoldering in a fire pit. It nearly took the breath out of him.

Grace would soon own half of the plantation. Was this why the doctor had come? Was he enamored with the plantation? Ethan offered to take the ledger back to the house. But Cameron was no fool. He knew better than to let a total stranger get his hands on the field ledger. The doctor likely wanted to see how much sugar moved to the markets. Cameron pulled off his straw hat and brushed his pants with it. The breeze cooled his head before he jammed it back on.

He glanced back at Denzel, who stayed behind in a slow lope. Cameron nudged his horse, disappearing around the bend of the fields.

That evening, Dinah put the last bowl on the table before Cameron came in from the fields. "'Bout time you got in. Sit down before your supper gits cold."

"I've got to wash up. Go ahead and start without me." He glanced toward Grace's seat and found her staring at him. Truth to tell, she looked miserable. It served her right. He placed the field ledger on the sideboard and went through the kitchen door. He grabbed hold of the metal hand pump by the sink and pumped it. After several tries, the cold water flowed. He dried his hands, then pushed open the kitchen door again. Ethan sat beside Grace, who leaned away from him. Ethan eyed Cameron victoriously.

No one spoke, except Aunt Katy and Josie. Their prattle seemed to go on without end and for once he wished for silence. It was the longest dinner hour he'd spent in a long time.

"Has the captain returned from the Borjeaux's?" Cameron asked no one in particular.

"He's been gone all day," Josie said.

Grace pushed her food around her plate. Her appetite had fled.

Cameron took his last bite of pork roast, and left the room.

Ethan stood as well. He scooped up the field ledger from the sideboard and went out the front door.

Distraught, Cameron forgot he'd laid the field ledger on the sideboard. He scanned the office. Then he went back to the dining room. Seeing the ledger was not on the sideboard he turned to Grace. "Where's Ethan?"

She tilted her head toward the porch. "Out there."

Cameron went out onto the porch. Ethan stood with the ledger tucked under his arm. "Nice evening. Have a seat." Ethan sat down and put the book on his knees.

Cameron held his tongue and glanced out over the flowering plants that bordered the porch. "How long are you staying?"

"'Till Christmas. In the meantime, I want to explore the plantation." Ethan raked Cameron with a hard glance. "Why do you ask?"

Cameron had no intention of allowing Ethan the privilege of exploring the grounds. "The ledger." Cameron retrieved it from Ethan, and walked back into the house.

When he entered the foyer, Grace stood at the top of the stairs. He peered up for a long moment. She turned and walked away.

FORTY-TWO

GRACE STOOD ON the balcony letting the breeze soothe her wretched soul. The scent of jasmine and honeysuckle wafted up the trellis. In the rooms below, one man demanded she return with him to Charleston, while the other, the one she loved, would let her go without a fight. Her mind told her she should go for the man who wanted her. Her heart, however, wanted the man who filled her every waking moment.

A crescent moon graced the grounds with a faint light. She left the French doors open to let in the cool night air and mixed scents of tropical flowers. Miserable, Grace climbed into bed and pulled the cool sheet to her neck. Smitty crept to her face, purring loudly in her ear. She scratched the cat's head for a moment, and then turned over to bury her sorrows in her pillow. Smitty found his spot at the foot of the bed, his feet kneading her ankle as he worked himself into a comfortable position. Before long, he settled into deep slumber. And so did she.

Grace awoke to an odd sound. Her eyes closed, but her senses awake, she lay still. Something wasn't right. A cool breeze wafted over her and she pulled the sheet tighter around her neck. Smitty lay at the foot of the bed. She heard the odd noise again, a sound she'd never heard before.

A low growl filled the room. Smitty? Her eyes snapped open. The cat's growling sent a chill up her spine. Grace squinted and struggled to see in the darkness. Faint light streamed through the open doors that led to the balcony. It missed the bed, leaving Smitty and Grace in darkness. She sat up to light the kerosene lamp.

With shaking fingers, she scratched the match on the wooden box. But only a spark lit and went out. She struck another match and it hissed to life, illuminating the bed. Smitty growled louder. She found Smitty standing in the middle of the bed, puffed up to about three times his normal size. His back arched and every hair on his body stood straight up. Ears tilted back and at full attention, his growl grew. His front claws extended further than Grace would have thought physically possible.

Grace looked out beyond the bed. She saw nothing. Yet Smitty's claws extended further. All at once a man in a stocking cap stood at the foot of her bed. His silhouette seemed distantly familiar. Every muscle in her body tensed. Before tonight, Grace was certain someone kept tabs on her every move. Now, right here, right now, in her bedchamber stood an intruder. She darted a glance around the room, considering each object she saw as a weapon.

The prowler seemed almost as startled as she felt. Then she realized he wasn't looking at her. He hadn't taken his eyes off the cat.

The match burned down the thin wooden stick and singed her fingers. She shook it out, tossed it on the table next to her bed, and trembling uncontrollably. Grace scratched another match to life.

Smitty's growl rose in both volume and pitch. He wouldn't back up. Instead, he crept forward, toward the intruder.

Grace knew if Smitty attacked this man, she wouldn't be able to stop him. The only question was how clawed up and bloodied this intruder, or herself, or both of them, would get in the process. He was barely visible in the dim light.

She opened her mouth to scream, shaking the low-flamed stick in her hand before it burned her fingers again.

"Don't do that." The man spoke for the first time. She'd heard the voice before. Where?

All at once the clouds parted and the moon lit up her chamber.

Hesitating for the briefest instant, Grace looked over at Smitty. *Be like Smitty*, a voice in her head urged. *Act tougher than you really are.*

"Get out of my room!" she screamed. "Help! There's somebody in my chamber!"

With a loud hiss, Smitty thrust the whole weight of his body forward. His right front leg stretched out far and fast. His claws extended, glinting like scythes in the moonlight. They slashed at the intruder's face, missing by a fraction of an inch as the man snapped his head back. The stocking cap slid up. Still clawing, Smitty scratched a long gash into the left side of his face, sending him stumbling backwards. The man raised a palm to his face and saw blood on his hand. His head shook with fury as he turned and ran out the doors. Smitty, tail upright, leaped from the bed and raced after him.

"Smitty!" Grace shrieked. "No!"

She slid from her bed and ran after them. Who knew what this man would do if he saw Smitty's talons coming at him a second time? She feared Smitty would not walk away unscathed again.

When Grace reached the balcony, the intruder was nowhere to be seen. Smitty's head poked between the spokes of the balcony. He raised his back and held his tail as stiff as a pipe cleaner. She scooped the cat up in one hand. The staccato pounding of his heart alarmed her, even though her own chest rose and fell at a fast pace. Smitty flailed his front claws, catching the skin inside Grace's forearm and raising angry, red welts. She hurried into her room.

"Grace!" Cameron called, rushing in. His hair stuck straight up. Momentarily, Aunt Katy stood beside him, gaping. Kindra and Josie stood by the bed, anguish in their eyes. Stealthily, Tia moved to the side of the door and gazed over Cameron's shoulder.

Ethan bounded into the room. "What's happening? Where's

Grace?" He slipped on the floor rug, his arms waving to catch himself. He bumped his head on the bedpost. His palm went to his forehead.

Smitty panted, his rib cage expanding and shrinking in rapid succession. He stretched and arched his back and flicked his tail disdainfully.

"There was an intruder!" Grace pointed to the balcony. "Smitty jumped him and he fled."

Cameron pushed forward and grabbed Grace by the shoulders. "Are you all right?"

"Yes." She shuddered. "I'm fine."

"Who was it, Grace?"

"It was Jesse. I'm sure of it."

Cameron glanced at Aunt Katy. "Sit with her."

Aunt Katy removed her shawl and placed it around Grace's shoulders. "I think you'd best sit down. Good Lord, what else is going to happen in this house?"

Aunt Katy glanced at the others in the room. "You can all go back to bed. We have everything under control here."

Kindra nodded. "I'm glad you're all right, sister. She hugged Grace. "Come for me if you need me."

"I will." Her sister left, but Tia stood at the door, her ice-blue eyes piercing Grace. Grace held her gaze, not backing down.

"You too, Tia," Aunt Katy said.

Tia raised her chin and left the room.

As the others filed out of the room, Ethan backed away. He moved into the sitting room, in the dark, and waited.

Aunt Katy shut the door and sat by Grace on the vanity bench.

Moments later, Cameron came through the chamber door. "Jesse's gone." He pulled Grace into his arms and searched her eyes. "He didn't touch you, did he?"

"No, Smitty held him back."

Cameron kissed her forehead, her nose, and then her lips. "I shouldn't have been angry with you, Grace. Forgive me." He brushed her tousled hair back with his hands.

His words were a balm to her soul. She heard the aching tightness in his voice. It was true. He loved her with a vengeance she couldn't deny.

Ethan stepped out of the shadow. Cameron and Grace stared at him.

"I believe you are out of line, Cameron. Take your hands off my woman."

"Ethan!" Grace said in surprise.

"I'm talking to *him*." Ethan jabbed his finger in the air. She saw hatred fill Ethan as he moved toward Cameron. "You owe me an apology and a duel."

Grace turned to Ethan. She pushed her palms against his chest. "Ethan, stop it!"

In a flash, Ethan backhanded Grace and sent her sprawling on the floor.

Cameron loomed at him with fist flying. In one powerful punch, Ethan went down. He was out.

When Ethan left for Charleston a few days later, Grace watched him go with no regrets. She'd given her heart to Cameron. Would there come a day when he would approach her with a proposal of marriage? She would wait. If he was the right man, God would work it out.

FORTY-THREE

A FEW DAYS later, Grace woke with an urgency to finish the business of her father's will. They had waited far too long. Her uncles would be in Riverbend in the next day or two. This time they'd had the courtesy to inform her of their arrival.

Still wearing her nightgown, Grace walked to the door, pivoted and walked past the foot of the bed to the lace curtains, turned and walked back to the door. Her long, airy nightgown swished as she turned to pace in the opposite direction. Hedy's wide, brown eyes gaped at her mistress.

"Hedy."

"Yes, Missy?"

"Fetch my traveling dress. I'm going into town." Grace darted for the bathroom door.

"Yes, Missy."

"Wait." Grace peeked back out into the bedroom.

"Yes, Missy?" She jumped back and stared at the mistress.

"Before you lay out my clothes, send word to Nate to get the carriage ready."

"Yes, Ma'am." Hedy dashed out of the bedchamber.

Grace left the bathroom moments later. Hedy returned and went into action. In no time she had her mistress dressed and had piled Grace's hair in a becoming style.

When Grace descended the stairs, Zeek opened the door and escorted her to the waiting carriage. Nate helped her into the plush seat. She would pay a surprise visit to her father's attorney, Desmond Rothschild.

In Desmond's office, Grace leaned over the desk to touch the will. "What does it say?" She felt sadness and anticipation.

"Given your situation and the fact that you've waited far too long to hear the reading of the will, I'll read it to you now." He removed his spectacles and rubbed the bridge of his nose. "You say your uncles arrive tomorrow?"

"Yes."

"On Captain Harding's ship?

"That's right."

"Then Drew Harding will be present." He slid his glasses in place.

"Yes."

"I'll be out to Cooper's Landing tomorrow night. I want everyone present for the reading. Furthermore, this should put any doubts your uncles have to rest."

"I understand."

"There's some legal prattle in the beginning." Desmond said. "Then it declares you as one of Phillip's heirs. You know he has another daughter?" Desmond looked up from the document.

"Yes, I know. I figured it out shortly after I arrived."

"Good." He cleared his throat and continued. "He was also fond of his foreman, Cameron Bartholomew." He peered up again.

"I'm aware of their relationship, as well."

"He was like a son to Phillip."

"I know." She smiled.

"The three of you are the main heirs of your father's will. He has split up his estate as follows: You are the sole heir of his half of the

Great House as well as his half of the sugar plantation at Cooper's Landing." He glanced over his spectacles. "Are you aware your father sold Cameron half of the plantation?"

She nodded. "Yes, I was told my father granted this to him as a birthday gift several years ago. That is also when they became partners in the business at the Landing."

"That might not have taken place had your father known about you." He rocked back in his leather chair. "I've known your father a long time, handled most of his legal affairs, as well. He was concerned about who would take a real interest in the plantation when he was gone."

"I understand." It didn't hurt in the least that her father sold Cameron half of the land. She agreed with her father. Cameron earned it.

"As to be expected, your father left a vast fortune in funds he kept in a bank in Bath, England. He left the majority of those funds to you. I'll draw up a legal document so you can draw from that account."

"He left a quarter of his funds to Cameron."

Desmond removed his spectacles. "There is one clause where Phillip mentioned your half sister." He steeped his fingers together with his elbows on his desk. "Your father set aside separate funds for Kindra, a bank account made out in her name. The money has been accruing through the years. It is an enormous sum of money. Your father wished Kindra to know he loved her and hadn't forgotten her."

"He finally told her so," Grace whispered.

He glanced down at the document before him. "Your father has another plantation in Barbados that has served him well. A tobacco plantation that continues to flourish. He left this to Kindra. A foreman and his wife oversee the work and live on the grounds at Kindra Hall. Kindra may want to move to Barbados after the will is read."

Grace gasped in delight. Kindra Hall? Her father had Kindra in mind all along. It warmed her to know he hadn't forgotten her.

Then she asked, "Does he mention Tia?" Grace bristled.

"There's no mention of the mother of his child."

A heavy silence slipped between them.

Desmond shuffled through the papers. "There's also the matter of your father's fleet of ships."

Would there ever be an end to the surprises her father held? Grace gave the attorney her full attention.

"Your father owned twelve vessels."

"I'm aware of this," she said. "I handled the books before he passed. We've talked about his adventures on merchant ships. His favorite vessel was the *Savannah Rose*."

"Which brings me to the subject at hand." Desmond's eyebrows rose as he read the document. "One of his captains became a dear friend."

"Captain Drew Harding?"

"Yes, Mr. Harding."

"My voyage to Jamaica was on the *Savannah Rose* with Captain Harding in charge. He is a capable man. His crew has great respect for him."

"Your father shared your sentiments." He smiled. "Which is why he left the *Savannah Rose* to the captain. You, on the other hand, have been given ten of the finest merchant ships to sail the Caribbean Sea, save the *Savannah Rose*. Your father also gave Kindra one of the vessels. It brings in a handsome profit, as well."

Grace set her peacock fan in motion and glanced at Mr. Desmond. She shook her head as if to shake off the enormity of her stake in the will.

"Do you have any questions, Miss Cooper?"

"Does my father have any outstanding debts?"

"No, he does not. Your father was an astute businessman when it came to paying his debts. He was never comfortable owing anyone. This inheritance comes with no unpaid account prohibiting you from receiving it free and clear."

"I'm relieved to hear that. It seems my father took care of

everything. Is there anything else?"

"There is one more thing."

Grace leaned forward expectantly.

"He put in a clause that states should you die without an heir, the entire estate granted you would transfer to Kindra." He coughed, and then closed the folder.

Why had her father put such a clause in the will?

"Thank you for going over the papers with me." She smiled. "Please join us for supper tomorrow night before you read the will." Grace held out her hand.

"It would be my pleasure." He shook her hand.

"Good day."

"And good day to you." He saw her out of his office.

Grace was so pleased she hardly needed the carriage to drive her back to Cooper's Landing.

The next evening Mr. Rothschild read the will after dinner. Grace's uncles sat stiff-necked, with their attorney residing beside them. Tia's crystal-blue eyes were like ice as she trained her gaze on the attorney. Grace tried not to look at any of them.

When Mr. Rothschild had finished, Tia stood up.

"Phillip would never have excluded me. This is the doings of his young brat!" Tia turned toward Grace with hatred in her eyes ready to flee the room.

Grace said nothing, but her heart pounded wildly in her chest.

Cameron stood. "Enough! Tia! "We have not dealt with the fraudulent will you sought to blind-side us with. I'll see you in the study first thing in the morning."

Tia held his gaze a beat, then stormed out of the room.

"As you can see," Desmond Rothschild continued, "there is sufficient proof that Phillip owed no debt to his father." Desmond held the document in the air, then sat down.

"Here, here," said Uncle Henry. "I dare say this reading of the will seems a bit outlandish! Have none of you questioned the validity of the woman who sits here proclaiming to be Phillip's daughter? And furthermore, I've never heard of such a thing as giving a slave an inheritance such as you say our brother has given this good-for-nothing, who sits here dressed as if she were of an elite class!"

"Excuse my clients outburst," Henry's attorney stood, and buttoned his jacket over a rotund belly. He addressed Desmond Rothschild. "Shall we have breakfast together on the morrow? Bring the will with you. I'm certain we can clear all of this up."

"You'll not only clear this up!" Henry's outburst resounded through the drawing room, "you'll serve papers to these paupers to leave this property immediately!"

"Enough!" Cameron broke in. "Our attorneys will meet in the morning. If you have anything more to say, I suggest you wait until after they confer with each other."

Henry glared. "I believe we've heard enough. Let's go." The two uncles and the attorney stood and took their leave.

"I'll be on my way as well." Desmond reached for his suede hat. "Good evening." He bowed and slipped out into the night.

"Grace, Cameron, congratulations," Drew said. "God has shown favor to the two of you."

"Thank you, Drew," Cameron said.

"And God has given you the desire of your heart, has He not, with the *Savannah Rose* now your own vessel?" Grace smiled warmly.

"Indeed. It gives a man a lot to be grateful for. Phillip was a friend whom I was honored to work for. This gift is bittersweet, in that I now own a profitable ship on the high seas. But I've lost a dear friend." His lips quivered, and he flushed lightly. "I believe I'll retire for the night." "Good evening Cameron, Grace." He left them with her aunt and cousin.

Aunt Katy and Josie hugged the couple. "Congratulations, you two," Aunt Katy said. "Come, Josie, let's give them time alone to rejoice. Besides, I want to take a walk."

"In the dark?" Grace asked.

"Yes. There is a full moon and the sky is glinting with millions of diamonds. They are so much closer here than in Charleston." She stopped and touched Grace's shoulder with one hand. "We'll be leaving for Charleston soon. I want to enjoy the tropical nights while I can imprint it on my mind so I'll remember it forever."

"I don't blame you." Grace smiled. "Be careful."

Cameron proposed a toast. "To Pip, one of the finest men who ever lived!" He and Grace raised their crystal glasses and clinked them together. After they sipped the wine, Cameron swung Grace around and set her on her feet. "We can now get on with the business of Cooper's Landing without the hounds barking at us."

"Yes. Good riddance." Grace laughed.

A moment later the servants appeared from the kitchen with wide smiles on their faces.

Grace noted their steps were lighter as they flew in and out of the kitchen. Grace suspected their ears were pinned to the kitchen door and they heard every word the attorney said.

Tia was furious that Phillip had cut her out of his will. She had deliberately kept her gaze from Cameron. All her attempts to attain Phillip Cooper's holdings had failed. She was livid.

She had been working on a plan the past few days. She would get rid of Grace once and for all. Phillip may have stripped her of any rights to his estate, but she still had Kindra. Grateful for the clause that if Grace died without an heir the inheritance would go to her daughter, Tia smiled wryly. Grace would soon be out of the picture, and Kindra's fortune would double. She would have to move fast if her plan was to work. Tia slipped out of the room and disappeared into the night. She

Forty–Three

sent a note to Jesse to meet her at the back of the Great House, and to bring an extra pair of men's clothing.

FORTY-FOUR

THE FOLLOWING NIGHT the tropical rain had ceased and the winds had calmed. With Ethan and her uncles gone, Grace wanted to wander the gardens and praise God for his marvelous works. The giant flowering shrubs loomed as she headed for the cobbled path.

She still had concerns about Tia. The woman was livid when she stormed out of the house the previous evening. Would she seek revenge? Grace knew she wouldn't know a moment's peace until the mistress was dismissed from the house.

Leaves rustled in the bushes behind her. Was someone in the garden? Grace tensed and heard the shuffle of feet a moment too late. A hand clamped over her mouth before her body hit the ground. She struggled to pull loose as she heard the tearing of cloth. As she kicked, night air touched her legs, back, and shoulders. She bit a thumb, tasting blood.

"Stop it you nasty brat!" A man's voice . . . one she didn't recognize.

He grabbed her hair and yanked her head back. A dark figure loomed and slapped her hard. Stunned, she fought with all she had. Hands seemed to be all over her. The sound of material ripping from her body filled her ears.

Grace squirmed and again bit the hand that covered her mouth, letting out one desperate yell before the hand clamped over her mouth again. "You best get the wench in the wagon soon, afore she mangles me hand!"

All at once, Jesse's eyes jeered at her in triumph. A long scratch trailed down his left cheek. Smitty's mark. Her heart sank. She closed her eyes. When she did, she heard a familiar voice behind her, Tia's.

"Did you bring the clothes?"

"Right here,"Jesse hissed. "If we can get the girl to stop kickin' long enough, we'll get her dressed. Though I might say, I ain't in that big of a hurry."

Grace struggled in the vise grip of her captor, her eyes wide. Whoever covered her mouth with a rough hand, also had a handful of her hair at the back of her head. She couldn't move, couldn't look behind her. All she could see were Jesse's dreadful eyes, leering. A damp rag covered her nose. Cold air wrapped itself around her body. She shook her head, needing to gasp for fresh air, needing to scream for help. But no cool air filled her lungs, and no one came. Darkness pulled her in.

Cameron set down the field ledger and stretched before heading to the kitchen. He went through the swinging door. "Anybody seen Grace?" he asked.

"She done gone out for a walk, Mastah Camp." Gemma shoved a stack of bowls onto the shelf.

"She went out 'bout a half hour ago. She should be back fore too long," Dinah said.

"I think I'll go look for her. Maybe she'd like some company." He grinned.

"You gonna sit out by the light of the moon?" Gemma chuckled.

"Not a bad idea. She might like that." Cameron shoved on his hat and went out the kitchen door to the side of the house. When he reached the long drive, he found Nate standing on the road holding his head. "What's wrong, Nate?"

"Something mighty bad be happenin' tonight, Mastah. Somebody come up and hit me in the back of the head. I just come to. The wagon and the horses be gone. When I be coming to, I heard a scream, not loud like. Muffled is what it was."

Cameron's blood ran cold. "Where's Grace?"

"Don't know."

"Where'd you hear the cry come from?" Cameron scanned the area. The moon hid behind a dark cloud. Shadows lurked all around.

"Over theah." Nate pointed toward the garden.

"Go get the captain."

Nate stumbled toward the house.

Cameron made quick strides to the garden. His heart lurched as he spied a wad of material crumpled in a pile on the damp ground. He rushed over and picked up the dress. It belonged to Grace, and it had been slashed repeatedly. He swallowed. Where had they taken her? The moon slid out to reveal fresh tracks from the wagon wheels. It dug into the ground near the place where the dress had been, and something else. A dirty piece of damp cloth lay near a tree trunk. He picked it up and took a whiff. His head jerked back. Whatever this foul smelling rag held, they must have used it to put her out, and taken her in the wagon. But where?

Grace. Where are you?

Captain Harding slowed to a stop as Cameron held up Grace's dress.

Drew sucked in a deep breath, eyeing the gown slashed to shreds. "Oh, my Lord," he cried. "We don't have time to waste."

The two men ran from the shroud of the garden to the stables. Within moments, horses' hooves beat it out to the main road.

Hidden and obscure, Jesse sneered at the dock loaders. It was only moments before that he'd boldly walked out to the dockyard where marauders loaded crates onto Morgan Blissmore's ship, the *Bloody Mary*. Jesse had turned from the dock, shouting to one of the loaders to be careful with the crate. "Whatever's in there, Morgan Blissmore will hold your miserable lives accountable for."

He turned to the woman in the scarlet cloak. "We've got to move fast." Intending to drive the wagon back to Cooper's Landing, the two looked up at the sound of thundering hooves. Two horses pounded their way down the center road, riding at breakneck speed. Jesse grasped the woman's arm. "We've no time. Follow me." They hid behind barrels and worked their way up the gangplank of the *Savannah Rose*. Slinking behind the ship's rails, they bobbed their heads long enough to see Cameron and Drew pulling on the reins of their horses, skidding to a stop on the harbor below. Darkness swallowed the pair on the ship as they hid under cover.

Grace felt as if she were cooped up in a cocoon. She slid to one end as her cocoon tipped up, then slid back when the cocoon lowered. Then sheer darkness.

A while later she awoke. She felt around her. The walls were crude and smelled of cedar. Was she inside a long wooden crate? Yes, long and narrow, though it seemed to be spacious above her. She stretched her arm and felt the crude lid of what must have been a large shipping crate. She remembered feeling cold earlier and touched herself to see if she had clothes on. She did. It felt like an oversized shirt. She ran her bare feet over her legs and felt the rough wool breeches. Good. Then she listened. Was that water sloshing outside the box? She felt the sway from the swell in the sea. Then she knew.

I'm in the hold. I'm packaged like cargo in the hold.

"Help!" she screamed. "Somebody help me!"

She called until her voice grew hoarse. No one came. She lay scrunched on her back and brought her knees close to her chest. She pushed against the lid of the box. It wouldn't budge. She repositioned her bare feet flat against the lid. After three tries the lid made a crackling sound and popped off. She glanced out into the dark room and sat up to look around. She could barely make out the formation of crates in the hold around her.

She tried to stand, but her head spun. She scooted to lean her back against the wooden crate. *Whose ship am I on?* After several moments, she tried to stand again. This time she was able to get her bearings. She stepped out over the long crate onto the wooden planks. Something ran over her foot. Grace squealed and jumped back. Rodents! The hold was crawling with rats.

She climbed back into her box and pulled the lid down. For now she'd wait. Thankful for the small air holes in the crate, she tried to curl up, listening to the sound of the ocean and the patter of rats running between the wooden crates. She stared into blackness, tears streaming down the side of her face and falling onto her hair.

Why God? Why am I here?

A while later, voices and a thin crack of light penetrated her crate. Someone walked nearby, pushing crates to one side. She heard a match strike, smelled acrid smoke. She lay still. More crates moved across the floor. Before long, her crate jostled to one side. She held her breath.

The smell of cigarillos wafted through the air. Her eyes smarted, but she didn't move. After some time, the men left, blowing out the lamp. She waited.

Grace pushed against the lid and peered out. No one. She lifted one foot, then the other as she crept over the rough boards, feeling her way in the dark. She touched a small pile of wool clothes. A slim line of light showed through the crack of the door.

A knitted cap lay on a long board. She shoved her hair under the cap and looked down at her chest. For once she was glad she wasn't blessed with an over-abundant bosom. The loose breeches threatened to slide off her hips. She searched the hold for a thin rope, working her way around the crates until she found one hanging from a hook on the wall.

The door to the hold opened again. She crouched behind a crate and waited. Was it the same two men? She leaned to one side and peered down the line of crates. They talked low while they sat and smoked.

This time, when the men went out, Grace crept to the door. She ran the rope through the belt loops of her breeches, and tied a knot as she listened to sounds on the deck above. Step by step, she crept up the stairs. She pushed the door open a tiny crack and peered out. Two sailors looked out over the water. She nudged the door open and hunched behind a barrel. She stifled a gasp and gawked at the huge man with a fringe of greasy black curls beneath a gaudy head scarf, his brows grim above dark eyes. Another man stood against the rigging. He looked much the same, but over his head scarf a floppy black hat bearing the caricature of the devil sat lopsided on his head. He wore a wrinkled black shirt and loose breeches of black canvas. Both of the men bore a brace of pistols and a cutlass in their belts. Grace peered up at the ship's flag and moaned. *Morgan Blissmore's ship.* She'd been smuggled onto the vile captain's ship! He was known for smuggling African slaves and selling them off to American soil. She cringed. Had she been deposited in a crate as a slave to be sold?

Grace looked for something she could use to protect herself. A club leaned against the wall by the door. Chains coiled on the wooden deck a few feet away. The moon shone on an object a few feet away. She bobbed her head over to have a look. A sword. She crawled over to the chest where the blade lay. Her hand curled around the handle and she lowered the weapon to the deck.

One of the men turned back. "Did you hear something?"

"Course I heard somethin' you fool." The other guffawed. "The waves been a sloshin' on the sides of the hull all evenin'. We're in for quite a squall."

"I mean did you hear something on the deck?"

"Go on with you. You're actin' like a woman."

"No I ain't. Cap'n said for us to keep our eyes open."

Grace held her breath as she peeked through a crack between the crates. A door swung open. Light spilled out. A group of men stumbled out, laughing and hollering. She shrank back as far as she could into the shadow. How was she going to get out of this mess?

FORTY-FIVE

CAMERON BARTHOLOMEW AND Drew Harding stopped at the edge of town. To their dismay no one had seen anything out of the ordinary. They rode on, frantically searching the streets. Cameron rode up one road, while Drew took another. They hadn't a moment to waste; Grace's life depended upon them. When the wagon didn't turn up, they led their thundering horses down to the harbor.

"Is that it?" Drew pointed toward a wagon parked next to a bleak shack on the wooden pier. In the murky waters the *Bloody Mary*, Blissmore's ship, moved slowly out to sea. The men looked at each other and ran for the gangplank of the *Savannah Rose*. Captain Harding's voice boomed as he roused his crew.

Cameron stood at the rail looking across the darkening blue waters toward Blissmore's ship. Lanterns glowed golden and their sails grew ghostly white against the deepening twilight. He watched the ship slipping away. "God preserve her." Drew's men worked to raise the main sail. The crew worked swiftly. They couldn't afford to waste any time.

Before long, the *Savannah Rose* sliced slowly through the water in the direction of the *Bloody Mary*. The captain gave orders, "hold back and lay low. We must get close enough to Blissmore's vessel without his knowing it."

Four ships lay staggered in the inky water, as if sleeping in the wake from the *Bloody Mary*. The *Savannah Rose* had favor with the trade wind and made good time. "Lower the sails," the captain ordered, his voice barely audible to the crewman as he peered through the telescope at the *Bloody Mary* a short distance away.

The *Savannah Rose* mingled with the sleeping vessels, seeming invisible to their adversaries, who moved through the dark sea. Drew's vessel slipped between the ships at a crawl. A hush fell over the deck as the men waited to see if they'd been spotted. Captain Harding stood at starboard, a somber look on his face. Moments later, he gave the command, "Lower the longboats."

The crew hurried to the side of the vessel and lowered two boats. Drew turned to his first mate, Erik. "You're in charge until I get back." He pointed at his crewmen. "You four come with us."

Cameron, Drew and the four crewmen climbed down the rope ladder into the longboats bobbing in the choppy water. They dipped their oars and moved toward the *Bloody Mary*. Clouds roiled overhead. The rough water made rowing difficult.

The six men, three in each boat, sat in deep silence, making quick strokes with their oars. The boats rose and fell with the swells of the waves until the *Bloody Mary* loomed large and ominous before them.

"Well, what 'ave we here?" A pirate reached down and pulled Grace to her feet by her shirt collar.

She stared wide-eyed at the ill-kempt seaman. His lecherous grin revealed he had several teeth missing.

"We got us a lad astowin' on the *Bloody Mary*," he hollered out to the others. "Captain Blissmore don't take kindly to stowaways." He scowled in her face.

Grace kept silent, lest her voice betray her. She was thankful for the knitted cap pulled low over her ears, and the baggy shirt and breeches that hid her figure. On the other hand, if they thought she was a boy, they might throw her overboard, and she couldn't swim. She tried not to show fear. If they knew how weak her knees were right now, they'd likely feed her to the sharks for the sport of it.

Grace backed up and touched the cold metal of the sword with her bare toe. Several of Blissmore's men strode over. One ugly brute leered down at her. She tried to still the trembling of her body. She shook so badly, she feared her teeth would chatter.

"How did you board this ship, you caw dawg?"

Grace clamped her mouth tighter; so tight, her teeth felt like vise grips. When she didn't speak, the ruffian shoved her with a large hand. She slammed into the chest of another, who guffawed and pushed her into the grip of a large, smelly sailor, who bounced her back to the former crewman. Grace's body was tousled and rough-handed. Her arms became tender as one sailor after another shoved her stumbling form across the coarse deck in the ring of vile men. Humiliated, she held back tears that threatened to give her away. One of the privateers slapped her back, sending her stumbling to her knees. When she hit the wooden deck, her eye caught sight of the sword shining in the moonlight. In a desperate fight for her life, she lunged for the weapon, and in a flash, she was on her feet pointing the blade at the seamen.

"The lad wants to spar, does he?" One of the pirates growled and drew his sword. The rest of the men backed up.

Grace thought back to what Mr. Laws had taught her. She circled around until the corsair jumped forward to swipe his saber across her face. The metal hissed the air, a hair's breadth from her cheek. She backed up in time to dodge the tip of the blade.

The two walked in catlike movements as the scallywags laughed. "How much experience can a young boy have?" jeered the ill-kempt sailor, jabbing his saber toward her as he licked his lips.

Grace ignored his gibes and prepared herself to parry his thrust. The sword was heavy, so she couldn't move as smoothly and swiftly as she did with a foil. He advanced. She stepped back. His blade sliced the air as he tried to make contact. She moved on light feet, but the man's experience excelled. His saber flashed in the moonlight and swiftly pulled her sword from her hand. She heard it clang to the deck and slide out of reach.

A marauder grabbed her arms, the swordsman's blade at her throat. *"Think fast!"* Grace told herself. "I demand to see the captain!"

The beast lowered the blade, and his robust frame shook with laughter. "She demands to see the captain!"

Grace jerked out of the swab's hold and spun around, staring at the shiny blade. "Yes. I demand to see Captain Blissmore!" She pulled off her cap and shook her long auburn tresses over her shoulders. The freebooters drew back in surprise. The swordsman waved his blade, a sly smile on his lips. Another sea dawg from behind gripped her arms. Grace elbowed his ribs and squirmed out of his hold. She quickly moved to one side, eyeing the privateers like a caged animal.

I must put up a bold front, she told herself. *If not, I don't stand a chance.* Grace squared her shoulders, placing hands on her hips, "Get back, you sea dawgs, before I have your despicable heads hanging from the gallows!"

The crewmen laughed and shoved each other. "Bold words for a scraggly-lookin' damsel!" A giant brute stared down at her, eyes gleaming.

"And who might you be, sweet thing, that you be so brazen as to hurl such orders at us?" asked the swordsman, his blade extended towards her.

"I'm Phillip Cooper's daughter." She spied the fallen sword from the corner of her eye, and inched toward it.

"Grab the wench." The smelly crewman waved his saber toward the toothless man.

Toothless reached out with massive hands and pulled Grace to his mountainous frame.

The corsair leered down at her. "Do you be havin' proof you be the daughter of the notorious Phillip Cooper?"

Notorious Phillip Cooper? She held her eyes steady.

"Until the captain be seein' you, you'll be held prisoner." He turned to one of the freebooters. "Bind her up and throw her in the hold."

Grace tried to wrench free. "I demand to see the captain!"

Laughter filled the deck. A great wave lifted the vessel. Her footing slipped. Before she knew it, she'd flown back into the hard chest of toothless. His eyes shone as big as silver coins while he held her steady.

"Let go of me you . . . you . . . you!"

Laughter continued as the scallywags ogled her.

"Enough of this!" The swordsman shoved the toothless man aside and touched the blade to the top button of Grace's oversized shirt. The button severed and fell to the deck, rolling until it met a crack and disappeared.

A wry smile crossed the swordsman's lips. "If you're not who you be sayin' you are, Missy, more's the pity for you." He raked the length of her with wild eyes.

"Hold your tongue, you dirty snake!"

The freebooters hooted and howled.

"You're in no position to make demands, little Missy." The blade lingered near her throat.

"What goes on here?" A booming voice broke through the crowd. The sound of waves smashed the side of the ship. The marauders parted.

Grace looked up to see the rogue she'd seen on the boardwalk in Riverbend. She'd learned he was Captain Morgan Blissmore, a slave smuggler on the coast of the Caribbean Sea.

The captain strode over to Grace. His eyes took in the baggy breeches and oversized shirt and the long tresses falling over her shoulders, then came to rest on her face. His expression hardened. Fire glinted in the darkness of his narrowing scowl. The stony gaze of the big-chested man made her knees go weak.

Blissmore boomed, "I demand an explanation for this slip of a wench standin' on my ship."

Toothless leered. "She be a stowaway, Captain. I found her hidin'" on the deck." He stepped up from behind and gripped her arms again.

"That's not true!" Grace stormed. She looked the captain in the eye. "I was kidnaped and thrown on your ship. I was merely trying to find a way to escape."

The captain's eyes widened.

"Let her go," he commanded the man gripping her arms. "I want to know what the devil you're doing on board the *Bloody Mary*."

"I . . . I told you." She licked her lips and eyed the sword on the deck flooring and turned away from it, stepping back.

Grace stood with her back to the rail while the crewmen stepped aside as the captain commanded. Blissmore loomed large before her as he glared down at her. "Send her to my cabin. I'll deal with her there. I think I like the sassy little wench."

In a flash Grace bent down and sprang up with the blade pointed at the captain's throat. "If anyone makes a move toward me, you'll die."

His broad hands reached for her.

"Don't!" She shoved the sword against his neck, denting his skin.

He lowered his hands and squinted at her.

Two men moved hastily toward her. She whirled around, slashed the sleeve of one man's shirt, drawing blood. She raised the sharp blade and brought it down swiftly and cut off the ponytail of the other man, missing his skull by a hair's length. In a flash, she reeled back and held the sword to the captain's chest, the blade drawing a trickle of blood.

"I mean it. Touch me and you'll pay," she snapped.

Grace knew she had only seconds before she would be overtaken by the group of men, but they were seconds she planned to use to her own advantage. She spied an opening, just enough room to flee. Beyond them was a clear path that led to the stern. She tried not to panic.

"Seize her!"

Grace heard the captain's shout. Without hesitation, she dropped the sword, and slipped between the two staggering seamen before her, and ran toward the stern of the ship.

Like a wild animal, Grace rounded a barrel, leaped over rigging, ropes, and obstacles that stood in the way of her escape. She couldn't swim, but she'd not be held captive by a bunch of renegades who'd have their way with her.

The ship was in pandemonium when Cameron and Drew climbed over the ship's rail.Cameron heard Captain Blissmore shout orders as he charged after her. He watched Grace jump feet first without a moment's hesitation. Captain Blissmore shoved a crewman overboard, "Go after her!"

Cameron shot a glance at Drew. "She can't swim!"

FORTY-SIX

STUNNED, GRACE THRASHED in the murky darkness. She came up gasping for air. The crewman grasped the back of her shirt and yanked her down into the water. She struggled in the black sea as the rough hand held her down. She held her breath until she felt her lungs were going to explode. She fought to push his hand away, only to feel its perilous assault shove her further down into the depths of the watery grave.

Is this how my life is going to end?

She kicked her feet and flailed her arms. *Lord save me from this wretched sea!*

All at once, a hand lifted her up, up, up from the bowels of the treacherous sea. Her head shot above the water. She gasped as she sucked in a great gulp of air, then coughed and spurted, as she was pulled through the roiling ocean.

"Hold on!" Cameron shouted as he hooked his arm under her chin and swam through the choppy water. But she fought against him. The longboat reached their side. He lifted Grace into the waiting arms of a crewman, and then hoisted himself in behind her. Drew pulled himself into the opposite side of the boat moments later. The crewmen rowed for the *Savannah Rose* while pistol shots rang through the night air.

Slugs pierced the water, missing them by mere inches.

Grace hurled herself away from Cameron with the look of a frightened animal. He secured her flailing arms, only to have her bite his forearm. He jerked back in pain. "Grace, it's me! Stop! Let me help you."

"No! Leave me be!" she swung at him and backed away.

"She's in shock!" Cameron shouted, and kept a watchful eye on Grace.

As soon as they reached the ship, Cameron slung her across his shoulder and mounted the ladder. He expected her to pommel his back with angry fists, but it seemed all the fight had gone out of her. When they reached the top, he climbed over the ship's rail. The ocean tossed the ship like a tiny cork.

"Get her into the second cabin. I'll bring some towels," Drew yelled.

Cameron shut the door and placed Grace on her feet. She looked as if she wanted to bolt. Exhausted, he had his doubts he could contain her. She stared at him like a wild boar. He wanted to protect her, to hold her, but for the moment, he kept his distance.

Grace shook uncontrollably. Cameron glanced frantically around the small cabin and spied a blanket on the cot. He moved to the cot, not letting her out of his sight, and pulled the blanket off the bed. "Let me put this blanket on you, Grace. You're shaking like a leaf."

Fear began to leave her eyes and he gently draped the blanket over her shoulders. Recognition began to dawn in her eyes. Grace took one step forward, and he pulled her into his arms to warm her. They couldn't wait long. She was cold and wet. And she shivered uncontrollably.

The door opened after a brief knock, and Erik entered carrying two steaming buckets. For the next ten minutes, a succession of crewmen delivered hot water for Grace's bath. All the while Grace stood in Cameron's arms, shaking.

Then he led her toward the screen where she'd change before she could get into the tub. "Let's get you warmed up before you get sick."

Grace clung to Cameron, her teeth chattering. "The . . . thank . . . you for s . . . saving . . . me once again." She gazed up at him, basking in his hold. Grace looked around the familiar cabin. She was safe, safe on the ship and safe in Cameron's arms.

"Sweet Grace, I thought I'd lost you in the tempest of the sea," he whispered over her head.

"But . . . you saved m . . . me." She leaned back on shaky legs to look at him.

"I'll never let you go again." He kissed her forehead, her nose, and then gently, her lips.

They didn't linger. Grace's chilled body trembled violently.

Cameron stood back. "You've got to get into the tub and warm up. We can talk later." He turned reluctantly and walked out of the cabin.

Grace wished for Hedy as she prepared to get in the tub. Hedy would have perfumed her water and soothed her.

She took a deep breath and tried to calm the frantic beating of her heart. She shivered so violently she could hardly remove her soaked clothes. Grace stepped into the water as soon as she was undressed. She gasped, as the heat of the water seemed to scald her skin. Some minutes passed before she was able to let her body sink low, and she closed her eyes as the water washed over her shoulders.

A half hour later, she stood in the middle of the cabin holding a towel around her. She crept over to the wall hooks and found Josie's blue-printed day dress that she had forgotten. She donned the dress and shook out her damp curls, running her fingers through her tresses to get the tangles out. She glanced around the cabin and thought back to when she had first sailed to Jamaica. Much had happened in four months. She lost her father and found love. She fought for the right to be on her father's plantation and gained a sister.

When she'd left the banks of America, she harbored bitter resentment toward her mother for deceiving her about her father. Now on Jamaican soil, she found love and forgiveness for both parents. Her life was full.

Yet there were those who stood in the way of her happiness. Those who wanted her gone. She had to find a way to end this strife. Having been rescued from the perils of the sea gave her a new energy for living. Through God's mighty hand, she would conquer the fiery darts that assailed her. She would put on the armor of faith and the shield of righteousness. She would rest in the shadow of the Almighty.

She remembered Psalms 91. Angels would watch over her, lest she dash her foot against a stone. Refreshed in her spirit, she left the cabin to search for Cameron.

As Grace stepped over the threshold, a cold hand clutched her elbow and swung her into the shadows near the ship's rails. Grace turned. The scarlet hood hid Tia's face against the night's chill, but a diamond necklace glittered against her dark throat from the moon's glow; the diamond solitaire Phillip had given Grace before the ball. Tia swung her arm over Grace's shoulder and pinned her against her chest. "Don't make a sound," she whispered hoarsely.

Grace stiffened. The hooded cloak belonged to Tia, but the voice did not.

Paralyzed by fear, Grace glanced across the vessel. Where was Cameron?

Just then, he and the captain rounded the corner and stepped onto the main deck.

"Hey!" Cameron lunged to free Grace, and then stopped.

The woman had whipped out a knife and held it against Grace's throat. "Get back." She scooted away from the men, dragging Grace with her.

The ship plunged in the choppy water. The waves tossed the crewmen against the side of the rails. The main sail flapped hard against the strong winds. Another swell rocked them. Sailors gripped the rails as they watched the scene before them.

Grace struggled to pull free, but the cold blade dented her skin at the bottom of her throat. She sucked in her breath, wide-eyed. The pitching of the vessel was her worst enemy at the moment.

"Hold still! I'm not done with you yet!"

A blast of wind tore the hood off the woman. The crew gasped.

Cameron stood bolted to the deck, fists clenched at his sides. "Minerva!"

"Yes it's me, you imbecile." She threw back her head and laughed. "I had you fooled all along, didn't I?"

Grace trembled in the mad woman's hold. The knife pricked her skin. A trickle of blood ran down her throat. "You poisoned my father, didn't you?" she rasped.

"He had it comin'."

"And you tried to poison me with the tea." A shudder passed through Grace.

"Yes, you deserve to die."

"But why? What have I done to you?" Grace swallowed hard.

"You robbed my sister of everything that was rightfully hers. Before you came, Mastah Phillip would've given Tia the world. But you ruined everything."

The iron hand of fear gripped Grace's heart as she watched Cameron, flanked by a body of crewmen. They all eyed the evil woman like a pack of hyenas waiting to strike their prey.

From out of the darkness, Jesse Simmons stepped to the fore, a sword in his grip. As Minerva held Grace, Jesse circled in front of the crew with a snarl on his lips. His eyes flickered over the men and settled on Cameron. "You planned to see my neck in a noose, did ya?" He pointed the sword with the Cooper coat of arms toward the foreman. "It won't be me who be swingin' by the gallows. Afore the night's over, it'll be you."

Grace saw frustration in Cameron's expression. He was caught off guard with no gun, no sword. So intent in rescuing her, he'd let his defenses down. Now she saw his eyes swerve from Jesse to Minerva and back to Jesse. Would he be able to get her out of this predicament?

"You're not thinking straight Jesse. You're outnumbered, in case you haven't noticed." He moved away from the side of the barrel and flung himself in front of Grace, arms outstretched.

Jesse lunged toward Cameron, sword extended. An angry growl escaped his throat as he charged.

Cameron swerved, intending to knock the sword from Jesse's hands, but missed.

At the same moment, Grace threw her left arm up, and elbowed Minerva's rib cage with her right. For a split second she turned to face the evil woman and spied the diamond solitaire against the black woman's throat. She snatched the necklace and Minerva's arms flew out as she slammed against the ship's rails.

Grace plunged to the deck and rolled from Minerva's reach. Cameron threw his body on top of Grace's. A giant wave tossed the ship and a blur passed them as Jesse flailed before Minerva, plunging his sword into her abdomen.

Minerva threw up her hand in an outstretched arc, and the blade meant for Grace, passed over and slashed Jesse's throat. The two tumbled over the ship's rails into the roiling sea.

In stunned silence, Grace saw their bodies tossed into utter darkness. Cameron rolled to the deck, and Grace leapt to her feet and ran to the rail in time to see the two bodies floating face down in the swirling water.

Cameron came to her side. His arms went around her. Her eyes jumped to the now vacant spot where Minerva once stood.

"She's gone, Grace. They're both gone." He held her tight. Grace trembled. The crewmen waited in numb silence.

"Let's go home," Cameron called to the captain.

"Wait!" Grace stepped back and looked out over the waters toward the shore. "What of Tia? She wanted me dead."

"I know." Cameron pulled Grace back into his arms. "We have a rocky road ahead of us. Tia will be booked for the fraudulent will. She won't be able to stalk you any longer. She'll serve time in jail. I promise you."

"But Kindra– "

"She'll get over it. Her mother deserves to pay for her misdeeds."

"You're right, Cameron. Let's go home."

Men flew into action, turning the ship toward the shores of Jamaica. Cameron held Grace to his side as the men pulled the rigging to tighten the sails. Captain Harding shouted orders in the windy night. Soon, the lights of the shore came into view.

Grace turned to Cameron. She saw the need in his eyes. She backed away and let a smile spread across her lips.

He pulled her into his arms. "My darling Grace," he whispered in her ear before burying his face in her hair.

When he finally pulled back, he held her waist to steady her. "Are you all right?"

"I am now," she whispered.

"Marry me," Cameron said.

Grace gazed into the eyes of the man she loved. "Are you asking, or telling me?"

"I'm telling you."

She breathed in his scent. "I shall let you have your way this time, Cameron Bartholomew."

Cameron moaned as he pulled her into his hard chest. He brought his head down. His lips claimed hers as his own.

When they raised their heads, silence reigned. The two glanced back. The crewmen watched with smiles on their faces.

"She said, yes!" boomed Cameron to their friends.

A loud cry of joy filled the air.

Grace looked up at the billowing sails as the wind moved the vessel to shore. All the hurt from her past ebbed away as she leaned into Cameron. She was headed for a safe, secure harbor in her heart and in his arms. The winds of grace sailed through her soul.

A high moon shone through parting clouds. "Let's go home, Grace."

She turned her face up to his. "I've waited a long time to call

Cooper's Landing my home. To share it with you makes it worth the wait."

Cameron smiled wholeheartedly, and before she knew it he'd swooped her up and carried her down the gangplank with a group of well-wishers watching from the ship's rail. He kissed her soundly and then set her into the waiting carriage, bound for home.

The Winds of Love Series

  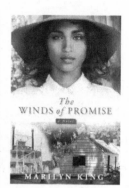

Hearts of Home Series

Thank you for reading!

Dear Reader,

I hope you enjoyed The Winds of Grace, book one. I have to tell you I really love the characters Cameron and Grace, and Denzel and Kindra. Be sure to stay tuned because book four is in the works. Will the drama end? No! Will Grace and Kindra find a happy ending? I sure hope so.

As an author, I love feedback. Tell me what you liked, what you loved, even what you hated. I'd love to hear from you. You can write me at Marilynking6318@gmail.com and visit me on the web at www.marilynking.net.

Finally, I need to ask a favor. If you're so inclined, I'd love a review of The Winds of Grace. Loved it, hated it–I'd enjoy your feedback. Reviews can be tough to come by these days, and you, the reader, have the power to make or break a book. If you have the time, here's the link to my author page, along with all my books on Amazon: http://amzn.to

http://goo.gl/qXSY2Dhttp://www.marilynking.net.

Warm Regards,
Marilyn King

Made in the USA
San Bernardino, CA
17 November 2017